THE VANISHED SEAS

THE VANISHED SEAS

CATHERINE ASARO

THE VANISHED SEAS

A Baen Books Original

Baen Publishing Enterprises
P.O. Box 1403
Riverdale, NY 10471
www.baen.com

ISBN 978-1-9821-2471-7

Cover art by David Mattingly

First printing, July 2020

Distributed by Simon & Schuster
1230 Avenue of the Americas
New York, NY 10020

Library of Congress Cataloging-in-Publication Data

Names: Asaro, Catherine, author.
Title: The vanished seas / by Catherine Asaro.
Description: Riverdale, NY : Baen Books, [2020] | Series: Skolian Empire: Major Bhaajan
Identifiers: LCCN 2020015801 | ISBN 9781982124717 (trade paperback)
Subjects: GSAFD: Science Fiction.
Classification: LCC PS3551.S29 V36 2020 | DDC 813/.54—dc23
LC record available at https://lccn.loc.gov/2020015801

Printed in the United States of America

10 9 8 7 6 5 4 3 2 1

To my husband,
John Kendall Cannizzo
The love of my life
In cherished memory

Acknowledgments

My thanks to Aly Parsons for critiquing the entire manuscript and to the Aly Parsons writers group for their critiques on selected scenes: Aly Parsons, Bob Chase, Carolyn Ives Gilman, John Hemry, J.G. Huckenpöhler, Simcha Kuritzky, Mike LaViolette, Bud Sparhawk, Connie Warner, Kelly Dwyer, and Mary Thompson; to the amazing Lina Perez, who somehow managed to keep me organized; to my editor Tony Daniel for his superb editing suggestions; to my publisher Toni Weisskopf for her patience and compassion; to Ben Davidoff for his excellent copyedit; to Alex Bear, Corinda Carfora, Elizabeth O'Brien, Christopher Ruocchio, Carol Russo, and all the other fine people at Baen for making this book possible; and to David Mattingly for his inspired art on my covers and for his kindness. My thanks to my agent, Eleanor Wood, of Spectrum Literary Agency, for her much-appreciated support and kindness; and to my publicist Binnie Braunstein for her enthusiasm and hard work on my behalf.

A heartfelt thanks to the shining lights in my life, my husband John Cannizzo, whose loving support made me the writer I am today, and to our daughter Catherine Jr., whose love, support, and care makes all the difference.

THE VANISHED SEAS

✛ CHAPTER I ✛
VANISHING ACT

Light glittered through the crystal columns in the ballroom of the Quida mansion. Women in sleek clothes and men in sensual black and silver filled the room, all with the ageless beauty that wealth and power could bestow. Music played while the glitterati danced.

So yah, these people were rich.

To say I didn't normally attend parties with Imperialate nobility was like saying it didn't normally rain in this region of the world Raylicon. I mean, this place was a freaking desert. The few humans who lived here had built the gleaming City of Cries, the stark jewel of the empire, a paragon of modern civilization and all that. Not that it wasn't true. The City of Cries, despite its name, wasn't a place where people wept, at least not where you could see.

Tonight the planners had done themselves proud in this reception for Scorpio Corporation, a simple name for a conglomerate that was anything but simple, an empire of commercial industries and military contracts. I'd attended as a guest of the Royal House of Majda, because, well, who the hell knew why. Majda wanted a private investigator present, so I went. After all, they paid me an exorbitant retainer, not to mention the penthouse they'd given me in Cries. Although I'd never been at ease in their stratospheric world of influence, I'd adapted during the two years I'd worked for them, Earth years, the human standard. To fit in tonight, I'd even worn an evening gown, chic and shimmering gold, the type of clothes I usually avoided like a techno-plague. I was normally a black leather and muscle-shirt gal.

3

The Quida mansion stood on the outskirts of Cries in the foothills of the Saint Parval Mountains. Attending the gala had started out as one of my easiest jobs ever, just go to the party so I could later tell the Majdas if I noticed anything "unusual." They apparently wanted me to judge how the guests reacted to whatever big announcement the Scorpio slicks had planned for tonight.

With so many of the Imperialate's mighty gathered together, none of the invited guests noticed when Mara Quida disappeared. It told me a lot more about this supposed esteemed gathering than they probably wanted me to know. As Vice President for Sales and Marketing at Scorpio Corporation, Quida was the guest of honor at tonight's gala.

You'd think they would have noticed when she fucking vanished.

Four of us gathered in an alcove upstairs, hidden from the ballroom while the gala continued downstairs, its entitled guests blithely partying. The small room here gleamed, white with silver accents. Detective Talon, the head of security for Scorpio Corporation, paced across the alcove, rigid in her gray uniform, with silver hair and silver ribbing on her sleeves. She surveyed our group as if she were trying to fix us in place with her stare. Screw that. I had no patience for people who expected to intimidate me instead of earning my respect.

Besides myself and Talon, our group included two other people: Colonel Lavinda Majda, third in line to the Majda throne; and of course Mara Quida's husband Lukas Quida. We were isolated from the gala; Lavinda's "aide," the redoubtable Lieutenant Jo Muller, stood hulking at the bottom of the sweeping staircase that led from this alcove down to the main floor, out of earshot but not out of sight, pretending to be the colonel's assistant. Yah, right. Majda bodyguards were about as discreet as power-hammers.

"Who knows Mara Quida is gone?" Detective Talon demanded. She spoke to Colonel Majda, which made zero sense. How would Lavinda know?

Lukas answered. "No one is aware of her disappearance yet except the four of us." Light from the chandelier glinted on his silver hair. He was too young and too rich to be going gray; that metallic look had to be deliberate. The effect was gorgeous. So was he, the trophy husband, with his broad shoulders, narrow waist, and handsome face.

Lavinda spoke coolly to Talon. "Why does it matter who knows?" She looked every bit a royal heir, with her dark coloring and aristocratic features. The green tunic and trousers of her dress uniform were sharply pressed and gold bars gleamed on her shoulders. Her dark eyes, high cheekbones, and smooth skin showed no trace of irregularity. I recognized her upright military carriage because I also stood that way, but only in part. I'd never exuded that sense of authority, a self-assurance so ingrained, I doubted she even realized the confidence she projected. I'd always respected Lavinda, in part because she never tried to intimidate anyone. She did it anyway, to put it mildly, but it wasn't deliberate.

Talon's discomfort actually seemed more with Lukas than the Colonel. The detective glanced at Lukas when he spoke, then looked away quickly and talked to Lavinda instead. "It could help to know. None of our searches have given any clue why his wife vanished. She might have had her own—personal reasons."

Ouch. That was as subtle as thwacking Lukas with a hammer. I doubted his wife had run off with another man. Why do it in the middle of this gala intended to honor her? Lukas wouldn't have asked for our help if he believed it was anything that simple, not to mention humiliating. That he'd called us here suggested he had good reason to suspect trouble.

Lukas spoke with restraint, but his body had gone so tense, he seemed like a band of elastic ready to snap. "She didn't have a 'personal' reason."

Talon grunted, and she still wouldn't look at him. Seriously? The atavistic era was long gone when matriarchal queens owned their men, when no woman could speak to a highborn man unless she was a member of his family. Modern culture gave men equal rights with women. In the Skolian Imperialate, a star-spanning civilization with nearly a trillion people, almost no one followed the ancient customs, only a few of the most conservative noble Houses—including the Majdas. Since they cloistered their princes, hiding the prized fellows from the rest of the universe, some families among the highest society here followed similar customs. Although legally they couldn't get away with keeping their men in full seclusion—they weren't

Majdas, after all—they could still be ridiculously sexist. Lukas had asked us to come here, though, so I doubted he had any use for those barbaric constraints.

I spoke directly to Lukas. "How did you discover your wife was gone?"

He turned to me, his shoulders coming down from their hunched position. "Mara was about to announce the Scorpio contract with Metropoli. She intended to present the Metropoli execs with a scroll, a ceremonial parchment. She went to get it about an hour ago. When she didn't return, I looked for her." He raked his hand through his hair, messing it up, which revealed more than he knew. He didn't care about his appearance, he just wanted to know what the hell had happened to his wife. "She wasn't in our room," he continued. "The remains of the scroll were on the bed. It was ripped up, like it had been caught in a fight."

Talon frowned as if he were a lying child. "Those ceremonial scrolls are museum pieces."

For flaming sake. What was wrong with Talon? He finds the bedroom in shambles and her only comment is about the damage to a *thing*?

Lukas met her gaze, neither averting his eyes nor stepping back. "What's your point?" He looked ready to explode.

I spoke quickly, before Talon could cram her foot farther down her throat. "Your wife went to a lot of trouble for this gala. It must be quite an achievement, what she arranged on Metropoli."

He took a deep breath, waited a moment, and then spoke in a more even voice. "Yes, it is. She was about to make the announcement. Scorpio will be managing the usage franchises for the northern continent on Metropoli."

Holy shit. No wonder Mara Quida wanted to party. "Usage franchises" meant Scorpio had just taken over the electric and optical utilities for the largest continent on the most populous world of the Imperialate. A contract like that would involve billions of people and trillions of credits. Nothing could hide the admiration in Lukas' voice, and I had the impression he appreciated what she had achieved because of her accomplishment, not because he expected to gain from it in financial or social terms. He offered a refreshing contrast to the other guests I'd met tonight.

"I see," Talon said. She watched me with poorly disguised suspicion. People in Cries claimed I had a "wild" quality, whatever that meant. It was true I could go places no Cries citizen dared visit. No one here knew that, however. Besides, I was the least dangerous person in this room. These people took "threatening" to an entirely different level, one that would terrify any sane person who understood how the technocrats of Cries navigated the currents of power in their glittering city. I wasn't one of them and I never would be no matter what my Majda ties.

Well, tough. If Talon thought she could intimidate me into leaving, she had no idea. I met her stare, and her expression hardened.

Someone coughed. Talon turned away and spoke to Lukas. Although she sounded awkward, at least she looked at him this time. "We need to trace your wife's actions, everything she did for the past day."

"I'll go over it with you," he said. "Anything you all need, just let me know."

Max, are you getting all this? I thought.

Yes, I am recording. The thought came from Max, my EI, or Evolving Intelligence. I used my neural link with him for privacy. He usually "lived" in my gauntlets, but tonight he resided in the slender bracelets I wore instead. He sent signals via sockets in my wrists along the bio-optic threads in my body to bioelectrodes in my brain. Coated with protective chemicals, the electrodes fired my neurons, which my mind interpreted as thought. Tech-induced telepathy. I wished I actually were telepathic, so I could figure out what everyone here thought. I had to rely on intuition and my ability to read body language, voices, and facial expressions.

Talon took Lukas through every detail of the gala preparations. Security had searched the bedroom, looking for a body. They found nothing. They also checked their monitors. Big surprise, the footage for those vital moments in the bedroom was missing, with no clues yet as to why.

"What I don't get," Talon was saying, "is why someone destroyed the scroll. It's as valuable as your wife, maybe even more so."

Lukas stiffened, and I stared at the detective. Was she brain dead? She continued, oblivious to the pain she was causing Lukas.

"Whatever ransom they can get for her would be greatly increased if they also held the scroll hostage."

"That assumes this is a kidnapping," I said, more to shut her up than because I actually thought something else had happened.

Lukas turned to me with a jerk, as if he were trying to escape Talon's words. "What else would it be?"

"To answer that," I said, "I need to look more at the bedroom."

Talon frowned at me. "This is an internal Scorpio matter. We will take care of it ourselves, officer—" She paused as if waiting for my name, which pissed me off, because as the chief investigator here, she would have checked my identity with her EI the moment we met. Her refusal to acknowledge my name was an insult more effective than any words she might have used.

Diplomacy, I reminded myself. *Be courteous.* I said only, "Major Bhaajan, army, retired. I'm not a police officer, I'm a PI."

"And why are you here?" Talon spoke with disdain, in an accent that sounded Iotic, the language spoken by the nobility. It also sounded fake. I wasn't impressed.

Lavinda turned her cool gaze on Talon and spoke in a true Iotic accent, which I doubted she even thought about. "Major Bhaajan works for the House of Majda. I requested her presence."

"Oh." Talon closed her mouth.

I wondered what stake Lavinda had in this. As a sister of General Vaj Majda, the Matriarch of the House of Majda, she operated on a level of power I could only imagine. She was also a colonel in the Pharaoh's Army; I doubted she had either the interest or time to involve herself in her family's corporate dealings. The third sister, Corejida Majda, ran their finances. I hadn't expected such a highly ranked Majda to attend the gala, but given what I'd just heard about the Metropoli deal, I saw now why they were interested. They controlled the city, and that meant knowing everything that went on at its highest levels.

It was also obvious why Lukas requested Lavinda join us. He was no fool; he knew whose presence would get the police snapping on this case.

"Can you help?" he asked me. Smart choice. Asking an heir to the Majda throne would be presumptuous, but addressing the Majda rep acknowledged their sway.

"I'll do my best," I said. "I'm good at finding people."

Talon spoke tightly. "We are grateful to Majda for offering this aid in our investigation."

She didn't sound grateful, she sounded like she wanted to throw me out the window.

The bedroom looked like hell: cracked tables, shattered holoscreens, and mirrors in jagged shards on the ground. A filigreed nightstand had broken in two. The scroll lay on the bed, torn and crumpled, but even with that, I recognized its value. I'd grown up in the ancient ruins under the city, a buried world rich with the remnants of past ages, and I'd learned to respect such artifacts. This one didn't look native to Raylicon. It probably came from the planet Parthonia, the seat of the Imperialate government, which made it even more valuable. I had to admit, Talon had a point. Who in their right mind would destroy that scroll? Mara Quida plus the artifact would bring the kidnappers more wealth than Mara alone.

Max, I thought. *Make a record of all this. Use my eye filters.*

I'm recording in the optical spectrum, he answered. Also infrared and ultraviolet.

Good.

A holoscreen on one wall was cycling through views of the room. I blinked, startled. I barely recognized the tall woman it showed, a statuesque figure in a shimmering gold evening gown with a cloud of black curls falling down her back. Yah, that was me. Strange.

My walk around the room gave Max many views of the wreckage. I paused by Talon. "Can you send me the police reports after their analysts finish their work here?"

The detective turned her cold stare on me. "Aren't you making your own recordings?"

"Yes. But I can't get the same detail as their experts." Talon knew that.

"It's up to them if they send you their report." She turned back to her work, ignoring me.

I gritted my teeth. She knew perfectly well that if I asked for the report, as the Majda rep, she had to send it to me. *Let it go,* I told myself. I had no interest in getting involved in her turf war.

Lukas paced the room, restless, never pausing, but he stayed back, respecting our space. He had class, this one. I didn't want to like him, on principle, because I'd grown up in poverty and these people were all too rich. But I couldn't help it. He seemed like a decent fellow.

When he caught me watching him, he came to where I stood with Talon. "What do you think?" He directed his question to us both, letting us figure out whatever hierarchy we were inflicting on each other. Smart. I wouldn't want to get between me and Talon, either.

"Your wife clearly fought with her captors," Talon said.

"It's possible," I said. "But something is off." I motioned at the mess scattered across the floor. "It doesn't look like anyone stepped on this debris. Those broken mirror shards are like knives, but none of them show any sign of blood. And it would take more force than two fighters slamming into that nightstand to break it in half."

Lukas went very still, hope warring with fear on his face. "You don't think they fought with Mara?"

I gave him the truth. "I'd say an explosion blew apart this room."

Talon spoke quickly. "I doubt it." Before I could respond, she walked away.

Well, screw that. I tamped down my anger. The last thing Lukas needed was to see the investigators on his wife's case at odds. I even understood why Talon left so abruptly. It wasn't just to piss on the PI trespassing on her jurisdiction. She didn't want to tell Lukas his wife could have died. I realized then her rudeness with him came from awkwardness rather than insensitivity. She had no clue what protocol applied to a man with his high rank, and yah, with his beauty, too. He rattled even me, and I'd thought I was immune to that sort of thing. She obviously wasn't comfortable talking to him without his wife present.

Lukas spoke quietly to me. "I haven't received a ransom demand."

"That isn't so unusual," I said. "She disappeared less than an hour ago. It could be hours before they contact you."

His face paled. "And if this was an explosion?"

I spoke as gently as I could. "We've found no trace of blood or any clue that she suffered injuries." It was the closest I could come to reassuring him.

Lukas rubbed the heel of his hand over his eyes, smearing away tears. "I just—I don't understand." He lowered his arm, watching me as if willing us to make sense out of this nightmare. "We planned so long for tonight. She was so happy! I can't believe it ended like this."

"I'm sorry." I meant it. "I swear to you, we'll do everything we can to bring her home."

"Thank you, Major." He went back to pacing.

I exhaled, fearing I'd raised his hopes too much. This didn't look good. No, that was too mild a word. It looked like bloody hell. I continued my investigation, not only of the bedroom, but also in the surrounding areas. I stopped on the landing of the curving staircase near the foyer and stood at the rail, studying the foyer below.

Talon joined me. "The police analysts are here. We've also set up monitors in case Del Quida gets a ransom demand."

Del Quida. She used a high title of respect for Lukas, only a hair's breadth below Lord. She had to get me the report, so she wasn't telling me much, but at least she was trying to be civil. Maybe with Lukas somewhere else, she could relax.

I touched the crystal sphere at the top of the banister. It was just the right size to rest your hand on as you started down the stairs. "Someone twisted this."

Talon peered at the ball. Light from the chandeliers refracted through the crystal, creating a rainbow on the rail. "Looks normal to me."

I tapped the stem of the ball. "See that mark? Someone turned the sphere."

Talon straightened up. "I doubt it means anything."

"Probably not." It just struck me as odd that in such a perfectly kept mansion, this ornament was out of place.

Lukas came over to us. "I don't see any way someone could have broken into the bedroom."

"We'll figure it out," Talon said, gazing at his shoulder.

His voice cracked. "She has to be all right."

Talon finally looked at him. "We'll do everything we can to find her."

Lukas just stared down the staircase. The guests had left, and the robo-servers that cleaned the mansion were waiting patiently for the police analysts to finish their work. Yah, I knew the cleaners were machines, that "patience" didn't come into it, but they looked that way, robots of all sizes and shapes arrayed in a silent row while human analysts applied yet other machines to study the crime scene.

Lukas took a deep breath. "I should check on things."

"You go on," Talon told him. "We'll let you know if we find anything."

Lukas nodded and headed downstairs, gripping the railing. He was damn convincing as the distraught spouse. At a gut level, I believed him. I had to think about the rest of it, however, that he and Mara Quida had no children. He was his wife's sole heir.

Lukas had a lot to gain if she died.

The desert night drowsed with a crystalline purity of air. I stood outside the mansion, one of the last people to leave after the gala. A few light globes floated off to the right, above a patio the guests had deserted hours ago. I walked along a path paved with blue stones. Lawns dotted with tiny white flowers lay on either side and the delicate scent of night-blooming jaz filled the air. It wasn't that I didn't appreciate the gardens; I just knew too well the other side of that tender beauty. Except for the jaz, everything else growing here came from offworld. Native plants were spiky and tough, better suited for desert survival than making gardens pretty.

I pulled up the shoulder strap of my dress. The blasted thing kept slipping down my arm. *Max,* I thought. *Have the city transport authority send a flyer.* It would be good to get home and take off this outfit.

Done, Max answered.

I headed for the curving driveway about a kilometer from the house, where I could meet the flyer. Silence surrounded me; not only was the Quida mansion on the outskirts of Cries, but sound dampeners also muted the hum of the city.

I stumbled on a rock in the path and caught myself. *Damn heels. Damn dress.*

You wear them well. Max supposedly didn't have emotions, but his amusement was all too realistic. I don't think I've ever seen so many men try to pick you up before. Or women.

I'd never gotten used to the way upper-crust types found me sexy in what one fellow called an "untamed way." I stopped and pulled off my heels. Holding them in my hand, I continued in bare feet. *Max, you need to learn some new idioms. English has some good ones.*

Why ever would I need to learn English idioms?

This one: Silence is golden. Especially from EIs who find my sex life so amusing.

I am an EI assistant. I don't experience amusement. He didn't sound one whit less amused.

I stopped, distracted. The silence was too golden here at the mansion. Concentrating, I trying to pick up a sound. *Any* sound.

What's wrong? Max asked.

Turn up my ear augs. Any good investigator had biomech augmentation, including enhancements to her ears, eyes, skeleton, and musculature. I'd received the basic combat mods when I enlisted, and an upgrade when I transitioned into the officer ranks. It was invaluable in my work, and I kept my system at the top of the game.

As Max activated my ear mods, sounds intensified, the scrape of leaves against leaves, a breeze whispering over the lawns, and the buzz of pico-ruziks, tiny flying reptiles that lived in the desert but sometimes wandered into city gardens. Normally my enhanced hearing was too intense to use for long, but tonight the gardens still seemed too quiet.

A faint clink came off to my left.

I dove into the garden and rolled, my legs tangling in my stupid dress. In that same instant, the lilies next to the path where I'd been standing lit up in the blast of a nail-laser.

Damn! I jumped to my feet and dropped my shoes. Grabbing my dress, I hiked it up to my hips, holding it with one hand while I sprinted through the garden, my stride stretched out to its full length. I clenched my little gold purse in my other hand, not because I liked little gold purses; I hated the things. But it contained useful stuff.

Combat mode toggled, Max thought. I'm activating your internal microfusion reactor.

Somewhere behind me, the garden hissed with a nail shot. I ran harder, doubling my speed. Rocks jabbed my calloused feet. As I dodged back and forth, a lawn at my side flared with another shot.

Max! With my free hand, I shook my purse open. *Have the beetle shorten this damn dress.*

A little green beetle bot zipped out of my purse. It extended its blades and proceeded to cut off the bottom half of my dress while I ran. Its AI managed to keep it from chopping me up, too, despite the way I bounced it around. Within seconds, I was running in a gold shift that fell around my hips in tatters. As I dodged onto a lawn, the dirt next to me hissed with a nail shot.

I sent a command to the beetle through my link to Max. *Find out who is shooting at me.*

The beetle whisked away into the night.

A public flyer is waiting for you on the driveway, Max thought.

Why hasn't security kicked in? The city monitors should have whapped the shooter.

Someone must have deactivated security.

No shit. To block city security required a clearance higher than anyone in this investigation could claim—except for Colonel Lavinda Majda.

I ran out into the sweeping curve of the driveway. A silver flyer waited there. As I sprinted for it, darting back and forth, a nail shot exploded the ground. The hatch of the flyer snapped open and I threw myself inside.

"Get us out of here!" I yelled.

With my enhanced speed, it looked as if the pilot was moving in slow motion. To her credit, she took off without hesitation, the craft leaping into the air as the hatch snapped shut. I slid across the deck and plowed into a passenger seat.

Within moments we were above the city. As I pushed up on my hands and knees, the pilot looked back at me. "You pay *now*," she said. "And you give me your clearance."

Combat mode off, Max thought.

My sense of speed returned to normal. "Clearance for what?" I climbed into the passenger seat, doing my best to project a calm, civilized appearance. I doubted it worked, with my hair in a wild mess, my dress in tatters, and my breath coming in gasps.

"Hell if I know." The pilot turned back to her controls. "You give me a reason why I should help a raggedy-assed woman running out of a mansion with people shooting at her."

"Look at your screen." Max would have already sent my ID, to pay for the transport.

A ping came from the cockpit. "Well, shit," the pilot said. "Majda."

As uncomfortable as I felt within the Majda realm of influence, I couldn't deny that being on their payroll had advantages. "Take me to the city outskirts." I gave her coordinates for the entrance to the Concourse, a great underground boulevard in the desert beyond the City of Cries. The Concourse was supposedly part of the Undercity, the ancient ruins that lay beneath the desert, but in reality it just served as a glitzy source of revenue for Cries. The true Undercity where I'd grown up existed far below the gleaming Concourse.

While the pilot brought the flyer around in a long arc, I pondered the Majdas. They had sent me to the gala and called me in on the investigation when Mara Quida disappeared. They were also the only ones who could have deactivated the city security monitors. Coincidence? I doubted it. I needed to find out what was up.

My life could depend on the answer.

I strode onto the main floor of the Black Mark casino. No one blinked at my ripped gold scrap of a dress. I fit right in. Holographic roulette wheels spun in the air above the tables, glowing in neon colors while patrons bet and lost. Other gamblers sat around tables in chairs with diamond accents. Dealers who were far too beautiful dealt them cards, cubes, spheres, disks, rods, or whatever game pieces the players wanted. The games were all holographic, run by the house. I mean seriously, who would bet on games of chance controlled by a house mesh system? It always beat you, unless it calculated it needed to let you win a few times to keep you coming back. In the end, you lost, lost, and lost again. You could lose your soul to the Black Mark if you weren't careful.

A man in a silver shirt and tight black trousers lounged against a table, watching me. I ignored his predatory gaze. Yah, I recognized his arrogant body language, knew the aristocratic sheen of his glit-rags. He was probably among the wealthiest of the wealthy in Cries, illicitly coming to the Black Mark in the depths of the true Undercity. Sure, he had plenty to offer—gifts, drugs, and who knew what the hell else. I didn't care. I stalked past him without a glance.

Someone caught my arm. I swung around, raising my fist, my adrenalin surging—and froze. A bartender stood there. Her slinksuit showed more skin than it covered, her makeup glittered, and the holo-stars in her black hair sparkled.

"Eh." I lowered my arm. I had no intention of slugging my best friend. "Dara."

She pulled me over to the bar and spoke in the terse Undercity dialect. "What goes? You look ready to blow."

"Need talk to Jak," I said. "Fast." He always had his ear tuned to the Undercity whisper mill. If any rumors were going around about what had happened at the gala, he'd know.

"I get. Stay here." Dara sped off, soon lost amid the patrons and holos. Taking a deep breath, I leaned against the bar, surveying the clientele to see if their behavior offered any useful info they didn't know they were revealing. I recognized a few guests from the gala, come here to slum it in the Undercity's infamous den of vice. I watched them discreetly, but no one did anything interesting.

The other bartenders left me alone, though they did glance my way when they thought I didn't notice. It would be all over the Undercity whisper mill tomorrow: *Bhaaj showed up at the casino dressed like a blitzed out city slick instead of like Bhaaj.*

A group of slicks wandered over to me, two men and two women, all dressed in scraps of metallic cloth that covered almost none of their bodies. They looked like cyb-fibs, a weird trend among the wealthy in Cries, pretending they were machines rather than people. One of the men had a gold face, and the woman with him had eyes the color of polished titanium coins. The other woman had a cybernetic arm that glowed with tech-mech. It looked like solid gold, but more likely it used some hardened alloy that wouldn't dent. The second man had implants in his ears that flashed in light patterns I knew were supposed to make me dizzy. They didn't have the intended effect any more than the swirling holos in the casino could entice me to gamble. I'd never been particularly susceptible to suggestion, and the biomech in my body further blocked the effects.

The man with ear implants leaned against the bar next to me and gave me a once over, letting his gaze linger on my body. I felt like punching him. He leaned in closer, bringing his lips to my ear, and spoke in the Cries dialect. "You've good cyb. I've got better. Try it out."

"Fuck off," I said, ever the epitome of tact. I didn't have to act civilized at the Black Mark, and after some city slick had just tried to kill me, I had no intention of pretending otherwise.

The woman with the cyber-arm laughed at her friend as she tilted her head at me. "You won't get honey from that kit."

Kit my ass. I might look young, but I was probably twice their age.

The man took my arm. "Your accent is Undercity. You're a dust rat, aren't you?"

I twisted out of his grip and pulled his arm behind his back while I swung him around. "Touch me again, asshole," I said in a perfect Cries accent, "and I'll break your elbow."

"Hey!" The woman with the cyber-arm pulled him free. "Get your respect together, rat," she snapped at me. "Or you'll regret it."

She had that tone I hated. I tensed, my fist clenching—

Bhaaj, stand down, Max thought. *Let it go.*

I took a deep breath and stepped back from the group. "Not interested."

"He didn't ask if you were interested," Cyber-arm said.

The other woman shook her head at her friend, probably her equivalent of Max telling me to stand down. To me, she said, "Your loss."

Ear-plants looked me over avidly. "You got pump," he told me, whatever that meant. He sounded like he intended it as a compliment. "Come with us. We'll make it worth your time."

"Seriously?" He thought I'd go with them for gifts? I probably had more wealth than the four of them combined. After living the first sixteen years of my life in poverty and then twenty years in the austere life of the Pharaoh's Army, I saved my earnings with an obsessive intensity these slicks would probably never understand, given the gilded life they most likely took for granted. I was annoyed enough, though, that I couldn't resist baiting him. "Worth my time how?"

"What do you want?" He sounded sure of himself again, in familiar territory, offering to buy whatever took his fancy. "Credits, jewelry, hack, bliss. You name it."

Bhaaj, cut it out, Max thought. *Leave them alone.*

Oh, all right. "Sorry," I told Ear-plants. "Not interested."

"You won't find better," he told me. "I mean it. Whatever you want."

A dark voice spoke behind me, sensuous and smooth, but with a steely undertone of eagerness that said, *push me, go ahead, see what happens.* "She already has everything she needs."

Their gazes shifted to a point beyond my shoulder—and they froze. I turned. A man stood there, tall and leanly muscled, dressed in black, from his sleeveless muscle shirt to his rough trousers to his thousand-credit belt. An old scar stretched down his cheek that he'd never bothered to get fixed, and a gnarled scar snaked across his left bicep. Violence simmered in his gaze. He was menace and sexuality incarnate, with the face of a threatening god and the aura of a man who'd earned his wealth from the dark side of human nature.

Jak had arrived.

He spoke to the cyb-fibs in a terrifyingly pleasant voice. "I see you met my wife."

His *wife*? Where the bloody hell did that come from?

Ear-implants looked ready to shit platinum bricks. "My apology sir. We meant no offense. We were just leaving."

"Yes, just leaving." Cyber-arm spoke fast, stepping back.

"You're welcome to keep enjoying my establishment." Jak was practically purring. He lifted his hand, indicating the worst of his rigged roulette wheels. "Please. Be my guest."

The cyb-fibs all bowed to him, I mean, *bowed*, for freaking sake, after which they made a fast retreat, heading off to his tables to lose more money and make him happy.

I swung around to him. "Your wife? Fuck that, Jak."

A slow, drowsy smile spread across his face. "Yah, Bhaajo, sure."

I strode past him, headed for the back of the room, to a discreet stairway without any gleams or glitz. I didn't look back as I went up the stairs. Holos activated in front of me, just enough to light the way, and then went dark after I passed. I headed into the secret depths of the casino owned by Mean Lean Jak, the most notorious criminal kingpin in the Undercity.

Jak leaned against the wall of his office, a darker shadow against its ebony surface. Diamonds glittered on bowls in niches in the walls, on the black furniture, and dusted across the plush black rug. Tendrils of smoke curled up from the bowls, scenting the air with carmina, a euphoriant that could make you feel as if you were drifting in clouds of pleasure. The nanomeds in my body were working overtime to keep me from having fun, because I felt no effect of the drug. I didn't have Max tell them to stop, though. I needed my wits tonight.

"Someone tried to shoot you?" Jak asked. "I thought these people hired you to protect them. Why kill you?"

I paced back and forth, unable to stay still. "Fuck if I know."

Bhaaj, Max thought. You're doing it again.

Doing what?

Cursing.

So fucking what?

You asked me to stop you.

I wanted to use my choicest language to let him know just what I thought of that, but I held back. I had indeed asked him to help me clean up my act, at least with my elite clients.

This is Jak, I thought. *He's smooth.*

You said you wanted to break the habit. That means with everyone.

Yah, well, not tonight.

At least come up with something more original. He sounded amused again.

Max, go away. I walked over to Jak. "I got a new job. Find a missing glitz. Scorpio."

He looked suitably intrigued. "When she'd vanish?"

"Tonight." I banged my fist on my thigh. "We got no record. Zill, zilch, zig. Glit-flit is just gone. I searched, checked, talked to guests. Then I left. That's when the shooter tried to nail me."

"Where?"

"Garden. Glit-flit's digs." I lifted my hands, then dropped them. "Why nail me?"

"Easy to see why." Jak waved his hand as if to encompass more than the room. "The Undercity. You know it. All of it. Like no city slick."

He had a point; I alone of the Quida investigators could reach the true Undercity. No one from Cries could enter these ruins without one of our dust gangs escorting them, to keep their wealthy butts from getting mugged or worse. Sure, some city dwellers knew about Jak's casino; it was the one place in the Undercity that slicks could visit. But they couldn't do it by themselves. Jak required any outsider coming to or leaving his establishment to wear sight and sound canceling goggles. They went blind and deaf. If they refused, no one would bring them to his elusive casino.

Nor could city monitors detect us in the Undercity. Our cyber-riders hid our community with shrouds that Cries engineers couldn't even understand, let alone defeat. If Cries tried to raid the Undercity, our population would retreat deeper into the endless ruins that honeycombed the ground below the desert. With enough resources, the authorities would eventually find some of us, but to what point? They had little interest in our world.

Until two years ago.

That was when the army discovered we had something they coveted—the highest concentration of empaths in the Imperialate. No one knew that little gem of data, though, except for a few highly placed officials. I doubted anyone at the Quida gala fell into that select group. Although I didn't think any of them knew I came from the Undercity, I made no secret of my history. Did my ability to come and go here threaten whoever had taken Mara Quida?

Max, I thought. *Find out if any of the other investigators were attacked tonight.*

Will do, Max answered.

I considered Jak. "You hear anything tonight about missing city slicks?"

"Nothing." He shrugged. "I'll keep an ear to the whisper mill."

I nodded, deep in thought, walking back and forth.

Jak watched me. "Stay tonight. Relax."

I went over to him. "Think you can settle me down, eh?"

He laughed, not with the menace everyone knew, but a deep, hearty laugh he showed no one else, a sound I'd loved since I first met him, when we were both three years old. "Yah, Bhaaj," he murmured. "I can settle you down."

I felt like poking his chest and saying he wasn't my husband. I mean, where the hell had that come from? Oh, I knew, he wanted to have fun with the city slicks. Maybe we were even married by common law. But of course we never discussed it. Marriage was a custom for the wealthy in Cries. Although my people did form bonds by a ceremony we called handfasting, Jak and I had never bothered.

We knew what we had. I had to admit, though, if one of us ever did propose, he had chosen a dynamite way, pissing me off and making me want to laugh at the same time.

I smiled, a genuine smile, as rare from me as from anyone else in the Undercity. "Yah. I should stay." I never gambled here at Jak's casino. I knew all too well how he fixed the games.

The Black Mark, however, offered better reasons for me to stay the night.

❖ CHAPTER II ❖
VETERANS ADMINISTRATION

I sat sprawled in a chair in the sunken living room of my penthouse, my legs stretched across the floor and light pouring in the window-wall. Outside, far below the tower, the panoramic view of the Vanished Sea Desert spread to the horizon. Inside, the white carpet shimmered with a glossy finish that was actually a holoscreen. Currently, a holographic replica of the Quida mansion filled the room. The images came from Max's recordings and the police analysis Talon had finally sent me. The scene looked the same as I remembered from last night.

"I don't get it," I said. "Still no ransom demand?"

"Not a word." Max spoke using the comm in my wrist gauntlets. I preferred talking when we were alone. Of course, that was only after I'd deactivated any nosy Majda tech trying to watch the penthouse. It was the price I paid for accepting this gorgeous place; it belonged to the Majdas, so it included their security monitors. Fortunately, I was better at outwitting their spy tech than it was at spying on me.

"Maybe Mara Quida went offworld," I said.

"Not according to any flight record I've found," Max said. "The police, Majda security, and Scorpio Corporation also did checks, not just of who bought tickets or boarded ships, but also a visual analysis of every passenger on any flight."

"With her resources, she could have paid for anonymity."

"For what purpose? She had every reason to stay."

It certainly looked that way. Last night should have been a coup for Mara Quida. I got up and walked over to the holo of the crumpled scroll. "The negotiations were finished, right? Quida had already finalized the Metropoli deal."

"That's right. The contracts have been signed and processed."

I passed my hand through the holographic scroll. "Her disappearance could make Metropoli doubt Scorpio Corporation, maybe even spur them to question the contract."

"According to every report I've received or intercepted, the deal is proceeding as planned."

Intercepted. That sounded like Max-speak for cracking other people's secured systems. "Anything from the beetle bot I sent after whoever tried to shoot me last night?"

"Nothing yet. Wherever it went, it's either out of my range or shrouding its systems."

I noticed he left out the other possibility, that the shooter had caught or destroyed my bot. I scowled. I liked that little beetle. "Let me know when you make contact." I paced through the holos as if they were ghosts. "Do you think Lukas Quida killed her? He inherits everything, all her assets, connections, real estate, even her place on the Scorpio board of directors."

"He is the obvious choice," Max said. "Maybe too obvious. Several hundred people saw him at the gala before, during, and after her disappearance."

"Yah, well, he could have hired someone to whack her."

"True. But why be so obvious about it?"

"Maybe that's the point. Make it look absurd to suspect him."

"No body has been found," Max reminded me. "We don't know she is dead."

"I hope not." Her husband had seemed genuinely agonized last night. He didn't strike me as a good suspect, but I did have some questions. "Set up a meeting with Lukas Quida later today."

"What about your appointment at the Veterans Administration?"

I stopped pacing. "What appointment?"

"With Adept Sanva."

"Oh, that." I shifted my weight. "Reschedule it."

"You've already rescheduled twice."

I went to the wall console and smacked my palm against a panel. The holos in my living room disappeared like an Undercity thief evading the cops. It left me surrounded by the elegance of a penthouse I never would have chosen myself, as much as I liked it. I'd always felt like a visitor here, never truly at home.

"Bhaaj?" Max asked.

"What?"

"You should go to your appointment with Adept Sanva."

"Why?"

"Because if you don't, you'll be angry at yourself."

What, now my EI was analyzing me? "You're a biomech brain, Max. Not a psychologist."

"I have entire libraries dedicated to psychology. I also have many years as your EI. I know you."

Great. My EI was pulling the *I know you* card. Even worse, he was probably right. His brain evolved as we interacted, and after more than ten years together, it did sometimes seem like he knew me better than I knew myself.

"All right," I grumbled. "I'll go see Sanva. But get the meeting with Lukas, too. I want to talk to him as soon as possible."

The Veterans Administration stood in the Commodore's Plaza in Cries. All the buildings here served the army, fronting on an open area paved in white and blue stones. A fountain in the center showed the ancient goddess of war with her wings spread and her head tilted back as she blew into a battle horn. Water spumed out of the horn into the air and cascaded down her body in glistening drops.

It never ceased to amaze me what people in Cries took for granted. We lived on a dying world where the seas had dried up ages ago. Raylicon had no surface water; you had to dig deep to find it even here in the north, the most livable area of the planet. Deadly chemicals poisoned the water, making purification plants the most lucrative business on the world. In the Undercity, we had several grottos, even an underground lake, but none of those contained drinkable water. To survive, we scrapped together filtration machines and siphoned energy from Cries to run them. Yet this city boasted so much wealth, her people could waste water in a fountain that sprayed huge amounts of the life-saving liquid into the air. Cries probably even filtered it. No one wanted to get sued if someone drank from the fountain and ended up in the hospital or died.

I crossed the plaza to the VA building. In Cries, the army topped the city hierarchy, separate but equal to the corporate big dealers. The VA reflected that status, a tall building with displays on its outer walls showing confident soldiers in spotless fatigues, their heads lifted with pride. Too bad we'd never actually looked like that. Most of my time in combat, I'd been dusty, covered in mud, soaked to the bone, or drenched in sweat. Nanites in the cloth tried to clean our fatigues, which maybe helped boost morale, but it didn't stop you from dying, both literally and emotionally, bit by bit, until you built so many defenses, you became numb.

Inside the VA, I found a lobby with consoles at chest height. Benches lined the walls and four people sat on them, two women and two men, all looking bored. They were like the soldiers I'd enlisted with. Like me. None of us had been considered officer material. Many of the higher-ups hadn't believed I'd survive basic training. A dust rat? Ludicrous. My response had been *Just watch me.* I refused to give up, and eventually I'd made the supposedly impossible leap to the officer ranks. The army used my skills well, putting me on task forces to solve problems in weapons and strategy. I retired after twenty years and became a PI, intrigued by the idea of solving problems for a living. But I never forgot where I came from, below the city.

I stood at a console and pressed my finger against the screen.

"Name and rank?" the console asked.

"Major Bhaajan, retired. I have an appointment with Adept Sanva."

"ID verified." A holo flashed, the Majda insignia, a hawk soaring through the sky. It vanished as fast as it came. Huh. It looked like the console had flagged me as a Majda employee.

"An escort will be out to take you to your appointment," the screen said.

I glanced toward the bored vets waiting their turn. "Other people are ahead of me."

The screen didn't answer, probably since I hadn't asked a question, or maybe it just found my comment irrelevant. I scowled, then stalked over to the bench and sat down with the others.

A man in fatigues walked under the archway across the room and headed in my direction. He looked like the people in the images on the walls, perfect and professional. He stopped in front of me. "Welcome, Major Bhaajan." Lifting his hand, he invited me to follow him. "This way please."

I motioned toward the other people, who were watching with varying degrees of irritation and resignation. "They were here first."

The man blinked, looking confused. "You are next."

I didn't want to give him a hard time. He was just doing his job, following orders and the city hierarchy. Apparently my Majda connection or my retired officer status put me on top of this little pecking order. Screw that. I'd spent a substantial portion of my life being treated as if I were less than nothing, and I wasn't about to inflict that on other people.

"You can take them ahead of me," I said. "I'll wait my turn."

He stood awkwardly, as if hoping I'd change my mind. When I stayed put, he left the room. One of the other vets nodded to me, the barest motion. Then we all went back to our boredom.

The console's voice spoke in the air. "Sergeant Mazo, proceed to room fourteen for your appointment with Doctor Raven."

A man stood and left the room through the archway. The rest of us continued to wait.

Eventually, after the other three people were called, the console announced my name, to meet Adept Sanva in room three. I headed for the archway, reminding myself I didn't feel nervous about talking to a neurological adept. I normally had no problem with healers, including doctors who specialized in neuroscience and psychology. But she applied her training to empaths. Psions. Kyle operators. Whatever you called them, it meant the same thing. I had absolutely no desire to use my abilities as an empath. The last thing I wanted to experience was other people's moods. Hell, I had enough trouble understanding my own emotions. I'd always suppressed my empathic ability.

It made survival easier.

Adept Sanva turned out to be an older woman with gray hair and an unlined face that suggested her body carried nanomeds to delay her aging. The large desk where she sat had glossy holoscreens for its surface. The room was airy, with flowering plants in pots and windows that let in sunlight.

Sanva looked up as I entered. "Welcome, Major." She motioned to a smart-chair. "Make yourself comfortable."

I sat down, about as comfortable as a sand-hawk caught in a prickle-pot.

She considered me. "I understand you would like to redo your Kyle tests."

"Not exactly." I didn't want to answer. She was supposed to be an empath. She should know what I felt, right? Except it didn't work that way. Everyone had natural barriers in their mind, and mine were stronger than most.

"Not exactly?" she prodded.

"The army tested me when I enlisted." I pushed my hand through my hair, tousling the black mane around my shoulders. "They said I have zero Kyle ability."

Sanva tapped her desk and hieroglyphics flowed across it in a glowing river of data. "Actually, it doesn't say zero ability." She looked up at me. "It says 'none detected.'"

So yah, apparently "none detected" didn't mean "no ability." I'd never realized that until last year. "The Majdas believe my tests were wrong. They think I might be an empath. I want to find out if that's true." I didn't really, but I'd hidden from this for too long. If I was even a marginal empath, it could be useful in my business, not to mention in life in general. Besides, it was ridiculous that I could be so good at solving other people's mysteries and so bad at facing my own.

"Yes, they put a flag to that effect in your file." She sat back in her chair. "Have you noticed anything to make you think they are correct?"

"Well, no." That wasn't a lie, not exactly.

Sanva waited. After a moment, I added, "I may have suppressed any ability because, uh—"

"Yes?"

"Because of my birth." I felt stupid saying the words.

She regarded me curiously. "You can't remember your birth."

"Not literally." I shifted my weight on her "smart" chair, which seemed pretty dumb. No matter how much it readjusted to make me more comfortable, nothing worked. "An EI helped me reconstruct the events and their implications."

"And?"

"My mother died." I spoke curtly. "It was in a cave. She bled to death. Apparently she was an empath. She tried to reach my mind, to comfort me while I cried. We made a link. When she died, I felt it. That left mental scars." There. It was said. I waited.

Sanva stared at me. "You were born in a *cave*?"

That was all she got out of my miserable little story? Everyone in the Undercity lived in caves. Those homes could be works of art, but, yah, they were caves. The surprise wasn't that my mother gave birth in one, but that it had been rough and cold, and she had been alone, with no help. I had no idea why, since no records existed of my father or other relatives.

"Yah," I said coldly. "I was born in the Undercity." She knew that. It was in my files.

"I didn't realize the conditions." She spoke in a gentle voice. "I could see how such an experience might damage your ability to make empathic connections."

I took a moment to breathe. It wasn't her fault that talking about this made me jittery. "I don't know that I want to fix it. I've been fine. But it seems I should find out how it affected me."

She touched her desk, bringing up a new display. "According to this, a recent medical exam picked up traces of the neural transmitter psiamine in your brain. Only psions produce psiamine, and only when they are using the Kyle structures in their cortex."

"Does that mean I was, uh—feeling moods?"

"Possibly." She spoke in a friendly manner. "Did you notice anything?"

"I'm not sure." Her calm nature made her easier to deal with than I'd expected. "I mean, I'm good at reading people. You have to be, to survive in the Undercity. But it's more reading body language, facial expressions, that sort of thing."

"Have you ever heard someone else's thoughts?"

"Just my EI. But that's all tech." Dryly I added, "That's annoying enough."

I am most certainly not annoying, Max thought.

Sanva read the data floating above her desk. "You have a biomech web in your body." She looked up at me. "And a spinal node?"

"Not in my spine." I raised my gauntleted wrist. "In here. When I click the gauntlet into my wrist sockets, it connects to my brain."

She didn't look surprised. "An ability to use that tech indicates your brain is well suited to the process. Not everyone can link with a neural EI. You may be drawing on the Kyle structures in your brain without realizing it."

I hesitated. "There is one other thing."

"Yes?"

"It's just that—very rarely, I get flashes of, well, I don't know what you'd call it." I stopped, feeling stupid.

"Flashes of what?"

She was certainly patient, I'd give her that. "The glimpse of a possible future. It only lasts a few seconds."

"Precognition?"

"I don't know." Gods, I sounded like an idiot.

"It's rare." She seemed intrigued, as if I were a puzzle. "More so than empathy. It's due to the quantum uncertainty in time and energy. The better you know the energy of an event, the more uncertain the time."

"Those are tiny uncertainties." I'd had to take quantum engineering during college. "Way too small to notice on any human scale." As small as Planck's constant, which meant even our best instruments couldn't measure the uncertainty in time.

"Yes, generally, that's true," she said. "But apparently for some people, the Kyle bodies in their brain interact in such a way to increase the temporal uncertainty."

I grimaced. "Can you translate that?"

"Your brain increases the uncertainty enough for you to glimpse the future." She spoke as if this were a perfectly natural event. "It's one reason people experience déjà vu."

It didn't sound real, but then, up until a few years ago, I wouldn't have expected to have this conversation at all. "Do you think it's worth pursuing any of this?"

"That depends. Do you want to?"

Good question. I wanted to say no. I'd come here for help, though, and she couldn't give it if I closed up like a water clam in the desert. I spoke awkwardly. "My people don't talk about our emotions. But I can't hide forever." After a pause, I said, "So yes, I want to pursue it."

"All right. We'll see what we can do." Sanva tapped another panel on her desk. "I'm sending you a file with some exercises. Try them. Let's meet again in a few days."

"Exercises?" How the blazes could you exercise being an empath?

"Just relax your mind for a start."

"I'll try." I might as well. People were always telling me I needed to relax. I stood up. "Thanks."

She stood as well. "Good luck, Major."

I nodded. Then I escaped her office.

I walked out of the VA into a perfectly sunny day. We never had clouds unless we created them ourselves using weather machines. As someone who'd spent the first sixteen years of her life underground, I never stopped marveling at the open sky, the city towers reflecting its blue expanse—

A silver glint flashed in my side vision. I dove to the side, but not fast enough to avoid being hit. Pain flared in my chest as I smashed into the blue-tiled plaza.

Mist blurred my vision. Impossible mist. I groaned and rolled onto my back. The clear sky stretched above me. Someone was shouting. I tried lifting my arm—felt like lead—it dropped onto my chest. My palm squelched on wetness there.

Bhaaj, don't move, Max thought. *You've been hit by a knife. It tore an artery near your heart. I have contacted the hospital and summoned emergency med-bots.*

Hurts . . . I couldn't form coherent thoughts.

A man's face came into view above me. He looked familiar.

"Major, we have help coming," he said. "Stay here."

Like I was going somewhere? I recognized him now; he was the well-meaning fellow who had offered to take me in to see Adept Sanva.

I closed my eyes and passed out . . .

"Stay put!" Doctor Raven looked ready to tie me to the hospital bed. "Major, if you don't lie down, you'll reopen your wound."

I glowered at her from where I sat on the edge of the bed with my legs hanging nearly to the floor. "I'm fine," I repeated.

"You aren't even close to fine. You nearly died."

"You fixed me up. Now I have business to attend." Like finding the asshole who kept trying to kill me, and had nearly succeeded this time.

Raven crossed her arms. "You're not going anywhere. And you have to talk to the police. Security from Scorpio Corporation wants to see you, too." In a more subdued voice, she added, "Also Colonel Lavinda Majda."

Well, good. "So go get them."

She didn't budge. "You woke up thirty minutes ago. You aren't ready to see anyone."

"You refusing Majda?" I was so annoyed with my enforced bed rest, I was even willing to invoke their name, which I normally avoided like indigestion.

She didn't look the least intimidated. "Using the Majdas to get around me won't work. If you'd like, I can contact their doctor."

Well, damn. I knew the Majdas' personal physician. She didn't take shit from anyone, including me. "Fine," I growled. "When can I see all these people?"

Raven lowered her arms. "I'd like you to rest for another few hours. I injected specialized nanomeds into your body. Give them time to repair your artery. I'll check on you later this afternoon. If you're healing well, you can talk to your visitors."

A few hours. I supposed I could live with that. I felt more worn out than I wanted to admit. With a grunt, I lay on my back and stared at the sky-blue ceiling.

Rustles came from across the room as she did whatever doctors do when they check their machines to make sure you aren't dying or misbehaving. Eventually her footsteps receded as she left the room, until only the distant hums and clicks of the hospital kept me company. I turned on my side and gazed at the landscapes glowing on the walls, images of the Vanished Sea. Eons ago, long before humans came to Raylicon, an ocean had filled that great basin. Another image showed the ruins of the alien starships that had brought our ancestors to Raylicon six thousand years ago. No one could visit those ships except the military and a few scientists cleared to study them. They'd sat in the harsh desert sun for millennia, all that remained of whoever stranded humans on this world.

I closed my eyes and drowsed, thinking about the ruins. My ancestors had built an interstellar civilization using the libraries on those ships, but their Ruby Empire had fallen thousands of years ago. In this modern age, an elected Assembly ruled the Imperialate; the

Ruby Pharaoh's position was only titular. She led the House of Skolia, just like the Majda Matriarch led the House of Majda, but she no longer ruled.

Except . . .

We called ourselves the Skolian *Imperialate*, not the Federated Worlds of Whatever. If it ever came to a challenge between the Assembly and the Ruby Dynasty, the military might well throw their formidable power behind the dynasty. The Pharaoh's Army was its oldest branch, with six thousand years of fealty to the empire. And yah, many people still considered Skolia an empire, not a democracy. So sue us. The Majda Matriarch also served as General of the Pharaoh's army, one of the four joint commanders of Imperial Space Command. That alone placed her among the Imperialate's most forceful leaders . . .

Sometime later I became aware of someone watching me. I opened my eyes to find Jak sitting on a stool by the bed, his dark clothes and hair a sharp contrast to the sky-blue room.

"Eh," I said.

"Eh, Bhaaj." He was verbose today, using two words for his greeting.

"How'd you get in here?"

He shrugged. "Easy. Cyber-rider shroud."

Ah, good. A well-constructed shroud could help hide him from monitors, including optical, ultraviolet, infrared, radar, microwave, and neutrino sensors. I used one when I went to the Undercity, to keep the Majdas or anyone else from spying on me. Shrouds that hid you that well tended to be military grade and not available to civilians. That never daunted our cyber-riders. They'd provide Jak with top-notch protection using smuggled parts and black-market tech.

"You got knifed." Jak leaned forward. "Stupid. Almost dead stupid."

I sat up, more startled that he called me stupid than annoyed. "Not stupid."

"Walking in plain view."

"City has defenses."

"City has crap."

Normally I'd have challenged him on that. Cries had military-grade defenses even for the civilian population. Not that I would call it a military state, because, you know, you didn't say that, not where anyone could overhear. Besides, its wealthy population wanted protection even if it meant giving up some of their privacy. Yet despite all that, in the last day someone had twice nearly managed to kill me.

"Yah, stupid," I decided. My attacker was smart. Too smart. No one could trick the defenses in Cries that well. They had to be part of the same security infrastructure they were outwitting, which placed them high in the city hierarchy.

"You need to be more careful." Jak switched into the Cries dialect, which he always did when he wanted to stress a point with me. "Someone big is after you."

"Someone in Scorpio security or the city police."

"Or Majda." His dark gaze simmered.

"Maybe." I didn't see why Majda would want me dead. Nor did murder seem like their style. They had more subtle ways to achieve their goals. I'd never met any other group so adept at doing whatever the hell they wanted without breaking laws, at least not in ways you could trace. "Scorpio seems more likely."

"Police don't like you, either."

"Yah. But they wouldn't throw knives. They'd shoot."

He shook his head. "It's easier to hide a knife from the city monitors."

Doctor Raven's voice came from across the room. "How the hell did you get in here?"

Jak looked past me and spoke in his deepest voice, a tone meant to sound pleasant, but that came across as menacing more than anything else. "My greetings, Doctor."

I turned to see Raven walking toward us. She frowned at Jak. "You have to leave. The major is recuperating."

Jak almost smiled. He didn't, because he didn't know her, but apparently he found the concept of me obediently lying here to recuperate funny enough that he stopped being irked at the doctor. "She's too ornery to stay put."

I scowled at him. "You heard her. Leave."

He did smile then. "Go with care, Bhaaj." With that, he vanished. Not literally; I could make out a slight ripple in the air in the shape of his body. He'd activated the holographic portion of his shroud, which used screens and tiny light sources in his clothes, and holo-dust on his skin, to project images of his surroundings. It showed realistic views of the room behind his body instead of him, so he seemed to disappear. The shroud had limitations, especially close up, but the farther away the viewer, the better the camouflage.

"What?" Doctor Raven blinked at the place where Jak had vanished.

"He does that sometimes," I said.

She spoke wryly. "Major, you are not the world's easiest patient."

I could have told her that.

"I don't know who threw the knife," I repeated.

Detective Talon from Scorpio Security was recording my statement with her wrist-cam. She stood near my hospital bed where I sat with my legs dangling. Lavinda Majda had accompanied her. Although it made sense for Majda to check on me, given how much they paid for my services, I hadn't expected Lavinda. She showed respect by coming here when she could have sent an underling. The colonel stood back in the room, tall and silent by the entrance arch. Gold mosaics bordered the doorway, another indication this was no ordinary hospital, but a high-end clinic.

"Then you didn't see anyone?" Talon asked me.

"I didn't have a chance," I said. "I barely managed to dodge in time."

"How did you know to dodge?" Talon frowned. "According to our footage of the incident, you had no warning."

I'd wondered that myself. "I saw a flash."

"No flash shows in our recordings." From Talon's suspicious tone, you'd have thought I was the criminal rather than the victim. "And yet somehow you threw yourself down in the exact moment your attacker threw the knife."

I leaned forward. "I should be asking how someone got that close to me with a weapon."

Talon's expression turned bland. "That portion of the city is monitored by army security, not Scorpio Corporation."

Lavinda came forward. "Our security didn't pick up anyone with a knife."

"Why not?" I asked—and immediately regretted my tone. My recuperating brain was worse off than I realized, because I'd just disrespected someone I admired. "Colonel, I apologize for my discourtesy. I didn't mean to sound rude."

Lavinda didn't look offended. "You ask a good question. The knife should have set off warnings. Yet whoever threw it didn't register on our monitors. We're checking on it."

"Has anyone else in the Quida investigation been attacked?" I asked.

"Only you," Lavinda said. "We'll get this figured out, Major."

I nodded to her, and she inclined her head.

"We could get you a Scorpio bodyguard." Talon spoke as if that idea smelled bad.

"Or a military escort," Lavinda said.

"No, that's all right. I'll take precautions." I was probably better at being a bodyguard than most anyone they could provide, besides which, it would hamper my investigation to have someone following me around. If I showed up in the Undercity with a bodyguard, no one would talk to me.

"Maybe you should leave the investigation to those of us trained for this," Talon said.

Well, screw you too. I'd looked at her record. She didn't even come close to my experience. I couldn't tell if she didn't like me nosing around her jurisdiction or she just plain disliked me. Lavinda was harder to read, but she should know I never backed down. It was one reason the Majdas hired me. I could be as tenacious as a byte-bull infecting a mesh system.

I said only, "I'm sure I'll be fine."

Whoever tried to kill me had made this personal, and no way would I let that go.

❖ CHAPTER III ❖
SHADOWS

Grief honored no boundaries. When it stepped into our lives, it could hit like a hammer, smother like fog, or crouch like a beast, waiting to attack. As soon as I saw Lukas Quida, I knew it had invaded his heart and left him no refuge.

We met at the mansion. He was pacing in the media center, a white room that produced a pleasant, almost inaudible hum. Holoscreens on the walls projected starscapes of interstellar clouds in vibrant colors against the backdrop of space. The room consisted of wide spaces with luminous white consoles and smart-chairs that resembled modern sculptures. A crystal vase on one table held three green stalks with red flowers. Normally I appreciated clean, brisk architecture full of light and space, but when Lukas stopped pacing and stood there, watching me with exhausted anguish on his face, all that pristine beauty seemed barren. His wife's absence felt tangible in the air.

"Major Bhaajan!" He strode over to me. "Have you heard anything?"

"My honor at your presence, Del Lukas," I said. "That was actually my question for you. You still haven't received a ransom demand?"

"Nothing." Disappointment flooded his face. He took a breath, then let it out slowly. "My apology. I don't usually yell at people when they walk into the house."

"No worries. I'd have reacted the same." I actually tended to become very quiet when I worried, but I sympathized with his reaction. "I'm sorry I don't have better news."

His assistant was standing a few paces away from us, a young man who looked like he wasn't long out of university. He asked, "Would you like me to stay, sir?"

Lukas glanced at him. "No, that's fine, Bessel. I'll comm you if I need anything else."

Bessel bowed and left the room. He had an assured air, one that didn't blend into the background. He also had the black hair and eyes prized among the Cries elite because it meant you looked like Skolian nobility. I wondered if he knew he also had the same name as an ancient mathematician from the planet Earth.

"Why hasn't anyone contacted us?" Lukas asked. The dark circles under his eyes were even worse now than last night. I wondered if he'd slept at all.

"We're working hard to find her." I did my best to sound reassuring, but I doubted I fooled him. It had been too long; if she had been taken for a ransom, her kidnappers would have made contact by now. "No news is better than bad news."

He twisted the cuffs of his shirt. "I can't stand not knowing."

"It would help if I could ask some more questions."

"Anything. But I'm afraid I've said everything I can think of. I talked to you, security, the police, everyone." He took a ragged breath. "Hell, I'd talk to the walls if it would help find her."

I motioned toward the chairs. "It's quieter now, with less people. Let's go through it again. Maybe we missed something last night."

Lukas dropped into a chair, sitting on its edge. He looked like a model, but he handled himself as if he had no clue how he appeared and didn't care. He'd worked as a financial advisor before he married Mara Quida. From what I'd seen of his background, he seemed more of a reticent scholar than any sort of glitterati. I sat in the chair opposite him, and it shifted, trying to make me more comfortable. Both our chairs were working overtime in their futile attempts to do their jobs.

"Did you get the police analysis?" Lukas asked. "I asked them to send it to you."

"Yes, I got it." So it had been him, not Talon, who had the reports sent. Lukas had guts, asking the police, who didn't have to do squat about what he said, particularly given that he was their top suspect. Even more interesting, they had done what he wanted. Maybe I wasn't the only one who didn't find him credible as a suspect.

"Their analysis included a DNA scan of the entire mansion," I said. "Hundreds of people have been in your house, far more than at the party last night."

"We entertain a lot." He made it sound more like a duty than a pleasure. "Scorpio Security went through the list with me. We can account for everyone."

Although I hadn't found anything unusual either, I didn't know all of the names. "Was anyone listed who shouldn't have been at the gala?"

"Yes, many." He raked his hand through his hair. "The analysts tell me they can't time-stamp most of the ID scans to say for certain if the DNA came from last night or an earlier time."

"What about visual records?" They'd sent me interminable recordings showing rich people having fun while everyone else, human and robotic both, worked hard so the partygoers didn't notice how much effort it took to host the event. "Did you see anyone you didn't expect?"

"No one. Everyone there was supposed to be there."

I leaned forward. "What about those few minutes in the master bedroom when your wife disappeared." Convenient, how all trace of those records had vanished.

"Whoever deleted the record knew what they were doing. No one can reconstruct the missing part." He sounded so tired. "And yes, I know, I'm one of the people best positioned to dispose of them. I didn't do it, Major. I'll take any lie detector test you want."

"No need. I saw the results of your tests with the police." They'd found no indication he was lying. I wasn't surprised. His appearance made it difficult for me to be objective, though. Those sculpted cheekbones, his perfect skin, the dark coloring valued by the aristocracy, and his luxuriant hair, which was black today instead of silver—it was difficult to see past his exterior. I'd grown up in a place where that kind of beauty didn't exist. Life in the Undercity destroyed perfection.

"I realize lie detector tests aren't enough to clear me," he said. "But surely it's enough to motivate considering other possibilities."

"Yes, it is." I wondered how hard the other investigators were coming down on him, that he seemed worried we wouldn't investigate anyone else. "I see several possibilities. The kidnappers may have been guests at the party. Or maybe they found a way to get in and out without leaving a trace." I didn't tiptoe around the last option. "Or your wife left by her own choice."

"She wouldn't do that!" He lifted his hands as if showing me his frustration. "Major, I know I'm a cliché, the youthful husband everyone thinks married his powerful wife for her money. And yes, I know the whispers, that people think she wanted to trade me in for a newer version." He dropped his hands. "I doubt anything I say will change what people want to believe. But it wasn't that way between Mara and me. We were good together."

I hated what I had to say next. Lukas didn't deserve any of this. But I had to speak. "Unless she wanted to disappear, even fake her death. She could have set you up to look guilty so she could run off in secret with her lover."

He stared at me for a full five seconds. Finally, he spoke in a slow, cold voice. "You know nothing about my wife, to accuse her of something that cruel. She didn't have an unkind atom in her body. Yes, she could be hard-hitting in her job. But she was a good person, the kind of good that goes deep."

Two facts jumped out at me: He defended her without a word about himself, and he used the past tense. He already believed, at least subconsciously, that she had died.

I spoke quietly. "Del Lukas, are you a Kyle?"

He blinked at me. "What?"

"Are you a Kyle operator? A psion. An empath or a telepath."

"Well, no. I'm not." A smile gentled his face. "Mara was a strong psion. She was like—like a presence in my mind. An incredible presence. She became part of me."

His words sounded like what Jak used to say about me when we were young. I spoke with care. "Why do you think your wife died? Do you feel her absence?"

"She's not dead!" He rose to his feet. "She *can't* be dead." He sounded more desperate than convinced.

"I'm sorry." I hated these questions. "We still have the other option, that the kidnappers took her without leaving a trace."

He took a deep breath and sat down. "As far as I know, that's impossible. Our security is better even than the best military protections."

It didn't surprise me. I'd seen the high level of protection these technocrats could claim. "What about option one? Could it be someone you invited?"

"I didn't personally know every guest who attended. But we have recordings of what everyone was doing when she disappeared."

"Except in her bedroom."

His mask of restraint slipped, and for a moment I saw the man terrified for his wife. Then his expression shuttered as if he had closed a door. I understood. The elite of Cries were known for their emotional reserve, and he would honor that custom even if it came less naturally to him.

"The only DNA the police found in the bedroom was mine and hers." Lukas spoke as if that were good rather than yet more evidence against him. He saw only that it meant she had been true to him and their vows.

"That assumes security here is as good as you think," I said. "If someone did get in, then the lack of evidence means they could eliminate any trace of their presence. It's difficult to erase all hint of a person's DNA, but not impossible. High-end nanobots can be programmed for specific DNA. If they're well shrouded, they can fly in, do their job, and leave without anyone knowing."

He lifted his hand, palm facing me, as if to block my words. "This house can counter all bot species."

"All known species." It could be something new. "Is it possible someone threatened her? Or you? If she feared for your life, would she do what they wanted?"

"Yes, I think so." He spoke awkwardly. "Our marriage started as a financial merger, but it soon became more. We were well suited. Do I believe Mara loves me? Yes, absolutely. I can't imagine being without her, and she often said the same about me. If they threatened me, I believe she would do whatever they wanted."

"You clearly mean a lot to her." I actually had no idea how she felt, but the words needed saying. Although he might be the world's greatest actor, I didn't think so. He wasn't faking how he felt about his wife.

"She would never have destroyed that scroll," he added. "If someone took her, they must have ripped it up. But why? It serves no purpose."

"Maybe they tried to subdue her. They might have ruined the scroll to show they meant business." On the surface, it seemed the most plausible explanation, but at a gut level, I wasn't convinced. It looked like the fringes of an explosion had caught that scroll. "Del Lukas, I'd like you to think back to your conversations last night with your guests. Did anyone say anything that struck you as odd? Not necessarily hostile. Just strange, off-kilter, not the usual."

"Not really." He considered the idea. "Even Jen Oja was on her best behavior."

"Who is Jen Oja?" The name sounded familiar.

"Another Scorpio exec." He shook his head. "She resented Mara. Jen felt she deserved the Metropoli contract. She didn't like Mara, but she's always professional in her interactions."

"What was Oja doing when your wife vanished?"

"Getting dessert, actually." Lukas sounded calmer now. Talking about last night seemed to help. "I looked for her because I feared she might, well, I don't know. Try to undermine Mara's success. But she didn't do anything. She seemed to enjoy the party."

Max, I thought. *Do you have records of a Jen Oja from last night?*

Yes. Nothing is flagged as suspicious.

Have the files ready for me to check. To Lukas, I said, "I'd like you to put a list together."

"All right. Of what?"

"Anyone who didn't like your wife."

"I did for the police. It should be in the files they sent you."

"It is. But I want you to think about it again. Include anyone you don't trust."

He spoke dryly. "That's a long list. My wife is a powerful executive in a harsh business."

"You never know what will help." I had one last request. "Do you remember the crystal sphere at the top of the banister? The one I thought someone had turned."

He nodded. "The police checked. Apparently one of the housecleaning bots turned it."

"Apparently?"

"The deleted record includes that area just outside the bedroom." He rubbed the back of his neck, working the muscles as if they ached too much for even the nanomeds in his body to relax. "We have a record of a bot cleaning the banister just before the deletion."

It sounded routine. But still. "Would you mind if I took the sphere with me?"

"What for?"

I wasn't sure myself. It bothered me, that one detail in their perfectly arranged house. "I'd like my people to take a look at it."

"Sure, you can take it. Whatever you think will help."

Lukas took me through the halls and up the sweeping staircase. At the top, on the banister, the sphere sparkled, refracting light into prismatic colors. He unscrewed the orb and gave it to me. "Here you go."

"Thanks." I was glad he didn't ask what I was going to do with it, because I doubted he would approve of what I planned for this pretty chunk of rock.

I walked across the bluestone plaza that bordered the outskirts of Cries. Beyond the plaza, the red desert stretched to the mountains that edged the horizon. Cries lay behind me. I'd amped up my biomech sensors, and I carried a backpack with a jammer that shrouded me from would-be assassins. I hoped.

Max suddenly spoke through my wrist comm. "I've made contact with your green beetle-bot."

Finally. "Where has it been hiding?"

"It's currently flying over the city. I don't know yet where it was before that."

"Send me its memory files."

"All of them? It's been sixty hours since you released it at the mansion."

"Yah, I'd better look at it all. For now, condense it down for me."

"Working."

I continued walking. "I keep thinking someone is going to try shooting me out here."

"Even if you weren't shrouded," Max said, "it would be difficult to manage, given the increased security in the city."

I grimaced. "That doesn't do me much good if the people who attacked are in charge of the city defenses."

"True," Max admitted. "However, I am also monitoring this area."

"Good." I trusted his sensors. "You get anything useful from the green beetle?"

"It was hiding because its target had good sensors. The beetle wanted to evade detection."

"Smart little bot. What did it find?"

"It encrypted its records in case they caught it. I am doing a decryption."

"Let me know when you finish." I kept walking. I longed to jog, but Doctor Raven insisted I take it slow while the specialized meds she'd injected did their repairs. My knife wound still ached.

"Someone is tailing us," Max said.

I turned around, surveying the landscape. It looked empty. This was the middle of the forty-hour daylight period, so most people were in their midday sleep. "I don't see anyone."

"Your follower is coming from the city." Max activated my heads-up display. Crosshairs appeared in my view, centered between two buildings on the outskirts of Cries, about a kilometer distant. "They're using a holo-shroud."

"Is it Jak?"

"I don't think so." He magnified my view until it seemed like I was only a few meters from the target. Now I could see a ripple in the air, the faint outline of a human figure.

"That's not tall enough for Jak."

"Whoever it is, they are headed toward you."

I turned and resumed my walk toward the desert. "I'm supposed to be hidden."

"So are they," Max said. "I almost didn't detect that you had acquired a shadow. However, I am good at my job."

"So you are." Interesting. He'd never simulated pride before. "Keep monitoring them. Let me know if they speed up."

I headed for the entrance to the Concourse in the desert beyond the plaza. The Concourse supposedly served as the highest level of the Undercity. Yah, right. The wide boulevard offered a tourist trap where boutiques sold fake Undercity goods and cafés served fake Undercity food. Taxes on the goods offered a lucrative source of income for the city, and the upscale vendors made a fortune from tourist shoppers. The Cries police monitored the Concourse to make sure no person who actually lived in the Undercity ever sullied the boulevard with their presence.

It pissed me off. The Cries authorities fought my efforts to secure licenses for Undercity vendors, but our merchants had every right to sell their goods there. Even if my people could get licenses, though, they seemed unable to fathom the idea of selling goods to outsiders. We did everything with bargains, just among ourselves. City vendors didn't want us there, either. It wasn't only that they considered us the lowest of life. The savvier merchants also knew genuine Undercity goods could outsell their fake goods. They didn't want the competition, not even on commission. I was fed up with it all and determined to make changes.

"Max," I said. "Is my beetle close enough to check out whoever is following me?"

"Yes, it's in range."

"Good. Have it spy on them."

"Will do." Max paused. "Perhaps you should run."

I set off at a jog, relieved to get moving. Air brushed my cheeks, hot and dry. "Why?"

"Your shadow has speeded up."

"Won't my jogging give away that I know someone is there?"

"She probably can't tell how fast you're moving, since you're also shrouded."

"She?"

"Yes, I think so."

I kept running. Although it strained my bandaged abdomen, it wasn't too bad. To save energy, I thought to Max instead of talking. *Any sign she's armed?*

She hasn't drawn a weapon.

Send me a heads-up display of whatever my beetle is recording.

Done.

An image appeared in front of me like a ghost moving through the air. It showed a woman jogging across the plaza. She looked fit and athletic, but without the upright carriage I associated with the military. Like most people in Cries, she had dark hair. Her eyes were harder to see in the blurred image, but they looked hazel, which suggested she wasn't related to a noble House.

Can you ID her? I asked.

Not yet. She's hidden her mesh footprint. No worries; I will defeat her obfuscations.

I smiled. I didn't know anyone else who actually used the word obfuscation. *Good work. Let me know if she does anything threatening.*

I will. Right now, I detect no weapons on her person.

Although that didn't mean she had none, Max had excellent sensors, especially with the beetle augmenting them, and the city had ramped up security since yesterday. My shadow would be hard-pressed to hide anything dangerous.

I reached the edge of the plaza and ran down the short staircase to the desert. Red sand swirled around my feet. A few meters away, an archway rose out of the ground, glowing like moonstone, a contrast to the barren land that surrounded it. It had no door, just a shimmer that hid whatever lay beyond. I tried to step through the shimmer, as I had done hundreds of times—and it pushed back, refusing me entry.

"What the hell?" I said. "What's with the barrier?"

Max spoke aloud, taking his cue from me. "The shimmering effect you see is a molecular airlock, a modified lipid bilayer with nanobots doping its structure. Applying an electric potential across the membrane causes enzymes within it to alter shape and lock into receptor molecules. That changes its permeability. Such airlocks can be made impermeable to air, solids, even people—"

"Max, for flaming sake, I know how it works." I pushed the membrane. "It's not supposed to stop anything here. It's just for show or an emergency." I stiffened. "What's going on? Is there a problem down on the Concourse?"

"I find no indication of a problem."

I glanced toward the city. I couldn't see my pursuer.

"She is still there," Max said. "I calculate a ninety-percent probability that she hacked this archway and sent a signal to change its permeability. She's trying to slow you down. I am sending a signal to reset the membrane."

I was tempted to go ask my shadow why she was following me. *Toggle combat mode.*

Toggled, Max thought, unfazed by the way I switched between thought and speech. I'd become so used to communicating with him, even I didn't always know why sometimes I wanted to talk and sometimes I wanted to think.

As my body switched into combat mode, I became aware of every sound. The wind keened. Pyro-geckos scuttled through the sand and hissed out their fiery breath. The desert came into sharp focus, its grains of sand distinct, with the sparkle of blue azurite scattered in the red.

I'd advise you not to engage your pursuer, Max added, as if he could read my mind, which he sort of could.

Maybe she just wants to talk to me.

Max wasn't fooled. It's not her I'm worried about.

He knew me too well. After the attempts on my life, talking ranked low on my list. I wanted to hit something.

If she just wanted to talk, Max continued, she could easily contact you. You shouldn't take risks. You could tear open your wound, damaging your internal organs and suffering a blood loss that could become life-threatening—

All right! I'll behave. My hand, which was resting against the membrane, suddenly passed through the shimmer. *You fixed the molecular airlock.*

Yes. You can use it now.

As I walked through the membrane, it trailed along my skin like a soap bubble. I came out at the top of a staircase, and I ran down the stairs to the spacious lobby below. Bright images glowed on the sky-blue walls of the lobby, ads showing people laughing, dining, and shopping. Soft voices told me I wanted to buy this or that, especially expensive bottles of filtered water.

I jogged across the lobby and through a wide archway that led to the Concourse. The many tourists who thronged the wide boulevard spared me no more than a glance. In my trousers and pullover, I probably looked like a guard. A few did watch me uneasily, as if they weren't sure I belonged here. Even when I dressed like a Cries citizen, apparently I never looked fully civilized.

I passed many upscale boutiques at first, but I soon entered the maze of back streets behind the glitzy shops. Narrow alleys snaked between the buildings, with arches spanning the roofs above, turning the passages into tunnels. The Concourse sloped downward slightly. The avenue was long enough, over a kilometer, that by the time I reached the end, I would be hundreds of meters below the surface. As I ran, the buildings became dingier and the clamor of voices from the main boulevard receded. Even the most naive tourist knew better than to go this far down the avenue.

Max, I thought. *Is my shadow still following me?*

No, you lost her after you left the main Concourse.

Good. Have you figured out who she is?

Not yet. But I will.

I kept going, headed for my true home—assuming no one else showed up to kill me.

✜ CHAPTER IV ✜
THE AQUEDUCTS

Darkness that engulfed my senses. No light reached this far underground, not even a stray hint that might reveal the barest outline of my hands when I held them in front of my face. Silence filled the air, deeper than a sea, as if the world had gone mute, unable to speak its secrets. I brushed my hands along rocky walls on either side of my body as I walked, and the faint whisper of their touch might as well have been thunder. No voices broke the silence, no footsteps, nothing to indicate anyone existed in this dark, cool realm.

I knew better.

I'd hung a light stylus around my neck, but I didn't flick it on. My hands hit a barrier. I felt along it until I found a tall crack in the stone. After I squeezed through the crack, I continued walking. My hands scraped over rippled rock formations. If any light had revealed their stark beauty, I'd have seen stalagmites that rose in cones from the ground, and stalactites that hung like stone icicles from the ceiling. Mineral-saturated water had created them eons ago, dripping relentlessly. No trace of that water remained; this cave had dried out long ago. The air smelled of dust, an aromatic scent from traces of benzene compounds, nothing poisonous, but enough to tinge the air. I loved it. I'd grown up assuming dust smelled good. That was before I shipped offworld at seventeen to train with all the other grunts in the stinking grit of other worlds.

Even in the darkness, I knew when I reached an open space. I tapped my stylus and light flared. After all the darkness, it might as well have been the blinding glare of a flood lamp. Gradually, as my eyes adjusted, the intensity eased until it was no more than a dim sphere around my body. I could see again—and it was worth the wait. I'd always loved to come this way, through the dark, revealing the beauty at the end in a flare of radiance.

This was the Undercity.

I had come out into an underground canal, part of what we called the aqueducts, though I'd never understood that name. This conduit was far too big to be an aqueduct, besides which, if water had ever flowed through here, it had disappeared ages ago. All that remained was a wonderland of canals, caves, and stone lacework that honeycombed the ground below the desert for many kilometers in every direction near the City of Cries. The Undercity dwarfed Cries, but most of it remained inaccessible unless you knew the ways and people of this hidden world.

I stood on a midwalk, a pathway large enough for two people to walk side by side. It was about halfway up the wall of the canal, midway between the ground and the rock ceiling. Arched supports reinforced the canal. At intervals, a long-dead artist had carved statues into the wall, ancient and detailed, work that survived the eons with the careful attention of the Undercity population. The statues showed deities and their spirit companions from the pantheon our ancestors had worshipped millennia ago.

Ixa Quelia, goddess of life and fire, stood near me with her hair streaming along the wall, engraved into the stone, her features chiseled, the high cheekbones, straight nose, and large eyes associated with the nobility. She held the embers of life, a quartz circle embedded in the rock. The statue beyond showed her spirit companion "Chaac," a name my people spoke in the ancient manner, with glottals at the start and end of the word, a pronunciation rarely heard among modern Skolians. Chaac looked human from the waist up, but she had tufted ears and the body of a hunting cat. She held the axe of lightning and a shield painted with gold, red, and white rings, the colors kept bright by those of my people who tended these statues.

Modern sculptures stood in the canal below, shaped from dust and hardened by chemical applications we'd had passed down for generations. One showed a woman and man standing back to back, both turned forward. Muscled and beautiful, with their daggers drawn, they were modern-day warriors. They mirrored an ancient statue above them on the midwalk, a female warrior in a similar pose, holding a sword at the ready, her body turned forward. She had one hand on the shoulder of a man who sat facing the canal, his head lifted, his clothes those of a barbarian prince. The contrast of the men in the two statues spoke volumes. Cries might struggle to reconcile modern society with the ancient ways, but my ancestors had left those traditions behind thousands of years ago when they retreated to live underground. We had neither the interest nor the luxury of secluding our men. Even the older statue on the midwalk had a different quality. Although the man had a less aggressive pose than in the modern sculpture, he leaned forward with a fierce intensity that hardly fit the notions of cloistered, protected princes from the history books.

The entire scene glittered as the light from my stylus struck crystals embedded in the stone, thousands of them sparkling like a multitude of tiny stars. It was breathtaking, and it was *ours*, hidden deep beneath the desert. Even the archeologists who came to study the ruins, those few my people allowed to visit the aqueducts, had never discovered these depths of the ruins.

I set off jogging along the midwalk, settling into a familiar rhythm. An entire city of ruins existed here. Our ancestors had built some of this thousands of years ago; the rest dated from a time before humans came to this world, a reminder our species hadn't originated on Raylicon, but on a blue-green paradise called Earth.

The legend of our home world had grown misty with time. Six thousand years ago, an alien race had taken humans from Earth, stranded them on Raylicon, and then vanished, leaving the lost humans fighting to survive. Nothing remained of that unknown race except three crumbling starships on the shores of the Vanished Sea. However, those ships contained the library of a starfaring race. Much of it had been destroyed; what remained described sciences unlike anything we used today. Although it had taken centuries, my ancestors developed star travel from those libraries and went in search of their lost home. They never found Earth, but they built an interstellar empire. Based on poorly understood technology and plagued by volatile politics, the Ruby Empire had soon collapsed, and the ensuing Dark Ages lasted for millennia. Eventually we regained space travel and formed today's Skolian Imperialate.

When Earth's people finally reached the stars, they found us already here, building empires. We rejoiced to reunite with our lost siblings. Our origins remained a mystery, however. No civilization from six thousand years ago on Earth matched our culture. Our ancestors seemed too advanced to have come from any group in that time frame. But we could never be sure. Before they achieved space travel, the people of Earth had fought what they called the Virus Wars, which acted in both the cyber and biological arenas, devastating Earth's population and her digital history. If a memory remained of our ancestors there, we had yet to find that record.

Here in the Undercity, my people lived with famine and wonder, pain and joy, deep below the desert in the magnificent ruins of an alien civilization that had been ancient before humans ever walked this world.

Torches shed light across the canal, set into the walls in metal scones that looked like roaring beasts. Their fiery light revealed two fighters on the floor of the canal locked in a sparring match. Red dust swirled around them and only the thud of muscle on muscle broke the silence. Three other fighters stood back, intent on the bout. Together, these five ranked as my top tykado students. They were in their early twenties, considered adults in the aqueducts even though by Imperialate law, they wouldn't reach the age of majority until twenty-five. Down here, children grew up fast.

The two in the sparring match were members of the Ruzik dust gang, a tall woman named Tower and a man called Byte-2. Ruzik himself stood leaning against the wall with his arms crossed, studying the fighters. At twenty, he was the youngest of the five, but that took nothing from his leadership. Tats covered his shoulders, stylized depictions of his namesake, the giant reptilian beasts called ruziks that ranged across the desert above. People from Earth compared the creatures to a Tyrannosaurus Rex. So maybe a ruzik looked sort of like that dinosaur, but its front limbs were longer and more powerful, and iridescent scales covered its body.

Ruzik's girlfriend Angel stood next to him. Dressed in dusty trousers and a torn muscle shirt that showed her well-defined abs, with her muscular arms crossed, she looked about as angelic as a barbarian warrior-goddess from Raylican mythology. The third fighter watching the match was Hack, Ruzik's best friend. Hack fought well, yah, but his true genius was at creating tech-mech. He had become a cyber-wizard unequalled by anyone else in the Undercity even among the surreally tech-savvy cyber-riders.

These were my tykado experts, five violently beautiful youths, all surviving into adulthood, a rarity here. I stood by the wall, dressed like them, studying their technique as they fought. They called this canal Lizard Trap and claimed it as their territory, which they marked with dust sculptures of ruziks rearing up on their back legs. It reminded me of the gang I'd run with in my youth, protecting our circle of kith and kin. Ruzik's gang looked after a large circle: ten children ranging in ages from a baby to older adolescents, and also a group of adults that included Hack. As the cyber-rider for the circle, Hack played the meshes for them like a virtuoso.

Tower dropped into a roll and kicked Byte-2 in the ankles. With a grunt, Byte-2 tripped and slammed into the ground. As Tower jumped up, I walked over, holding up my hand to stop her. I spoke in the Undercity dialect, short and succinct. "Illegal move."

Tower scowled. "Good move."

Byte-2 stood up. He looked more pissed at me than at Tower, even though she was the one who had cheated against him. "Smart move," he said in his gravelly voice.

"Illegal," I said. "Tykado rules forbid."

Angel glowered at me. "Screw the rules. Move works, move good."

Patience, I told myself. They knew tykado wasn't the rough-and-tumble of their gang fights. Sure, they were good street fighters, and they'd been refining their skills all their lives, practicing every day for the sheer love of the challenge. They'd learned tykado fast when we started two years ago, but that didn't mean they were ready to earn their first-degree black belts. Tykado was about more than knocking down your opponent. It was a way of life.

I crossed my arms. "No rules, no black belt."

"Fuck black belt," Angel rumbled.

I knew they'd never admit they were nervous about testing with an elite Cries Tykado Academy, grouped with city students who came from a wealth and privilege these five could barely imagine. So they blustered. They also worked hard, practicing every day.

A wicked smile played around Ruzik's lip. "Not the belts," he told his girlfriend.

Angel laughed, her tension easing. Then she remembered she was pissed and gave me a look that could have melted steel. "Tykado rules shit."

"Only one rule," Byte-2 offered. "Win."

"Yah." Tower brightened. "We fix tykado rules. Make them better."

I could just imagine what the ITF, or Interstellar Tykado Federation, would say to that idea. "Tykado rules fix you. Make you better."

Angel gave me an exasperated look. "Always you say this. How am I better?"

"Smarter than city slicks," I said.

That answer got approving looks from them all. Ruzik spoke quietly. "We'll do their rules better than them. Don't need special treatment."

The others quit arguing then. Ruzik had chosen a good approach; it was a point of pride for them to achieve the same honors as Cries students without special consideration.

I called a rest, and they gathered on stone benches by the wall. Statues of winged reptiles supported the seats, their heads tilted back, their fanged mouths open in roars, their massive tails curled on the canal floor. The works sold by Concourse vendors didn't come close to this artistry. I couldn't interest any of those vendors in taking work by our artists on commission, though. Even if they'd been willing to share profits with Undercity artists, which they weren't, they didn't believe my people could make anything worth selling. They thought the craftwork I showed them was fake, that I meant to cheat them. The few who realized they were seeing the genuine article were even less willing to sell them. They'd rather refuse whatever they could earn than admit Undercity artists created better works than them. Well, screw that. It just strengthened my determination to get Concourse licenses for my people.

As the fighters did their cool down, I went to another bench. The gash in my abdomen ached, and I needed a pause, so I sat and considered our options. My students had participated in two tykado tournaments, the first ever sanctioned events between Cries and the Undercity. Before that, interactions between our cultures had consisted of Undercity kids sneaking to the Concourse to steal food, cops chasing them back to the aqueducts, clandestine visits by the Cries elite to Jak's casino, the drug trade, secret trysts between forbidden lovers, and other whacked out misbehavior. Those two tournaments, for all their simplicity, were unprecedented. They almost hadn't happened because no Cries academy wanted anything to do with Undercity teams. That changed when Lavinda Majda offered to give out the awards. She was the closest I had to an ally in the House of Majda. It also helped that another ally of mine, Professor Ken Roy from Cries University, knew people at the Cries Tykado Academy and put in a word for us. With two such distinguished supporters, CTA agreed to a tournament. Their students had expected to win easily, but the fights had been close and my group bested them in several matches.

My fighters sat together now, dark hair shaggy about their faces as they talked about their technique. Good. They'd caught the interest of the Cries coaches, so I was negotiating for them to test for their official tykado belts. But which ones? They trained every day, often for hours, far more than most Cries students. They hadn't started out in tykado, though, and they still had gaps in their technique. Although they already had the equivalent of the lower belts, they hadn't earned them at a school accredited by the ITF. The Cries Tykado Academy agreed to test them for first-degree black belts anyway, because in return I agreed to work with the academy students. It was a good bargain: As a sixth-degree black belt, I needed to teach as part of the training for my next level. I worried, though. As much as I didn't want to hold back my students, who burned with dreams, if I let them test too soon and they failed, it could backfire. These five were trailblazers, informal ambassadors from the Undercity to Cries. The last thing I wanted was for them to feel humiliated in front of the city students, who already considered them inferior.

Footsteps sounded down the canal, muffled by dust. I looked up to see a huge figure walking in the shadows beyond the golden torchlight. As I stood up, he came into view. He towered, with wide shoulders, powerful arms, and legs like tree trunks. Yah, Gourd was big. Fortunately he liked engineering better than beating up people.

Of course, no one here called him an engineer; our dialect didn't even include the word. He was a mech wizard.

"Eh, Gourd," I said as he came up to me.

"Eh, Bhaaj." He nodded, and a curl of gray-streaked hair fell into his eyes. When had it started to change color? It seemed only yesterday we'd been kids, running with Jak in our own gang. We were both in our forties now, but he had no nanomeds in his body to delay his aging.

My efforts to improve medical care in the Undercity sometimes felt like wading through quicksand. Cries preferred to forget about the inconvenient slum under the desert. My people wanted nothing to do with Cries and would never accept anything they considered charity. Although I'd been making progress, seeing Gourd's graying hair brought home how far I still had to go.

Gourd settled next to me onto the stone bench. "Heard whisper. You looking for me?"

"Yah," I said. "You need to see Doctor Rajindia."

"What for?"

I touched his hair. "Get health meds."

He shrugged. "Feel fine. Like my hair."

"Meds keep you always feeling fine."

Gourd grimaced. "Don't want them in my body. They never go away."

I understood. I'd been uneasy when I got mine in the army. But now I took for granted the advantages of having little molecular laboratories cruising my bloodstream, taking care of my health. "Worth it. Live better, live longer."

He crossed his huge arms and scowled. "Jak says this, too. Him and his meds."

I'd never figured out where Jak got his, but I was glad he had them. "So yah, it's good."

"Won't take charity."

Again we came to that. He wouldn't take anything for free, and he was one of the few people in the Undercity who understood how much meds cost. I knew how to reach him, though.

"Make a bargain," I said.

He uncrossed his arms and regarded me curiously. "You get me meds, I do what?"

"Work for me. Do research."

"Like what?"

I reached behind the bench and grabbed my backpack. Opening it up, I took out the sphere from the Quida mansion. "This."

Over on the other bench, Angel lifted her head. "Pretty," she said. She and the others nodded their greeting to Gourd, who nodded back. They then went back to their tykado talk.

I handed the sphere to Gourd. He turned it around, letting it catch glints of light. "Bright."

"Puzzle," I said.

"Why?" He tossed the ball into the air and caught it. "Round. Puzzle solved."

I smiled. "Check it out for me."

"Check for what?"

"Not sure. Was twisted."

He gave a hearty laugh, deep and rumbling. "What, evil or just kinky?"

I couldn't help but grin. "No kink. Just turned on its post. It was on a stair rail."

"In a Cries place?"

"A mansion."

He snorted. "Pretty and useless." It summed up how most of my people felt about the city.

I took the ball and stuck it on my thumb. "Should fit like this." I twisted the ball around, lifting it slightly. "I found it like this. Strange."

"Why care?"

"Got job. City job. Woman gone. City exec." I paused. "Maybe dead."

He stopped smiling. "And this ball matters?"

"I don't know. Cops say it's fine. Cleaning bot twisted it." I offered him the ball. "Seems wrong."

He held the ball, testing its weight. "Wrong why?"

I wished I knew. "Not sure. Bots are smart. Wouldn't move the ball. But it's moved. You find what cops missed, eh?"

"I'll look. Problem might be the cleaning bot, though."

He had a point. Although the police had found no problems with the bots, you never knew. Even so. Gourd could maybe come at it from a different angle. "We'll see. Check, yah?"

He slid the ball into a pouch hanging from his leather belt. "Will do."

I nodded my thanks. "Got good news, too. For water."

He perked up. "You can get new mech for my filters?"

"Get you city mech. Top-notch."

He stopped looking interested. "Not news, Bhaaj. I always get city mech."

"Not stolen mech. Not salvage, either. Legal and new."

"Nahya!" He thumped his big fist on his thigh. "No charity."

"Not charity."

He still didn't look interested. "Can't buy it. Don't have optos. Don't want optos."

"Don't need optos." Most Imperialate economies used opto-credits, a currency transferred through electro-optical systems. You never saw an opto, which was why my people considered them a scam. The Undercity economy worked on an exchange of goods or services. Gourd either traded his skills for what he needed on the black market or else mined salvage from the city tech-mech dumps. If people in Cries threw it out, then taking it wasn't charity.

"Got a trade," I said. "With Ken Roy. You talk to him."

"Why?" He sounded more puzzled than anything else. "Ken looks at ruins."

"Not exactly. Not an anthropologist. Terraformer."

Gourd smirked at that. In our dialect, using a word with two syllables was considered emphasis. Three syllables either meant the speaker wanted to show importance with the word, as in "aqueducts," or else they meant it as ridicule. A four-syllable word implied incredible importance, a great insult, or a huge joke. My people considered Undercity two words: Under-city. The words I used to describe Cries amused them no end. I'd given up trying to explain I wasn't insulting Ken Roy when I said he chaired the Terraforming Division at the university.

Gourd waved his hand at me. "Jibber, Bhaaj."

I regarded him sourly. "Not gibberish. He wants talk to you."

"Why me?"

"For his study on the aqueducts." I'd met Ken Roy last year. He was studying the failure of the terraforming on Raylicon, as our world slowly became uninhabitable. He wanted to understand what motivated my ancestors to move underground, retreating to these ruins so many millennia ago. Of course, no one in the aqueducts wanted anything to do with him. So he was trying to work out bargains they would accept.

"Talk to Ken," I said. "Get good tech in return."

Gourd considered the idea. "Need new filters," he acknowledged. "Need more drinkable water. Many new births. That doctor you sent, she helps babies survive."

Ho! That was welcome news. Our population had one of the highest mortality rates in the Imperialate. Convincing a doctor to visit the aqueducts had taken some doing, but now that the military realized we had value to them, with so many empaths among us, they were more willing to help. Of course the charity business had reared its head, but Doctor Rajindia was no slouch. She learned fast how to bargain in the Undercity. She never came down without permission and the protection of a gang. She would treat anyone who asked for help, and in return, she asked to study the psions among us. Rajindia remained discreet and careful, never intrusive with her bargains, and gradually she earned the trust of my people.

Change was coming to the Undercity.

❖ CHAPTER V ❖
ABOVE CITY

"It happens every time I hear a sound in the house," Lukas said as we walked through the Cries park. Sprinklers misted water across the feather-grass and cooled our skin. "I jump, thinking she's come home. But it's never her." He waved his hand at the gardens as if to encompass its entirety of velvety lawns and imported trees wrapped with diaphanous vines that fluttered in the breezes. "How can this all look so beautiful? How can the world go on as if nothing happened?"

I started to lift my hand, to lay it on his arm, offering comfort. Then I stopped myself. Of course I couldn't touch him. The elite in Cries lived by such coldhearted customs to isolate a grieving man this way, but violating those traditions was no better. He didn't need the implied insult of my invading his personal space. I thought of the friends I'd lost to illness, hardship, and starvation in my youth, desperate in the Undercity, or the soldiers I'd fought with and lost to the violence of wars that never seemed to wane no matter how "civilized" humans became. It never stopped hurting, never stopped creating those empty spaces inside where grief crept with silent cruelty.

"I'm sorry." I wished I had something better to tell him.

Lukas started to speak, stopped, and then said, "You asked me before if I felt her presence. Major, I almost had a convulsion that night, at the gala, after she went upstairs and never came down. It was like a mental tsunami blasted through my mind."

I stared at him. "Why didn't you tell us?"

He spoke bitterly. "In my experience, comments like that from trophy husbands are relegated to the realm of 'high-strung neurotic.'"

"Del Lukas, you have never once given me the impression of anything but a sound mind."

He hesitated. "This may sound strange, but both she and I believed the neurological processes of our brains had become linked."

I thought of Jak. We'd grown up together, loved, fought, starved, triumphed, and failed together every day of our lives until I joined the army. He'd often infuriated me in our youth, the way he'd disappear for days without a word, off gambling or caught up in some scheme. Yet after I'd enlisted, I felt disconnected without him. The day I finally acknowledged that yes, I'd loved this man my entire life, it felt as if an undefined link became complete. Had some interaction between our brain waves become second nature? I had no idea. Jak wasn't an empath as far as either of us knew. This much I'd never doubted; if Jak died, then no matter what distance separated us, I would know.

"I think people connect to each other in ways we're only beginning to understand," I said.

"A few times I've dreamed we were together again, taking a walk or talking." Longing touched his voice. "It felt so real. As I woke up, just for an instant, I could have sworn she was lying next to me." He drew in a shaky breath. "Then I realize I'm alone."

That had to hurt. "Lukas, I can't tell you I'll bring her home. But I can promise you this. I won't stop investigating until I've done everything in my power to get you answers."

He looked at me without trying to disguise the pain of his loss. "Thank you, Major."

Somehow, someway, I had to find closure for this anguished man.

Jen Oja refused my attempts to set up a meeting. Tough. I strode across the spacious lobby of the Scorpio Corporation tower. Aqua-blue panels stretched from the floor to the ceiling three stories overhead, showing oceans on other worlds. A balcony bordered the second level, its transparent floor and rails designed to look as if water filled them. Several people stood up there, taking a break from work while they watched visitors come and go as if we were sea creatures within an ocean.

A robo-server blocked my way, humanoid in shape, with a transparent body that looked as if it were filled with water. Holo-fish swam within his interior. "Do you have an appointment?"

I walked around him, headed for the lifts. "No."

"Please stop." He moved in front of me again. "You must have an appointment."

"Look in your files for Major Bhaajan."

Blue lights flickered in his eyes. "Retained by the House of Majda," he told me, as if I didn't know. He moved aside. "Please proceed."

Well, so, that worked. I wondered how it felt to grow up as a Majda, with every door open and every desire met. It made a jarring contrast to my own childhood, with its crushing poverty. I'd wrestled with anger when I first came back to Raylicon. I managed better now because I could see progress in my efforts to improve life in the Undercity. The Majdas were even willing to help, and to follow my lead rather than trying to force their ideas on my people. I'd convinced them that such flexibility served their needs; they shouldn't risk damaging whatever created so many psions among our population.

When I reached the lift, its blue doors whisked open and I stepped into a round car. Its walls, ceiling, and floor showed holo-scenes of water rippling while sunlight slanted through the clear blue depths. Aquatic animals drifted past, gold and crimson. As the lift went up the tower, I felt as if I were rising through an ocean. It was all painfully beautiful on a world where the only body of water on the surface of the entire planet was an artificial lake at the Majda palace. Scorpio projected a clear message: They offered their elite clientele services as valuable, and as rare, as limitless water.

Maybe my ancestors had named the canals in the Undercity "aqueducts" because water meant power on Raylicon. Hell, that could explain a subconscious choice on my part when I'd dressed for this face-off with Jen Oja. My designer skirt, blouse, and jacket were all aqua blue.

The lift let me out in a corridor that smelled of fresh water. How did Scorpio do that? Pure water didn't have a smell. Yet as I walked along that spacious hallway, the air reminded me of freshwater lakes. The walls showed images of Scorpio Towers on other worlds, all near rivers or oceans. A fountain in a niche of the wall burbled with water, and blue-glass tumblers sat on a ledge. I tried to walk past it, but I couldn't resist. So I stopped, filled a glass, and drank deeply. Damn, that was good. When I set down the glass, it moved into a wall niche and vanished. Another glass slid out, taking its place. Feeling guilty for taking part in such a display of excess, I walked away. It was hard to believe drinking a glass of water was such a mundane activity on other worlds.

Jen Oja had a large office at the end of the corridor. Its colors matched the hallway, and a large window stretched across the far wall of the room. Niches in the walls displayed offworld artifacts. I hadn't realized just how high the lift had taken me until I saw the panoramic view. Cries spread out below, its towers elegant against the pale blue sky.

"Who are you?" a cold voice asked.

I pulled my gaze away from the spectacular view and focused on the woman I'd come to see. She sat at a large holo-table to the left. She looked exactly like the images I'd found of Jen Oja: black hair pulled into a sleek roll on her head, a face of sharp angles, and a lean build. She wore a tailored suit in that pale color people called ivory, whatever that meant. It looked to me like white and yellow got together and had a baby, but what did I know. Everything about her whispered elegance. No metallic hair, no vivid colors, no loud words from this Scorpio luminary.

"My name is Major Bhaajan," I said. "I'm an investigator working on the Quida case."

She considered me like a queen checking out a lizard scuttling through the sand. "I told your assistant Max I didn't have time to see you."

I walked into her office, and discovered I rather enjoyed the way she took such pains to hide her unease. Apparently even my expensive blue suit didn't make me look civilized. She tapped a panel on her table. "Security, send someone to escort my visitor out of the building."

The voice of the robo-server answered. "I'm sorry, Del Oja. She has clearance from Majda."

Oja scowled at the table as if the robo could see her. Hell, probably it could, given all the security here. She tapped off the comm and rose to her feet, facing me. "What do you want?"

I went to the table. "I'd like to talk to you about Mara Quida."

"I already talked to the authorities." Her voice was perfectly controlled. "I don't know what happened to her. I was downstairs when Mara did her little vanishing act."

"I'd still like to ask some questions." I kept my voice courteous. I'd already pissed her off, to see if it stirred anything useful, but if I took that too far, she'd have me kicked out, Majdas or no.

"I have work to do," she said.

"Just give me five minutes. Then I'll go."

At first, she said nothing. Then she let out an annoyed breath and motioned to a chair across the table. As I sat down, she settled into her big chair. "What do you want to know?" she asked.

"Were you surprised Mara Quida invited you to her party?"

"Why would I be surprised? She invited all the execs."

"My understanding was that the two of you weren't on good terms."

"I didn't think she deserved the Metropoli account, if that's what you mean." Oja frowned with impatience. "It doesn't matter. We all knew she would get it."

Interesting. Most people I'd spoken with liked Mara Quida and considered her an excellent choice for the job. "Why would she get the account if she wasn't qualified?"

Oja met my gaze. "She puts on the pleasant act, the hard-worker, loving wife, all that. It's bullshit. People aren't that nice in our profession."

"No one last night mentioned that."

"Mara isn't the only one who plays that game. Everyone pretends. Gods, that pretty husband of hers. Where the hell did she get some kid like that to marry her?"

Ho! Jealousy reared its vicious head. "You don't like him?"

"How would I know? He never talks to anyone."

"He's shy."

"It's all an act." She snorted. "You can't look like him and be shy. I mean, seriously? People practically fall over their feet when he walks into the room. And Mara knew it."

"You think she held that over other people?" That didn't fit with my impressions.

Oja spoke grudgingly. "Actually, no. She was surprised he'd

married her, too." She exhaled as if she were releasing a defense. "Major, it's true, I don't trust her. Would I like her to go work somewhere else? Yes. But I don't wish her ill. I would certainly never cause her harm."

That sounded more genuine than her other comments. "What about the other three execs she pushed out of line for the Metropoli contract? How do they feel?"

She regarded me as if I had the intelligence of a scuttling lizard. "I've no idea."

I waited. When the silence became awkward, she added, "I doubt they did anything, at least not Zeddia Vixer or Daan Bialo. I've known them for years. They're crafty, sure, but not vicious. I can't see them arranging a kidnapping."

Max, are you getting these names? I asked.

Yes, I've recorded them, he thought. Both were at the party and both were downstairs in the ballroom when Quida disappeared.

"That's only two people," I said to Oja.

"The third was Exec Tallmount. I don't know her. She's new."

I thought of the artifacts Oja had on display here. "How did you feel when you learned about the destruction of the scroll Mara Quida planned to give to the Metropoli reps?"

"It's a crime." Oja leaned forward. "It's not just the monetary worth, but the loss of such a rare item. It can never be replaced."

For gods' sake. She cared more about the scroll than Quida. "It must be hard to arrange for such a valuable gift."

She waved her hand in dismissal. "Some professor at the university helped her."

"Do you know her name?"

"His. Roy, I think." She drummed her fingers against the table. "Major, I'm busy."

If Ken Roy had helped her arrange the deal, it would be an honest one. I stood up. "Thank you for your time, Del Oja."

She nodded, her mask of cold composure in place again. "You can show yourself out."

So I did, out of the cool office and down to the ocean-blue lobby of Scorpio Tower. I wondered who had come up with the bizarre idea to name this cool-as-the-sea corporation after an Earth desert creature that killed with its sting.

Then again, it did seem apt for the people who worked here.

I ate my steak in pleased silence. The dinner table stood near the window-wall in my living room, letting the bronzed rays of the setting sun bathe me in light. The mosaic of a sunset also inlaid the table, and the legs were blue, lighter at the top and shading into the purple of oncoming night at the bottom. Even after decades of living aboveground, I'd never lost my love of the sky. Or of steak. Normally I was a vegetarian or I ate synthetic meat, which tasted all right, but every now and then I treated myself to the genuine article, despite its huge cost. The health nanomeds in my body got rid of bad cholesterol and any other junk the doctor told me to avoid.

"So Max," I said. "Why is it taking so long to decode the records from my beetle bot? When will I know what it saw when it went after the asshole who shot at me?"

"The files are corrupted," Max said. "I don't know why. I'm still working on them."

I speared a chunk of desert-succulent drenched in pizo sauce. Who'd have ever thought cactus could taste so good? "What about the woman who followed me out of Cries this afternoon?"

"I haven't identified her yet, either. The image resolution is terrible." He sounded frustrated. "I'm trying to clean it up."

"Show me what you have so far."

"This is the woman who shot at you in the garden." A holo formed in the air across the table. It showed a blurry figure running along a garden path under trellised arches draped by vines. The runner must have been wearing a skin-suit woven from holoscreens that analyzed the surroundings and projected images to match the landscape. For someone moving so fast, the suit couldn't completely hide her, but it blurred her beyond recognition.

"It looks like a woman," I said. "Dark coloring." That didn't help, given that it described pretty much the entire female population of Raylicon. Those of us native to the Undercity were a bit paler since we needed less melanin in our skin, but almost no one had light brown or red hair. I'd never seen a blond until I shipped offworld. "Could she be the person who followed me today?"

"I don't think so. Your shadow today was stockier than this woman."

The runner in the holo left the mansion and jogged along a lane that wound through the foothills of the Saint Parval Mountains. Every few minutes she passed a driveway that curved up to a mansion set back from the street.

"Can you clean up the resolution?" I asked.

"I already have as much as I can," Max said. "Watch this next part. It's odd."

I watched the woman for a few more moments. "She's just running."

"Yes, but where?"

Good question. The street sloped upward. "She's going into the mountains. Those mansions are in the foothills. If she goes any higher, she'll be above them." Wryly, I added, "She won't find anything there except even thinner air than in the city."

"She spent an hour jogging," Max said. "She stopped at a hut and slept for a few hours. Then she continued into the mountains."

"What for? Nothing is up there." I stopped, feeling cold. "Except the Majda palace."

"A flyer eventually picked her up," Max said. "A gold-and-black vehicle."

Damn. Majda flyers were gold and black. *Only* theirs. I didn't want to believe it. "Why would the Majdas send her to shoot me? I work for them."

"I don't know. It's also odd they made her run for so long first."

"Maybe they didn't want anyone to see them pick her up."

"Your beetle saw them."

"Did it follow the flyer?"

"It tried. Something happened that corrupted its record. Its AI isn't advanced enough to fix the problem, so it came home."

"I can't believe the Majdas are involved." I ate the last piece of cactus. "They want that Metropoli contract. It makes Scorpio look good, and since Scorpio is headquartered in Cries, that makes Cries look good, and anything good for Cries is good for Majda. They sent me to the gala to help make sure it all went according to plan."

"The attack on you doesn't make sense to me, either." He paused. "I have a partial ID on the woman who followed you out of Cries today."

I sat up straighter. "Who is she?"

The holo of the blurry runner swirled away, replaced by the image of a woman with a face that looked as if it were molded from clay without details.

"That doesn't look real," I said.

"It's the best I've managed so far. I've narrowed her ID to about three hundred people."

"Can you pare it down more?" I had no desire to investigate three hundred people.

"I'm working on it. Her physique suggests she's an athlete."

I took a swallow of ale, tart and golden. "Think she could be in the army?"

"Some of the possibilities are military personnel, active or retired."

"Let me know if you find out more." I pushed back from the table.

"You should sleep," Max said. "It will help your injuries heal."

I stood, leaving my dinner for the house bots to clean up. "I don't have time to sleep."

I had another matter to attend to—figuring out why the Majdas might want me dead.

I'd stayed at the Majda palace two years ago, when they first hired me. They'd given me a suite to make my work easier, or so they said, but it also made it easy for them to keep an eye on me. They had wanted me to find their runaway prince.

The House of Majda cloistered their men in full seclusion. On the rare occasions when a prince left the palace, he went robed and cowled, covered from head to toe, accompanied by guards. If a woman trespassed, even just trying to glimpse his face, her sentence was execution, or at least it had been thousands of years ago. I doubted the Majdas were going to kill anyone just for looking at one of their men, but they could make her life miserable.

Two years ago, Prince Dayj had run away. His lack of experience with anything beyond the palace nearly got him killed when an Undercity weapons dealer kidnapped him, but I managed to find him in time. Although it took his nearly dying for his family to realize they had to let him live his life the way he wanted, they finally accepted his wish to attend university. Last year, he'd left Raylicon to attend college on the world Parthonia.

During my investigation, it had fast become clear I couldn't do my job with Majda looking over my shoulder. So I moved out. They gave me the penthouse in Cries, where they still looked over my shoulder, but at least they were discreet about it. Fortunately, I was even better at avoiding them. I doubted they realized just how well I'd learned to outwit their monitors.

Today I hiked up the mountains. Nothing grew at this high elevation. The thin air never bothered my Raylican-bred lungs; the atmosphere on other human-habitable worlds seemed too rich to me. I came out on a ledge about half a kilometer from the palace. The mountains plunged down from my feet in black stone streaked by red. The palace stood on a mesa below, surrounded by a valley and lush with the green canopy of the imported trees. I had no idea how the Majdas grew plants this high in the mountains, but what the hell. Managing miracles was their forte, or at least they liked the rest of the universe to think that. Mirror Lake shimmered in the sunlight, with trees trailing vines into the blue water, and red water lilies floated in their shadowed bower. And yah, "bower" was the right word, not that I'd ever known what it meant before Max used it to describe these gardens with their leafy, shaded alcoves.

Terraced gardens stepped up from the forest to the palace. The building reminded me of images I'd seen of the Taj Mahal on Earth, with towers that rose at its corners and a majestic dome topping the roof. Sunlight bathed the golden work of art, making it glow like a testament to the glory of human architecture. I could almost forget that the their ancestors had built it during one of the most barbaric eras known to my people, when the queens of Raylicon were atavistic warriors who spread mayhem with their conquering armies.

Majda security should have stopped me long before I got this close to the palace. However, when I'd lived here, they'd given me the security codes so I could come and go. Although they'd changed them since then, Max had created a trapdoor into their systems that allowed him to access the new codes. I approached without incident. So far, so good.

I made my way down a steep trail, using the jammer in my backpack to shroud my presence. I'd dusted my face with holo-powder, which networked with the holosuit that covered me from foot to neck to wrist, projecting holos so I looked like my surroundings instead of like me, at least from far away. The suit's inner surface kept me warm while the outer surface matched the temperature of the icy air. It confused infrared sensors; if they couldn't register the heat I generated, I became invisible to them. Sonic dampers in my jammer muted sounds. It could even fool neutrino sensors, now that neutrino detection had become feasible for smaller devices. If someone searched using the full palace resources, they could probably find me, but so far I hadn't given anyone reason to look.

At the bottom of the trail, I walked onto a lawn. I kept to the shadows under overhanging trees, making it easier for the shroud to hide me. Curling fronds brushed my face, fragrant with the scent of rich green life. A gardener had sculpted the trees to resemble mythological creatures, like Azu Bullom, spirit companion of the god Izam Na, with the powerful body of a mountain cat, a human head, and horns that spiraled around his ears. It was easy to climb the terraces, using staircases of blue stone with sculpted railings. Pink and gold flowers bloomed everywhere. Most of the plants were imported from gentler worlds, but desert stalks grew here, too, with red blossoms hanging from their curved tips like bells. Gods only knew what resources it took to provide enough oxygen to grow these gardens in such a harsh environment. It was too lovely, so exquisite it hurt, a painful reminder that this dying world had once been a place of beauty.

On the top terrace, I crossed to the garden behind the palace, still in the shadows. Voices drifted through the air. I froze under an arch with hanging vines. *Max, crank up my hearing.*

Done.

Every noise became louder. The spray from a sprinkler pattered. Crackles came from closer by, what sounded like a smart-rake sweeping up dried leaves. The distant voices jumped into focus. A man was speaking Iotic, an ancient language used in modern times only by royalty or the aristocracy. I'd learned it in the army because some of our COs came from the noble Houses. Everyone spoke Skolian Flag of course, the universal language of our people, but an ability to use Iotic made you look good, and I'd been an ambitious young fireball in those days.

"—so the vote of confidence against Bak Trasor is coming up tomorrow in the meeting for the board of directors." His deep voice rumbled. "I think we've enough support to get rid of him."

"Good," a woman said. "It's about time."

Damn! I knew that woman's voice. It had as much power today to scare the hell out of me as it had the first time I'd heard it, two years ago. It belonged to General Vaj Majda, Matriarch of the House of Majda, General of the Pharaoh's Army, a joint commander of Imperial Space Command and one of the most powerful people in the Skolian Imperialate.

I was dead.

✥ CHAPTER VI ✥
IN THE HALL OF THE MOUNTAIN QUEEN

I held my breath, afraid to inhale, even though they were far enough away, at least fifty meters across the garden, that they couldn't hear me.

"It won't be easy," the man said. "We don't want to antagonize his supporters."

"You're the expert," the general said. "I'll trust your judgment."

Breathe, I told myself. In the two years I'd known Vaj Majda, I'd never heard her talk in such a relaxed manner. I'd met only the authoritative General, a force to reckon with in the halls of Imperialate power. *I'll trust your judgment.* I couldn't imagine her saying that to anyone, let alone a man.

Unless—

Ah, hell. Yah, she might say that to one man, someone rumored to sit on the boards of several powerful corporations. Of course he never appeared at any meeting, but he was present even though no one could see him. Vaj Majda would take his advice because he would only ever give it to her in private, when no one else could hear them. Yah, one man fit that bill. Izam Kaaj Majda. Her husband.

The Majdas no longer ruled Raylicon. Supposedly. In truth, their power had become even more formidable in this modern age. Now they held sway over a financial empire, controlling more wealth than the combined governments of entire planets. The arranged marriage between General Majda and Izam Kaaj had involved many factors, including his high birth, background, appearance, and fertility. He was a son of the House of Kaaj, which also cloistered their men. Almost no one realized he was also a financial genius. Vaj might be conservative, but she was no fool. She knew the advantage of having a husband who could increase the already stratospheric wealth of her House. Izam was a power hidden behind the metaphorical throne of her influence.

Yah, like the Majdas needed more wealth. They already had more than any other family in human history, including even the Ruby Dynasty, whose members seemed more interested in math than finances. While the Ruby Pharaoh solved equations, the Majdas made money.

Are you talking to me? Max asked.

I hadn't realized my thoughts had become intense enough for Max to pick up. *No. I'm just panicking. I'm dead.*

You don't look dead to me.

I'm spying on the most powerful woman and the most guarded man in the Imperialate. If they find me, I'm dead.

You are indulging in hyperbole. Besides, the Ruby Dynasty has more power than General Majda.

General Majda is more experienced at wielding it. I wondered how she felt knowing the Imperator was a man. He commanded Imperial Space Command, the combined military forces of the Imperialate, so as a joint commander, Vaj answered to him. I'd always figured it must bother her, but I wondered now if she accepted his title because of his dynastic heritage. He was the nephew of the Ruby Pharaoh. Although Prince Izam operated in secret whereas the Imperator was a public figure, they had more similarities than I'd realized. Power stayed in the family. Regardless, right now I had trouble. I hadn't even realized General Majda was on Raylicon. I certainly hadn't expected to run into her chatting with her husband about some corporate coup. My presence here had become more than simple trespassing; it verged on treason.

I suggest you leave, Max thought. Fast.

No kidding. I walked in the other direction from the speakers, toward a back entrance to the palace. Breezes whispered over my skin. I stayed among the trees, adding their natural concealment to the shroud provided by my jammer. Somewhere a pico-ruzik whistled its eerie cry.

I meant leave the palace, Max thought. *The risk is too great.*

Yah, well, if the Majdas are trying to kill me, that risk is bigger. I need to know, and I can't find what I need off-site. Their protections are too strong.

Max had no response for that.

I reached the back entrance with no further incident. A molecular airlock shimmered in its archway, keyed to the DNA of the Majda family and staff.

Max, I asked. *Double check that the house system still recognizes my DNA.*

I checked earlier. I can do it again. Give me a moment; I need to ensure the trapdoors I put into their mesh systems weren't discovered and set with ambushes. After a few seconds, he said, *I found one ambush. I have avoided it. Shall I access their mesh?*

Yes. They still might detect us in their mesh system, but Max was good at what he did, enough that I was willing to take the risk.

We're in, Max thought. *And yes, the system will accept your DNA.*

Interesting. Their security couldn't have overlooked my having access to their mesh; they were too efficient to make that mistake. That meant the Majdas still intended to let me enter their home. It made sense if they wanted me to continue working for them. Then again, they might keep my ID in their system to deflect suspicion if my corpse turned up somewhere.

I edged forward, staying out of sight until I reached the archway. When I slipped through the airlock, it slid along my skin like a soap bubble. The corridor inside had floors tiled in white, blue, and gold hexagons. The ivory walls gleamed, with mosaics running along them at waist height. Tall vases with flowering plants stood in niches in the walls.

I headed into the palace.

The palace suite where I'd lived looked the same, though nearly two years had passed since I'd stayed here. A palm-reader I'd forgotten still lay where I'd left it on a table. With my heightened senses, I smelled the trace of disuse in the room. It wasn't dust: Cleaning bots would keep this room spotless. Places that had stood empty for too long had a scent I could only describe as aged.

Probably no one had been here since I left; the palace had hundreds of rooms, and no one needed this one. Wasting that much space struck me as about as sensible as standing on your head and blowing bubbles, but what did I know.

A dark red rug carpeted the living room, plush and dusted with holo-sparkles. Holoscapes glowed in front of the walls, images of the sun setting over the desert, with the sky darkening to cobalt above the luminous bands of red and gold. The black lacquer tables stood low to the ground, surrounded by pillows brocaded in sunset colors. I loved images of the sky, especially the brilliant colors of the setting sun. My apartment also reflected that taste, but light filled its open spaces. I hadn't realized the darker tone of this suite. I wondered if it reflected a buried unease I didn't know how to express, staying in a place so lavish it felt like a crime.

I didn't turn on lamps; I could see well enough with the dim light from the holoscapes. The console stood on the far side of the room, curved around a control chair. I went over and sat down.

Max, I'm ready.

I'm not, he answered. I'm studying the palace security. It has changed more than I realized. I need more time.

We don't have more time. Someone might find me.

Someone is more likely to find you if I trip an alarm.

I schooled myself to patience. *Do what you need to do. And turn on my IR.*

Max didn't answer, busy with his checks, but he easily multitasked. The room took on a blurred glow as the infrared filters in my eyes activated. They let me see at wavelengths longer than visible light, like those produced by heat. Cold areas were dark; hot areas were bright. The room mostly looked dark blue, including me, with my holosuit matching the air temperature. The console, however, showed a lighter shade of blue.

This console is using too much energy, I thought. *It shouldn't be warmer than the room.*

According to my sensors, it's been active since you were last here, Max thought.

For more than TWO years?

Yes. Palace mesh systems don't hibernate. They are always ready for use.

Gods. The energy this console used could run Gourd's water filtration machines for a year. My people were dying of thirst while this fucking console consumed resources by doing nothing.

Given the energy usage of the entire palace, Max added, they probably don't even notice the energy drain of a single console.

I gritted my teeth. *Good for them.*

I'm sorry. His thought had a subdued feel.

Any luck with security?

Yes, I'm ready. I've created a shell within your old account. As long as you operate within that shell, your activities on the Majda mesh shouldn't be detected.

Good. I'd known my account remained active because I used it from my apartment when I needed it for a job. The moment I linked in from an outside location, however, it activated monitors in the Majda system. Tonight I couldn't risk accessing their mesh from the outside. I had to be inside Majda security to shroud my activities at a deep enough level.

I pulled a cord off my belt and clicked one end into the console. The other went into my gauntlet, which connected to the socket in my wrist. Although I could have used wireless, it was a bit less secure and slower than this direct link.

Accessing the Majda mesh, Max thought.

Another thought came into my mind, androgynous. My greetings, Major Bhaajan.

My greetings, Jan, I thought.

What can I do for you? Jan asked.

I need for you to leave.

I don't understand your meaning. I am an EI. I can't go anywhere.

I need to go under your programming. Put yourself inside a shell.

You are already in a shell, Jan thought. If I put myself inside a shell that is also inside yours, I will be unable to interact with you, and I will also be hidden from the Majda network. Jan no longer sounded friendly. You are not allowed to operate in this covert manner.

Secondary shell activated, Max thought.

Jan went silent.

Thanks, Max, I thought. *Did I distract her enough for you to erase her memory of my entry?*

Yes. But we can't maintain these shells for long. Please search quickly.

Will do. I tapped the console screen. *Bring up the root directory for this console.*

I recommend a direct mesh-to-brain link rather than using the screen. It's more secure.

I wasn't a fan of jacking directly into systems I didn't trust. Who knew what spamoozala it might download into my brain. For a short time, though, I'd take the chance. Better that than increase the risk the Majdas would discover me slinking around their mesh.

All right. I closed my eyes. *Show me the files.*

An array of icons appeared in my mind. Cyber-riders called such images *thumbers,* apparently from the old-fashioned word "thumbnail." When they liked whatever function the image represented, they sometimes replaced it with the thumbs-up sign so popular on Earth. If they were pissed, they turned the thumb into a third finger. Here the icons portrayed athletes doing random stuff. The one that showed a running woman had the name *error-free systems.* A thumber labeled *under diagnosis* pictured the runner sitting on the ground with a medic treating her foot.

I scrolled through the records, looking for security monitors. Nothing, nothing—there! A group of thumbers came up with names like *console monitor, intranet monitor,* or *submesh monitor.* These mostly looked like bugs, of the insect rather than the mesh variety.

The thumber for the intranet monitor showed a web like those created by sand-weavers, industrious little creatures that lived in the desert, neither reptiles nor insects, but something between. They wove their webs out of the sand and a glue their bodies produced. I'd heard they covered the starship ruins on the shore of the Vanished Sea with those corrosive webs, forcing the army techs to keep cleaning the hulls.

Max, bring up the intranet monitor, I thought.

The picture grew in size and then faded, replaced by an array of names like *IM-processor-usage, IM-diagnostics,* IM-this and IM-that. I looked for something that would get me access to the larger mesh that spanned the palace. Using a subsystem of their own mesh to reach the main system rather than accessing it directly would better hide my actions. I hoped.

The sand-weaver image came up again, this time with the title *IM-full-mesh.*

Open, I thought.

The thumber expanded to fill my view and then morphed into the image of a foyer with corridors radiating outward in every direction like the spokes of a wheel.

Max! I thought. *Where do these pathways lead?*

Some have labels, he answered. An overlay appeared marking each hallway with phrases like *kitchen intraweb, north garden intraweb,* and one called *disposal intraweb* that showed a man wrinkling his nose in distaste.

These don't look promising, I thought.

I dug up something else. Several new passages appeared to my left, each closed by a stone door with an old-fashioned padlock. These were hidden.

As I focused on the locked passages, they grew in size until they dominated my view. *Unlock,* I thought. Nothing happened, big surprise there. *Can you open them?*

I'm investigating. Max paused. I'm also avoiding probes. They regularly sample every region of the palace mesh. So far, we're fine, but we won't stay hidden for long.

Got it. I concentrated on the locked pathways. *Something is off-kilter here.*

What do you mean?

I'm not sure. I brought up the full foyer again and scanned the other corridors. They led to domestic functions, things like the laundry or utilities. Of course none of them had titles like *secret intraweb.* Those would be hidden, like the padlocked passages Max had found. Without his help, I doubted I could have located them. Those had to be what I needed.

Yah, right.

Max, I thought. *Open the disposal intraweb.*

Why? It will detract from my investigation of the locked systems.

Exactly. It's the least likely pathway an interloper will investigate. A spy would look at subtle attempts to hide data, like unlabeled pathways that are discreetly hidden.

Well, yes, he thought. That's exactly where we should look. Not at the sewer system.

Max, think about it. Those hidden pathways weren't really hidden.

They were very well hidden. Only systems sophisticated enough to spy on the Majda intraweb from the inside could find them. Like me.

Exactly. It's a decoy meant to distract the best spies. These Majda security types are smart.

Maybe. Or maybe you're overthinking it. I can look at the sewer or I can crack open the locked pathways. We don't have time to do both.

I understand. I'm afraid we have to visit the sewers.

Very well. He was doing an annoyingly good job of simulating resignation.

The thumber with the man wrinkling his nose expanded until it filled my view—and then it faded into a long corridor with black walls, nothing else, just a hall that stretched out forever.

I don't like it, Max thought. Where are the menus for waste disposal functions?

I headed down the corridor. *Let's see where it goes.*

Even more probes are sampling this region. We don't have much time.

I'm hurrying. I deepened my concentration, which manifested as me jogging. The black walls streamed by, nothing, nothing—wait, was that a red streak that flashed by?

I went back to the streak. It formed a line of writing: *First access.*

First access to what? Max thought.

I've no idea. Can you open this door?

What door?

This one. I focused on the wall, and the outline of a door appeared.

Just a moment—it has locks—all right, I'm opening the file.

I pushed the door, and it swung open, revealing a white space, as if I were standing in bright light and nothing else.

Open security files, I thought.

Nothing happened.

It must need an access code, Max thought.

If I give it my Majda password, will that set off alarms outside this shell?

It shouldn't, but I can't guarantee that. The shell is weakening.

My password only let me access the outer levels of the palace mesh. I was never meant to go this deep. However, now that I was here, it might help open the locks. Unfortunately, it could also leave a trail that pointed to me.

We don't have time to find a work-around, I thought. *Give it my password.*

Done.

Open security files, I thought.

The brightness solidified into a circular chamber that glowed white. Hieroglyphics in blue and gold flowed across the walls too fast to read.

Slow transmission, I thought.

The thumbers slowed until I could make out file names. They had nothing to do with me. *Just show files linked to Major Bhaajan.*

Most of the thumbers disappeared, leaving only a handful. One labeled *Bhaajan-hiring* showed me descending to the palace roof from the flyer that had brought me here for my first job. Another called *Bhaajan-accommodations* showed me relaxing in cushions around a lacquered table in this suite. Another caught my attention. It was just my face, which wouldn't have seemed interesting, except for the title.

Open Bhaajan-clearance-history, I thought.

The image faded into a list of menu items organized by date. Ho! The records went back to the year I'd been born. Even I didn't have files that old. Did the Majdas know my lineage? My mother had died giving me birth, and no one knew anything about my father. Someone had left me at the Cries orphanage with a note that read, *She is the jan of Bhaaj.* That was all I knew, that I was the daughter of a woman named Bhaaj. I'd run away from the prisonlike orphanage with the help of an older girl when I was three, and from that day on I had gladly called the Undercity my home. For all my searching, I'd never learned anything about my parents.

A chill went through me. *Open birth file.*

We don't have time, Max thought. We have to go. Now!
Copy every file in the records the Majdas keep on me.
It will take too long.
Do it! Fast.
Copying. Max displayed a bar filling with green to show his progress. Ten percent. Twenty percent. Normally he copied files a lot faster, but he would have to outwit the protections on these. Forty percent.

The thumbers flickered.

A probe just brushed our shell, Max thought.

The progress bar showed sixty percent.

Did it detect us? I asked.

I don't think so. However, it did register an energy blip we may have caused.

Keep copying.

The bar showed eighty percent. The room wavered and began to fade.

Bhaaj, we have to get out. The probe is aware of our shell. It's trying to delete it.

The progress bar increased to ninety percent.

Finish your download, I thought.

We have to get out.

Not yet!

The bar increased to one hundred percent.

Download complete, Max told me. NOW GO!

I ran from the white room. The entrance was solidifying as I raced through it. I got stuck in the thickening wall and wrenched my way out into the corridor. As I sprinted down the hallway, it dissolved around me.

Max, delete all record of our operations. Erase all trace of your deletions, and erase the record of those erasures. It's a three-stage process here; our trail won't truly disappear unless you sweep all three levels.

Erasing, Max thought.

As I reached the end of the corridor, it melted around me. Opening my eyes, I jerked my cable out of the console. *Are we out of the Majda mesh?*

We're clear and the deletions are done. However, the probe knows someone infiltrated the mesh.

I jumped up. *Does it know it was me?*

I don't think so.

With the palace on alert, its motion sensors would become even more sensitive. Any tiny movement, even people breathing, would register. However, hundreds of people lived in the palace. If I acted normal, as if I were part of the staff, my walking shouldn't trip alarms. Even if my shroud didn't hide me completely, it would blur my identity.

I crossed to the closed door. *Do you detect anyone on the other side?*

No, I'm not getting life signs.

Is my jammer still operational?

Yes, you're good.

I reached for my pulse revolver in my shoulder holster—and found nothing. I'd deliberately come unarmed. Shooting anyone here would be lunacy, and bringing weapons increased the chance security would detect me. Even so, I felt naked without my gun.

I opened the door. The foyer outside was indeed empty. Taking a deep breath, I headed to the hall beyond, walking normally.

Someone is in the corridor ahead that crosses this one, Max thought. You need to hide.

I stepped into an alcove just off the hallway, staying behind its ivory-and-gold wall.

Sit on the bench, Max said. Fix your shoes or something, so it looks like you had a reason to come in here.

I sat down and fooled with my boots. The voices of two people talking drifted to me as they passed in the other hallway. When their steps receded, I thought, *Safe now?*

Yes. Go.

I resumed my walk. I wanted to run, but I held back, schooling my breathing, my pace, everything to be as normal as possible.

Bhaaj, Max suddenly said. The probe just contacted the human security chief and informed her that a trespasser may be on the premises.

Damn! *Are they shutting off the palace exits?*

Yes. You have to get out another way.

What way? The roof?

No, they've closed the landing pad. You need a way out

that isn't public. He paused. I found an option, but it won't be long before they close that exit, too. Turn left at the next corner.

Got it.

Max sent me into the servants' wing. Normally, that wouldn't have helped, since most buildings used bots instead of humans, which meant my presence would stand out like a bruised thumb. Only the Majdas were wealthy enough to afford a full human staff and conservative enough to want people rather than machines waiting on them. I had to hide several times, but I made it undetected to a storage room heaped with cleaning equipment. Max directed me to the back of the room—where I faced a blank wall.

This is a dead end, I thought sourly.

Look under your feet.

I looked. I was standing on a trapdoor, the physical equivalent of the secret entrances Max had left in the Majda mesh.

Max! That's a garbage disposal chute.

I'm sorry. But you can get out this way.

Well, fuck that.

I would hope not.

I knelt on the ground and felt around the edges of the trapdoor. *How do I open it?*

Can you feel a series of buttons?

Yah, seven of them.

Good. Push them in the order I give.

I entered the combination, and the door slid to the side, revealing a square chute that angled downward, then made a sharp turn into a horizontal passage. I couldn't see beyond the place where it leveled out.

This isn't a disposal chute, I thought. The Majdas dissolved or incinerated their trash in a manner that didn't damage the environment. Everyone in Cries did, though I suspected it was more because they liked their living spaces pristine than because they were paragons of environmental virtue. If my memory of the palace served, this chute would come out a horizontal cliff face. The Majdas would never throw their trash so cavalierly down the mountain.

I've figured it out, Max thought. This is for their pets. The animals come and go as they please. Filters clean them. Any dirt or waste is absorbed by the walls and incinerated.

Oh, that's charming. I get to use the Majda equivalent of a pooper scooper.

Essentially. It is, however, clean. You must get going.

It won't work. This can't be an exit. They don't want their pets running away.

If my guess is correct, you can get out this way.

Your guess? You don't know?

Bhaaj, you must go now or it will be too late.

You better be right about this. As I slid down the chute, it closed above me. I hit the flat place where it turned horizontal. *How do the animals come and go?*

The entrance door is tuned to recognize them. It opens when they approach. I believe this passage is designed to be fun for them to slide down.

Yah, great fun. At least the level portion of the passage was large enough to let me stand. *What pets do they have?*

Two fluff-bears.

Well, damn. Yah, those bears looked adorable. They'd also tear you to shreds if they didn't like you. I walked along the passage. *They let their kids play with fluff bears?*

Yes. The animals are trained to protect the children.

The tunnel wasn't lit, except by starlight; I could see an opening about a hundred meters distant that showed the night sky. *How does this passage end?*

It opens up onto a railed ledge with facilities for the bears.

I didn't want details about "the facilities." *It cleans up after them, right?*

Yes.

So why don't the bears leave? Why return to the palace?

They can't leave.

Then how can I? I reached the end of the passage and walked into a circular area under the glittering night sky. I crossed to the rail that bordered it—and I understood why the fluff-bears didn't run away.

I was screwed.

Of course the bears didn't take their fluffy, intimidating selves off to some other place. The only way to leave this ledge was down a cliff. Above me, the cliff rose in another horizontal face.

Max, I have to go back. Better the Majdas catch me than I die.

You can't go back. One of the bears is coming this way. They don't like strangers.

As if this couldn't get any worse. I turned to see a large creature lumbering into the circular area, like an Earth teddy bear with floppy ears and big eyes. Yah, charming—until it growled and raised its huge paws, unsheathing claws longer than my fingers. It headed straight for me.

I didn't waste time cursing. Grabbing the rail, I vaulted over it and came to a stop with a hard jerk, hanging from the rail, stretched out along the cliff. Scrabbling with my feet, I tried to find a toehold. My boot caught on a crack, and I wedged in my toe. With a grunt, I let my weight settle on my foot, giving my arms a rest. A growl rumbled above me. I looked up to see the bear leaning over the rail. It trailed its claws along my arm as if to say, "You're dead meat."

With a grunt, I let go of the rail with one hand and grabbed for a handhold in the cliff face. My other arm ached from supporting my weight. Catching a projection, I hung on tight. The bear raised its arm, extending its claws. I released the rail and grabbed the projection in the wall with my other hand. So far, so good. Easing my foot out of its toehold, I let my body slide down the cliff face. I couldn't find another toehold—sliding—the projection I was clutching with both hands wouldn't support my full weight—

My boots hit a ledge, nothing more than a ridge barely wide enough for the balls of my feet, but it did the trick. I stopped sliding, my arms stretched above me. For a moment I just clung to the cliff face, afraid to move. Air whistled past me. The fluff-bear leaned further over the railing, but I was beyond its reach. It growled, baring its fangs in all their sharpened glory.

"I don't like you either," I muttered.

The bear's head retreated out of view.

They can't talk, Max thought. It can't tell anyone you were here.

Yah, well, I'm still here.

You have to climb down the cliff.

Are you fucking insane?

I am not insane, reproductively or otherwise. The distance you have to climb is about a third of a kilometer. Three hundred meters. You can manage.

Yah, right. I could create a few galaxies, too, while I was doing the impossible. Given that I had no other choices, however, climbing would have to do. I slid my left hand toward my right arm until I touched the gauntlet on my wrist. When I pushed a stud there, a blade snapped out of the leather sheath. Repeating the process with my other hand, I snapped a second blade out of my other gauntlet. I moved my hand down until it was level with my shoulder and worked the knife into a tiny crack in the cliff, then repeated the process with the other knife. Reaching down with one foot, I searched until I found a crack that held my weight. With a breath of relief, I eased both feet onto its support. That entire process took me down the cliff about one fourth of a meter.

Good job! Max offered, simulating cheerleader mode.

Yah, right. Only two hundred ninety-nine and three-fourths meters left to go.

So I went, using my hands and toes, and the blades from my gauntlets. I was fortunate the cliff wasn't as smooth as it looked, if anything about this mess could be called "fortunate." Eventually I found a ridge large enough to support my full weight. I paused, leaning against the cliff, catching my breath. It felt like I had been climbing forever—

The ledge collapsed.

"Ah!" I was suddenly hanging by my hands and the knives shoved into the stone. My left hand pulled off the spur I was holding, adding my weight to the knife, which snapped out of the rock. With my entire weight pulling on only one blade, the second knife yanked out as well. I plummeted down the rock face, scrabbling frantically for a handhold. My boot hit a projection and I flipped away from the cliff.

It isn't supposed to end like this, I thought.

❖ CHAPTER VII ❖
THE FOOTNOTE

I hit the ground *hard* and grunted as the air went out of my lungs.

Bhaaj! Max actually yelled in my mind. Are you alive? Then he added, Oh, yes, of course you're alive. I'm monitoring your vital signs. He sounded scared, Max, my emotionless EI.

I lifted my head. I'd landed at the base of the cliff. It looked like I'd slid several meters and fallen several more, enough to do damage, but not enough to kill, at least not my ornery, rock-headed self. The smart knives had retracted into my gauntlets rather than stabbing me. The ground here sloped down toward the foothills of the mountains, sparsely clothed in scraggly cactus vines. An overhang of the cliff hid my view of the palace.

I'm okay, I told Max. *Do I have any broken bones?*

I don't think so. Your fall smashed some of the tech-mech in your gauntlets, however.

Are they fixable?

Yes. I suggest you don't use a Cries vendor for the repairs. The Majdas might find out and wonder what happened.

Good point. I could bargain with a cyber-rider to work on it. *How is the jammer?*

Your backpack protected it. Your shroud still works. Can you walk?

I struggled to my feet and took a step, easing my weight onto my foot. Nothing cracked or otherwise gave away. I just hurt all over. My second step worked almost as well, except for jabs of pain in my foot.

The holosuit was torn in several places, including a long gash that stretched along my abdomen. It had ripped open the knife wound, and blood soaked my clothes.

"I need to get home." My head hurt, so I spoke instead of thinking.

We shouldn't talk out loud, Max thought.

Is Majda security still searching for the intruder?

Undoubtedly. However, I disconnected from their system so I don't know for certain.

That made sense. The faster we got out of there, both physically and digitally, the better. I limped down the hill in the dark, staying concealed under overhangs, and headed home, hoping to make it without collapsing or being arrested for treason.

I opened my eyes into the dark, my head throbbing. Where—?

It came back in a rush: my spying and near-fatal escape from the palace. I'd walked home, forcing myself not to limp, in case a city monitor picked me up. Once here, I'd collapsed into bed. I'd have berated myself for the stupidity of my actions, except I now had a goldmine, all the files the Majdas had put together about me. It had been worth the trouble.

At least, I thought I had them. I spoke into the darkness. "Max?"

"Good evening." His voice came from below me.

I peered over the edge of the bed, trying to get my bearings. I didn't remember undressing before I passed out, but I must have because my gauntlets and clothes were lying on the floor.

"Is your record of the Majda files intact?" I asked. They might have primed the files to delete if copied. Their security was better than I'd expected even after my assumption it would be exceptional. Any system that outwitted Max so soon after we snuck into their mesh was damn good.

"That's your first question?" Max asked. "Not 'How injured am I?' or 'Are you all right, Max?' Yes, I'm good, I wasn't damaged in the fall, thank you for asking. And yes, the files are intact."

I smiled. "EIs aren't supposed to scold people."

"I'm not scolding. Also yes to the other question you should have asked. I have checked, double-checked, and triple-checked the protections in your domicile here against spying. We have privacy.

Which is good, because I don't think you should use your neural interfaces for a while. You overextended yourself at the palace."

"Thanks for checking." I smiled. "You're the only person I know who ever says 'domicile.'"

"I'm not a person, but thank you." He sounded pleased.

I sat up in the dark, rubbing my temples. "My head hurts."

"That is because you hit it when you fell."

No shit. I swung my legs off the bed and picked up one of my gauntlets. With caution, I stood up. My head swam, but I stayed upright. "I feel like I went through a meat pounder."

"What is a meat pounder?"

"I think I made it up. That's how I feel, though." I walked across the room in the dark. The few people from Cries I'd allowed to visit my apartment thought it odd that I chose a penthouse with such a small bedroom. It was just big enough for the alcove with my bed, a console against the wall, and an open area about eight paces across. The archway at the foot of my bed opened into a bathing room with a "bathtub" that took up more space than this entire bedroom.

Jak never asked why I slept in a small, enclosed space. He knew. We'd grown up as part of a dust gang, two girls and two boys who protected a circle of children and young adults. They made the cave where we all lived into a home, with handwoven rugs and tapestries, sculptures carved from the rock, and bead curtains. Jak and I had some privacy due to our status as protectors. We slept in a nook behind a half wall of rock. This bedroom was the closest I could come to what I'd known then. A large room wouldn't feel safe. Logically, I knew that made no sense, but never mind. This kept me happy.

The archway across from my bed opened into the spacious living room, which filled with light during the day. Right now, starlight trickled through the doorway. That meant I hadn't slept through the night. Of course, that wasn't saying much given that the night here lasted forty hours.

"How long was I out?" I asked.

"About five hours. You could use more sleep."

"After I clean up." I walked into the bathing room, and its light came on gradually, letting my eyes adjust. Blue, gold, and aqua tiles covered every surface. The pool lay to the right, with a mist hanging over the warm water. I'd never felt comfortable knowing this "bathtub" contained more fresh water than I'd ever seen in one place in the aqueducts. I intended that to change. My people wouldn't take fresh water for free, but I was finding bargains they'd accept, like in my work with Gourd. The water filtration systems he built would far outlast any handouts from Cries. More than that, it showed we could do it ourselves. Change had to come from within the Undercity if it was going to last.

I set my gauntlet by the pool and slid into the shallow end, submerging to my shoulders while I slouched against the side. Soap-bots swam around me like silver and blue fish.

I closed my eyes. "This is good."

"I wish I could advise you to see a doctor," Max said. "Unfortunately I can't."

"No one can know I'm hurt." Not now, with the Majdas trying to figure out who'd been prowling around their palace.

"As far as I can tell," Max said, "you are only banged up. However, the gash in your abdomen aggravated your knife wound from yesterday. You should take extra care with that."

"I will. Is anyone looking for me?"

"Scorpio Security would like to know if you have any leads on Mara Quida."

"So would I." I laid my head back against the edge of the pool. "Can you reach Lukas Quida?"

"He's probably sleeping."

"If he is, my message will go into his queue, waiting for a more civilized hour." I doubted he was asleep, though. I remembered the nights in my youth when Jak would disappear. I'd pace and pace, agonized that he gotten himself killed.

"I have Del Quida on comm," Max said. "He's asking if you'd like audio or both audio and visual."

"Which would he prefer?"

"He didn't say. But based on my analysis of his voice, I think it's a good bet he'd like both, for the company. I can make an appropriate holo of you to converse with him."

"All right. Go ahead."

The tiled floor of the room glimmered as its holoscreen activated. An image of me dressed in trousers and a pullover appeared. I looked as if I were relaxing in a chair in my living room. The image Max created showed me with no sign of fatigue or injury.

Lukas' voice came into the air. "Major Bhaajan?" He appeared in a chair opposite mine as if we were both in my penthouse. Dark circles of fatigue showed under his eyes and his face was even more strained than the last time I'd seen him. No trace of his fashionable silver hair or elegant clothes remained; tonight he dressed in worn trousers and a simple gray pullover. He dark hair was tousled and stubble showed on his face. He looked more like a graduate student than a member of the sparkling Cries elite.

He nodded to me. "My greetings."

"My apology for disturbing you," I said. "I know it's late."

"It's all right. I can't sleep." He leaned forward in his chair. "Have you found anything?"

"I'm working on some leads." I wished I had more to tell him. "I was wondering if you were all right."

He looked startled. "Thank you." With self-deprecation, he added, "I feel like a violin string. Every time any comm in the house buzzes, I twang. It's never good news."

"You should rest. You look so worn out."

Lukas smiled wryly. "This is what I really look like, Major. I mean, not this tired, but that polished man you met at the gala isn't real. As the Earthers would say, I'm just a nerd."

I wondered if his wife pushed him to glamorize his appearance. She wouldn't be the first exec to use her spouse as a decorative accessory. "Did you feel pressured to put on an act?"

"By Mara?" He gave a startled laugh. "Never. She didn't care. When we first started seeing each other, she was as shy as me." With affection, he said, "She never pushed me to impress her friends. She doesn't think that way. That's why I enjoyed doing it for her, because she never asked. She loved me just the way I was when we met, an absentminded analyst with no more fashion sense than a freight tug."

I smiled. That fit with the picture I'd been forming. "The Scorpio investigators seem to think the two of you are some sort of glitz duo."

"Detective Talon isn't interested in my view of my own life. She likes hers better." Anger edged his words. "Mara wasn't faking how she felt about me. And gods, I'd never hurt her."

"What did Talon say?"

"She thinks I killed Mara." He lifted his hands, then dropped them. "My lawyer believes the police are going to arrest me for killing Mara."

"What the fuck?" Remembering myself, I added, "My apology for my language, but that's bullshit. They have no evidence to arrest you for anything, let alone murder."

"My DNA is the only trace they found of anyone else in our room." He grimaced. "Talon has brought me in for questioning twice since the gala. She keeps telling me they will 'go easier' if I confess."

Damn it. Talon had "neglected" to tell me they were interrogating him as a primary suspect. "Lukas, listen to me. Don't ever talk to them without your lawyer."

"I haven't."

More gently, I added, "And it's a good sign no one has found a body."

"I hope so." He sounded miserable, not hopeful. "Why are you up so late?"

"I get restless when I'm trying to solve a case." At least I did when I cared about it as much as this one. I liked to think of myself as hardened, and I fooled most people into believing it, but I couldn't fool myself. "I wanted to know if you had any updates. I'm sorry I don't have more news."

"Nothing here, either." He let out a breath. "It helps to hear from someone who doesn't think I'm a monster or a toy."

"Gods, Lukas, never let them make you believe that."

He breathed in deeply. "I'm trying."

We talked a bit longer and then signed off. I sat then, thinking about Talon. Yah, Lukas was the most obvious suspect, but he hadn't done it, and the detective was an idiot to think otherwise.

Then again, I wasn't the most impartial observer.

"It's hard to be objective in this case," I said to the cool air. "He's so appealing, I don't want to believe he did anything wrong."

"Appealing?" Max asked.

"You know. The beautiful, grieving spouse. Maybe I'm letting that influence my judgment."

"What beautiful?" Max sounded confused. "He looked and sounded like hell. And that was a raw holo feed."

"A what?"

"His holo wasn't doctored," Max said. "With sophisticated enough techniques, an advanced EI can tell if the images coming in on a holo feed are genuine. Yours weren't; they were doctored to make you look rested and alert."

"Well, yah." It wasn't the first time I'd pulled those tricks. "His wasn't?"

"Not at all. If he were trying to play on your sympathies, he could have easily presented a more compelling image."

"He didn't look so much like a kid tonight."

"He's actually a year older than Mara Quida."

"Really? That I wouldn't have guessed." Then again, very few people in Cries looked their age. "Her colleagues seem to think he's a lot younger. You think he does that on purpose?"

"Based on my analyses, I doubt he cares what they think. He's just blessed with good genetics." Dryly he added, "And good health nanos."

"Yah, well, so am I." As much as I might resent the access the Cries elite had to such superb health care, I'd be a hypocrite to deny how much I appreciated it now that I had it too. "I don't believe Mara Quida ran out on him, that he killed her, that someone kidnapped her, or that a guest at the gala ambushed her. So what the bloody hell happened?"

"A good question."

"Someone somewhere did something," I muttered.

"That was certainly specific." Max sounded amused.

Just what I needed, my EI razzing me. I had to find answers soon, before Talon destroyed Lukas Quida's life by accusing him of a murder he didn't commit. His behavior could be a well-crafted act, but my instincts said otherwise.

"I have to figure out what happened," I said. "For his sake. Hell, for mine. If I'm wrong about him, I'm nowhere near as good of an investigator as I think."

"Actually, you're supposed to figure it out because the Majdas hired you to do so."

"Well, yah." I had to report to them, but I had nothing to say, at least not without risk. "Did you find anything in the files you got from their palace about why they might want me killed?"

"Nothing. Just the opposite, in fact."

I sat forward. "What do you mean?"

"If anything, they are exceptionally motivated to keep you alive."

"Seriously? That's hard to believe."

"Apparently it connects to an insult you gave last year to the Ruby Pharaoh."

"For gods' sake." Not this again. "I did *not* insult her. The fact that the Majdas think I did says more about their prejudices than anything about the Pharaoh. She didn't mind at all."

"Bhaaj."

I stood up and stepped out of the pool, dripping. "'Bhaaj'? What does that mean?"

"You suggested that Her Majesty the Ruby Pharaoh descended from the Undercity."

I stalked into my bedroom, flinging around drops of water. "I don't consider that an insult. Besides, it turned out to be true." I smacked a panel in the wall, and the light came on. A cabinet opened with my clothes.

As I dressed, trying not to aggravate my wounds, I thought about the Pharaoh. She had developed the interstellar meshes that spanned human-settled space—and the meshes controlled civilization. People called her the Shadow Pharaoh for good reason; she knew the opto-digital world better than anyone else alive.

I hadn't understood until I went offworld that our civilization couldn't exist without the meshes that networked our lives. They ranged from webs spanning entire star systems all the way down to the nano-nets within our bodies. They even extended into another universe. People called it Kyle space or psiberspace. Either way, it existed as a Hilbert space spanned by the quantum wavefunctions that described a person's brain. In other words, your thoughts determined your location in the Kyle. It operated according to different laws than our spacetime universe. You couldn't physically visit; you accessed it through a neurological link. People thinking about the same subject in the Kyle were "next" to each other there even if light years separated them in our universe. In other words, Kyle space made instant communication possible across light years, defying the speed of light. It held our interstellar civilization together. Unfortunately, only trained Kyle operators could operate the network, and they were prohibitively rare.

Enter the Undercity.

We were no more than a footnote in scholarly texts, if we appeared at all. People outside our insular world had no idea that a thriving, hidden culture existed under the desert, not only in the aqueducts, but even below the canals, in the Down-deep, where the population had become so isolated, their skin and eyes were almost translucent from millennia of living in the dark.

We wanted nothing to do with the rest of the Imperialate. They didn't like us and we didn't like them. However, a good bargain always appealed to my people. Last year, in exchange for a free meal and medical care, hundreds had agreed to let the army test them for Kyle traits. I suggested the exchange when I began to suspect that the strong Kyle abilities among the nobility might have origins no one wanted to admit, specifically, in the genetics of my people. No one expected any drastic result, however, including me.

We had all been wrong.

Historians claim my ancestors retreated into the ruins under the desert because they were homeless and unable to endure the heat without technology they couldn't afford. So they sought refuge in the cooler aqueducts. We knew the truth now. They fled the rest of humanity because they were psions and couldn't bear the pressure of so many minds. The Undercity offered mental surcease. Over the ages, psions in the wider Skolian civilization learned to protect themselves by blocking other minds, but before those techniques were developed, the Undercity must have seemed the only escape for my ancestors. And so we had lived for thousands of years, interbreeding within our population. New genes came into our pool from sporadic trysts between my people and partners outside the Undercity, but we still carried a great deal of our original DNA.

In modern Skolian populations, the rate of empaths was one in one thousand at best, and became rarer for stronger empaths. Telepaths, those psions who not only felt moods but could pick up a few of the strongest thoughts associated with them, were one in a million. Those strong enough to work the Kyle webs were one in ten million.

And in the Undercity? *One third* of us were empaths. One in twenty were telepaths, a rate *fifty thousand* times greater than the rest of humanity.

It was one of the most valuable discoveries in known history. Of course the authorities wanted us to work for them. Well surprise, almost none of my people wanted the "opportunity." Where did the powers of Skolia get the whacked-out idea we'd suddenly give up our lives, culture, and everything else that mattered to labor for a government that had neglected, ignored, suppressed, and even denied our existence for thousands of years?

Last year, the Ruby Pharaoh had hired me for a job. When I met her, I was struck by the almost translucent quality of her skin and her green eyes. It reminded me of Down-deepers, so I asked her about it. To say my idea displeased the Majdas—who revered the Ruby Dynasty and no one else—was the understatement of the year. Of the century. Of forever. I thought they would eviscerate me. They didn't, because the Pharaoh told them to cool it. She had herself tested and surprise, her DNA included Down-deeper stock. It reversed that fairy tale where the pauper girl discovers she's a queen. Our queen was a pauper. After that, the Majdas went silent on the subject. I had to sign the nondisclosure agreement from hell. In fact, they buried the data so deep, no one else would ever discover that little factoid about the Pharaoh.

"Bhaaj?" Max asked.

"Sorry. I was thinking. Why does that change how the Majdas feel about me?"

"You also have some Down-deeper DNA."

"So?"

"So you come from the same stock as the Pharaoh, albeit distantly."

I shrugged. "That doesn't mean squat. She sits on the Ruby Throne. I don't."

"Actually there is no throne. It was destroyed thousands of years ago."

"Max."

"Your DNA makes them more likely to want you alive."

Yah, right. "So why did a Majda flyer pick up my would-be assassin in the mountains?"

"I don't know. According to the palace files, you weren't the only Majda agent at the gala."

"You're kidding."

"Not at all. They also sent someone named Sav Halin. She matches the description I've put together of the person who shot at you."

I recognized the name from the list of guests. "Halin is a Majda agent? I wouldn't have guessed." She'd seemed as nondescript as her name, a reporter for a popular mesh publication. I snapped on my gauntlets. "Why would they tell her to shoot me?"

"Nothing in the files indicates they even wanted her to notice you. She was just supposed to do her job, writing an article about the event. They wanted her to make everyone look good."

No surprise there. Majdas never stopped optimizing their finances. I thought of what Jak had said about my being the only person on the case who knew the aqueducts. "Does this Halin person have Undercity connections?"

"I haven't found any."

"I take it I'm not supposed to know she works for Majda."

"The only reason she appears in your files is because you were both assigned to the gala."

I walked into the living room. The window-wall facing north had turned transparent as the sky lightened with sunrise. The panoramic view of the predawn desert soothed the jagged edges of my thoughts, all of that distance stretching to the edge of the word. Now that I'd rested, I could think more coherently about the palace.

"Max, I need to look into Halin without revealing I know about her." I thought for a moment. "It's natural for me to check the background of everyone at the party. I've been meaning to do it anyway. So try this. Do the checks according to occupation." I needed to be oblique about my approach, to avoid suspicions I'd seen the Majda files. "Don't start with reporters. Check other jobs first. When you do get to Halin, find something that gives me a valid reason to ask the Majdas about her. Mix it up with other people so it doesn't sound like I'm investigating her in particular."

"I can do that," Max said. "Also, a message just came in from Jak."

I blinked at the abrupt subject change. "What does he say?"

"Here's the recording."

Jak's voice came into the air. "Bhaaj, I just saw Gourd. He looked at the crystal sphere you gave him. He didn't find anything unusual."

Oh, well. "Send Jak a message. Ask him to thank Gourd for trying."

"Can't you tell Gourd yourself?"

"He never responds to a page from outside the aqueducts. He stays off-grid." I finally asked the question that had tugged at me since we cracked the Majda palace security. "Max, what about those Majda files from my birth? What do they say?"

"If you mean, did the Majdas identify your parents, the answer is no."

"Oh." The disappointment hit hard, more than I expected. No records existed for most people in the Undercity. It was one of the few places a person could live free of the interstellar meshes. I realized now I'd secretly hoped my father was an Imperialate citizen who had a liaison with an Undercity woman, that he might still be alive or have family somewhere. If my DNA linked to any such Skolian citizen, though, the Majdas would have discovered it.

"No big deal," I lied. It wasn't to anyone else, just to me.

Max spoke in an unexpectedly gentle voice. "I'm sorry."

"No need to be." I had to change the subject. "Make sure you keep those files secured. I'll look at them in more detail later." Max rarely missed anything important, but he lacked an ability to think outside the box, whereas I pretty much lived beyond its confines.

Another thought came to me. "What about that person General Majda and her husband were talking about in the palace garden? Some CEO named Bak Trasor. You have anything on him?"

"No. And I don't intend to look him up."

"Why not?"

"We heard his name when you were at the Majdas committing semi-treason."

"Semi-treason?" I smiled. "As opposed to what, pseudo-treason?"

"Bhaaj, listen to me. You can't do anything that might suggest you were at the palace. So far I've no indication they suspect you, but they're surely focusing all their resources on the search."

I stopped smiling. Majda resources were formidable. "I see your point." Trasor probably sat on the board of some company the Majdas controlled. "Max, you regularly look over my financial holdings, don't you?"

"Yes. Every day."

"I think you need to look over them now."

"I could. Why?"

"Well," I said, "maybe while you are doing that, you might notice if Bak Trasor sits on the board of any corporation where I have assets."

"Ah." He sounded satisfied. "It's true, you've invested in many places."

I didn't know the full shape of my portfolio; Max kept tabs on its constant flux. But I never spent a single credit I didn't have to part with. I knew what it was like to live in poverty, scrabbling just to eat. Never again.

"Analyses done," Max said. "Bak Trasor is the CEO of Suncap Industries."

"I take it that means I have holdings in Suncap."

"Yes. Fairly significant, in fact."

I grimaced. "I should sell them now, before Trasor gets deposed in a corporate coup. The value of the stock will probably drop."

"You aren't going to sell squat," Max said flatly. "You want another reason to get arrested? You don't have enough already?"

"What are you talking about?"

"It's called insider trading. Using confidential information to your financial advantage that you obtained through trespass into the residence of the General of the Pharaoh's Army is so feloniously criminal, my normally unemotional processors are feeling ill."

Unemotional, my ass. I knew he was right, both ethically and for common sense, but after the way I'd grown up, the fear of losing everything never left me. I also hated to think what that loss could mean to the resources I was so carefully building in my efforts to help the Undercity.

"How badly do you think it will damage my holdings?" I asked.

"Your investment firm uses top-of-the line trading algorithms to manage your portfolio. They will minimize your loss as much as possible." More quietly, he added, "You'll be fine. This sort of thing happens. Normally you wouldn't even know."

Quit overreacting, I told myself. "I think I'll get breakfast."

"Wait, I'm getting a page." Max paused. "You have an incoming from Majda."

I froze. Shit! Had they figured out what happened?

"It could be nothing," Max added.

Nothing the Majdas did was nothing. "Put it through."

The confident voice of Lavinda Majda rose into the air. "My greetings, Major Bhaajan."

"And mine to you." It amazed me how calm I sounded. "Do you have more information about the Scorpio case?" I didn't know why Lavinda would contact me; she wasn't one of the investigators. But I had to pretend everything was normal. I couldn't say what I wanted to ask, which was, *You know, don't you? You found me out.*

"I'm afraid we have a new problem," Lavinda said.

I felt as ill as Max's unemotional processors. "What's the problem?"

"Another person has disappeared."

✤ CHAPTER VIII ✤
SHADOWS

"She was here!" Inna Starchild stood in her living room, her white tunic and trousers a soft contrast to the blue rug. Her furniture consisted of elegant antiques, from tables carved with vine patterns to wingchairs with gilded upholstery. She came from old wealth, nothing sleek or modern here. Her artwork glowed in the air above crystal tables, delicate holos of desert-stalk blooms. I'd heard that her work, and the protections needed to prevent it from being copied on the meshes, went for millions. She had little in common with Lukas Quida except that her powerful executive spouse had also disappeared.

Chiaru Starchild, her wife, sat on the board of another corporation, Abyss Associates. They built stuff, a lot of it, some of the top architectural wonders in the Imperialate. She and Inna had married two years ago. Today the head of Security from Abyss had shown up, Patrik Laj, a lanky fellow with red hair. I wondered how he felt about being one of the few people on the planet without dark hair. I didn't get the sense anything ruffled him. He presented the picture of cool efficiency.

"She went to the kitchen," Inna said. "Just to get a glass of wine."

"How long was she gone before you looked for her?" Patrik asked.

Inna twisted the ends of her cloth belt around her hand. "Maybe ten minutes? We were watching the holo of a news show. When it ended, I wondered why she hadn't come back."

Detective Talon, the head of Scorpio Security, stood near the sofa, watching Inna Starchild intently. Given the similarities of this case with the Quida disappearance, I could see why Talon was here. What I didn't understand was why Lavinda Majda had also showed up. Sure, the Majdas kept watch on any significant event in Cries. Keeping track, however, and sending a royal heir were two very different things. Lavinda stayed back, an imposing but discreet figure in her army uniform with her black hair swept up onto her head. A tendril of hair had escaped, though, and hung by her cheek. Interesting. Usually every aspect of her appearance was in perfect place.

Talon grilled Starchild with curt intensity. Although Patrik had a gentler approach, his questions were essentially the same. Inna's story never changed. She'd gone to the kitchen and found the place in shambles. I'd seen the room; it looked as bad as Mara Quida's bedroom. Inna claimed she hadn't heard any noise. The kitchen was far from the living room, and she'd had the holo-vid going, so it could be true. I didn't know if I believed her, though. It looked like a rubble smasher had blasted through the place. No trace of Chiaru remained, nor could we find any security footage for those moments she vanished, just like what happened with Mara Quida.

Lavinda joined me while Talon and Patrik talked with Starchild. "Major, my greetings. I'm sorry we had to meet again under these circumstances."

I nodded to her. "My greetings."

"How are you feeling?" She pushed back her wayward strand of hair. "I hope you're recovering."

"Yes, I'm good," I answered, pretending my injuries didn't hurt like hell. My meds were doing repairs, but I didn't let them give me pain relievers, which dulled my brain. I just smiled at Lavinda. It wasn't a real smile, because in the Undercity we never smiled at people we didn't trust. I had nothing against Lavinda. In fact, I rather liked her. But I had no intention of trusting her.

"Does your family have connections to Abyss Associates?" I asked.

"No. I'm just here to follow up in case this relates to the Scorpio case."

I still didn't see why she needed to come in person, instead of sending an aide or security officer. I motioned toward the staircase to the second story. "Think we can look up there?" Maybe I could get her talking if we had more privacy.

"I'll check." She went over to Inna Starchild. "Do you mind if we look upstairs?"

Inna nodded, her dark hair rustling. "Yes, please feel free." Although she seemed upset, her concern didn't have the intensity I felt from Lukas. If I'd had to define the difference, I'd have said Lukas lost the love of his life and Inna lost a valued lover and friend. Unlike Lukas, she had no obvious motive for murder; she was the one who had brought the wealth into the relationship.

As Lavinda and I headed to the stairs, she asked, "What's happening with the Quida case?"

"No ransom demand." To Max, I thought, *Give me a fact on the Quida investigation that relates to the Majdas. Something it would make sense for me to ask her about.*

"It's odd." Lavinda climbed the stairs with me. "If it's not a kidnapping, then what?"

"Malice? Maybe some sociopath is blowing up execs."

"Then why no trace of either Quida or Chiaru." She took a ragged breath. "No blood, no tissues, nothing. What happened to them?"

Gods. Her voice was shaking. Although I'd known her long enough to realize she has a great emotional depth beneath her controlled exterior, I'd never seen her like this, vulnerable and raw, traits no one associated with the Majdas.

I said only, "It does seem unusual."

"It's better to find nothing rather than—than their remains."

"That's true." Why did these cases matter so much to her? Maybe it linked to her being an empath. Although members of the noble Houses let the rest of the universe believe they were all great psions, most had only traces of the abilities or none at all. Lavinda was the only full psion among the three Majda sisters. I'd learned to guard my mind in her presence. I needed no Kyle abilities, though, to see that this case had hit her much harder than the Quida disappearance.

I found a useful fact, Max thought as we reached the top of the stairs. Exec Tallmount was at the gala. She's one of the Scorpio execs that Mara Quida pushed out of consideration for the Metropoli contract. A few tendays ago, Tallmount spoke about the Majdas, saying they wielded too much control in Cries. It was controversial.

Thanks, Max. To Lavinda, I said, "I'm looking into the background of the people at the Quida gala." I paused at a rail on the landing of the stairs and looked down at the living room where the investigators were talking with Inna Starchild. "I'm checking everyone."

Lavinda stood with me at the rail. "Anyone stand out in particular?"

"Maybe. A Scorpio exec named Tallmount. She was passed over as a manager for the Metropoli contract."

"That sounds familiar." She paused. "Ah, yes, I remember. A critic of my family."

"I'm sure she meant no offense." I actually wasn't sure at all, but it seemed the tactful response. Anyone who criticized the Majdas risked her career. Tallmount was right, though; the Majdas did wield too much influence. Although they took industry here to a higher level, which benefited Cries, their control amounted to a monopoly over the entire city.

Lavinda smiled wryly. "She has guts. I rather liked that."

Ho! I hadn't expected that reaction. "She may have resented Mara Quida."

"Let me know if you find out more." Lavinda watched as Talon grilled Inna Starchild below. "This house has a different feel than the Quida mansion."

"What do you mean?"

"I'm not sure how to explain." She spoke with compassion. "Lukas was dying inside. Inna is worried, yes, but more like someone in the verge of a divorce."

Where had *that* come from? "You think Inna wanted to get rid of her wife?"

Lavinda glanced at me. "I don't mean it like that. I'd heard rumors they were in the midst of an amicable breakup." She actually looked sheepish. "I suppose we all succumb to a bit of gossip."

Hah! Even a Majda heir. I smiled. "Yah, me too." Immediately I felt embarrassed at using Undercity slang for the word *yes*. As much as I tried never to drop my defenses with the Cries elite, I tended to relax with Lavinda.

If she noticed, she gave no sign. "Shall we take a look around up here?"

"Sounds good."

We exited the landing into a hallway with tiles cut from red desert stone. I liked that Starchild used native materials rather than importing wood from offworld.

"Do you have any reason to think Tallmount might want trouble for your family?" I asked.

Lavinda's face took on an inwardly directed expression, a look many of us got while we talked with our EIs. I waited.

"My family holds shares in Scorpio." She focused on me again. "One of my cousins sits on the board of directors, in fact. Anything that hurts Scorpio could hurt my family."

No wonder they'd wanted me at the gala. They had a lot invested in Scorpio. "I'll let you know if I find anything else."

"My EI can't find any link between Mara Quida and Chiaru Starchild." Lavinda walked with me into a suite at the end of the hallway with two bedrooms, a sitting room, and a library. "Except the obvious, that they're both execs."

Max, did you find anything? I asked.

They belonged to the same private club in the city. The Desert Winds.

I knew little about the club, except that they'd never allow a lowly PI like me past their esteemed doors. "I've dug up one connection. They both belonged to the Desert Winds."

"That place?" Lavinda shrugged. "My sister Vaj is a member."

Ho! That placed the Winds among the elite of the elite. "It might be a good idea for your sister to take extra precautions with her safety, in case Winds membership connects with these cases." Gods only knew what would happen if the General of the Pharaoh's Army disappeared.

"That's a good idea. I'll have an aide from the palace contact you to talk about your recommendations."

"Sure, no problem."

We continued to look around, walking past antique tables under sparkling chandeliers. We found nothing out of place, not even a crystal knob. Max recorded while I examined everything. If Chiaru and Inna Starchild were having marital problems, maybe Chiaru had just deserted her spouse and the explosion in the kitchen had no connection to her absence. I doubted it, though. The two cases were too similar and the crime scenes too violent.

Someone was making the elite of Cries disappear.

I lay on my back in my bed at the penthouse with the room darkened.

Are you ready? Max asked.

No, I thought.

Max waited.

I tried to feel empathic, whatever that meant. It didn't work. I'd never wanted to be an empath, but this case had me stymied. Anything that would help me read the people involved would help. *Do you have the files from Adept Sanva? I mean the exercises for, uh, being empathic.*

Yes, all of them, Max said. Which would you like to start with?

I have no clue. Until two days ago, I hadn't even known you could do empath exercises. *Does she recommend any?*

Meditation. When you reach a relaxed state, try to sense how you feel, physically and emotionally.

Oh, Max. It sounded like the freely-feely nonsense currently trending with people who had too much money and went to hot-goop spas. *I'd feel stupid.*

It's not like you have anything to lose. Meditation is healthy. And you could use the rest.

I supposed he had a point. I closed my eyes. *How do I meditate?*

Center your mind.

I have no idea what that means.

Visualize a place that relaxes you. Breathe evenly. Imagine each part of your body relaxing, starting from your toes and moving to the top of your head. Keep your mind smooth. Don't think about solving problems.

All right. I imagined Mirror Lake at the Majda palace, one of the most tranquil sights on the planet. It didn't work. My thoughts on the Majdas were anything but tranquil, given the mixed signs they were giving about whether or not they wanted my sorry ass dead. So instead I thought of a grotto where Jak and I had often made love in our youth. Its crystals sparkled in torchlight, covering the lacy stone formations that had formed around the small lake over the eons. The water was poisonous but the grotto breathtaking, an apt metaphor for the aqueducts, both deadly and beautiful.

I tensed and relaxed my toes. Then the balls of my feet. Soles . . . heels . . .

I opened my eyes. Jak was sitting on the edge of the bed, watching me. Light from the living room trickled around him.

"Eh." I sat up and slid my arms around him, laying my head against his shoulder. "Mmm."

He held me. "You're in a good mood."

"Yah. Guess I was tired." I drew back from him. "How long have you been here?"

"About ten minutes. Max didn't want me to wake you up."

Max spoke from my gauntlet comm. "She needs rest." He sounded annoyed.

I stretched, feeling better. "How long did I sleep?"

"Four hours," Max said. "Do you feel more empathic?"

I laughed. "No, not one bit."

Jak tilted his head. "More what?"

I told him about Doctor Sanva and her exercises, which made him smile, and then I told him about what happened at the palace, which he found less amusing.

"Are you out of your fucking mind?" he demanded. "No one spies on the Majdas."

"I had to know."

"You already know." He gripped my arms as if that could stop me from doing stupid shit. "If they wanted you dead, you'd be dead."

"I'm not so easy to kill."

"That knife attack was too public. It isn't their style."

I swung my legs off the bed and he moved so we were sitting side by side. "Jak, have you heard of the Desert Winds?"

"Sure. Why?"

"Do any of their members go to the Black Mark?" He always checked out the glitz before he let them into his casino. His customers probably had no idea how much he knew about them.

He spoke to the air. "Royal, who do we have from the Desert Winds?"

The sensually deep voice of Royal Flush, Jak's infamous EI, came out his gauntlet comm. Jak had named Royal after the legendary poker hand that had netted him enough winnings to start his casino. "Several members of the Winds patronize the Black Mark." Royal gave two names I didn't recognize, then said, "Chiaru Starchild, Daan Bialo, and Mara Quida."

"Holy shit," I said. "That's the connection."

"What connection?" Jak asked.

I told him about Chiaru's disappearance. "Daan Bialo is another Scorpio exec. He was in line for the Metropoli contract and got passed over in favor of Mara Quida." I spoke to the air. "Max, send a message to Detective Talon at Scorpio. Tell her they need to protect these execs: Jen Oja, Daan Bialo, Zeddia Vixer, and Tallmount. One of them might be the next to vanish."

"Max, stop!" Jak turned to me. I'd never given credence to the phrase "blazing eyes," which sounded dumb to me, but if a gaze could burn, Jak's was on fire. "Your EI isn't sending anyone shit about my casino."

"I'd never reveal anything about the Black Mark," I said. "We need to protect Daan Bialo. If this connection is real, Bialo is the only one in danger. I gave the other names as a cover, so it looks like I singled them out because they all got passed over for the Metropoli deal. That has nothing to do with the Black Mark. It's a logical precaution." I regarded him steadily. "If I do nothing and Bialo vanishes, that's on me."

"You'll keep the Black Mark out of it?"

"You have my word."

After a moment, he said, "All right." With those words, he gave me a trust I'd never seen him show any other living soul.

"Shall I send the message?" Max asked.

I glanced at Jak and he nodded.

"Go ahead," I said.

"You have to be careful," Jak told me. "You're the only person with the connections to see the link between these cases and the casino. It's no wonder someone is trying to whack you."

"And you should close up the Black Mark." The entire casino was designed from an illegal composite. Doped with designer nanobots, the place could take itself apart faster than a desert whirlwind and rebuild wherever else he wanted.

"I can't close up," he said. "People will wonder why."

He had a good point. "You be careful, too, yah?"

"You worried for me, Bhaajo?" he murmured.

Damn, he was using *that* voice, a sensual rumble that could make me forget any other man existed. Seeing his body limned in sunlight from the front room was erotic in a way that people who'd always lived aboveground would never know. I lay down on the bed, pulling him with me in the bronzed light of Raylicon.

Daan Bialo, Zeddia Vixer, and Tallmount met me at a café on the Concourse. I chose the place to see how they reacted to being on the edge of the Undercity. Of course we were nowhere near the true aqueducts, but I doubted even Bialo knew that, despite his visits to the Black Mark. Although I wanted to talk to all three of them, his reactions were the ones I most needed to gauge.

We sat at a round table on a balcony. The Concourse lay below, a wide boulevard with boutiques, jewelry stores, and cafés. Although night had fallen in the desert above, the avenue remained bright from street lamps and overhead lighting. Across the boulevard, a bridge arched over the only canal in the Concourse. This aqueduct was better kept than those in the true Undercity, at least "better" according to people in Cries. It had no dust. The city kept it so clean, it no longer looked like part of the ancient ruins. They also paved it with flagstones cut from stone in the Vanished Sea, which would never happen in the true aqueducts. Clubs and party plazas lay beyond it, their lights dimmed for atmosphere but still glittering with people stroll-lolling at their leisure.

"All these kids." Daan Bialo watched the clubbers. "They think they're slumming it."

Zeddia Vixer snorted. "Well, then, so are we." Her nasal voice grated on my ears.

"I used to like the clubs when I was younger." Daan took a swallow of his whisker-run, a blend of whiskey and cacao. "I know this Undercity. It makes you feel alive."

Yah, right, I thought. *You have no idea.*

I don't think they realize you come from the Undercity, Max thought.

Tallmount sipped her water, then set down her emerald-hued

glass. She looked stronger and more fit than the others. Her file said she ran marathons. She spoke to me in a resonant voice, much easier to listen to than the others. "You wanted to ask about Mara Quida."

Interesting. She made it a statement rather than a question. Although I hadn't told them why I wanted to meet, it wasn't a stretch, given my position as an investigator. Still, she didn't miss much.

"We haven't found her yet," I said. It had been too long, two days, one hundred sixty hours.

Zeddia looked bored. "You think her disappearance connects to Scorpio?"

"If you mean, could you be in danger, then I hope not. But we have to be careful." I motioned to the cop by the wall of the café and his two mini-drones floating nearby. "That's why we have officers assigned to each of you." I considered them. "I understand you were all in consideration for the Metropoli account, along with Jen Oja."

"It was mostly Jen." Zeddia glanced at Tallmount. "Though I thought you had a shot at it."

Tallmount said, "I had a sense—"

"Hey!" Daan interrupted. "We all had a shot at it. Mara just pushed us out."

"Yah, she was definitely a bitch," Zeddia said.

Such compassion for their missing colleague, Max thought.

They don't seem to like her much. Most people do, though.

Jealousy, I suspect.

I focused on Tallmount. "Did you want the contract?"

"I thought about it," she said. "It certainly would have been a good career step."

"Of course we all wanted it," Daan said. "But if you're asking would we hurt Mara over it, then hell no."

"Is that what this is about?" Zeddia snapped. "You think one of us took revenge? That's a load of slop-shit."

"Someone might have," Daan mused. "Mara is a fucking pain, the way she's always ahead of everyone else."

Max sent me an amused thought. Their Els need to tell them to clean up their language.

Not likely. Unlike me, these execs had nothing to prove. They probably spoke more conservatively at work, but the Scorpio higher-ups would know everything about the execs they were considering putting in charge of a deal worth billions. Neither Daan nor Zeddia struck me as smart choices. I had a better impression of Tallmount, though.

Daan finished his drink and waved over a floating servo-orb. As it swooped to our table, he held out his empty glass. "Get me another."

"Right away, sir." The orb unfolded a silvery arm from its body and took his glass, then hummed back to the café.

"They call that service?" Zeddia snorted. "So sloppy. Too much association with the dust scum under the city, I'd wager."

Daan laughed. "It's a matter of breeding, Zeddia dear."

"What breeding?" Zeddia said. "They ought to clean out the ruins, get rid of all that human trash." She paused. "Do you suppose the people down there are fully human? I doubt it."

Fuck you, I thought. This time, Max didn't object.

Tallmount was watching me. To Zeddia she said, "Maybe they feel the same about Cries."

"That's ridiculous," Daan said. "They like us."

I'd have laughed at that absurdity if I hadn't wanted to punch him. "Why do you say that?"

He waved his hand at the Concourse. "The vendors make money off us."

"None of the Concourse vendors come from the Undercity," I said.

"Of course they do," Zeddia told me. "If it wasn't for us, they wouldn't have a living. They should be grateful."

Grateful? My hand clenched around my water glass.

Tallmount spoke quickly. "I suspect the Undercity is far different than any of us know."

"It's not a big deal." Daan wiped sweat off his forehead. "This is a boring subject."

Maybe. More likely, it made him uneasy. From what Jak had told me, Daan spent far too much time and credits in the Black Mark. Although most worlds allowed gambling, here it was a felony punishable by prison and large fines.

The servo-bot brought him a new drink, and he took a deep swallow.

"I need to go." Zeddia was looking across the bridge at the clubs. "Time to enjoy the night."

I motioned to the two police mini-drones. "Stay with one of them. Don't go alone."

Zeddia laughed as we all stood up. "Could be an interesting night for that drone."

I tapped my gauntlet, sending each of them a holo-mail. "If any of you think of anything else about Mara Quida, you can reach me with the code I just commed to you."

Zeddia was already walking away. She waved her hand over her head, apparently her goodbye. Daan waited, shifting his weight back and forth. Tallmount looked at me, at Daan, then back at me. She said, "If I think of more, I'll let you know."

I wondered what was up. "That would be good. You can reach me anytime."

She nodded, still pausing. Daan stayed put, so Tallmount nodded to us and left.

Max, I thought. *Schedule a reminder for me to contact Tallmount when I have a chance.*

Done.

"Did you want to talk to me?" I asked Daan.

He squinted at me. "Do you really think we're in danger?"

"It's possible." Especially him.

"But—do I have to stay with the cop or the drones?" He cleared his throat. "What if I, uh—have a native guide?"

Good gods. He wanted to go to the Black Mark even now. Jak always sent an Undercity guide to bring in his clientele. He required the city slicks wear blindfolds and sound dampers so they could neither see nor hear while their escort led them on a circuitous route through the aqueducts. Without that guide, they'd never find the Black Mark; they'd end up mugged or killed instead. His clients mostly loved the thrill of danger, but I doubted they realized the true risk. Most of them had a sense of entitlement that blinded them to the harsh reality of the Undercity.

If Daan wanted to sneak off to the casino, he'd have to give the cops the slip, which would put him in danger. I'd seen what addiction did to people. Jak considered his casino like a bar where patrons enjoyed a night out with friends. He didn't deny some people had a problem, but he didn't believe he was responsible for a gambling addiction any more than a bar owner was responsible for alcoholism. It bothered me, especially given that Jak's own gambling habit could destroyed him if he hadn't been so damn good at poker, and if becoming owner of the Black Mark hadn't changed his path in life. He also employed many of our people, paying high wages and seeing to their health and families, which earned him their fierce loyalty. I'd never made peace with the cognitive dissonance of my lover being both a criminal kingpin and a hero to our people.

"Where would this guide take you?" I asked Daan.

He stared down at the Concourse. "Some places people go, they don't want to be followed."

"Daan, look at me."

He met my gaze, suddenly defiant. "It's not your place to judge me."

"Whatever you're planning to do, it's not worth risking your life."

"I didn't say I was planning to do anything."

"Fine. Whatever you're not planning to do, don't do it. Daan, I'm serious. Your life could be in danger."

The servo-bot hummed up to us. "Would you like another drink?" it asked Daan.

"No. I'm going." He looked relieved at the interruption. "Send the charges to my account."

"Done, sir." As the bot floated away, Daan nodded to me. "Good night, Major."

I hoped it stayed that way. Although I didn't particularly like him, or at least his views on the Undercity, I had no wish to see him become the third casualty in the disappearing elite of Cries.

I was crossing the bridge on the Concourse when Max thought, Your shadow is back.

I paused at the top of the span and rested my hands on its rail. The canal stretched out below until it faded into the smoky mist at the end of the avenue, a kilometer distant. *What shadow?*

I think it's the person who followed you out of Cries yesterday.

Apparently I hadn't fooled her with my nondescript appearance. I had on city clothes today, boring enough to blend with the crowds.

When I dressed this way, people here tended to assume I was some sort of law enforcement protecting them against nefarious Undercity types.

I looked around, but saw nothing out of place. *Where is she?*

Across the Concourse from the café where you met the execs. See the open-view counter?

It took me a moment to figure out what he meant. A festive stall stood near the bridge, topped by a roof of bright blue cloth with gold tassels hanging from its edges. The proprietor stood behind a counter heaped with pottery glazed in swirls of color.

Do you mean the man selling pots? I asked. *I thought my shadow was a woman.*

No, look to the left side. I'll magnify. See that ripple in the air?

As Max accessed the lenses in my eyes, the counter grew larger as if I were walking toward it. I did see a ripple now, one in the shape of a person standing only a few paces from the stall. *The owner doesn't seem to know anyone is there.*

If he checked, he'd probably notice, Max answered.

I headed the other way, down the bridge toward the glitz-clubs. *Is my shadow following me?*

Yes, she's coming up the bridge.

At the bottom of the bridge, I blended in among the crowds. After a ways, I turned down a narrow alley with no lights except holos dancing on the buildings on either side. The club on my right shimmered with red and white polyhedrons, all these geometric shapes twirling around, pleasing but weird. On my left, cascades of purple light flowed down the wall like a waterfall.

Behind the buildings, a narrow lane went past storage huts. They weren't lit except by a faint overflow of light from the clubs. I kept going, farther from the main boulevard, deeper into the back alleys. Eventually I reached the Concourse wall, a barrier that rose to the ceiling far overhead. Tourists never bothered to visit these places where the shiny nightlife faded into the practical construction that supported the underground world. The darkness had become thick.

My shadow still trying to disguise herself with holos? Here in the dark, the light she needed to produce holographic images would make her stand out like a beacon.

No, she deactivated her holosuit. She's still shrouded from UV and infrared sensors, however, and she's using a sound damper.

Walking along the wall, I trailed my fingers across it until I felt a familiar set of ridges. I tapped them in a pattern that had passed from generation to generation of dust gangers. When I pushed the wall, it moved inward just enough to let me squeeze through the open crack.

Send out my red beetle. I had two drones, one red and one green. Although both were the same model with rudimentary AI brains, they'd developed differently over the years, which meant they might pursue their targets in different ways. I was curious to see if the red bot gave me different insights on this person following me than the green had already produced.

The droid rose out of my jacket pocket, rustling the leather, and flew off. I closed the hidden door, leaving me inside the wall and my shadow outside. Max used the sensors in my gauntlets, so my going inside the wall limited what he could detect. The droid could reach him, though.

Have the beetle follow my shadow, I thought.

It's registering her pulse and respiration. She stopped walking. I'd bet she doesn't know how you vanished.

Good. I stayed put. Even with my sound dampers working, I didn't want to risk her hearing me. Shrouds worked best at a distance; this close, it was harder to fool people.

She's moving again, walking along the wall away from us, Max thought.

I waited a few moments to put some distance between us, then opened the door enough to slip back into the darkened alley. *Keep me shrouded, except for the holosuit. Don't activate anything with a light.*

You're hidden. She's headed toward the Undercity.

Connect me to the beetle.

Done.

I was suddenly in the air above the Concourse, watching the alley with infrared vision. The scene appeared dim and translucent, superimposed on my normal vision. The woman below had matched her suit temperature to her surroundings, making it difficult to see her in IR.

I still don't recognize her, I thought.

I'm getting a bit more detail, enough to refine the image I made yesterday.

Check it against every database, including any offworld networks you can reach.

That's trillions of records. It could take a while.

Take whatever time you need. Find out who she is. She can't be completely off the grid. No one is. That wasn't one hundred percent true, but the few wizards who could manage that feat wouldn't likely be skulking around the Concourse.

My shadow headed toward the end of the Concourse, where it exited into the real Undercity. A sign there warned any tourists to go no further, at risk to their lives. It was the only true sign about the Undercity on the entire Concourse. Before my shadow reached that point, though, she stopped. When she spoke into her comm, my beetle picked up some of her words.

"...not here...lost her again." She paused. "No, Bialo left with the cop." More silence. "Why would he give his guards the slip?" Yet another pause. "All right...I'll take care of him."

Damn. *They're going after Bialo. We have to get to him first.*

How? It sounds like he ditched his guards.

It doesn't matter. I know where to find him.

If I wasn't too late.

✤ CHAPTER IX ✤
LIQUID ROCK

The Black Mark was in full swing, awash in purple light and glitz-dust floating in the air. It was mesmerizing, at least for anyone without military biomech in their body blocking subliminal invitations. I wandered among the tables looking for Daan, with no success. I'd changed into my usual clothes, a black muscle shirt and trousers, with my pulse revolver plainly visible in its shoulder holster. No one bothered me tonight.

"Eh, Bhaaj," a woman said.

I turned to see Dara in her glitz makeup. If I hadn't known her so well, I'd never have guessed this was the same woman who looked after a family of five, including her two daughters, her two adopted children, and her husband Weaver, one of the most gifted artists I'd ever met. Jak paid her well, enough that she could provide a stable life for her family, a rarity in the aqueducts where many adults didn't even live to see their children grow up.

"Eh, Dara," I said.

"Got a whisper today," she told me. "Good news."

I smiled, another rarity. Dara was my closest friend, and good news for her was good news all around. "What's the buzz?"

"Weaver's license," Dara said. "Doctor Rajindia told us. License is ready to pick up."

My mouth dropped open. This was more than good news. It was a freaking miracle.

I'd worked with Weaver for two years to get him a license to sell his tapestries and glassware on the Concourse. We'd even arranged for him to rent a stall, not a fancy area, but respectable. And for two damn years, our work had gone nowhere, because the blasted Cries licensing authority blocked us at every step.

Nor was it only the bureaucrats. Convincing Weaver it was worth the effort had been almost as tough. He didn't like city slicks, he didn't like the cops who patrolled the Concourse, and he didn't believe the credits that people in Cries would pay for his work meant squat. You couldn't see credits. You couldn't hold them. They had no trade value in the Undercity. I'd resisted my urge to push. He had to want this himself, not because anyone told him that he should do it. He was setting a precedent, a huge step for my people. He would be the first true Undercity merchant to sell his work on the Concourse.

In the end, it was his oldest daughter, fourteen-year-old Darjan, who convinced him. She loved to learn and often bargained with me, teaching tykado to the youngest children in return for my getting her schoolbooks. Weaver listened to her. He'd still needed time to adapt to the idea, but he had more than enough, because it was taking so long to work through the bureaucracy. Had he finally succeeded? I was almost afraid to rejoice.

"Doctor Rajindia brought news?" I asked. "How? She's a healer. Not burrow-rat."

Dara smiled tolerantly at my idiot pun about bureaucrats. "Doctor Rajindia came to see kids. Check their health." She walked with me across the main floor. "Weaver told her about the license. She said she'd ask. Came today to check on me and Weaver. Told us the news."

"Good news, yah." Incredible.

Dara's smile faded. "Got to go to the city to get the license. We can't."

I understood. Like many of my people, Dara never left the Undercity. The first time I'd stood under the open sky, I couldn't even see it all. The neurological pathways in my brain had needed to rewire themselves so I could comprehend that incredible vista. On the rare occasions when adults among my people ventured out, some hated all that open space. Others adapted, but most returned home with relief. In the past few years, though, more of our young people were sneaking up to the desert, going at night first, when it was easier to deal with so much space. Our children adapted faster. Maybe if we showed our babies the sky, their brains would learn early to accept that vast land and sky.

"I go with you and Weaver," I told her.

Relief showed in her gaze. "Is good."

"Got a question for you. Looking for a city slick."

She snorted. "Room full of slicks."

"Man called Daan."

"Not know." She motioned around at the main room. "See him?"

"Not here." I tilted my head toward a hallway that led to the high-stakes poker rooms. "Maybe private."

"You go." She headed to the bar, then looked back with a grin. "Come drink later, yah?"

"You bet."

I headed for the poker rooms.

I searched four games before I found Daan. He sat at a round table with five other people who varied from dissipated youths to glitz-fibs to older execs. A handsome young man with blue hair dealt them cards. I knew the dealer; Bez lived with one of the smaller dust gangs. He put the wages he earned here toward food for their circle of kith and kin. In this game, he dealt real cards, not holos. You could only join these backroom games if Jak invited you, and every player went through a tech search to make sure they weren't bringing cheats. The lights were dimmer because Jak turned off his hypnotic holos. Stakes went high in these games, but they were the only way you could get a fair shake in the Black Mark.

I stood in the shadows, watching. Daan looked discreet tonight, in simple dark clothes, as if he hoped to avoid notice. That wasn't going to save his ass if someone tried to explode him.

"More cards?" Bez asked.

"Two." Daan set two cards on the table and the dealer gave him new ones.

As the round progressed, most of the other players folded, until Daan was facing only an older woman with a too perfect face and black hair pulled back in a sleek braid. She watched him intently, and he avoided her gaze. With the barest hint of a smile, she tapped the table. The holo of a ten-thousand-opto chit formed in front of her, glowing blue and purple.

Daan let out a breath. Even for a high-powered exec, that was a large bet. I'd never understood how they could squander their wealth that way. I hung onto every opto I earned. To risk so much just for a game was beyond my ability to comprehend.

"Raise, call, or fold?" the dealer prompted him.

Daan finally looked at his opponent. She met his gaze with confidence.

"You going to play?" She sounded smug.

"Call." Daan tapped the table, and a chit for ten thousand optos appeared in front of him.

"Show your hands," the dealer said.

"Fine," the woman muttered. She tossed down her cards. "It's yours."

Murmurs of appreciation went around the table. "Well played," someone said.

Daan's mouth fell open, which made me suspect he hadn't been sure she was bluffing. Then he grinned. I walked around the room, staying in the shadows until I was opposite Daan, in his view. Then I leaned against the wall to watch them again.

Daan glanced up—and froze. "Fuck!"

Surprise, I thought.

The others at the table stiffened as they looked around. Their gazes scraped over me as if I were part of the scenery. Daan's face, however, went pale.

Bez glanced at me, at Daan, at me again. "Got a problem?"

"Nahya," I said. "All good." I spoke to Daan in his Cries dialect. "We should get going."

"Uh—we should?" Confusion washed across his face. He stood and tapped the cash-in panel on the table so the casino could send the opto credits to his bit-disk. He'd figure out later what to do with them, but for now no record existed, except on his disk, that he'd just made ten thousand credits.

Daan walked with me back to the main room. He didn't say a word. The smell of some oil he wore wafted around me, a subtle scent. It smelled good, but it seemed, well, I didn't know what. Not natural. Out of place. My people never wore cologne.

Ironically, with so much action in the main room, we had more privacy than in the private game. Everyone here was intent on their own fun: gambling, watching holos, getting doped, hacked, or drunk, or otherwise indulging their vices. They didn't even glance at us.

Daan spoke in a low voice. "What are you doing here?"

"Looking for you."

His face tightened with anger and something uglier. "You talked like a fucking dust rat to that dealer. And you look like one, dressed that way. What's wrong with you?"

Drill you, I thought. "What stupid shit are you doing, dumping your guards and coming to a place where you're practically begging to get whacked?"

"Don't talk to me like that."

I'd heard that tone before. I tensed, gritting my teeth.

Bhaaj, let it go, Max thought. You have a job to do.

I took a moment to breathe. Then I said, "If you want to get out of here alive, stay with me." I angled toward the bar.

Daan followed without more argument. I stopped in front of the bar, where abstract holos in purple and blue rotated lazily above its dark surface. Dara stood on the other side, watching me as she polished a glass. It swirled purple light around her hands.

"Eh," I said.

"Eh." She glanced at Daan, and then back at me. "Got a friend."

Not likely. "He's leaving. Needs an escort."

"Angel is on the job tonight."

Good. As one of my future tykado black belts, Angel was one hell of a fighter, and as a Dust Knight, she'd sworn to the Code of Honor, which included no drugs. I could trust her, and she'd be alert.

"Comm her?" I asked.

"Yah, can do." Dara set down her glass and tapped a code into the counter.

"What language is that?" Daan asked me. "I can't understand you."

"It's the same language as in Cries," I said. "Just a different dialect, a more compact form of speech. The accent can be hard to understand if you aren't used to it."

Dara was reading a message scrolling across the counter panel. "Be a while. Angel is bringing in another slick." She looked up at me. "You want I get someone else?"

"Nahya. Stay with Angel. She gets here, let me know."

Dara nodded, her curiosity practically tangible in the air. "Got it."

I glanced at Daan. "Come with," I told him.

His forehead furrowed. "What did you say?"

I hadn't even realized I was still using my dialect. I switched to Cries speech. "Come with me. I need to talk to someone before we leave." I led him around the bar, to the discreet staircase.

"Hey." Daan stopped at the bottom of the stairs. "We can't go up there!"

"You'll be fine." I started up the stairs. "Just stay with me."

"Are you freaking bats? I'm not going up there."

I turned around. "Would you please quit the hell arguing with me and come up the stairs?"

"You're a lunatic," he muttered. He did join me, though.

At the top, we followed a private hallway. Holos of stars floated into view as we approached and darkened behind us. At Jak's office, I tapped a code on the door panel, including a tag to let him know I wasn't alone. The door slid open, revealing the black-and-silver room with tendrils of blue smoke curling in the air. Jak lounged at his big desk chair, watching holos of the rooms downstairs that floated above his desk. As I walked in with Daan, the door closed behind us.

"You got a city slick." Jak tapped his desk and the casino holos vanished.

"He's leaving," I said. "When Angel gets back."

Jak stood up, studying Daan, who stared back like a terrified fluff-pup.

"Why bring him here?" Jak asked me.

"He had guards. Idiot slipped the cops to come here and lose money."

Jak spoke to Daan in Cries speech. "Why are the police guarding you?"

Daan pushed his hand through his spiked hair. "Another exec at the corp, I mean the place where I work, she vanished. Kidnapped, they think, or—or murdered. They think I could be next."

Jak scowled at him. "The cops better not have tried to follow you here."

Daan's face turned ashen. "I'm sure they didn't."

"How are you sure?" Jak asked.

"I mean, I don't see how they could have. I was careful."

Jak didn't look angry so much as puzzled. His guides would have known if Daan had cops following him around, and they wouldn't have brought him to the casino.

Jak turned to me. "Got a worry?"

"Yah." I rubbed my eyes, tired. My torso still ached where the knife had cut me yesterday. I tilted my head toward the back wall of his office. "Private."

Jak spoke to Daan. "You. Stay there." Daan nodded, his gaze wide.

Jak and I walked to the back wall together. Jak's shrouds were running, so Daan couldn't catch our words, not even if he had enhanced hearing. But we took no chances. I turned so Daan couldn't see my lips and spoke to Jak in a low voice, describing my meeting with the execs, and the shadow who had followed me afterward.

"It all ends up here," I said.

He didn't look pleased. "You think those slicks are doing dirt in my casino?"

"Somehow, yah. Maybe they meet here. Secret. No way to trace."

"Could be." Jak glanced at Bialo. "Got to get him out of here."

"I'll take him, with Angel. You close up shop. Got a cover story now. Daan came here. Cops were guarding him. Too risky to stay open." Jak could have his super-nanos disassemble the casino and reassemble it as a plain black wall somewhere else, until he decided to reopen. The Black Mark was a ghost.

"Will do." He glanced at Bialo. "Other execs vanished from Cries, though. Not from here."

"So far. But, listen: All three come here, all three go to the Desert Winds. Got a connection."

"What about Scorp-corp and Abyss?" Jak asked. "They linked?"

"Not really." I thought for a moment. "Need to look at other corps, other execs who come here. See if any more have links."

Jak spoke in a low voice, his head turned away from Daan. "I'll check."

Such a simple statement—for such an explosive idea.

Jak had just put words to his deadly secret, that he could cross-reference members of the most elite club on one of the most powerful worlds in the Imperialate with the list of who frequented Raylicon's most notorious criminal establishment. A blackmailer couldn't find a more lucrative list, and he had just offered it to an investigator for the royal family. Gods, no wonder people wanted me dead. Him too, if they realized he knew.

Jak's gauntlet hummed, and Royal's voice floated into the air. "Angel is downstairs."

"Good," Jak said. "Got a slick for her."

"Eh, Royal," I said.

The EI's voice deepened into a sexual rumble. "Good evening, Major."

I raised my eyebrows at Jak. "You tell your EI to talk to me like that?"

He laughed, another deep and sensual sound. "He talks how he wants." His smile faded as he tilted his head toward Daan. "Get him home, fast."

Angel met us in a foyer that sometimes served as an exit from the Black Mark. Hexagonal in shape, with a high ceiling, the room moved within the casino to wherever Jak wanted it. The only light came from wall niches that gave off a red glow. Each held a human skull, its teeth inlaid with diamonds and its eye sockets bejeweled with rubies. Angel leaned against one wall, taller even than me, her body backlit by the red light, her muscled arms crossed, her trousers tucked into boots covered with red canal dust. A pair of goggles hung off her belt and she wore her knife in a finely tooled leather sheath.

As Daan and I entered the foyer, he gaped at Angel. The door closed behind us and the hum of motors rumbled under our feet.

"This is Angel," I told Daan.

"Her name is *Angel*?"

"Yah," she said. "Angel."

Normally we didn't reveal our names to outsiders, but Angel got a kick out of the effect hers had on Jak's clientele. She nodded to Daan. He stared back at her, apparently not realizing she had just offered him the Undercity equivalent of a friendly greeting.

"Pretty," she told him.

Daan's face turned red. He looked like he didn't know whether to be afraid or fascinated. Our ancient bloodlines ran strong in the Undercity, undiluted by civilization; Angel was a throwback to the warrior queens who had ruled Raylicon thousands of years ago. Still, he had nothing to fear from her. If anything, she felt protective toward the handsome slick. I doubted she'd feel so generous if she knew what he thought of us, but as long as he kept his mouth shut, he'd be fine.

Angel gave the goggles to Daan. He turned as pale as a moonstone when he took them, but he didn't protest. Any slick who visited Jak's illicit den knew this drill. They all had to do it, no matter how great their wealth or power. Say no and you'd never find the casino.

Daan pulled on the goggles and adjusted their silencers over his ears. The eyepiece was still transparent, letting us see his uneasy gaze. Angel tapped her gauntlets and the goggles went dark, making him deaf and blind. They also locked into place on his head so he couldn't remove them. His posture became so tense, the tendons in his neck stood out.

Angel glanced at me. "You come with?"

"Yah." I tapped the wall in a place no different than the rest of the room, unless you were one of the few people the foyer recognized. The hum of its engines stopped and a doorway opened onto a maze of twisty rock passages. Light trickled from the foyer into the darkness outside.

Max, I thought. *Crank up my senses.*

Done.

The passages outside became easier to see as my night vision amped up. The augmentation could blind me in brighter light, but here it worked fine. I became aware of dust rustling in the air currents, which blew through a web of conduits that came down from the desert and extended throughout the Undercity. Our ancestors had designed that network thousands of years ago to keep our air fresh, and in these modern times, our structural wizards rigorously maintained the system.

Angel guided Daan outside, and I followed. The Black Mark closed up, leaving us in darkness so complete that even with enhanced vision I couldn't see squat. I touched my gauntlet, turning on a dim light embedded in its leather. The casino blended so well with the stone around us that if we hadn't known it was there, we wouldn't have seen it. I doubted it would be here for more than another hour or two, however long it took Jak to send his patrons home and fold up shop. Then he'd disappear.

We headed into the tunnels, with Angel leading Daan. The passages were so narrow, they brushed my shoulders. A few times, we turned sideways to squeeze through. I knew the way; Jak and I had played here as small children, wandered this maze as older kids, and found hiding places for a different kind of play when we were older.

Daan never spoke. His unease felt like mist in the air. I tried to read his mood, relaxing my mind the way Doctor Sanva had suggested with her exercises. I felt nothing. Well, okay, I did sense that Daan was thinking about what to do with his winnings, but yah, what else would he be thinking about. He wanted to transfer his credits. No, that wasn't right. He wanted them in the Kyle mesh? That made no sense. Exasperated, I dropped my clumsy attempts to reach him.

So we went, trekking through tunnels under the desert. It amazed me that Jak's patrons were willing to go through all this to reach his casino. I supposed it added to the aura of mystery. Eventually we entered a more open area where we couldn't touch the walls on either side. The silence became too complete—

I grabbed Angel and Daan and threw us all to the side, smashing into a ragged stalagmite.

"Hey!" Daan yelled.

"Protect him!" I told Angel as I scrambled to my feet. In the same instant, the ground where we'd been a moment before *rippled*.

"Jump!" I yelled. "Both of you!"

As I leapt into the air, the ground beneath us roiled in a whirlpool as if it were liquid—and collapsed into the tunnel below.

❖ CHAPTER X ❖
HIGH MESH

I fell through the air and into the collapsing tunnel with a rain of broken rock. Dust went down my throat and nose, choking me. The ragged debris scraping my arms and face felt like fused rock. I slammed into the ground of the passage below and falling rocks pummeled my body.

"Angel!" I shouted.

"Here," she said from somewhere close.

"Daan?"

"Here, too," she said. "Can't hear you."

I climbed to my feet, knocking away the slag. It reminded me of shrapnel fused by plasma artillery. "He breathing?"

"Think so."

I needed better than *think so.* "Let him see and hear. We need to run."

"What the hell happened?" Daan said.

I exhaled with relief. "Can you hear me?"

"Yes." It sounded like he'd pulled off his goggles, which he couldn't do unless Angel unlocked them. "What threw us around?"

"The tunnel exploded." I could see now as the dust settled. Daan stood a few paces away, and Angel towered behind him, one large hand on his shoulder.

"Come on." I scooped up a handful of the slag. "We need to get out of here." The walls creaked around us. I had no intention of discovering if more of the tunnel was going to collapse.

"Don't know this level," Angel said.

"I do." I dumped the slag into my pack and slung it onto my back. "Follow me."

We picked our way free of the debris and took off running.

We raced for over a kilometer. Daan kept our pace, gasping as he ran. I didn't call a stop until we reached the Foyer at the top level of the aqueducts. We stood together in a clump, catching our breath. Daan bent over with his hands braced against his knees and gulped in air.

The Foyer was about fifteen paces across, with a ceiling as tall as two of me, one standing on the shoulders of the other. The walls resembled stone lace, created by mineral-rich water dripping in past ages. Rock stumps offered places to sit if anyone wanted them, which mostly no one ever did. My people had secret ways to come and go, and we avoided this entrance. It served as the "official" exit from the aqueducts to the Concourse, its archway opening into the lower end of the avenue. An ancient sculptor had carved arabesque designs around that exit so long ago, no one remembered who created that exquisite artwork. Beyond it, the Concourse was visible, draped in a smoky haze, the dregs of an alley that only became an upscale boulevard farther up its length. Its light filtered into the Foyer, along with tendrils of smoke from the braziers.

Angel gave me the goggles Daan had worn. "I go back."

"Yah. Tell the Knights." I didn't want to believe our attackers came from the aqueducts, but who else could have blown up the tunnel? Without a guide, outsiders never got below the top levels of the canals. Gangs harassed them from hiding places, throwing knives and taunts; drug punkers mugged them for their valuables; and cyber-riders screwed up their tech-mech, corrupting their systems. We had an unspoken agreement with Cries: As long as my people stayed put, without going onto the Concourse, Cries left us alone. Mostly it worked.

To reach the tunnels where we'd been attacked, an intruder would need help from someone who knew the aqueducts. We had to warn the Dust Knights: keep watch, stay on guard, protect. I regarded Angel in silence and she inclined her head, acknowledging my unspoken directive. She'd tell her dust gang, and they would tell the other Knights. The warning of what had happened would spread throughout the Undercity.

Angel jogged back toward the aqueducts, taking a wide path that sloped downward. A street lamp shone there, one of the few Cries maintained below the Concourse. It wasn't for those of us who lived in the Undercity; the city posted it for any tourist foolish enough to wander this far. I liked it, though. The post had an antique look, aged bronze, with a top that curled in a loop. Its lamp hung by a chain from the loop, shedding golden light on the path.

Daan straightened up, breathing more normally. "Where is she going?"

"Back to work." I turned to him. "You okay?"

He gave an unsteady laugh. "That was something! What happened? An avalanche?"

"I don't know. The ground blew up."

His smiled vanished. "What?"

"Something attacked us." I scowled at him. "Which was why you were supposed to stay with your police protection. You're lucky you didn't become another statistic in this business of vanishing people who have too much money and too little sense."

Daan squinted at me. "You shouldn't talk to me that way." He sounded a lot less certain about it than he had in the casino.

"For fuck's sake." Would it kill him to say *thank you for saving my over-indulged life?*

"I don't understand you." He seemed more confused than angry. "You sound like one of them. You shouldn't slum that way. I guess you have to if you're working a case, so you blend in. But you shouldn't act that way to me."

Gods. He still didn't get it. I spoke curtly. "I grew up here. I didn't leave until I enlisted in the army. No one from Cries could 'slum' here. You can't get anywhere without a guide. Even if you did manage without getting mugged or whacked, we'd know you weren't one of us."

"You're *from* the undercity?" He made the word sound as if it wasn't capitalized, like if I said he came from the city of cries.

"Yah, I'm from the Undercity," I said.

"That's impossible!"

"Is it now? How interesting."

"No, I mean, seriously, you can't be from here."

"And why is that?"

"You're too intelligent. Too educated." He shook his head as if to push away an indigestible idea. "You're physically superior to most people. You were an officer in the army. You're too beautiful to be a dust rat. I mean, you do have a wild quality, but I assumed you affected it to seem more exotic. You look too young to be a retired major who's been a PI for over a decade, which means you have health meds to delay your aging. I mean, come on. No way could a homeless nobody with inferior genes achieve even a small part of that."

I just stared at him. So much was wrong with everything he'd just said, I had no idea how to respond. If I said what I wanted, Max would chew me out for my profanity, not to mention my lack of originality. Yah, I needed some new curses.

"We have to go." I lifted my hand, indicating the archway that led out onto the Concourse.

His face went pale. "I can't go out there. People will see me."

Yah, well, tough. "It's the only way back to Cries."

"No, it's not. They brought me in a secret way. Take me out that way."

"Too dangerous." I met his gaze. "I'd have to put you in the goggles, which means you couldn't defend yourself if someone tries to kill you again."

"But they didn't really—" He stopped. "I mean, that wasn't a murder attempt, was it? It was just some Undercity gang prank, right?"

"No."

He waited, as if I was going to qualify the statement. When I didn't, he said, "Why would anyone want to kill me?"

"Good question. Maybe the same reason someone disappeared Quida and Starchild."

"This makes no sense! I barely know Mara and I've never met Chiaru Starchild."

"You all have two traits in common," I told him. "You belong to the Desert Winds and you gamble at the Black Mark."

He glanced away from me. "Oh."

I had no intention of letting that one go. "Does that have a translation?"

Daan looked at me. "I've seen them at the Winds a few times."

"Did the three of you ever do anything together?"

"No. We socialize in different networks."

"What about at the casino? You play in the same poker game? Make bets together?"

"I can't remember any time we were even at the same table." He regarded me uneasily. "You seem to know the proprietor. Perhaps he has, um, records?"

Given that Jak promised his clients secrecy, which was part of why they paid him so much, I had no intention of giving away the fact that he did indeed keep records of everything. I said only, "The Black Mark is completely off-grid." For Cries, anyway.

"I never went to the casino with either Mara or Chiaru," Daan said. "At least, not that I know. I was always blindfolded and deaf, so I couldn't say if anyone was with me."

"You ever sleep with either of them? Or both?"

"No!" He reddened. "They're married. Besides, Chiaru Starchild isn't interested in men."

"How'd you know that?"

He shifted his feet. "I heard it in the news broadcast about her disappearance."

"No, you didn't." The Starchilds kept their private lives exactly that: private. "How are you privy to details about her personal life if you've never met her and know nothing about her?"

He crossed his arms. "I don't need to tell you anything."

"Well, no." I tapped his forehead. "But if you want us to stop people from trying to blow holes in your head, I suggest you tell me everything you can." I lowered my arm. "Look, I know you go to the Black Mark. I'm obviously not going to tell the cops, since I was there too."

He thought about that. "Here's the thing." He stopped, started to speak, and stopped again. Finally he said, "All three of us are in the High Mesh. It's a smaller, uh, club. Invitation only."

"What does it do?"

He hesitated for so long, I wondered if he'd answer at all. Then he said, "Understand me, Major. This is confidential. If you relate what I tell you to anyone, I will report your activities in the Black Mark to the Cries police force." He gave me a look that was apparently supposed to appear significant, maybe even threatening. "To the Majdas, even."

Yah, right. I was shaking in my boots. The cops and the Majdas already knew about my association with Jak and his casino, since it helped me solve cases no one else could crack. I'd given the army full disclosure of my life decades ago. Still, if Daan thought I feared exposure, he might be more forthcoming.

"Understood," I said. "You keep my secrets, I keep yours." No one ever said Undercity bargains had to be fair, only that we had to make them.

Daan spoke with pride. "The High Mesh is a club dedicated to sponsoring new technologies that are under our control, both the research and deployment, without outside influence." He sounded like he'd been dying to tell someone.

He made it sound innocuous, just a "club." But technology was power. The more control they had over the methods, production, and creation of valuable new tech, the more power they gained. Just what we needed, a secret cabal of elitist, wealthy execs finding insidious ways to control human populations, as if the Imperialate didn't have enough of that shit already.

"I don't see the point," I lied.

He spoke too casually. "It's no big deal. Just an engineering club. Nothing you'd know."

Yah, right. My university degree was in mechanical engineering. "I'm sure I don't. What I do need to know is the link with the Black Mark." I had to protect Jak.

He cleared his throat. "Well."

I waited. "Well, what?"

"We get messages through the casino."

"What kind of messages?"

His gaze shifted away from me. "Nothing important."

"Sure it's not. That's why someone blew a hole in the tunnel." They'd done worse than collapse the passage; they'd somehow melted it, impossible as that seemed.

Daan rubbed his eyes. In the casino, he'd sported an elegant look, but now dust covered him, his clothes were torn, his hair straggled around his face, and sweat soaked his shirt, so much that its smart cloth couldn't keep itself dry and wrinkle free. "A dealer at the casino tells us where our next meeting will take place."

"A dealer? Of what? Drugs?"

"No. One of the card dealers at the poker table."

I couldn't believe someone on Jak's staff was passing messages for execs. "Who?"

"I don't know his name."

Him. That was a start. "What does he look like?"

"I don't know. Blue hair. Longish. Good-looking, I guess." He scratched his ear. "He was wearing a silver shirt. You know, like all the dealers dress, in tight clothes. Black pants, I think."

"Young? Old? Thin? Husky?"

"I don't know." He squinted at me. "Young, I guess. Women are easier to remember."

That was probably enough for Jak to identify him. "So you do see Mara Quida and Chiaru Starchild, just not at the Desert Winds or the casino. This dealer tells you where to meet. Then you all get together and talk about your projects." I underplayed what he'd told me. The more he thought I didn't understand what they were doing, the better.

"Something like that."

"How does a dealer at the Black Mark know where you're supposed to meet?" I kept my voice mild, almost disinterested, like a bored PI who had to do her job.

"I guess someone tells him."

"Who?"

"I don't know. I really don't. It's just a few of us. Like a hobby club." He smiled in an offhand manner. "We just share a common interest, you could say."

We could indeed. We were pretending this wasn't a big deal, but I felt chilled. Powerful people belonged to the Desert Winds, including General Vaj Majda, Matriarch of the House of Majda, General of the Pharaoh's Army, and the queen of a financial empire. If she also belonged to this High Mesh, it turned my view of the Majdas sideways. It still didn't make sense, though, that she would order Sav Halin to shoot me after the gala. If Vaj Majda was part of this High Mesh, she had a vested interest in discovering why two of its members had vanished.

I regarded Daan with fake sympathy. "I guess you'll have to give up this hobby club."

He stiffened. "Why would I do that?"

"They like to meet in secret. You know, like those clubs at

university." It wasn't the least bit like any honor society I knew, where the meetings weren't really secret, but a ritual to build camaraderie. If he thought I believed they were similar, though, that worked in my favor. "Once they know about what happened tonight, they'll kick you out."

He crossed his arms. "What, are you going to tell them?"

"Why would I do that? I don't want anyone to know I was at the Black Mark."

"Good." Relief flickered across his face. "I don't need to say anything, either. It will be our secret. No one needs to know." He almost looked contrite. "I'll stay with my police escort after this. I'll tell them I slipped away to meet a woman."

I thought of my work as a PI before the Majdas hired me. His excuse would actually work. "That's one of the most common reasons people sneak away from their bodyguards."

"I can imagine." He started to step toward the exit, then stopped. "If we walk onto the Concourse like this, people will know I've been in the Undercity. Rumors will start."

Well, damn. He had a point. As tempted as I was to make him walk the Concourse after his trash talk about the Undercity, I couldn't. I had to protect myself. If we went out there now, it would be obvious we'd been up to shenanigans down here. Rumors would spread like a desert whirlwind. It would probably scare the hell out of this High Mesh, making them wonder what I'd discovered. I had to keep a low profile, which meant sparing Daan the indignity of his walk of shame.

"Oh, all right." I gave him the goggles. "Put this on and I'll take you out the secret way."

He didn't look at all comfortable, but he donned the goggles and I activated them. Then we set off for the back ways through the Concourse.

If we were lucky, we'd stay alive for another day.

The window-wall in my penthouse didn't need to dim this early in the morning. With the sun rising behind the building, the desert below lay in shadow. I stood gazing at the view, drinking a steaming mug of cacao. The stark beauty of the scene soothed my thoughts. The land stretched in folds until it reached the jagged black mountains on the horizon. I tried to imagine an ocean filling that basin, its waves crashing on the shore. It would flood the City of Cries and drown the Undercity. That ocean had ceased to exist so long ago that even the geologists who studied Raylicon weren't certain when it dried up. The Vanished Sea: It felt like an apt metaphor this morning when I still had two missing execs and only opaque clues about what happened to them.

I'd slept alone last night, after the adventure with the exploding tunnel. Jak had the Black Mark to worry about, and I hadn't expected him to come here. I did miss him, though.

"Greetings, Max," I said. "Can you send a message to Tallmount? I need to talk to her."

"Good morning," Max said. "Message sent."

"Any news about the Majdas?"

"Nothing unusual. Lavinda Majda wants to know how the investigation is proceeding."

"Set up a meeting with her." After last night, I had plenty of questions about Majda involvement in this case. I couldn't risk asking them outright, but I had other methods.

"Message sent."

"Thanks." I rubbed my abdomen, wincing. All that activity last night had reopened my wound. Although I'd treated it when I got home, it still hurt. "Max, what kind of recording did you get in the tunnel last night?"

"It's choppy and dark. Do you want to see it?"

I nodded, then remembered he wasn't monitoring my head. "Yes. Run it above the carpet."

Lights glowed and a holo appeared in the air showing a dark, blurry image of Angel leading Daan through a tunnel. I could only see as much of myself as the cams in my gauntlets showed for my body. In the recording, I grabbed Angel and Daan and threw us against a stalagmite. Daan yelled and I told Angel to protect him as I drew my gun.

"Max, stop the recording."

The holos froze with Angel and Daan in the process of standing up.

"No one else is there but us," I said. "Who set the explosives?"

"It's too dark to see everything," Max said. "Someone could be hiding in the wall cavities."

"I suppose." I rubbed my chin. "I thought I heard a sound just before I threw us all to the side, but it isn't on this recording. Is it set to account for my ears being augmented last night?"

"Yes. You should be able to hear anything now that you heard last night."

"Huh. Weird. Continue."

The images moved again. I shouted, we all jumped, and the cave exploded.

"Freeze," I said. The replay stopped with all of us in midair, along with flying debris. "That explosion looks like it came from a bot-bomb."

"I'd say a class 4C bot," Max said. "Minimal AI, not fast enough to judge your location."

"That's a pretty stupid bomb." It didn't fit with my image of the High Mesh.

"It was a logical choice," Max said. "Anything larger could have brought down the ceiling."

"Yah, but even with a minimal AI, the bomb still should have caught us."

"It looked like you dodged in the exact instant the bomb launched. If you'd moved a second later, it would have hit you; a second earlier, it would have had time to recalibrate your position."

I squinted at my image. "How did you know?" I murmured.

"It just looks that way," Max said.

"I meant me. How did I know the exact moment to dodge?" A sound couldn't have warned me. By the time I heard someone throw a bomb, it would have been too late to dodge.

"Situational awareness," Max said. "It's always been one of your strong points."

"I know I'm good at it. But this needed too much luck."

"Maybe you sensed the shooter. You are an empath, after all."

"Not a strong one, and I've no idea how to use it." I studied the images. "Continue."

The holos moved again. The ground in the image liquefied, swirling like a whirlpool. It collapsed into the tunnel below us, solidifying into debris as it fell. We came down with a chaotic tumble of slag while debris rained over us.

"Freeze," I said.

The recording stopped with Angel tucking into a roll as she hit the ground, Daan flailing, and me flipping in midair. "Max, I *knew* it was going to happen, and it wasn't some weird empath shit." I walked around the holos, studying the scene. "Can you run it backwards, in slow motion?"

"Yes. Tell me when to stop."

The motion reversed, all three of us going upward in slow motion, and the cloud of flying debris contracting upward from the tunnel. The melted rock swirled in the other direction as the floor reformed beneath us. We came down—

"Stop! Max, look there, in the far corner. See? The rock whirlpool started turning at the edges of the open area in the tunnel. That's what I saw."

"You're right. It melted from the outer to the inner area and then collapsed."

I took a swallow of my cacao. "Run it forward again, slowed down."

The motion reversed again, showing the whirlpool forming as we leapt into the air. "I just don't get it. How could rock liquefy like that and then solidify again? It happened so fast."

"I don't know," Max said. "It would require an expenditure of energy and heat far greater than what was available in that tunnel or that you could survive."

"I brought back a chunk of the rock." I motioned at the holos. "You can turn this off."

The images disappeared. "Shall I send the rock to a lab for analysis?" Max asked.

"You do the analysis. I'll put a sample of the rock in my gauntlet."

"I can't tell much with just the gauntlet sensors."

"Do what you can. I don't want anyone else to know about what happened yet."

"Will do." He paused. "I have an incoming from Exec Tallmount."

"Put her on audio."

Tallmount's confident voice came into the air. "My greetings, Major Bhaajan. I understand you wished to talk to me?"

"My greetings. I had the impression yesterday that you wanted to talk to me."

"Yes, I did. But privately."

"This line is private, no monitors."

"Good." She paused. "It's about what the others said yesterday, that I was considered for the Metropoli contract."

"Jen Oja said as much, too." I thought back to our discussion. "She said five of you were in line for the account."

"That's what the higher ups at Scorpio claimed. I doubt I was ever really on the list."

"Why do you say that?"

"It's an impression." She paused. "I think only Mara and Daan had a chance. Someone at Scorpio wanted it to appear as if they were considering all of us, but it never felt genuine to me."

Ho! Mara Quida and Daan Bialo were the only ones who belonged to the Desert Winds club. "Did you resent that?"

"Not really. I never expected to get it. I'm new at Scorpio." She spoke dryly. "It appears I may not be here much longer."

"Why not?"

"I'm not discreet enough about politics."

Ah. Her Majda comments. "Do you regret that?"

She spoke as if she were tiptoeing through a field of broken glass. "I regret any offense I may have given to anyone in the city."

If she continued with that tact, she'd probably keep her job. I wasn't sure what to think of the Majdas, though. Until now, they'd been reasonable employers, intimidating but fair, Lavinda especially. Max claimed they wouldn't try to kill me, and I wanted to believe that, but I couldn't risk trusting them. I needed to find out more about Sav Halin, the supposed reporter who tried to whack me in the garden of the Quida mansion.

I pretended to speak in a relaxed manner. "It's those damn holo-reporters. They get every comment on the meshes no matter how discreet we intend to be. I avoid them like an ex-lover."

Tallmount laughed good-naturedly. "Hell, I'd take the ex first."

I sipped my cacao. "One reporter at the gala seemed nosier than most. Sav Halin."

"Halin? I think she's a friend of the Majdas."

I almost choked on my drink. How the hell did Tallmount know that little gem of data? "Really? I thought she worked for one of the city broadcasters."

"I saw her talking to Colonel Lavinda Majda. It looked like they knew each other."

That added another wrinkle this case didn't need. "Thanks for getting back to me. If you think of anything else that might shed some light on the case, let me know."

"I will. Be well."

With that, Tallmount and I signed off.

"Well, that was interesting," I said.

"Indeed," Max told me. "I'm not sure you're going to like this next interesting thing."

"What thing?"

"You have a call from the palace."

✤ CHAPTER XI ✤
SHADOWBOXING

Lavinda and I walked through the park in the city center of Cries. She was out of uniform today, dressed in blue trousers and a white silk shirt. Lawns sprinkled with small purple flowers bordered the path, and tiny fliers buzzed by us like miniature dragons from Earth's mythology. We passed an oxygen-producing hedge, and I glimpsed an oxygen mister in another arbor. Maybe that was how the Majdas grew their gardens high in the oxygen-scarce mountains, using imported tech and plants.

After I joined the army, I realized what an unusual world I came from. Only this narrow strip near the pole stayed cool enough for humans, and it still felt too hot. This world boasted only one modern city; with the planet becoming less and less habitable, it didn't make sense to build more. Cries survived because it was the first city established in the Ruby Empire, and it remained home to one of the most powerful families in the Imperialate. As long as the Majdas wanted to live here, the terraformers would find a way to make this small part of Raylicon agreeable. The mayor wanted to change the name of Cries to something more palatable for offworld tourism, maybe Saint Parval after the local mountain range, but to me it would always be the city where people wept, the last stand of humans on a dying planet.

As I walked with Lavinda, I outlined my progress on the investigation, leaving out Jak's casino and the High Mesh. I finished with, "I haven't found any link between Mara Quida and Chiaru Starchild except their membership in the Desert Winds."

"The Winds?" Lavinda gave me a startled glance. "I didn't know Chiaru belonged."

So. She was on a first-name basis with Inna's wife. "You know Chiaru Starchild?"

She looked out at the park, avoiding my gaze. "Years ago. We were in school together."

"But you don't go to the club?" I couldn't help my curiosity. I'd never come close to visiting a place as elite as the Desert Winds.

"I've been there a few times with Vaj. It didn't interest me enough to join." She seemed more pensive than usual. "I'm not comfortable there. It seems so, I don't know. Stuffy."

It surprised me to hear her talk so easily. "You prefer other places?"

"I'm a bit of an introvert," she admitted. "A quiet evening at home with my family is my idea of a high time."

"Mine, too." I understood better now why I felt that way; empaths tended to retreat from large crowds of people. "A glitzer, I'm not."

Lavinda smiled. "Can you imagine us as cyb-fibbers?"

I gave a startled laugh. What a thought, a Colonel in the Pharaoh's Army and a Majda heir to boot, decked out in torn glitz rags.

"I should try it sometime," she said. "Just to see the look on Vaj's face."

I grinned. "It would certainly shake up things."

Her smile faded. "Do you think Vaj is at risk for what happened to Quida and Starchild?"

"I hope not. But she should increase her guard." If someone disappeared the General of the Pharaoh's Army, this turned into a crisis of interstellar proportions. However, Vaj Majda had no connection to the Black Mark. She knew it existed, sure. The Majdas had an unspoken bargain with Jak; they ignored him as long as he remained silent about his clients, some of whom headed corporations owned by the Majdas. He never got busted because his clientele ran the city.

I'd never heard of any Majda at the Black Mark. For that matter, I'd never dug up any dirt in their dealings. Nor did the married ones screw around. The women could, given the way they cloistered their men, but as far as I'd seen, they didn't stray. Sure, the ancient laws required fidelity for members of the royalty and aristocracy, to ensure their heirs were genuine. Hell, those laws required men be virgins on their wedding night. I mean, seriously? If they followed those ancient laws nowadays, none of them could get married. But the Majdas stayed legal. It wasn't their conservatism compared to everyone else in the universe, but hardheaded common sense. They couldn't be blackmailed.

"Is your sister on Raylicon?" I already knew the General was here, making plans for some financial coup that was going to screw with my assets, but I had to pretend otherwise.

"She's visiting." Lavinda seemed preoccupied.

"We need to warn her."

Lavinda's face took on that distant I'm-accessing-my-node look. "I sent a message." She focused on me. "You mentioned Exec Tallmount yesterday. Have you found out anything?"

Hah! An opening. "I did talk to Tallmount. I don't think she harbors any ill will toward anyone." Wryly I added, "Except maybe holo-reporters. She regrets talking about your family."

Lavinda snorted. "Yes, well, maybe it's healthy for Vaj to hear a little criticism."

So Lavinda got a kick out of seeing her powerful sister called to task. She didn't sound resentful of Vaj, though. Lavinda liked her sister, loved her even. I couldn't imagine anyone feeling affection toward the imposing General, but then, what did I know. I was in love with a man the Majda police referred to as an Undercity kingpin when they were being polite.

All I said was, "Tallmount told me she was taking extra care at the gala with what she said around that reporter from the city network."

"You mean Sav Halin?" Lavinda waved her hand. "She's all right."

"You know her? I don't recall seeing her at the party." Which was true. I hadn't known anything about Halin until after she tried to murder me.

"She's come to the palace a few times to interview us."

I liked this less and less. You didn't get an invitation to visit the palace unless you worked closely with the Majdas.

Bhaaj, Max thought. We're being followed.

Of course we are. I tried to avoid that I'm-talking-to-my-EI look. I'm not talking about Colonel Majda's bodyguard. The person following us is shrouded. I think it's the same woman who tailed you before.

Well, shit. I glanced at Lavinda. "General Majda isn't the only one who should take extra care with her security. Have you had any problems?"

"Not at all." She wouldn't meet my gaze. "Should I?"

"I don't know." Her reaction puzzled me. She was holding back something. "You're not a member of the Desert Winds, and that seems to be the only link between the people who vanished. But since your sister might be at risk, it wouldn't be unreasonable for you to be careful, too."

"I will." She nodded to me. "And thank you, Major."

We parted at a grove of trees where several women in her retinue were waiting, as well as her supposed aide, Jo Muller, who looked as large and intimidating today as she had at the gala.

I headed toward the VA building where I'd met with Adept Sanva two days ago. *Is our shadow following me or Lavinda?* I asked Max.

You. Shall I activate your shroud?

Wait until I get behind that group of trees up ahead. The path I was following curved around a cluster of trees rich with green vines.

When I reached the cluster, Max thought, Shroud activated.

Good. I turned in a new direction, one I hoped the shadow wouldn't predict, and walked across the lawn, which was of course forbidden. As long as I didn't do it for long, the city monitors might not register a blur moving over the grass. Within a few moments I reached another bluestone path. I followed it, headed toward Commodore's Plaza.

Time to visit Adept Sanva again.

Sanva was watering the plants in her spacious office when I entered. She smiled at me. "My greetings, Major. Did we have an appointment today?"

"Sorry, no." I gave her one of my Cries smiles, the kind I'd learned to use when I wanted to convey friendly intent to people who weren't from the Undercity. "I was wondering if you could help with an investigation."

She motioned to a chair with white upholstery bordered by flowers. Copious sunlight slanted through the many windows, and leafy plants softened the decor. It all felt pleasant and airy, designed to make patients feel at home, except it wasn't like home, it was all imported. Nothing in this room came from Raylicon except me.

"What can I do for you?" Sanva asked. If I hadn't known better, I'd have thought she enjoyed seeing me. Actually, I didn't know better. I just didn't see any reason for her to like having me show up at her office without warning.

I sat in the chair as she settled behind her desk. "I wanted to ask you about the neurological basis for Kyle operators." The words felt clumsy on my tongue. In the Undercity, we said empaths, or even just feelers. *Kyle operator* sounded pretentious to me.

"Certainly," she said. "Anything in particular?"

I thought of the moment in the tunnels when I'd grabbed Angel and Daan. "Can you sense the presence of another person without knowing it?"

"Maybe." She tapped her desk and the holo of a brain formed above it. The image of a wave formed around it, the same shape as the brain but trailing off outside of it. "Your brain produces waves. Electromagnetic signals."

"The signals are weak, though, right? You have to be close to someone for your brain waves to interact with theirs."

"That's right." As she traced her finger across her desk, the holo faded. "Kyle operators have tiny organs in their brains called the Kyle Afferent Body and the Kyle Efferent Body. KAB and KEB. You also have specialized neural structures called paras. The KAB picks up electrical signals from the brains of other people and sends them to the paras using a neurotransmitter called psiamine. The paras interpret the signals. The KEB does the reverse, sending signals from your brain to other people. In most people the Kyle organs are either underdeveloped or nonexistent. In Kyle operators, people we call psions, the organs have more development."

I squinted at her. "A doctor who treated me last year told me she found traces of psiamine in my brain."

"I saw that in your files. It means your brain is using its Kyle organs."

"What about the noble Houses?" I asked. "They're all supposed to be psions." It was why they were adamant about marriages taking place only among the nobility, to strengthen the Kyle traits.

"That's what they claim." Sanva shrugged. "They aren't. They do have a higher incidence in their gene pool, however." She paused. "The highest rates of Kyle ability are among your people."

So she knew about the Undercity. I supposed it made sense. She was the adept the army had sent me to, after all. "I'm surprised the traits are so rare."

"It's genetic." Sanva relaxed back in her chair. "The abilities are due to a series of mutations associated with recessive alleles."

I tried to remember my biology class from university. "So a person isn't a psion unless they get the DNA from both parents?"

"That's right. Unfortunately, the genes also involve negative mutations, some of which are fatal."

That figured. "All this Kyle business seems more trouble than it's worth."

"Some people feel that way." She nodded as if confirming it to herself. "The traits probably persist in human gene pools because an ability to empathize with their children can make people good parents. It gives their offspring more chance of surviving."

I hesitated. "Do you know my Kyle rating?"

"My guess is that you're in the medium range for an empath. It's hard to say because you've suppressed the ability."

"I don't like it." To put it mildly.

She leaned forward. "Major, it doesn't have to be a curse. Empaths can learn to block emotions from other people. You already do that without realizing it. Your records describe you as a mental fortress."

Damn straight. Another thought came to me. "Wouldn't being a psion increase your ability to protect your tribe in primitive societies? You'd know if the enemy was sneaking up or planning an ambush."

"Yes, it could work that way."

"Could I sense that someone was about to attack me?"

She considered the thought. "During your military service, you showed a remarkable situational awareness. It's one reason you survived. One of your COs described it as preternatural."

I shifted in my chair. "What about other people? If I sense them, do they sense me?"

"Possibly, if they're psions." Dryly she added, "You're so protective of yourself, with so many mental barriers, no one is likely to pick up anything from you."

Relief washed over me. "Good."

She scowled. "It isn't good. You've walled yourself into an emotional prison."

I couldn't go there, not now. I stood up. "Thank you for your time, Adept Sanva."

She stood as well. "Major, your abilities really can enhance your life."

"I just need time to—" To what? I wasn't sure myself. "To adjust."

"Are you doing the exercises I gave you?"

I squinted at her. "Uh. Um."

Sanva smiled. "Does that have a translation?"

"It's just—I mean, I've tried a few times, the meditation thing, clearing my mind, relaxing. Nothing happens. I just fall asleep."

"Don't give up," she said. "The idea is to help your brain create new neurological pathways. That can happen even if you fall asleep."

"All right." I'd rather have stopped, but I'd initiated all this, so apparently I wanted to know myself better than I was willing to admit. Maybe my abilities *had* helped keep me alive. Many people I'd known in the aqueducts or army were dead now, yet I had defied the odds.

I intended it to stay that way.

After I left Doctor Sanva's office, Max thought, Lukas Quida would like to talk to you. He says he found something.

I stopped in the hallway. *Put him on.*

Lukas' voice came out of my comm. "Major Bhaajan? My greetings."

"Greetings, Del Quida. What did you find?"

"It's a note from Mara." He sounded better today. "She hid it on the house mesh. It's a present she had for me, one set to surprise me on my birthday. That's today. She got tickets for the two of us to vacation on Parthonia." He inhaled audibly. "I'd been talking about how I missed being with her when she was working on the Metropoli deal. This was her response."

From the sound of his voice I suspected he'd been struggling with the fear that she'd left him. This simple birthday note offered evidence that Mara Quida intended to continue her life as normal after the gala. People like that didn't fake their deaths and frame their husbands for murder. It didn't mean someone else hadn't killed her, though.

"That could be useful evidence," I said.

He spoke quietly. "I realize it doesn't help find Mara. But perhaps it will convince Detective Talon to drop this idea that I murdered my wife."

"Talon is *still* on that kick?" I'd had my fill of this blasted Scorpio detective. "I'll talk to her. And make sure you have an outside EI copy and authenticate the message you found before you give it to her team." I didn't trust Talon as far as I could throw her. If the message didn't fit her script, she might "accidentally" lose it. "My EI can do it for you, if you'd like."

"I'll send it to you." He paused. "Whatever the truth, I can face it. But I need to know."

"I'll let you know as soon as I find anything." I remembered losing a friend in my youth, when she died in a tunnel collapse. I'd agonized for days over her disappearance. It wasn't until we found her body buried under debris that the vise grip of my denial finally released. Lukas needed closure, and so far I'd failed miserably in giving it to him. I had to find answers, and soon, before Talon's zeal to implicate someone ended up getting him executed.

I stopped by the glass door of the VA, gazing at Commodore's Plaza. Last time I'd left this building, I'd been about five meters out the exit when the knife hit me. I paused, trying to sense any nefarious types lurking about. Nothing.

This Kyle business doesn't work, I thought to Max. The only "ability" I could manage was technology induced.

You should be at home, resting, Max thought.

I suppose. I have to get there without being followed.

I don't detect your shadow.

You figure out who she is yet?

Not yet.

It shouldn't be this hard. No one is completely off-grid.

Even I can't break into every grid, and I'm one of the best there is at such investigations.

Healthy ego there, haven't we?

Ego is not a property of Evolving Intelligences. I'm stating a verifiable fact.

All right. I sent him my amusement. Besides, he had a point. He was damn good at what he did. *I don't think she's the one who knifed me. She's not acting like a killer. More like a spy. Except she's not that good at spying, either.*

Why do you say that? She's managed to keep her identity secret.

Yah, but she hasn't hidden her presence from us. I pondered the thought. *I doubt she works for the military. She's probably a private contractor.*

That gives me some ideas for how to expand my search for her identity.

Let me know if you find anything.

I will. He paused. Are you going outside?

I guess I should. I settled my pack with the jammer on my shoulders. *Keep me shrouded.*

Done. His thought lightened. You look like a college student with that pack. Or a hiker.

That's my disguise. I stopped, hit with an idea. *Max, turn off my shroud.*

You aren't planning to leave the building?

Sure I am. I want my shadow to see me.

It's not safe.

After the attack yesterday, the city amped up its protection. I opened the door. *Besides, it would be stupid for whoever knifed me to try something in the same place the next day.*

I hope you're right.

You and me both. I stepped outside and stood there while breezes rustled my hair. With my awareness so heightened, the city looked incredibly vivid, its colors vibrant. The air smelled good, too, with no irritants or haze, just the delicate scent of the desert-blooming lilies in pots around the plaza.

Max, toggle my combat mode.

You aren't threatened, at least not at a level that suggests the need for combat.

I know. I avoided combat mode in non-hostile situations because my enhanced reflexes went so fast, I could end up attacking an innocent person before I stopped myself. *Trust me on this one.*

Mode toggled, Max answered.

I crossed the plaza, every sense sharpened. The scent of the lilies drenched the air. My boots clicked on the bluestone tiles and the city rumbled like muted thunder. The drone of a flyer growled in the distance, far enough away that I couldn't see it with all the city towers rising around me, their glassy surfaces reflecting the endless blue sky.

Your shadow is back, Max thought.

I headed down a path leading away from the plaza. *Where?*

She's to the east, standing by that grove of trees.

I glanced at the trees beyond a stretch of lawn. *I can't see her.*

Look at the feather-elm farthest to the left.

I still couldn't make her out. So I took out my green beetle-bot. It was why I wore a jacket in the middle of the desert; its climate controls kept me cool and I could hide stuff in the pockets. I tossed the beetle into the air. *Go find her. Max, transfer me to the beetle.*

I was suddenly seeing the park from higher up. As I neared the grove, a blur did indeed become visible by the tree Max had indicated. She didn't hide well, though. If she'd stood closer to the tree, under the feathery vines that draped its branches, it might have enhanced her camouflage enough that I couldn't have seen her.

Time to visit, I thought.

Visit what? Max asked.

My shadow. I left the path where I'd been walking and strode toward the trees.

You're going to get a ticket for walking on the grass. Max sounded irked. You are also going to get yourself beaten up or knifed again. You need to take better care of your health.

I'll be fine. Transfer vision back to me.

My aerial view vanished so I saw only through my own eyes. As I neared the trees, I focused on the tree hiding my shadow. She wasn't the only one who had noticed me. A small craft was floating across the park toward us, a robotic craft about one meter long and one meter above the lawn. Its little turbines flattened the lush carpet of grass.

That monitor is coming after you, Max thought.

If I can't walk on the lawn, I grumbled, *I don't see why those monitors get to fly over it. Their turbofans mess up the grass more than I ever could.*

Your shadow is retreating.

I was close enough now to see her blurred figure jogging across the grass. I broke into a sprint. As I chased to my shadow, the silver monitor closed on us both. When I was a few paces away from my shadow, she glanced back with enough panic that I saw the alarm on her face even through the camouflage of her holosuit.

Got you. I lunged forward and tackled her, throwing us both to the ground. She grunted as we thudded into the grass. Rolling over, she threw me to the side. I twisted away, grabbing her arm, and flipped her onto her back. Despite my augmented reflexes, my responses were off today, delayed by my injuries, and she twisted away. When she tried to jump to her feet, I kicked her legs out from under her, and she toppled like a felled tree. She grabbed my neck from behind, pulling my head back in a wrestling hold. Pain jabbed my side where I'd torn open the knife wound yesterday, and blackness swam in my vision. With a heave, I wrenched free. She struck me from the side, going for my kidneys probably, but she caught my stomach instead. Gritting my teeth, I slammed her onto her back. Raising my fist with enhanced speed and strength—

Bhaaj, stop! Max thought.

I froze an instant away from smashing her face. I was angrier than I'd realized, furious with these people shooting at me, throwing knives, exploding bombs. I really, really wanted to punch someone. She stared at my raised fist, her face flushed. This close, the shroud didn't hide her, it just blurred her features.

I lowered my fist and sat back on my heels. "Why the bloody hell are you following me?"

The monitor craft hummed up to us. Shaped like a teardrop, it kept its narrow end pointed in our direction. A drone-pilot with a silver dome for a head was installed in its back end. Red lights blinked all over the spherical body of the drone.

"You are in violation of city ordinance nine thousand six hundred and two," the drone said.

"Nine thousand six hundred two?" I asked. "Got enough ordinances, do you think?"

"Probably not," the drone said. "I have to give you a ticket. Both of you must deactivate any shrouds or combat enhancements you are using."

Combat mode deactivated, Max thought.

My shadow turned off her shroud. She looked stocky and fit, like an athlete. She'd pulled her brown hair into a braid that fell down her back. Her ordinary face would fit into any crowd so well, no one would notice her.

"This woman attacked me," I told the drone.

"Like hell I did." My shadow stood up and brushed off her clothes, a light jumpsuit.

"It appeared that you attacked her," the drone told me.

I clambered up to my feet. "I had to stop her from following me. You couldn't see it because she was shrouded from your monitors."

"My monitoring functions have been increased by three hundred percent since yesterday, due to a previous attack in this area." The drone paused. "In fact, according to my records, you were the victim in that attack."

"Yes, that was me." I motioned at my shadow, who stood glowering at both me and the drone. "I had to defend myself."

"Her following you doesn't constitute an attack." The drone swiveled its head to my shadow. "However, following a person without their permission while shrouded violates city ordinance three thousand nine hundred and eighty-six. I must also give you a ticket."

"For flaming sake," my shadow said.

"Giving her a ticket isn't sufficient," I told the drone.

"That seems sufficient," it said.

"We're resisting your authority. You have to arrest us."

"What the fuck," my shadow said. "I'm not resisting anyone."

"You are both arguing with me," the drone said. "Although this could be called resistance, that would be a rather severe interpretation."

"Even so," I said. "To be thorough, you should arrest us both and take us into the station."

I fail to see the point of this, Max told me.

Bear with me, I thought.

"An arrest isn't warranted," the drone said. "However, I will bring you to the authorities for questioning." It turned its teardrop car toward the east, in the direction of the Cries police station. "It isn't far. You are both fit enough to walk. Please follow me." With that, it hummed off, inflicting its turbine fans on the lawn. I was surprised Cries didn't have an ordinance about that, too.

My shadow stalked past me. "You'll regret this," she muttered.

I fell into step with her. "Why?"

She ignored me, staring at the monitor as it glided above the lawn. Tough. I'd let the cops ask her the questions I wanted answered.

Bhaaj, Max thought. *You're getting a message from an aide at the Majda palace.*

What do they want?

Apparently you are supposed to send them information about protecting General Majda. They'd like you to go to the palace and talk to security.

Well, shit. Great timing. *Tell them I can't now, but I'll be in contact soon.*

The drone left us with an officer in the lobby of the police station, a spacious room designed in chrome and glass. Its floor-to-ceiling holoscreens showed displays about the Cries police force, with cops who were far too good-looking and well-dressed to be real. The images included as many male as female officers, showing Cries gave equal opportunity to everyone. Yah, sure. One officer had blond hair, apparently proving you didn't have to look like a Majda to succeed here. I mean, seriously, this glossy tourist attraction was supposed to be a police station? Welcome to Cries.

The officer took us to a back room that looked like someone's office. The someone turned out to be a stocky woman with her black hair clipped sensibly short and the air of a police chief. She wore a blue uniform, crisp and neat, with the emblem of the city police on her arms, a blue triangle. When we entered, she was standing by a screen on the wall reading a display of statistics, like how many times the park lawns were mowed or how many evil criminals walked on the grass.

"So." The chief came over as our escort left the room. "I understand you two had an altercation in the park."

My shadow motioned at me. "She had the altercation. I was minding my own business."

The chief raised her eyebrows. "Is that why you were shrouded?"

"She's been following me the past few days," I said. "I have no idea why."

The chief glanced at me. "You were at the VA."

"That's right," I said. "I see an adept there."

She tilted her head, studying me. I just looked back at her. My doctor appointments were confidential and none of her business.

"You were the person attacked yesterday outside the VA," she said.

"That's right." I motioned at my shadow. "I thought she was going to attack."

The chief turned to her. "Why were you following her?"

"I wasn't," my shadow said. "I had the shroud up because I didn't want my employer to know I'd gone to the park instead of telecommunicating from my home."

Yah, right. A military-grade covert shroud so she could play hooky from work? Sure.

The chief didn't look like she believed it any more than I did. "I can't find your ID in the system," she told my shadow. "Why is that?"

I think I've identified her, Max thought.

"My name is Ti Callen," my shadow was saying. "I used to work on covert ops for the army. That's why I'm not in your database."

She's lying, Max thought. Her name is Tandem Walkerdale. She's a circus performer from the planet Metropoli.

And I'd thought this couldn't get any stranger. *A circus performer? Are you kidding?*

I'm quite serious. Nothing about her says military to me.

That could just mean she's good at going undercover.

A former operative wouldn't so easily reveal she'd been a spy.

"I'll need your ID chips," the chief told her.

A knock came at the door, which was still open. We all turned. The officer who had brought us here stood in the archway, her young face pale. "My apology, ma'am," she told the chief. "But we have, that is, I mean—someone is here. To pick up Major Bhaajan."

Pick me up? That made no sense.

"Are you all right, lieutenant?" the chief asked.

"Yes, ma'am." The lieutenant looked terrified.

"You can tell this visitor that Major Bhaajan isn't going anywhere." The chief frowned at me. "Not until I get to the bottom of this."

The officer gulped. "Ma'am, I—I don't think I can tell her that."

The chief put her fists on her hips. "And why is that?"

A woman spoke behind her in a resonant voice. "Enough of this."

A tall figure strode past the lieutenant and into the office. "So, Major Bhaajan," Colonel Lavinda Majda said. "You seem to be in trouble again."

✤ CHAPTER XII ✤
NEW STEPS

Lavinda frowned at me. "I don't see the point of tackling people in the park."

We were sitting on a bluestone bench in a courtyard by the station, cooled by the shadow of a modern sculpture with abstract curves. The thing looked far too artistic to be at a police station, but what the hell. I liked it. Or maybe I just liked that Lavinda had extricated me from the cops. I wanted to know more about Ti Callen, my circus shadow, aka Tandem Walkerdale, whatever that meant. What was she in tandem with? Still, I'd achieved my goal, to find out what Walkerdale had to say about herself.

"She's been following me for two days," I said.

Lavinda didn't look impressed by my excuse. She sat tall and easy, somehow managing to appear regal without being stiff. The breeze rustled her hair, tousling it around her shoulders.

"I'm sure many people have followed you," she said. "I doubt you beat them all up."

"Yah, well, no one was trying to kill me those other times."

Her annoyance shaded into concern. "How is your injury?"

It was a lot worse than it should have been, given my skulking around the palace and unceremonious exit down the cliff, not to mention wrestling with Tandem Walkerdale.

"It's fine," I said. "How did you know I was at the police station?"

"My aide told me you put her off when she contacted you. So I looked into the matter."

I reddened. "Sorry about that." She had that focused look she got when she was trying to read a person. I imagined my mind as a fortress with me inside and her outside.

Lavinda winced and rubbed her temple. "It's been a long day." She lowered her arm. "I checked into the Desert Winds club. I didn't find anything unusual."

"It's the only obvious link between Quida and Starchild."

"When I talked to the investigators on the Starchild case, they didn't mention any concern for my sisters or myself."

She was following this even more closely than I realized, if she'd questioned people about Chiaru Starchild. "I'm paranoid. It's a drawback of my profession."

Lavinda spoke wryly. "What are you not telling me?"

Good question. I had the same one for her. She had the look again, trying to read my body language, if not my mood. At least, I hoped she couldn't get my mood. I could bamboozle many people, but not Lavinda. I needed to tell her something, and it had to be at least a partial truth, because she was too savvy to fool.

So I said, "I think whoever attacked me is linked to the disappearances."

"Which may be linked to the Desert Winds, where my sister is a member." She considered me. "So you aren't sure you should trust us."

I couldn't tell her it related to the High Mesh. For all I knew, the Majdas had ties to them. I also had to protect Jak. "I can't break trust with my sources."

"You mean the Undercity, yes?"

"Essentially." Before she could press the matter, I added, "I did wonder about one thing."

She tilted her head. "What is that?"

I paused, uncertain how to proceed. Although no one had risked protesting when Lavinda told the police to release me, I'd clearly annoyed the chief. If I also annoyed Lavinda, she might send me back to the cops. "Please forgive if my question offends."

She spoke dryly. "Go ahead, Major."

"It just seems odd for you to be so interested in the Starchild case."

Her expression became unreadable, as if a shutter went down. "It's personal."

Damn. I'd just trespassed on the legendary Majda restraint. "My apology. I don't mean to intrude."

After a moment, she said, "It's all right. I knew Chiaru when we were young, after I graduated from the academy and she finished her business degrees at Cries University."

"The two of you seem very different."

"I suppose. But we're both empaths. Kyle operators tend to seek each other out." She paused. "It can be—fulfilling."

That sounded like more than friendship. "Can you sense her? It might help us find her."

She met my gaze with a look I couldn't quite place, one different from anything I'd seen with her before. "No, I can't sense her."

It suddenly hit me, that look. Lavinda was *afraid.* Not for herself, but for Chiaru, terrified even, that kind of fear that tore you apart.

"You're probably too far away," I said.

"I've always felt her presence." She took a deep breath, reminding me of Lukas Quida. "And now I don't."

"Nothing at all?"

She considered me for a long moment before answering. "Major, I realize you aren't a lawyer or a doctor. But our conversations are still protected."

"Yes, they are." The retainer I'd signed with the Majdas went on far more than I'd ever wanted to read about nondisclosure and the dire consequences I would suffer if I violated their stipulations. Regardless, I'd have respected her privacy no matter what. "Anything you say remains with me."

"It's just—I had a convulsion last night. My doctors are upset. No one knows what caused it." She paused. "I found out later it happened in the same instant Chiaru died. She—she was the one for me, Major, more than anyone else I've loved before or since. No matter where we were, what we did, we always sensed each other."

I stared at her. She'd just described a reaction more intense even than what Lukas experienced. No matter what scenario I might have imagined for this conversation, no way would it have included Colonel Lavinda Majda revealing that her greatest love wasn't her husband.

"Gods," I murmured. "I'm sorry." I seemed to be saying that a lot lately.

She spoke with difficulty. "After the convulsion, I slept for a few hours. I dreamed Chiaru was talking to me. It felt so *real*. For an instant, when I woke up, I could have sworn she was there, sitting in my room." Her voice cracked. "Then I remembered. She was gone."

I wished I knew how to ease her pain. "Maybe you don't feel her presence because she's too far away."

"Yes. Perhaps." She didn't look like she believed it any more than I did.

I'd assumed Abyss Associates and Scorpio Corporation had no link that affected this case. I'd missed the big one: the House of Majda. I could see why they'd wanted me at the Quida gala, now that I knew a Majda sat on the Scorpio board. The Metropoli deal impacted their financial holdings. They'd have grilled me after the party for my insights. But they had no link to Abyss.

No financial link.

Although marriage among the diverse peoples of the Skolian Imperialate included just about any relationship humans could imagine, Lavinda didn't have that freedom. Her marriage to Prince Paolo had been arranged decades ago. If even after all this time, she reacted so strongly to Chiaru, their relationship must have been intense. Had Lavinda been anyone else, they could have married. Not so for a Majda; they hewed rigidly to the ancient traditions.

Lavinda had done her duty—and lost the love of her life.

Jak stood with me on the midwalk of the Lizard Trap canal. Red dust had sprinkled across our clothes, my leathers and his trousers and muscle shirt. Ruzik and his people were on the floor of the canal talking trash with the Oey gang. Led by Pat Cote, the Oeys included Pat's lover Tym and two other kids. All in their late teens, they ranked highly among the knights in both leadership and tykado. Near them, a cluster of children were playing skip-jacks, throwing little stars carved from cacti-stalks, a native plant our ancestors had engineered to grow underground. Several adults sat on the midwalk across the canal cooking over a fire. Smoke rose in tendrils and drifted away through air vents in the ceiling. The aroma of grilled vegetables drenched in spicy pizo sauce filled the air, making my mouth water.

Chalkdust, an eleven-year-old girl, sat near the adults, engrossed in an algebra book with graphs floating above it. I'd bought the book from a school in Cries that would never let an Undercity child enroll. It didn't matter. None of the kids here wanted to attend such a school. It would feel like prison to them.

In my youth, I'd filched my education from the Cries education meshes. Hack, the cyber-rider in Ruzik's circle, had stolen time on the Cries University mesh to learn physics, until he reached a point where even I couldn't always follow his work. Previous to Chalkdust, though, no one in the aqueducts had *owned* a math book. Hell, many kids here couldn't read. No one liked it when I required schooling for the Dust Knights. The kids wanted to belong to the most elite fight club in the Undercity, though, so they learned. Chalkdust loved math. Our bargain was simple; I brought her the books, and she taught herself everything they had to offer. She'd blasted through pre-algebra in half the time it took most students, and now she was conquering algebra. Such a small thing to own her own math book— and such a large step for my people.

Jak followed my gaze. "You remember?"

I glanced at him. "Remember?"

"The math games we played. Me, you, at her age."

"Yah, I remember." I'd loved those games. "You calculated probabilities so fast, it was like you had a tech-mech brain." He'd kept winning big at poker, until none of the gambling dens would let him play. You could get killed for counting cards, and Jak was a master at it. I'd long suspected that was why he ran the high-stakes games at the Black Mark. At the glitz tables in the big room, he fixed the games in favor of the house, but the card games in the back rooms depended on skill. You could play however you wanted as long as you had enough credit for the buy-in.

"You find the worm at the Black Mark?" I asked. I'd told him what Daan claimed, that a dealer at the Mark was passing messages for these execs in the High Mesh.

"Yah, found him." Jak scowled. "Bez."

I remembered Bez from the card game where I'd located Daan. "He snitching?"

"Said a slick paid him to pass whispers."

"What whispers?"

"Secret place for meetings. In the desert, under the desert." He waved his hand as if shunting away the dealer. "Tonight I tell Bez. No more job."

"Jak, nahya. Don't kick him out."

He scowled. "Why? Betrayed my trust."

"Didn't harm the Mark."

"Harmed my trust."

"Yah. I ken. But Jak, you fire him, he tells the slick, we lose everything."

"Lose what? A bad deal?"

"My lead." The minute Bez told his Cries employers he could no longer pass messages, they'd know something was up. My lead would evaporate. "I need to follow. Find their meetings."

"Won't work. Bialo told you about the High Mesh. He'll tell the slicks you know."

"He won't. They'd kick him out." I shrugged. "Begged me not to tell."

"Think he can fool them?"

"For a while." Probably not long, though. I needed to move fast. "Tell Bez: He works for us, he keeps his job. Double agent. Bez tells you their next message. You tell me."

Jak considered the idea. "I could do. Bez is young. Not so smart." Dryly he added, "Doesn't ken optos. He's getting shit for passing messages. Could ask ten times as much."

It didn't surprise me, given how rarely we used opto-credits. Bez probably wanted them to buy junk on the black market. "You find any other execs who go to both the Black Mark and the Desert Winds?" My shoulders stiffened. "General Majda?"

He waved his hand in dismissal. "Majdas never come to the Mark."

"Anyone else?"

"Seven execs total, counting the three in your case. Also an artist."

"Inna Starchild?" I'd seen her artwork when we'd visited her home.

"Yah, Starchild. Only big names, famous, rich."

I thought of Lukas. "Mara Quida's husband?"

"Not him." He looked intrigued. "Someone else you know, though. Slick called Bessel."

I recognized the name. "Personal assistant to Lukas Quida."

"You going to follow these slicks?"

"Yah, you bet."

He touched my arm. "Only bet on what you can win, Bhaaj."

It was good advice. I wished I could heed it. I didn't like where this investigation was taking me, but I had to act soon. The longer it went on, the greater the chance people would realize how much I knew. Although it worked in my favor that Daan Bialo underestimated me, I doubted I would be as fortunate with the people in charge of this High Mesh.

Whoever they were.

The lowest end of the Concourse lay hundreds of meters below the desert, a cramped alley with faded stalls. I walked through the smoky air, headed toward the upper boulevard. As I continued on, the haze cleared and the street widened into an avenue. Higher quality stalls appeared, with yellow canvas walls and blue streamers hanging from their roofs, rustling in the air currents. I stopped at a stall between a café and a carpet stand, a small but respectable location. Nothing about it spoke of world-shaking events or even a little excitement. Nothing—except for the burly man standing behind the counter. Weaver. Today the first Undercity vendor in the history of Raylicon legally set up shop on the Concourse.

"Eh, Weaver," I said.

"Eh, Bhaaj." He motioned at the tapestries, glassware, and pottery stacked on the counters. "Got stuff to trade."

"Looks good." I nodded to him and to Dara, his wife, who had the day off from bartending to help out Weaver. Darjan, their fourteen-year-old daughter, had come as well. Dara seemed nervous, uncertain about this strange idea, her husband "selling" goods on the Concourse. Darjan looked delighted.

At this early hour, the Concourse was quiet except for the vendors setting up their stalls. I couldn't believe this day had come. Last year Weaver couldn't get a license because he had no birth certificate. Fixing that took time, but he finally got proof that yes, he had indeed been born. We spent another year caught in the Cries bureaucracy, which threw obstacle after obstacle in his path. I didn't ask the Majdas for help; the Undercity needed to make changes itself, without depending on outsiders to do it for us. Weaver had no interest in setting historic precedents; in the end, he persisted because it pissed him off that Cries made it so difficult.

Today he won that fight. Today the Undercity stepped into the world of Cries on the same footing as its privileged inhabitants.

"Stay a bit?" Weaver asked me.

I smiled. "Yah, I stay." I wouldn't have left for the world.

A chime rang, reverberating along the Concourse, the opening of the business day. A trickle of shoppers and tourists turned into a flow as people poured onto the boulevard. On a typical day, people thronged the street. A few would even go to the end, either out of curiosity or because they couldn't afford the pricier shops. I stood to the side, watching customers wander in our direction.

Before today, the "commerce" of my people on the Concourse had consisted of thieves stealing food, tech-mech, or trinkets. I'd been no different in my youth. Sometimes when our children ventured up here, the cops rounded them up and dumped them into the windowless orphanage in the desert. The kids either escaped or were freed by their kin and friends. The few who never made it back ended up as laborers on water farms in the desert, a miserable existence away from the beauty of either Cries or the Undercity. When the cops caught adults, they threw them in jail. The courts usually released them after a few days, except for the drug punkers, who went to prison. That had all worked against Weaver getting his license, but he never gave up, determined to prove to Cries that people like him existed in the aqueducts, a family man with a trade.

A woman came to the stall and peered at Weaver's glassware, especially the delicate vases glazed in desert colors. "These are beautiful." She looked up at him. "Do you have more? They'd make nice gifts for my family."

Panic flashed across Weaver's face. He'd been learning Cries speech, but in this moment, faced with his first customer, it looked like it all flew away. I hesitated, not wanting to intrude—

Darjan stepped forward and smiled at the woman. "Yes, ma'am," she said in an accented version of the Cries dialect. "My father has many vases. Other colors, too—blue, green, silver. Would you like to see them?"

The woman returned her smile. "Yes, that would be good."

Back in the stall, Dara let out a discreet breath. She seemed as nervous as Weaver.

The woman bought six vases, each for a hundred credits. She gave

Weaver a voucher for the amount. Darjan entered the woman's code into her mesh pad and registered the sale in the account we'd set up for Weaver's business.

After the woman left with her purchases, Weaver turned to me. "A number? This is the bargain? A *number*?" His scowl was thunderous. "Six vases. Worth three snap bottles of fresh water. I just lost that."

A feeling hit me that I didn't know how to describe. Triumph? Pride? Tears? "You got six hundred credits. Six *hundred*. Trade for two hundred snap bottles."

He stared at me. "What?"

"Yah." Darjan gave her father a classic look of teenaged annoyance. "You *know*. Told you. Snap bottle is three credits. You got six hundred." Her annoyance melted. "Good bargain."

"You ken these credits?" he asked her.

"Yah," Darjan assured him. "I ken."

I spoke softly. "Congratulations."

They all blinked at me, perplexed by the five-syllable word. They knew I had no intention to insult them or make a joke big enough to warrant such a word. The only other possibility was that I considered what had just happened worth that many syllables.

Dara sighed. "Ah, Bhaaj."

I grinned and she laughed, as much with relief as humor. Today life was good.

I rode the lift to my penthouse, feeling like a barbarian among all the elegance. Gold and black panels tiled the lower half of the car and mirrors graced the upper half. My reflection looked back at me, a woman in black trousers and a worn muscle shirt with no sleeves. A trace of dust covered my clothes. My gun sat snug in its holster and I carried my leather jacket over one arm. Tendrils of hair curled around my face, pulled out of the braid that fell down my back. I smirked, enjoying the dissonant image.

"Max," I said. "Find me everything you can on Bessel, the assistant to Lukas Quida."

"Will do. Also, Jak wants to talk with you."

I tapped my gauntlet comm. "Jak?"

"Bez got another message." Jak used the Cries dialect. We switched back and forth when we spoke to each other, depending on our subject matter, to the point where I often didn't notice which dialect he and I were speaking. "Bez was supposed to tell Daan Bialo to go to a meeting," he continued. "Except Daan never showed up, so Bez couldn't give him the message."

I tensed. "What meeting? Where?"

"You aren't going to believe this."

"Try me."

"The starship ruins on the shore of the Vanished Sea."

Ho! Why the hell would they meet at the ships? "They can't go there." The lift doors opened, creating an archway. I walked into my living room. "It's off limits to everyone except the army and a few scientists they let study the ships."

"Yah. But that's where Bialo is supposed to meet them. Tonight, in about thirty-five hours."

Not good. The army controlled access to the ships, and the Majdas controlled the army. If the High Mesh met there, that meant either the Majdas let it happen or else the Mesh was violating military security big time. "Let me know if Bez hears anything more, yah?"

"I will." Jak's voice darkened. "And don't do it, Bhaaj."

"Do what?" I knew what he meant, but I couldn't give him the assurances he wanted.

"Those ships are off-limits to you, too."

"Don't worry."

"I mean it, Bhaaj. Be careful."

"I will. I promise."

After we signed off, Max said, "He's right. You can't go out there." Then he added, "Not that such trivialities have ever stopped you."

"If you mean my job is dangerous, then yah. That's why I get paid so much." If I still had a job. "Can you bring up your record of the security mesh at the Majda palace?"

"You're changing the subject."

"Actually, I'm not. Look at the image they used for their security mesh."

After a pause, he said, "The image is the web of a reptisect called a sand-weaver."

"A repti-what?"

"Reptisect. It's a term for animals with traits similar to both reptiles and insects."

Huh. All the decades I'd lived on this planet, and I didn't know the animals were called that. "They're beautiful in a terrifying sort of way, like little shimmerfly dragons. They build webs out of the sand and some glue their bodies produce."

"Why do you bring them up?"

"A few years ago I read an article about how they weave their webs on the starships. The army has to keep cleaning them off. The sand-weavers are practically part of the ships."

"That doesn't mean the Majdas have a connection to this meeting at the ships. It could be coincidence that they use that symbol for security."

"Yah. It could." Except I didn't believe in coincidences.

The Vanished Sea looked less barren up close than from my penthouse. Its iron-rich sand sported many shades of red, from pale hues the color of an Earth peach to glowering crimsons. Blue azurite speckled the dunes and streaked the rocky patches. I jogged across the land, passing stone-vines with delicate tendrils stretching everywhere, like silver lace. Their roots extended under the desert for hundreds of meters, seeking water like miners searching for ore.

The folds of land were larger up close than they looked from my window, and isolated, untouched by most humans. I could easily hide here from visual scans. That didn't mean Cries ignored the Vanished Sea; the army monitored every meter of the desert this close to the starships. Those ruins had once housed a giant EI that destroyed whatever beings brought humans to this world. They couldn't defeat the EI, but they forced it to go dormant before they died. The rise of the human mesh activity on Raylicon had gradually awoken the monstrous intelligence. It attacked our electro-optic systems; humans were just a side-product of the infestation it wanted to eradicate. Left unchecked, it could have accessed our interstellar networks and wreaked havoc, even destroyed our civilization.

We'd just barely managed to destroy it. The authorities had secured the records of the event, afraid that if it became public knowledge, the resulting outcry might awake other malevolent EIs. Imperial Space Command intended to take no chances; the starship ruins remained off-limits to everyone except the soldiers who guarded them and a few scientists.

Why would the High Mesh meet out here? Gods only knew what they might wake up. It seemed unlikely any of them knew what had happened with the EI—

Unless their members included General Vaj Majda.

I grimaced as I jogged across the desert, using enhanced speed so I didn't have to hide a vehicle. After my foray into the palace mesh, I'd updated the jammer in my backpack, taking into account the newer protections we'd found there. It would give me an additional edge against the sensors at the ruins.

As I ran, I thought, *Max, did you look at my financial portfolio today?*

Yes, I did my usual monitoring.

Anything happen with my Suncap holdings?

Their value decreased substantially after the board ousted Bak Trasor, the CEO, in a vote of no-confidence.

Damn. *Did it impact my portfolio?*

Yes. However, your financial advisors are minimizing the effect. As long as you don't sell any Suncap assets for a while, your portfolio will recover.

Why did the Majdas oust the CEO?

The Majdas had nothing to do with it.

Like hell. We heard General Majda and her husband plotting to get rid of him.

Let me rephrase. As far as anyone else knows, the Majdas had no involvement. It's true that Prince Izam, General Majda's husband, sits on the board. However, he attends the meetings only via a mesh linkup. He never appears as a holo and he never speaks. His only participation was to cast his vote.

Against the CEO.

Yes, that is correct.

Well, wasn't that convenient. I wondered how long it had taken the Majdas to weave their influence throughout the financial structure of the Imperialate. Of course, their House had been around for six thousand years. They'd had more than enough time to perfect a stealth empire. *So why did the board oust the CEO?*

He lacked support for his vision of the company. Suncap manages water farms on Raylicon. The board wanted to extend their holdings to citrus farms on the world Parthonia. Trasor wanted to create more water farms here. He believes the demand for water is greater than for citrus fruit. The board pretended to go along with him, and then threw him out with the coup.

So the corporate rebels at Suncap betrayed his trust.

Essentially, yes.

Why would the Majdas care?

I can hazard a guess.

Hazard away.

They don't have a majority holding in water farms on Raylicon. However, they would have a majority holding in the citrus farms on Parthonia.

It all seemed so convoluted. *Their scheming better not put Suncap out of business.*

Suncap will be fine. Humans like citrus fruit, and the worlds where it grows best are Earth and Parthonia.

He had a point. I loved oranges, or I had when I'd lived on Parthonia. I never ate them here. They were impossible to import.

You're approaching the restricted area, Max added.

I stopped behind a rock formation that resembled the fingers of a giant skeleton reaching out of the ground. Peering around its edge, I could see what appeared to be three large dunes in the distance, about a kilometer away.

Toggle visual magnification, I thought.

The "dunes" jumped in size. Starships. The half-buried ruins each looked about the size of a small house. Millennia of wind-driven sand had scoured their surfaces, and a glistening mesh encrusted their hulls. It amazed me that they'd survived for six millennia. Whoever designed those ships had built well.

Pretty, I thought. *Haunted, though.*

Do you see the largest one on the right? That is the location for the meeting.

If anyone comes. Daan Bialo never got the message.

I can't detect anyone. However, I may be too far away.

I took the red beetle out of my jacket pocket. *Go on, little bot. Tell me who's out there.*

The beetle took off, humming toward the ruins.

Can you shroud it? I asked Max.

Not from here. The jammer is in your pack.

Have it stay back, then, enough to avoid detection. Let me know if it sees anything.

I'll do my best. After a moment, Max thought, The beetle has located four people. Two are outside the first two ships, cleaning off sand-weavers' webs. Two more are inside the third ship. I'm pretty sure three of these people are army officers. I don't know about the fourth.

How do you know they're officers?

They're communicating with each other via military-issue nodes in their spines.

You shouldn't be able to pick that up. Those spinal nodes have better security than you.

Apparently not. He sounded smug.

It always intrigued me what emotions he chose to simulate. *What about the fourth person?*

Based on what the beetle can read for respiration, heartbeat, and other vital signs, I'd say the fourth is older. My guess is that we have three army lieutenants guarding the ruins and a civilian scientist studying the ships.

I don't see how the Mesh can meet there, with all these other people around. Unless these four are also involved. That seemed unlikely with the lieutenants. *Link me to the beetle's cam.*

I "jumped" inside one of the ships, viewing it from near the ceiling. The low resolution of the beetle's tiny cam didn't provide much detail. The dimensions of the ship seemed wrong, designed for beings shaped differently than humans. Instead of a pilot's chair, several stools stood in what looked like a cockpit. Their arrangement would never work for a human pilot; they were too far from the controls. Someone in a green uniform stood near the hatch, probably a woman. Another person was sitting on the floor near the stools, examining panels there.

Ho! I know that guy on the floor. It's Professor Ken Roy from the university. His work to slow the failed terraforming of Raylicon helped keep this region of the world habitable.

You mean the man who helped you set up the tykado tournaments for the Dust Knights?

Yah, that's him. I wonder why he's here. He's a terraformer, not an archeologist.

Perhaps he's looking for clues about who terraformed this world and why it didn't work.

That was the billion-credit question. If the race that brought our ancestors here had intended to design this world for humans, they'd made some strange choices. The planet had no axial tilt, so no seasons. Atmospheric churning aided by our weather machines kept the climate livable, but the heat could be miserable at midday and midnights were icy. Humans on Raylicon had used a shorter hour before we rediscovered Earth, but once we adopted the Earth standard, a day on Raylicon lasted exactly eighty hours, with forty hours of light and forty of darkness. The year matched Earth's exactly. It all seemed too convenient for coincidence. If some race could move the planet in its orbit to set the length of the year, surely they could create a more habitable biosphere, without the lack of water, thin atmosphere, and poisonous native life. Either they never finished developing this world or else they'd intended it for some other form of life.

Those ships still have secrets, I thought.

You think Professor Roy is working with the High Mesh?

I doubt it. He has too much class.

You don't know him that well.

Well enough. He's a nice guy, Max. And he volunteers in the Rec Center. He can enjoy any advantages he wants in his free time. So what does he do? He goes to a place for underprivileged youth and mops tables. Would you say that fits anyone else involved with this High Mesh?

Not at all. Even so, you shouldn't make assumptions.

I'll be careful. I watched the lieutenant. She wasn't doing anything, just leaning against the hull watching Ken. My beetle hovered in the ship, its little engine in stealth mode. With enhanced hearing, the lieutenant might have noticed the bot, but she didn't act as if she'd activated her augmented senses. People using their biomech had a quality of hypervigilance in their body language and facial expressions. This lieutenant just seemed bored.

Ken was absorbed in his work. I'd have been surprised if he carried biomech in his body. He had no military connection, and that kind of invasive augmentation wasn't something people usually did without a reason.

I don't think either of them is expecting anyone, I thought.

I find no trace of anyone else, either. Just the three officers and Professor Roy.

Release my link to the beetle. As my view of the ship faded, I added, *Have it search the desert around the ships.*

Will do.

I need to get closer. Can you tell how much security they have?

I can only access the outermost layer of their security mesh. If I push deeper, it might detect my probes.

Do what you can. I set off at a jog, staying behind a ridge of the land, keeping to rocky ground where I didn't leave a trail. When I was about a hundred meters from the ruins, I paused. From here, the sand-weaver meshes that covered the ships looked like bronzed lace.

Someone else is here, Max suddenly thought. Three people.

I tensed. *Where?*

On the other side of the ruins, outside the third ship.

I moved behind the ridge, keeping low. *Why didn't you see them before?*

They're about fifty meters away from the ships. Max accessed my eyes and projected a heads-up display that floated in front of me, marking the position of the intruders with red dots. I headed in their direction. When the ridge tapered off, I ran across the ground in a crouch until I reached a ridge that ran parallel to the third ship. I slowed down as I neared the intruders.

Do the people at the ships know anyone else is out here? I asked.

I don't think so. I haven't detected any of them linking with the three intruders.

I don't see how the intruders could come here without the army guards knowing.

Why? You're here without their knowledge.

I know Majda security. It gives me an advantage. If this group had similar access, that suggested either the Majdas were complicit or someone inside their circle had betrayed their trust.

The beetle is getting a visual of the intruders. Max projected a translucent image of three people standing about thirty meters from my position and fifty from the ruins. An overhang concealed them, created by a rock formation that jutted up from the ground.

Toggle my ear augs, I thought. As my enhancements kicked in, I strained to hear the trio, with no success. *Can you crank it up more?*

Yes, Max thought. But it can damage your ears if you augment them too much for too long.

Understood. Warn me if you think it's becoming a problem.

All right. I'm turning it up.

"—without Daan if he doesn't get here soon," a woman said. She sounded familiar.

"My contact at the casino said he never showed last night." The man speaking also sounded familiar. "Apparently the cops are protecting him."

"For what?" the woman asked. "Do we need to drop him?"

"I don't think so." That came from a second woman with a crisper manner of speech. I didn't recognize her voice. "He's being careful. Keeping a low profile."

Max, can you identify them? I've heard two of them recently, which means you have, too.

Searching, Max thought.

The man spoke grimly. "Has anyone found Mara or Chiaru?"

"Nothing," the familiar woman said. "But that damn investigator, she keeps nosing around."

Does she mean me? I asked. *Or Talon, the Scorpio detective?*

She must mean you, Max answered. She is Detective Talon.

What! Holy shit.

I don't think her excrement has spiritual qualities.

Ha, ha, Max. Are you sure that's Talon?

I get a ninety-two percent match on her voice.

What about the other two people?

The man is Bessel, the assistant of Lukas Quida.

Bessel again. He kept turning up. *What about the second woman?*

I don't have a match for her. However, when I extend my search beyond the people you've met in the past few days, I find an eighty-seven percent match with Sav Halin, the reporter.

My would-be killer at the gala. *Extend how?*

I looked at news broadcasts she's done over the past few years.

How good do you consider an eighty-seven percent match?

I'd say it's probably her. People speak differently when they're being recorded for a public broadcast. If I account for that, the match goes up to ninety-three percent.

Bessel was talking again. "Without Bialo, we can't go any further. Only he can reach under-chambers from here."

Talon spoke. "He's afraid that what happened to Mara or Chiaru will happen to him."

"Have there been any attempts against him?" Sav Halin asked.

"Nothing so far," Talon said.

It sounds like they don't know about the explosion in the tunnel, I thought.

It also sounds like they aren't the ones making people vanish.

"I'll report back..." Talon said. The rest of her comment was garbled.

Max, did you get that? I'm losing contact.

You need to get out of this enhanced mode. You've used it for too long.

"—people in charge want to know what happened to Mara," Bessel said. "They're nervous."

Come on, I thought to them. *Hurry up. Tell me who is nervous.*

Bhaaj, I'm going to deactivate your augs, Max thought.

No! Not yet. I need to know who they report to.

"...can't find out," Sav Halin was saying. "—hit us like a mountain." The rest of her words were garbled. Then she said, "...Vibarrs don't want anyone to—" Her voice cut off.

Enhanced mode deactivated, Max thought.

I pressed my palms over my ears. *Damn it, my ears are ringing.*

You shouldn't abuse them that way.

It will heal, right?

Yes. You need to stop doing things that require healing, before you reach a point where your body can't heal itself.

I will. I think I got what I needed.

What is that?

The Vibarrs. They're a noble House. Not royalty, like the Majdas, but aristocracy. Their House dates back to the Ruby Empire. They live on the world Parthonia. They're a juggernaut, all bankers and lawyers and wildcatters determined to get richer than anyone else alive.

I hope that information was worth the price. I'm getting a message from the picoweb formed by your nanomeds.

I blinked. The picoweb couldn't do much besides help the meds maintain my health. It almost never sent me messages. *What does it say?*

You've stressed the hair cells that support stereocilia on the basilar membrane of your inner-ear cochlea. You need to remove all further stress if you wish your tinnitus to cease.

Does that translate into something I can understand?

Avoid loud noises. If you do, your ears should soon stop ringing.

I can do that.

You also need to leave here. Now.

I'm not done. I have to find out what they are going to do next.

What they are going to do next, Max told me, is look for you.

❖ CHAPTER XIII ❖
THE LEARNED HALLS

I froze. *They know I'm here?*

They've spotted the beetle-bot.

Do they realize it's mine?

I don't think so. However, they are embarking on a search. I suggest you leave. Fast.

Keeping low behind the ridged bank, I retreated back the way I'd come. When I reached the gap I had to cross between the two ridges, I stopped.

They're looking for the ripple effect in the air created by a holosuit, Max thought. If you go into the open, they might see yours.

He had a point. I couldn't stay here, though; they'd search until they covered this entire area. I took a breath—and sprinted across the open area. I reached the other ridge within seconds.

Did they detect me? I continued my retreat into the desert.

I'm not sure, Max said. I've moved the beetle out of their range. Based on their search pattern, I'd say they have no idea you're here. They are trying to monitor the people in the ships.

Good. The logical assumption, if they were hiding from the soldiers, was to assume my bot had come from inside the ruins. *I wish I knew why they came out here.*

They must want something with the ships.

Apparently. But they can't do anything here. I'd retreated to an area with dunes, enough to slow me down. I walked behind a ridge, hidden, my feet slipping in the sand.

You're leaving a trail, Max thought. You need to hide your footsteps.

I pulled out my green bot and tossed it into the air. *Have the bots smear away my tracks.*

They are rather small for that job.

True. But they move fast. And it will be a while before the trio gets this far in their search.

Smearing commenced.

Most of the land I'd crossed when I came out here from Cries consisted of rocky ground where my footsteps wouldn't show. I set off running. I could go for hours, my legs eating up the distance. I hid in plain sight, alone in the vast desert as it cooled toward the night.

I sat in my big, comfortable chair in my penthouse living room, resting after my trek through the desert. "Maybe the House of Vibarr wants to dethrone the Majdas."

"I see no indication they have that kind of power," Max said. "If they tried to overthrow Majda, it would be a huge political upheaval. They'd be inciting a civil war."

"I don't mean politically. Financially. Right now, Majda dominates the interstellar markets. But Vibarr isn't far behind." I put my feet on the low table in front of my chair. "So reporter Sav Halin, a Majda agent, is working with the High Mesh. And Detective Talon, too? No wonder they want me dead. I could blackmail their sorry asses."

"Blackmail, spying, and insider trading." If an EI could scowl, Max was doing it. "What other laws do you plan on breaking?"

"I didn't do either."

"'Either' implies you didn't do either of two things. I mentioned three."

"Yah, well, Max, if I need to spy on the Majdas to stay alive, so be it."

"You have to decide if you trust them."

"I don't trust them. What about our circus performer, Tandem Walkerdale? Was she a spy?"

"I haven't found any record of it, but I can't search most of the secured army networks."

"Replay what she said about Daan when she was tailing me on the Concourse."

Walkerdale's voice came into the air. "Bialo left with the cop." She fell silent. Then she said, "Why would he give his guards the slip?" Another pause. "All right. I'll take care of him."

"She didn't say she'd kill him," Max said. "Just 'take care of him,' whatever that means."

"Yah." Whoever blew up the tunnels could have been after me instead of Daan. I doubted anyone knew about Angel; the Undercity existed off the grid, including the dust gangs. "My guess is that Walkerdale is working for the High Mesh."

"A circus seems an odd profession for a spy."

"It's different, I'll give you that." Standing up, I stretched my arms, then went to the window and gazed at the desert. The ruins of the Vanished Sea starships were out there, too far to see from here. "Walkerdale comes from Metropoli. Scorpio just arranged a huge deal on Metropoli. Coincidence?"

"A lot of people come from Metropoli," Max said. "Ten billion of them."

"Yah, but almost no one comes *here*. Tourists, but they have to get permission. The only settlements of any size on Raylicon are Cries, the Undercity, and the Abaj Tacalique warriors who live out in the desert, running the planetary defenses. No villages, no other modern cities, a few science stations, a few outposts, and the ruins of the Vanished Sea starships. Nothing here is viable, not the biosphere, the economy, the social structure, none of it. It's a bunch of privileged people living in a beautiful city that couldn't exist without an exorbitant inflow of resources."

"You underestimate Raylicon," Max said. "The ruins on this planet—the Undercity, the starships, and the city of Izu Yaxlan—those are among the most important in the Imperialate."

"Yah. But most people can't visit those places." Although a small back and forth existed between the populations of the Undercity and Cries, offworlders never came to the aqueducts.

"I don't see your point," Max said.

"You can't immigrate to Raylicon." I stared at the spectacular landscape, forbidden to most of the Imperialate. "You can only visit if you're invited or a tourist, and those visas are hard to get. So why would Walkerdale come from anywhere to Raylicon, let alone a world like Metropoli that has everything we lack?"

"She might really be a spy, working for the army."

I thought back to the scene in the police station. "I didn't get the impression Lavinda recognized her."

"Colonel Majda masks her reactions well. How would you know?"

"Intuition, I guess." Lavinda had revealed more than I'd ever expected when she told me about Chiaru. "And no, I didn't sense it as an empath. Those exercises Adept Sanva gave me don't do shit."

"I suspect you use your abilities at a low level without realizing it."

"Maybe." I shifted my weight. "You find anything on this Bessel fellow?"

"A bit," Max said. "He's a mesh analyst in addition to being Lukas Quida's personal assistant. And I think he's associated with one of the noble Houses."

That didn't sound right. If Bessel came from nobility, he wouldn't take a job as a personal assistant. "Why do you say that?"

"When I analyzed his voice, I found traces of an Iotic accent. You can't hear it in his normal conversation, but it shows up in a more detailed check. His accent is pure, as if Iotic were his first language. Only the Ruby Dynasty and the noble Houses speak Iotic as a first language."

"That's odd." Maybe he was a Vibarr. "He must deliberately suppress his accent."

"Maybe he is also working undercover."

An interesting idea. "Can you do a facial recognition on him?"

"I'll try. I can compare him to public images of members from various noble Houses and royalty."

I continued to gaze at the Vanished Sea, soothed by all that panoramic space. "I wonder where he got his name. Bessel was an Earth mathematician. What people on Earth call Bessel functions we call Selei functions. Why name him after an ancient Earth theorist?"

"He can't call himself Selei," Max said. "It's the family name of the Ruby Pharaoh."

"Well, yah. But I'd have thought he would just pick another Imperialate mathematician."

"I will see what I can find out."

"Good." I pressed my palms against the window. "What about that melted chunk of rock I picked up after the tunnel exploded? Can you tell me anything about it?"

Max switched subjects with an ease most humans lacked. "I managed a cursory analysis using the lab niche of your gauntlet. To do a better job, you need a real lab. If you don't want anyone in Cries to know what happened, you could ask Gourd to look at it."

"I might. What did you find?"

"I verified the rock came from the Undercity. It has the right percentages of minerals." He paused. "I did find one odd result. I don't think it actually melted."

I'd wondered about that as well. "It didn't seem hot enough in that tunnel."

"Silicates become molten between six hundred and twelve hundred degrees centigrade."

Ho! "No way did it get near that temperature."

"It is strange," Max said. "I think the molecular structure of the rock was rearranged."

"That's just a fancy way of saying it melted."

"Not necessarily. It's not igneous."

"Ig-what?"

"Volcanic. Igneous rock forms through the crystallization of magma, which is molten rock."

"And you don't think this rock fits that description."

"Not at all." He stopped. Given that his processes worked far faster than the human mind, such a pause usually meant he was searching large databases. I waited, patient. He was the ultimate confidant for a PI. Years ago, when I'd installed him in my gauntlets, I'd considered calling him Watson, after a character in an Earth mystery series. I'd chosen Max instead because, well, I wasn't sure. Maybe for Maximum. Or Maximillian.

He spoke again. "This may sound strange, but I think the rock looks melted because it was taken apart at the molecular level and put back together incorrectly."

I blinked. "That's impossible, especially in that short of a time."

"I'm actually not sure how much time passed. My record of the explosion has a glitch."

I thought back to the recording he'd shown me. "I don't remember any glitch."

"I determine time according to an atomic clock, specifically the oscillation of an atom."

"I'm sensing a 'but' in there."

"I think my record of the incident has a gap in time."

"The record looks continuous."

"Yes, it does. But it is just slightly off from the planetary atomic clock, as if the atomic oscillation stopped for about one second."

That sounded nuts. "You can't stop atoms from oscillating."

"I'm not phrasing this well," Max said. "I read the time of day by linking to a standardized atomic clock. It works by electrons changing their energy level. For one second during the explosion, the atoms in the clock didn't change energy levels."

"Atomic clocks don't just stop." I thought about what that would mean. "You can't run mesh systems without them. If the official clock for this world stopped for one second, it would be a disaster. You know how often an atom resonates in one second? I'm sure it's millions of times."

"Actually, more. A cesium clock, for example, has 9,192,631,770 cycles per second."

Ho! "A lot."

"Yes. A lot."

"It couldn't have stopped for one second."

"I know. However, it did stop, and at the same time the tunnel exploded."

A chill went through me. "Max, is it possible you were the one who lost a second, rather than the clock?"

"I don't follow your meaning."

"Could you have been in a quantum stasis?"

"I don't have the capability to create a quasis field. That requires a starship generator or similar. It is beyond my ability."

"Not you. Maybe something else put the tunnel in quasis for one second." It was how pilots survived the killing accelerations of space battle. The quantum state of a ship in quasis remained fixed. The ship didn't freeze; its atoms continued to vibrate, rotate, and otherwise behave as they had when the quasis activated. But no particle in quasis could change its quantum state. On a macroscopic scale, that meant the object became rigid. Nothing could deform it. Ships used quasis for only a few seconds, and only in the relative vacuum of space. If your environment altered too much, then when you came out, the abrupt shift in the forces acting on you would tear you apart.

"It seems unlikely," Max said. "However, it could explain the glitch. Starship controls can correct for quasis pauses, but your gauntlets aren't sophisticated enough. If they went into quasis, my record of what happened would stop and only pick up again when I came out of quasis."

I grimaced. "If some idiot turned on a quasis generator in a planetary environment, gods only know what that could do."

"It was only one second. I doubt the tunnel changed enough in that time to cause the explosion we experienced."

He had a point. "Quasis doesn't change the atomic structure of an object, certainly not enough to make the stone look melted."

"I wouldn't think so. Besides, the energy required to put even a small section of the tunnel into quasis would be huge. Where would it come from?"

"I don't know. The High Mesh does develop new technologies."

Max spoke dryly. "Blowing things up is hardly new."

"Maybe it wasn't meant to explode." I turned around and leaned against the window-wall. I could never have done that in my youth, when I first left the Undercity. Back then, even drop offs of only a few stories unsettled me. The idea of turning my back on a view more than fifty levels up in a tower would have left me paralyzed.

"Can you send a message to Gourd?" I asked. "If you contact Royal Flush, he or Jak can get in touch with Gourd. Tell him what you found with the rocks in the tunnel. Ask him to analyze that crystal sphere again, this time to see if its molecular structure shows subtle signs of changes."

"Message sent."

"Thanks." I thought about what had happened in the tunnel. "Maybe the High Mesh is trying to develop quasis tech for use in a planetary environment."

"Why? It would be like using a planet smasher to crush a shimmerfly."

"For troop combat, maybe?"

"Combat armor would be more effective for close-in ground fighting."

"I suppose." In space, a ship could take two to four strikes from major weaponry before the quasis broke down. Huge strikes, far more than you'd get on a planet unless you were trying to destroy a substantial portion of its surface. In theory, nothing worked as well as quasis because an object in quasis couldn't change. Period. You could explode an antimatter bomb on top of it with no effect. But using weapons like antimatter bombs for infantry combat was dumb. They destroyed everything on both sides of the fight. For close-in combat, body armor or reinforced drones made more sense than a quasis field.

I pushed away from the window. "Whatever they tried to do, I think it failed. Miserably."

"What do you think they are trying to do?"

"I have no clue." I lifted my hands, then let them drop. "I wonder if even they know."

It was time to find out.

Cries University stood in the shadow of the Saint Parval Mountains on the western outskirts of the city. The starport lay to the south, far enough away that the noise of ships taking off didn't disturb the residents of Cries. As I walked to the Anthropology Department, I watched the sliver of a starship arrowing into the sky, the distant rumble of its leaving barely audible here in the foothills.

Every now and then I passed a bench shaded by feather-trees where students sat and debated whatever caught their interest. Columns fronted the buildings, suitably traditional, but sweeping curves of modern art also graced the quadrangles. The campus presented its elegance to the universe as if nothing illicit ever happened here, which I didn't believe for a second, but what the hell. It all looked civilized and right now I needed to feel civilized. It offered a respite from wondering when the High Mesh would try to whack me again.

I'd told the Majdas almost nothing. I had no evidence to support my conviction that both Mara and Chiaru were dead, blown up by some bizarre creation developed by a secret alliance of financiers without ethical constraints. I couldn't keep sneaking around, discovering more of what looked like a conspiracy, without telling some authority. Unfortunately, if I picked the wrong people, I could be signing my death warrant.

I needed answers. So off I went, to the university. The Terraforming Division took up the south wing of the Archeology Department. The halls had an antique quality, as if this stately building with its high ceilings had remained unchanged for centuries. A curving set of stairs led up from the lobby to a rotunda, and you could walk around up there until you found halls leading to whatever room you sought. Of course the building had plenty of tech, including lifts for people who didn't feel like taking the stairs. That was all out of view, though, so it didn't mar the atmosphere.

Ken Roy's office was on the third floor. I paused at the doorway. He was sitting at his desk reading a holomap of Raylicon that floated in the air. He looked so scholarly that I felt like a villain by intruding.

After a moment, I said, "My greetings, Professor Roy."

Ken looked up with a start. "Major! My greetings." He stood up. "Come in, please." He indicated a table across from his desk. The chairs there appeared exceedingly comfortable with their worn upholstery and plump cushions. Shelves stood against the walls crammed with books, *real* books, antiques, the kind that had words printed on a page. It was like being in a museum, except he actually used all this stuff. He matched my idea of a scholar, fit and athletic, but casual, dressed in a rumpled blue shirt and trousers. His hair had grayed at the temples. He also had a humble quality I'd always liked.

As we sat in the chairs, he asked, "What brings you to my world?"

"It really is like another world here," I said. "So different from the Undercity."

He smiled. "Less interesting, I'd say."

I supposed that depended on your point of view. "I wanted to let you know that my tykado students are testing for their belts in a few days. You helped sponsor several of them. If it wouldn't be an imposition, I'm sure they'd appreciate your coming to see the physical demonstration."

"Of course! That's wonderful." His face seemed to light up. "Which ones are testing?"

"Ruzik and his girlfriend are going for their first-degree black belts. Darjan is testing for brown." Several younger students were also testing, but Ken didn't know them.

"I'm afraid I'm still learning their names."

"My people don't give our names unless we know someone well."

They had to use their names for the tests, or I couldn't register them with the ITF, but I didn't feel comfortable telling him without their permission. I'd had time to ask Ruzik and Darjan before I came here, though, and that was enough. It offered a good cover for the other reason I wanted to see him.

"I think I remember Ruzik," Ken said. "The big fellow." Wryly he added, "Intimidating."

"He can be." Ruzik scared the hell out of people from Cries, with his large height, muscled frame, battle scars, and the crisscrossing tattoos on his arms that named him as the leader of his gang. "He's more civilized than people realize."

"He did ask about my research," Ken mused. "We talked one time after a tournament."

"Well, what you do is fascinating. How is it going?" I endeavored to sound sociable, rather than saying what I really wanted to ask, which was, *What the blazes were you doing at the Vanished Sea starships while nefarious types crept around outside?*

"Pretty much as usual." He relaxed back in his chair. "We're working on ways to increase the oxygen content in the air."

"It's never felt thin to me," I said. "When I first went offworld, the atmospheres of other terraformed planets made me dizzy, they had so much oxygen."

"The difference is only a few percent." He was warming up to his subject. "Eons ago, Raylicon had oceans and a thicker atmosphere."

"I never did get why the oceans dried up."

"The atmosphere thinned out, far more than now. The boiling point of salt water dropped too much and the water evaporated." He motioned toward the sky. "The ultraviolet light from the sun dissociates water vapor high in the atmosphere. The hydrogen probably escaped into space. The oxygen must have combined with minerals in the crust to form various compounds, especially iron oxide. That's why the deserts are so red."

This wasn't how I'd heard our history. "When our ancestors came here, the planet had an oxygen-nitrogen atmosphere."

"Yes! Someone or something created it, probably using the gas giant in this system."

"The fourth planet?" It was farther out from the sun than Raylicon.

"That's right. One of its moons has a great deal of water and nitrogen ice. We think whoever moved this world into orbit also fired a continuous stream of ice and nitrogen projectiles from that moon to Raylicon. They burned up in the atmosphere, giving this planet water and nitrogen."

"I didn't realize such a facility existed on any moon." In fact, I was sure it didn't. No way did we have the technology even now to do what he described.

He smiled at my expression. "You're right, it doesn't exist. If it ever did, it was gone long before humans explored this system." His smile faded. "That's the problem. Whatever produced this atmosphere ceased operating ages ago. It's been thinning ever since. If the oxygen content goes much lower, it won't support human life."

"So that's what you're working on? Making more oxygen?"

"That's one project." He leaned forward and tapped the table. "Would you like some tea?"

Tea? I never drank the stuff. Asking for ale didn't seem right, though, so I just said, "Sure."

He sent the order. "I'm also trying to figure out who terraformed this planet."

Ah! An opening. "I'd always assumed it was whoever built the Vanished Sea starships."

"That's one theory. I can't find evidence to support it."

I leaned forward, fascinated. I'd never had the chance to talk with a leading scientist about our history. "Because the libraries in those ships are ruined, right?"

"Not exactly." He paused as a bot rolled into the office, a cylinder on treads with a domed head and four limbs. It set our tea on the table and rolled out, blithely ignoring us. Logically I knew it didn't feel blithe anything, but I couldn't help thinking of it with human traits.

You're used to me, Max thought. An EI better at being human than a human.

For flaming sake, I thought. What, you're working on having an inflated ego?

He sent me a sense of amusement.

Ken poured two cups of tea. "Something corrupted the libraries in those starships. There had to be more ships, too. Those three could never have carried thousands of humans to Raylicon."

I was one of the few people who knew an ancient EI had

destroyed whoever dumped us here. It didn't surprise me that they'd lost so many records during their battle with the EI. I said only, "You talk as if you've been out there."

"I have, indeed." He offered me a cup of tea.

I took the cup. It was too delicate, this creation of glazed white porcelain with flowers painted around its rim. I felt like an idiot. Good thing no one in the Undercity could see me holding it. That would destroy my credibility with the dust gangs.

"What are the ships like?" I asked.

"Old." He took a swallow of tea. "Six thousand years old."

"Like the aqueducts." My curiosity jumped in. "Not all, though. Our ancestors built some of the Undercity, but a lot of those ruins came from before."

"Yes! So much is a mystery about all these ruins, including the ships, not only in them, but below them, too."

I wished I could tell him more. More than Undercity reserve held my tongue; I'd signed an ironclad agreement never to reveal anything I knew about the origins of the Vanished Sea starships, with good reason. The army didn't want to wake any more pissed off super EIs.

"I understand it's difficult to get permission to visit the ships," I said.

Ken grimaced. "It took me years of applications before they gave me limited clearance."

"Your team, too?" Maybe he associated with the High Mesh through academic channels.

"Just me, for now. I hope to publish my work this year, but I have to submit my paper to the military for clearance first."

I could just imagine what a scholar who was used to the freedom of research in a university felt about those constraints. "You're a patient man."

"Hardly." He gave me a wry grin. "You haven't seen me up here swearing and pacing."

"I can imagine. But I do I understand why they can't let many people visit the ships, though." I grimaced at the image of tourists flocking to the ruins. "It would destroy them."

"I know. It's a shame." He finished his tea. "The site is fascinating."

"I'll read your paper when it comes out." I would, too, assuming I came out of this alive.

He set down his cup with care. "I'm always afraid I'm going to break one of these."

I couldn't help but smile. "Me too." I sipped the tea. The warm liquid went down easy, tasting of citrus and caffeine. I blinked. "That's actually good."

Roy laughed. "You don't have to sound so surprised."

"Ale is more my style."

"Visit me at the end of the day sometime. I'll take you down to the faculty club."

It sounded so much like a place I'd never fit in, I immediately wanted to visit. "I'll do that." I set down my cup and rose to my feet. "Thank you for your time, Professor."

He stood up. "Call me Ken, please."

After I left, I mulled over his words. *Max, I don't think he's involved in any cabal.*

He doesn't seem like the type. But you never know.

I need to figure out how Detective Talon is involved. I thought of Lukas. *Her link to all this must be why she keeps pushing the guilty accusation on Lukas Quida. She's a major pain, but she's not stupid. It's obvious he didn't kill his wife.*

To you, maybe. Everyone has their own view of supposed true love.

I suppose. More likely, Talon was deflecting attention away from the High Mesh.

You just got a message from Gourd, Max thought. He says, "Bhaaj, the crystal has a glitch."

Interesting! *I'll go see him. Call me a public flyer.*

For the Undercity?

No. I took a breath. *First I have to visit the palace.*

✥ CHAPTER XIV ✥
QUEEN'S GAMBIT

"Are you sure you want me to keep going?" the flyer pilot asked. Sweat beaded on her forehead.

"I'm sure," I said, even though I wasn't. *Max, did your message to the palace go through?*

Yes. Their security knows you're coming. However, they haven't said they'll let you in. Then he added, I hope you know what you are doing.

So do I.

The comm crackled with a woman's voice. "You are entering restricted air space. Identify yourself."

"This is Del Jase, captain of public flyer H43," the pilot said. "My passenger says she has clearance for your airspace. I'm sending her ID."

I undid my safety harness, got up, and leaned over the captain's seat so I could speak into the comm. "This is Major Bhaajan, here to see General Majda and Colonel Majda."

The pilot's face went ashen. To her credit, she continued flying.

"ID confirmed," the woman said. "Captain Jase, we are sending coordinates for a landing pad on the palace roof. You will land, leave your passenger, and depart immediately."

"Understood, ma'am," Jase said.

As I sat down, Jase soared into the mountains. The palace came into view, golden and glorious in the sunlight. We descended to the pad, where two large guards waited.

After the pilot set down the flyer, she turned in her seat. "Good luck."

"Thanks." I was going to need it. Big time.

I opened the hatch and jumped down to the roof. As soon as I stepped clear, Jase took off.

I recognized one of the people waiting for me: Randall Miyashiro. I'd always liked him. He came from offworld, from a more egalitarian culture. Here, he was as the only male tykado instructor at the palace—but he was also the only seventh-degree black belt on the entire planet. Randall served as the Majda tykado master, the expert who trained their police and security staff, a highly coveted position. Vaj Majda had sought out the best for her forces, taking her search across the Imperialate. And when she found the best, she hired him, even though he didn't turn out to be the woman she'd undoubtedly expected.

Randall nodded to me, and I nodded back. He and the female guard fell in beside me, heading for my meeting with the Majda queens.

Vaj and Lavinda Majda were both in uniform, dark green tunic and trousers, and plenty of gold braid. We met in the Azure Alcove, a circular room with silver and blue mosaics on the walls. A chandelier hung from the domed ceiling and arched windows stretched from floor to ceiling. The room had no chairs, only a round table by one wall, all the better to keep guests from relaxing.

General Majda stood leaning by a window, her body backed by the view of the mountains towering outside, their peaks desolate against the sky. She was taller than Lavinda, taller even than me, fit and healthy, with black hair dusted by gray. Her high cheekbones and angular features defined the word aristocratic. She didn't seem pissed, but neither did I see any sign she wanted to hear what I had to say. Compared to her duties as General to the Pharaoh's Army, this investigation probably ranked at the bottom of the bucket.

Lavinda stood with me in the center of the room. I hoped that was a good sign.

"You have a report?" Lavinda asked.

I considered her, glanced at Vaj, then back to Lavinda. "First I need to know something."

"Yes?" Her face was impossible to read, as if she'd drawn a shutter over the window she'd opened to me outside the police station.

Keeping up my own mental shields, I took a breath and spoke before I had a chance to stop myself. "I need to know—does Majda want me killed?"

Vaj stiffened. "What the hell are you talking about?"

I turned to her. "Did you tell Sav Halin to kill me the night Mara Quida disappeared?"

"No," Vaj said flatly. "Why would I?"

"So I wouldn't find out about the High Mesh."

Lavinda stared at me, and the sudden tension in the room felt tangible.

Vaj walked over to me. "You have heard of the Mesh?"

"Yes," I said. "Are you a member?"

Her gaze never wavered. "What do you know about it?"

I plunged ahead. "It's a secret society of powerful executives, possibly also the Vibarr noble House. Their purpose is to develop and own new technologies in such a manner to increase both their wealth and their ability to manipulate human populations."

Lavinda and Vaj stared at me with a look I'd come to know well, an impassive expression that actually meant *How the bloody hell did you know that?*

Vaj said only, "The House of Vibarr? Take care whom you accuse, Major."

"I'm not accusing anyone of anything." I was too busy hoping I survived this.

"Why do you think we have anything to do with Sav Halin?" Lavinda asked.

"Because after I escaped, I sent one of my bots to follow her. She went into the foothills, stayed overnight in a backcountry hut that belongs to your family, and then met a Majda flyer the next day, which took her somewhere my beetle couldn't follow, because the flyer was putting out a signal that corrupted the bot's internal systems."

"Halin is a news broadcaster," Vaj said coldly. "Why would she want you dead?"

I met her gaze. "Why did a Majda flyer pick her up in the morning?"

"I have no idea." The general thawed a bit. "Are you sure it was Majda?"

"Black and gold, with the hawk insignia," I said.

"That sounds like Majda," Lavinda said. "Do you have the footage from your bot? We can see if we can identify the craft."

"I'll have my EI send it to you."

Sending, Max thought.

Vaj nodded to her sister, then turned the full force of her gaze back on me, that look I'd always felt could bore a hole into my brain. "What does this have to do with your investigation? Do you think the Mesh is involved with the disappearances?"

That she even had to ask that question suggested she wasn't involved—I hoped. However, she said, "The Mesh," which implied she'd heard "High Mesh" enough to shorten it. "I think the two execs who disappeared are members of the High Mesh."

Lavinda went very still. "Chiaru Starchild?"

Lavinda, I'm sorry, I thought. "Yes, both Starchild and Quida." I spoke to Vaj, doing my best to show no weakness. "Both are also members of the Desert Winds."

Vaj considered me. "As am I."

"Yes," I said. "As are you."

"A lot of people belong to the Desert Winds," Lavinda said. Although she hid her reactions, her shoulders had tensed.

I spoke carefully. "Chiaru Starchild and Mara Quida also met outside the Desert Winds."

"Met where?" Vaj asked. "And why?"

I just looked at her. I had no intention of talking about the casino.

"Who do they meet with?" Lavinda asked.

That I could answer. "For one, Daan Bialo at Scorpio Corp."

"Bialo is a member of the Mesh?" Vaj snorted. "That seems unlikely."

Lavinda regarded her sister with exasperation. "Why? Because he's young, male, and good-looking? Honestly, Vaj, you need to get out of the dark ages."

Vaj waved her hand in dismissal. "He's a party boy."

I kept my mouth shut. I knew no one else who would dare talk to General Vaj Majda the way Lavinda had just done.

The general considered me with a hard stare. "Who else is involved?"

Who indeed? Jak had told me about seven execs, Inna Starchild, and also Bessel. From what I'd seen, Detective Talon of Scorpio Security and Sav Halin were part of it as well.

A thought came to me. *Max!*

Yes?

Do any execs who go to both the Black Mark and Desert Winds work at Suncap Corp?

Checking.

"Major?" Vaj Majda asked. "Who else?"

Yes, Max said. **Ana Liara, the chief financial officer at Suncap, is one of the seven.**

"Holy shit," I said.

Lavinda smiled. "I hope that isn't a person."

I looked from her to Vaj. "Bak Trasor is a member, isn't he? That's the reason you wanted him out of Suncap!" He hadn't been on Jak's list, so I hadn't suspected him, but if his CFO went to the casino, she could give him any messages she got there.

Vaj turned icy. "I have no idea what you're talking about."

"Neither do I." Lavinda was no longer smiling.

You better find a reason for what you just said, Max told me. **Or you are in deep shit.**

"I have stocks in Suncap," I told them. "They took a dive yesterday because the board kicked out the CEO. Your husband is listed as voting against him." I was so caught up in fitting the pieces together, I almost forgot to be afraid. "Ousting Trasor benefits your House because you have more holdings in citrus than water. But that's not the real reason, is it? Both Trasor and the Suncap CFO are part of the Mesh."

Vaj stared at me. "Ana Liara is a member? Are you sure?"

"About as sure as I can be without asking her. Mara Quida, Chiaru and Inna Starchild, and Daan Bialo as well." I listed the other execs and then said, "Also Bessel, Lukas Quida's assistant."

"I've never heard of this Bessel," Lavinda said.

"What about Detective Talon at Scorpio Security?" I asked. "She has some link to all this."

"Not at the Winds." Vaj frowned. "She's the head detective on the Quida case, isn't she?"

"That's right." A head detective who seemed to be doing exactly zilch. "The last time I talked to her, she had no new information. No leads. No ransom demand. She seems more concerned about whether or not I've found anything than actually solving the case."

"We'll look into her," Vaj said. "Anyone else?"

I might as well go all the way. "Possibly someone named either Tandem Walkerdale or Ti Callen who is either a circus magician from Metropoli or a covert military agent."

"For gods' sake," Vaj said. "A *circus* magician?"

"Do you recognize either name?" Lavinda asked her sister. "Maybe she is an operative."

"I've never heard of the woman," Vaj said. "That isn't saying much, though. I don't know the names of every covert operative."

"I've no idea who she is," I said. "Just that she's been following me since I started working on this case."

Lavinda turned to me with a scowl. "She's the one you jumped in the park."

Well, yah. Although that action had served its purpose, it wasn't one of my finer moments. "I was trying to find out more about her. I figured she'd answer the police if I pushed it."

Vaj studied me. "How did you find the rest of this information?"

I just looked at them. The general knew I couldn't reveal my sources, or those sources would never trust me again. Instead I asked, "Are you a member of the High Mesh?"

She spoke bluntly. "No, I am not."

Of course she could be lying, but my intuition said no. "It's the House of Vibarr. They're the driver behind this Mesh."

"Vibarr?" Lavinda looked as if she wondered what drug I'd taken. "Whatever for?"

Vaj reacted differently than her sister. She turned and walked away, back to the window, where she stood staring at the mountains. Lavinda and I waited.

After a moment, the general turned to us. "It would explain a lot."

I could use some of that explanation. "How long have you known about the Mesh?"

"I never said we knew anything about them," Vaj said.

I waited. I could do that silence game, too.

Vaj came back to us. "You don't have the clearance to know more."

"She needs the clearance," Lavinda said. "She just told us more about the Mesh than we've managed to find out in the past year."

The past *year*? "Why didn't you tell me about them?" When neither of them answered, I let out a frustrated breath. "I *need* to know."

Lavinda and Vaj regarded each other with one of their looks, the kind only they understood. Maybe they were communicating via their EIs or maybe by thought. Sisters shared a closer bond than most empaths even if only one of them was a strong psion. The only outward sign they were interacting came when Vaj nodded to her sister.

Lavinda turned to me. "We didn't say anything because we didn't know either Mara Quida or Chiaru Starchild were involved." When she mentioned Chiaru, her eyelid twitched, a subtle response I would have missed if I hadn't been so alert. That Chiaru's involvement bothered her told me a lot of what they thought of the High Mesh, none of it good.

"So when you asked me to investigate the disappearances," I said, "you didn't know you were asking me to investigate the High Mesh."

"That is correct," the general said. "We wanted your insight on the behavior of the people at the gala to help us judge how the Metropoli deal was going to affect the Cries economy." She considered me. "I understand now why you've been so terse with your reports. We haven't sent anyone to assassinate you, Major."

"If that's true," I said, "then you have a security problem at the palace or on your staff. Someone is working against you."

Vaj gave me an appraising stare. "And you know that how?"

Careful, Max thought.

I will, I answered. *Don't talk to me here, though. I don't know what they can pick up.* It was an odd idea, that in the presence of the Imperialate's elite cyber-enhanced warriors, even my thoughts might not be private. "Three people associated with the High Mesh met at the Vanished Sea starships yesterday, Bessel, Sav Halin, and Detective Talon. Did they have clearance?"

"No," Vaj said. "How do you know they met there? You don't have clearance, either."

I breathed evenly, trying to steady my pulse. "I circumvented the monitors using my shroud, my experience as a cyber expert, and my familiarity with Majda security."

A sense of doom came from Max. He didn't have to say anything: *You just screwed yourself* felt the same regardless of whether or not he actually spoke the words.

The general frowned. "Major, your talent at going places where you shouldn't be seems to have no limits."

Lavinda looked more puzzled than annoyed. "Why were you all out there?"

"I was following them," I said. "They were waiting for Daan Bialo, but he never showed up. I couldn't hear everything they said, but I did catch the name Vibarr."

Vaj tapped her gauntlet comm. A woman's voice came into the air. "Lieutenant Ko here."

"Lieutenant, check the security records for the Vanished Sea starships," Vaj said. "Look at everything for the past two tendays. Let me know if you find any breaches. And I need any records you can find on a man named Bessel employed by Lukas Quida."

"Right away, ma'am. Also, we received the files from Major Bhaajan's beetle. The flyer that picked up Sav Halin is a Majda vehicle. According to the schedule, it never left the palace that day."

"Understood. Over and—" Vaj stopped when I lifted my hand. "Hold, Lieutenant." She tapped off the transmit panel on her comm. "Yes, Major?"

"Can you have her look up Ti Callen and Tandem Walkerdale?"

Vaj transmitted the request to her lieutenant and signed out.

"Tandem Walkerdale." Lavinda spoke wryly. "What the blazes is she in tandem with?"

I gave a startled laugh. "I wondered that, too."

"I once knew an officer named High-Low." Vaj actually smiled. "I never did figure out the history of that one."

Max sent me a sense of astonishment. I understood. It was the first time I'd ever seen Vaj Majda make a comment unconnected to business, let alone smile while she did it.

"This much I can say," Lavinda told me. "None of the three people you saw at the Vanished Sea starships are, to our knowledge, in the High Mesh."

"I'm almost certain Bessel is a member," I said. "Sav Halin and Detective Talon are probably just working for them."

"I'm still missing something here," Vaj said. "I see no motive for Sav Halin to kill you. No one attacked any of the other investigators."

I said nothing.

"It's the Undercity, isn't it?" Lavinda asked. "You're the only investigator with ties there."

"I have to ask you to trust me," I said.

Vaj crossed her arms. "This is a pattern with you, Major. You want us to trust your questionable methods without telling us anything."

I met her cold gaze. "You've asked me to trust you, that you aren't involved in the attempts on my life. I ask this in return."

"I don't bargain with—" She stopped as Lavinda laid her hand on her arm.

"Vaj, the bargain is fair." Lavinda glanced at me. "A trade, your trust for our trust."

Ah. A bargain. She was learning to understand the Undercity. It was a small step, but it meant a lot coming from a member of the royal family so high above the Undercity, she would have been in the clouds if Raylicon had any.

"It's a fair bargain," I said.

Vaj considered her sister, then turned to me. "I'd like you to work with our staff to block whatever hole allowed you, and apparently three other people, to break security at the starships."

"Yes, ma'am." I couldn't tell her no. Saying, *Excuse me, I need to be able to break your security to do my job* would go over about as well as a plutonium balloon. "It's more serious than a backdoor in your mesh. You also have a mole on the inside working against you."

Neither of them looked surprised. Lavinda said, "We're aware of the problem."

Feigning innocence, I asked, "What happened?"

Lavinda and Vaj did The Look again. Then Vaj said, "Someone broke into the palace security mesh. We don't know who or why." She regarded me with a distinct lack of enthusiasm. "You are on the list of suspects."

"It isn't me you need to worry about." That was true. Of course it was also true I committed the break-in. "Someone is working against you with the High Mesh. She's probably the one who picked up Halin. It has to be someone familiar enough with your security to hide that she took a flyer." Halin had also betrayed their trust, given that she worked for them in secret, but I couldn't say that without revealing I was privy to information I had no business knowing. In any case, it couldn't only be Halin. Someone had picked her up in a flyer that supposedly never left the palace.

Vaj considered me. "Do you have any idea how the House of Vibarr might be involved?"

"I wondered about Bessel's background. He has traces of an Iotic accent." I spoke with care. "Is it possible the Vibarrs plan to move against your House? They're an aggressive player on the financial markets, and Majda must be their greatest competition."

Vaj snorted. "Competition suggests they have achieved enough to be worthy opponents."

Lavinda gave her sister an annoyed look. To me, she said, "They do challenge us."

I waited, but she said no more. Vaj had turned back into an unreadable monolith. If they had dealings with the Vibarrs, they weren't going to tell me.

"General Majda," I said. "It might be a good idea for you to have an additional bodyguard." She needed someone she could trust. I thought about Randall. "Perhaps Captain Miyashiro."

Vaj gave me a look that suggested I had pudding for a brain. Yes, I knew the idea of a man protecting the General of the Pharaoh's Army probably offended her conception of the universe, but Randall wouldn't have become the master tykado instructor for the most prestigious police force on the planet if she didn't trust his judgment.

Vaj glanced at Lavinda, who looked poised to argue with her. Then, incredibly, Vaj actually smiled. Gods. Twice in fifteen minutes. I was surprised the planet didn't stop in its orbit.

"I've given you enough opportunities to scold me for underestimating the fairer sex," Vaj told her sister. "I'll refrain from providing you another."

"A wise choice," Lavinda said. "Miyashiro would be an excellent bodyguard."

For a moment I saw them simply as two sisters who, despite their differences, enjoyed each other's company. It was a side of the Majdas I'd never even imagined existed, let alone witnessed.

Vaj spoke to me. "This investigation has expanded beyond what we expected."

No shit. "Do you want me to continue?"

"Yes, that would be good." Her expression remained noncommittal. She acted as if this was business as usual, but I knew them well enough after two years to see beyond that mask.

"To do my job," I said. "I need all the information you've gathered on the High Mesh."

To my surprise, Vaj didn't go silent. Instead she said, "Less than what you've found, actually. We know it exists, and that they seek to undermine current power structures through the development of rogue technologies. What exactly that means, we don't yet know."

Lavinda spoke. "We discussed it with the First Councilor at the last Assembly session on Parthonia. She has asked for more details."

The Assembly—as in the democratically elected ruling body of the Skolian Imperialate? "You're talking about the leader of the government."

"Yes, that's right." Vaj focused even more intently on me. "Is that a problem?"

"I just hadn't realized it extended beyond Raylicon. The only person who isn't from Cries is Tandem Walkerdale. She came here from Metropoli."

"The Scorpio deal with Metropoli is substantial," Vaj said. "After they announced it, their stock value soared." She sounded quite satisfied with that result.

"I haven't found any link between the Metropoli deal and the High Mesh," I said. "I'm not sure the Mesh even knows what the hell they're doing."

Lavinda regarded me curiously. "What do you mean?"

I hesitated. "I've wondered if they're manipulating quantum stasis technology."

Vaj came to attention as if I'd said someone had threatened war. "You think they're building ships for combat?"

"No, not at all. I meant using quasis technology on a planet."

"To what purpose?" Vaj asked, incredulous.

"I don't know." I described what Max had found about the time glitch, except I implied it involved the crystal sphere at the Quida mansion. I said nothing about the Undercity or the explosion in the tunnel. "If they did try something," I finished, "it backfired spectacularly."

Vaj lifted her gauntlet to tap her comm. "I'll have our people look into it."

"No, wait!" I took a breath. "The moment we send people to investigate, we show our hand. Right now, the High Mesh doesn't realize I know about them." Except for Daan Bialo. I doubted he would break my cover; it would get him kicked out of the Mesh, and he thought he'd blackmailed me into silence. "If they think Majda knows, they'll panic. It will drive them underground. They'll also try to remove anyone they fear can do them damage." Like me, their number one irritant.

"We'll be covert," Vaj said.

Lavinda tilted her head toward me. "This is exactly what we hire her to do."

Vaj lowered her arm. "Very well, Major. Continue your work. You have our resources at your disposal."

Those "resources" were no small offer. "Understood."

"Good." Vaj had a look I recognized, the one that said *You're dismissed.* "We'll have one of our pilots take you back to the city."

I bowed to her. "Thank you, General."

After Vaj left, Lavinda walked with me through the palace, headed for the landing pad on the roof. She asked, "Do you have any idea who the mole might be on the Majda staff?"

I wished I did. "So far, no leads."

She watched me with one of those appraising stares that saw too much. "I'm the one in charge of the investigation about who broke into the palace security web a few days ago."

"Have you found anything?" I asked, all innocence.

She spoke quietly. "Major, no one in my family is trying to kill you."

Damn. Why would she tell me that in the context of the palace break-in? "Of course."

"I need you to work with our security people to fix the security holes in our palace system. Can you come back tomorrow morning, eighth hour?"

I didn't dare ask why she wanted my help. "Yes, certainly. I'll help catch your cracker."

"Hacker," she murmured.

Why would she specify that difference? A cracker broke into

systems where they shouldn't be, either with malicious intent or else the way I'd done it, to exploit the network for their own use. A hacker had similar skills or even more advanced abilities, but they didn't break into systems, they sought to further knowledge.

"I'll do my best," I said.

"See that you do."

She knows you're the one who broke in, Max thought.

Be quiet, yah? I thought. *We'll talk later.* Surely she couldn't know. If she did, she'd have me arrested. The only other option was that she trusted me enough to let it go, which seemed impossible. Her formidable sister would certainly never allow anyone to breach their stronghold.

For now, I could only sweat bullets, wondering if and when they'd find out what I'd done.

The pilot didn't talk as she flew me back to the city. I sat in a passenger seat, watching the mountains. Shifting my weight, I tried to get comfortable. The flyer that had brought me to the palace had smelled fresh and clean. This one had an unpleasant scent, a lightly pungent smell. Odd. The Majdas were usually scrupulous about their aircraft.

I spoke to the pilot. "Do you smell something?"

She didn't answer. I rubbed my eyes. So tired—

"Hey!" I pulled off my safety harness and stepped to the pilot's chair. "I smell gas."

No response. Leaning over her seat, I shook her shoulder. Her head lolled to the side. Damn, she'd passed out. The musty smell intensified in the cockpit, and my vision swam. I shook her again, trying to keep my balance as the flyer swerved. My legs buckled and I dropped to kneel on the deck. Dizziness swept over me.

"Max, release the oxygen masks!" I said.

"I can't," he said. "The system is locked."

"Well, fuck." I struggled to my feet and clawed at the overhead compartment that stored oxygen. Swaying, I clutched the handle on a bin next to my shoulder, trying to keep my balance.

The flyer lurched, losing altitude. *Can you fly this thing?* I thought, holding my breath. I scraped at the oxygen compartment. *We're going down.*

I'm trying to reach its onboard system, but it's locked up too. And you are about to pass out.

It would be so easy to collapse to the deck. *Toggle combat mode.*

Toggled.

The pungent smell intensified and my fingers tingled. No time for delicacy; I tore the cover off the compartment, ripping it from the ceiling. A blue mask dropped out, and I clamped it over my face. With a gasp, I inhaled the pure oxygen. For a moment, I just breathed. When my head cleared, I leaned into the cockpit. Grabbing the pilot, I pulled off my mask and clamped it over her face.

"Come on," I muttered. "Wake up. I don't know how to fly this thing."

The comm crackled with a man's voice. "Flyer M47, this is the Cries Transit Authority. What the hell are you doing? You're on a collision course with the City Arts Tower. Pull off!"

I looked out the forward window. The City Arts Tower rose in front of us, a soaring needle of mirrored glass that reflected the sky in luminous blue panels.

We would hit it within moments.

✤ CHAPTER XV ✤
NIGHT STALKERS

I spoke fast. "I'm a passenger. A gas was released in the flyer. Pilot passed out. I'm on oxygen."

"You have to pull off," the man said. "Now!"

I dropped in the copilot's seat. "How?"

"Your system is blocked," he said. "I can't access it from here. Find a blue panel the size of your thumb to the right of the pilot's screen. Push it."

I slapped the oxygen mask over my face and gulped in breaths as I scanned the controls. The holoscreen was obvious, a disk with glimmering lines. No blue panel—wait, there. I banged my fist on the glowing circle. "Done!" The CA Tower was so close now, I could see people inside running past the windows to escape the level we were about to hit.

The flyer abruptly swerved to the east, nearly grazing a window. A woman stood there, frozen in shock, her face clearly visible as she stared at us through the glass. Then we were past the tower and out in the open air.

I pulled away the mask. "Did you do that? We missed the tower."

"Yes," the man said. "You transferred control to me when you hit the panel. I can't land the flyer by remote, though. I'll more likely crash it. Is the pilot still alive?"

I glanced at the woman. "Yes, she's breathing. She passed out. I almost did, too."

"All right. I'll try to keep you in the air. See if you can wake her up."

"Understood." I put the mask over the pilot's face while I held my breath, and I shook her shoulder.

No response.

Glancing out the window, I realized we were above the plaza on the outskirts of the city, headed toward the desert. At least if we crashed, we wouldn't kill anyone but ourselves. Putting the mask over my face, I took several long breaths. Then I tried it on the pilot again.

"Ungh...." The woman stirred, her eyelids lifting.

"Wake up!" I said.

No answer.

I shook her again. "You need to wake up!"

The woman groaned. As she opened her eyes, she dragged herself upright, staring out the windshield with a blank expression. Then she took the mask and breathed deeply.

"Can you release your own mask?" I asked. "I need that one." The smell of the gas saturated the air, making me nauseous.

The pilot tapped her controls groggily, several times, until a blue mask dropped from above her. Moving more smoothly, she handed mine back and fixed hers into place. We were over the desert now, losing altitude despite the best efforts of the transit authority.

The pilot took the controls and spoke through her mask, her voice distorted. "This is flyer M47. Release control to me."

"Transferring control," the man said.

As the pilot took over, the flyer skimmed over the dunes, stirring up great swaths of sand. She brought up the nose of the craft only moments before we would have plowed into the ground. As we rose into the air, she banked in a large curve toward Cries.

The pilot spoke to me through her mask. "What the bloody hell happened?"

I moved the mask away from my face. "Some gas knocked us out. It must have released in the cockpit first, because it affected you faster than me." Either that, or I'd been less susceptible. "It smelled like an old-fashioned compound medics used as an anesthetic."

She concentrated on the controls. "Who did it? And why didn't it knock you out?"

"I don't know who did it." I talked through my mask this time, not wanting to inhale more gas. "As for why I kept going, I can hold my breath for a long time." In the army, I'd been astounded to discover that most human-inhabited worlds had water forever—lakes, rivers and oceans, real oceans, nothing vanished about them. I'd loved swimming underwater, staying as long as I could, always pushing for greater times, marveling that the universe could hold so much water.

"We were lucky," the pilot said. "We need to get back to the palace and have this checked."

The palace? Not a chance. So this happened right after I told the Majdas what I'd discovered. Yah, right, some "coincidence." It could be them or it could be whoever betrayed them, but either way, damned if I would trust them again.

"I need to rest," I lied. "Can you drop me off at the Sunrise Tower? I live there."

She gave me a skeptical look. "I will, but don't disappear. Security will want to talk to you."

I didn't doubt it. I had no intention of going near them.

Gourd and Hack sat with me on a pile of rubble in the tunnel that had exploded last night. Dust motes drifted around us, sparkling in the glow from the torches. Ruzik's gang were working on repairs, reinforcing the walls damaged in the explosion, their bodies bathed in the orange light. It looked like someone had taken part of the tunnel floor, swirled it around, and then smashed it into the tunnel below, leaving a jagged, gaping hole.

A charred smell filled the air. I couldn't get the idea out of my head that something living had burned here. *It's the torches,* I thought. *You smell the torches, that's all.* None of us had been hurt, aside from scrapes and bruises. After what happened today with the flyer, though, I couldn't escape my sense that death waited nearby, lurking in the shadows.

Gourd was holding the sphere from the banister in the Quida mansion. The crystal glittered with sparks of light. "At first, I found nothing," he said. "But I only looked at the big. Then Max tells about your rock. So I look at the small." He tilted his head at Hack. "He helps."

"What'd you find?" I asked.

Gourd grimaced. "The small is wrong. Built the same but different." Frustration washed across his face. "My words can't say."

Hack said, "Molecular structure." He spoke the Cries words with distaste.

I wished they knew the Cries dialect better. The Undercity manner of speech didn't have the words to express what they wanted to tell me. Hack often explored the Cries meshes, stealing his education. Sure, he knew words like molecular structure, but he'd never fully learned the dialect.

"Molecules wrong?" I asked. "Change to new molecules?"

"Not change," Hack said. "Same molecules. Frame broken."

I couldn't figure out what he meant. "Say in Cries words."

Hack shook his head. "Don't ken the words."

I tapped the sphere Gourd held. "Where frame broken?"

Gourd turned over the sphere to show the hole where it fit onto the banister. He touched its rim. "Only here. Like a mistake."

"A mistake in what?" The rim looked normal to me.

"Wrong frame," Hack said.

I still didn't see what he meant. "Say Cries word for frame."

"Lattice?" Hack used the term warily, as if it might bite him. "Nahya, not lattice. Quartz has a lattice. This ball, no lattice. Like glass."

Ah. Now I understood. The molecular structure of glass wasn't ordered in a crystal lattice. Despite its misleading name as "crystal," the ball didn't actually have a true crystalline structure.

"Not ordered," I said.

"Yah. Quartz is solid." Hack laid his hand on the ball. "This is liquid."

I blinked. "Not liquid."

He scowled at me. "Liquid."

How could he describe the ball as a liquid? "I don't ken."

"Not real liquid," he allowed. "More like liquid than lattice."

Okay, that did make sense. Glass had an amorphous structure between a liquid and a crystal lattice. "Not solid. Not liquid. Between, yah?"

"Yah." He took the ball from Gourd and weighed it in his hand. "Pretty, eh?"

I smiled. "Yah."

Hack touched the rim. "Different here. Not much. Few molecules." He stopped, then tried again. "Like someone pulls the molecules apart, then puts them back. But didn't put them back quite the same way." He held up the sphere. "A machine makes this ball, yah? So all must be the same. All same pieces."

"Pieces?" I asked.

"Tiny," Gourd said. "Too small to see. Needed Hack's tech-mech."

"Use Cries word," I said.

"Molecules." Hack paused. "Silica, lead oxide, potassium oxide, soda, zinc oxide, alumina."

Ho! Where had he learned all that?

Watching my face, Hack grinned. "Read Cries glassworks mesh to understand." He showed me the ball. "Same chemicals. But! Put together different."

I understood now. Nanomachines crafted these balls, constructing them atom by atom. They made every sphere in a lot the same, down to the molecular level. It was like a fingerprint. Something had disturbed the "fingerprint" of this sphere, taking apart a small bit and putting it back together with slight differences in the arrangement of the molecules. If I'd been a gambler, I'd have laid odds that the edges of whatever hit Mara Quida had also nicked this ball.

I glanced around the tunnel. Had the same thing had happened here on a more dramatic scale? Ruzik and Angel were working on the stalagmites that held up the ceiling, using silica-cement to reinforce the weakened areas. Tower was on the level below, clearing out the debris, while Byte studied the hole in the floor to see if it could be repaired. I doubted they could rebuild well enough to make it safe. Better to leave it open rather than risk its collapse when people walked through this tunnel.

Gourd regarded me. "Heard whispers about the bang here."

I had no doubt rumors had raged throughout the Undercity. "What hear?"

"No one set a bomb."

"Someone had to set." Bombs didn't spontaneously appear out of nowhere.

"No one came in," Gourd told me. "No one went out. Except you, Angel, and the slick."

That made no sense. Someone had to have set the explosion. If their weapon affected matter on a molecular level, they probably weren't from the Undercity. It wasn't impossible; Hack and his friends could create some bizarre tech. But they hadn't done this. If they had, rumors about their exploit would saturate the whisper mill. The silence implied outsiders set the bomb. Yet that remained impossible. Without a guide, they could never make it down here and back at all, let alone without leaving a trace. This felt as if ghosts had appeared, blown up the tunnel, and then vanished.

"No one saw intruders?" I asked. "Walking other tunnels maybe?"

"Nothing," Gourd said.

"Any bodies?"

"Almost you three," Gourd said. "No one else."

"No cyber trace, either," Hack said.

I hit my fist on my thigh. "Not possible!"

"Our own people wouldn't do this," Gourd said.

Hack said, "Offer good enough bargain, they might," but he didn't sound convinced.

I leaned back against the wall and closed my eyes. I felt so tired. Only a couple of hours had passed since that lovely excursion in the flyer. I'd come to see Gourd and Hack, sure, but I also wanted to avoid the Majdas and anyone else from Cries who might be after me.

I opened my eyes to find Gourd studying my face. "Stay here, Bhaaj," he said. "Stay with Jak. Don't go back above."

"Yah," I said softly.

Except no place seemed safe right now, not here, not Cries, not anywhere.

Mist curled over the desert and around my body. Impossible mist. The desert never had fog, yet here it drifted. Engines growled in the distance, starships it sounded like. I followed the sound, unable to see more than a few handspans in front of my face. The noise increased. Whatever ship they came from, it was in terrible condition.

I walked free of the mist—and stood facing the Vanished Sea starships. They rumbled as if they were trying to wake up. The closest stood before me, curving up and up, three stories high. A sand-weaver mesh covered it in red and gold lace. So beautiful, like mathematical artwork. A weaver scuttled across its web, a little dragon no larger than my hand, with filmy wings that could spread out twice the length of its body. They didn't look strong enough to bear the weight of the creature in flight. The weaver climbed down the mesh, down and down, until it reached the ground. It dug its way into the desert, going below the ship.

Below the ship?

I sat up in the dark, gulping in a breath. What the hell? Where—?

"Bhaaj?" Jak's sleepy voice came from beside me.

I closed my eyes. I was in Jak's room at the Black Mark, sleeping in his criminally luxurious bed. I lay on my back, my pulse slowing. I'd been dreaming, just dreaming.

Jak draped his arm over my waist and mumbled, "Go to sleep."

"Yah." I couldn't get the dream out of my mind. Sand-weavers and ancient ships. The little dragon had dug under the ship. Weird. Sand-weavers never dug, they just wove webs and ate the ill-fated creatures that got stuck in them.

Digging. Under the ships.

"That's it!" I sat up again. "I should have seen it earlier."

"What?" The sheet rustled as Jak shifted position. Niches in the walls of his room emitted a faint red light. "Too much talk," he grumbled. "Come sleep."

"I can't." I pulled away the sheet and swung my legs off the bed. "I have to go to the Vanished Sea starships."

"Bhaaj." He turned on his back. "You are out of your fucking mind."

"Yah, probably." I went over to the chair where I'd draped my clothes.

As I dressed, Jak sat up in bed, rubbing his eyes. "Why now?"

"I can't waste time."

"Wait until morning."

"Morning isn't for thirty hours. Too long." I knew he meant the "morning" that happened halfway through the forty-hour night. It didn't matter. I needed to reach the ships before anyone else beat me to it. What mattered wasn't in the vessels, but under them. Ken Roy had told me as much without realizing it: *So much is a mystery about all these ruins, including the ships, not only in them, but below them, too.*

"They didn't need to go *into* the ships," I said. "They said Daan

Bialo could reach 'under-chambers' from outside the ships. At least, I think they meant from outside the ship."

"Under-chambers?" Jak yawned and fell back onto the bed. "You mean the Undercity?"

I tugged on my pullover. "I doubt it. Could we reach the ships from here? Probably not. It's beyond even the Maze." That warren of twisting passages lay at the edge of the Undercity, far out in the desert. Almost no one ventured into the Maze, and those few who did often couldn't find their way out. People died in there. It might extend all the way to the starships, but that would be ten to twenty kilometers of nearly impassable tunnels crammed with debris.

Unless—gods damn it! I'd bet the High Mesh wanted to clear the Maze so they could reach the starships via the Undercity. Even if they dug a route, which I doubted was possible, it wouldn't do them any good. The army had undoubtedly increased security now that they knew we'd been skulking around out there. If the Mesh tried anyway, they'd also pose a threat to the Undercity. This was *our* world. Not theirs. They had everything, all the advantages of their power and wealth. Damned if we'd give them any part of the Undercity, too.

Jak sat up again, looking resigned. "You really going out there?"

"Have to." I tapped my temple. "Got ideas."

"Bhaaj with ideas." He spoke dryly. "Terrifying."

I smiled. "It happens, eh?"

"Not go alone."

Normally I'd have told him not to worry. With all that had happened, though, I didn't want to go by myself. "You come with?"

"Need sleep," he growled. After a moment, he said, "Yah, I come with. And bring some Dust Knights." He sounded pissed, but I knew his tells. His anger wasn't for me. He wanted to kill whoever kept trying to pulverize my life.

"Bring Ruzik and Angel," I said. If they'd come.

He walked over to me, dressed only in the sheet he held around his hips. "We go get them."

I tapped the sheet. "Like this?"

He smiled, a sexy curve of his lips. "You think, Bhaaj. Think what's under there, eh? Can't have it again unless we make it back alive."

When he looked at me like that, I almost forgot everything else. "Got to make it back, then."

He laughed, a brief rumble.

As we dressed, I watched him discreetly. Although he might not be my husband by Cries law, he had a point when he said we were married. It wasn't by common law; we didn't live together enough. It was by the unwritten laws of the Undercity. Maybe someday we'd formalize it according to all the legalities, but neither of us needed documentation.

I slid my EM pulse revolver into my shoulder holster, and Jak slung a Mark 27 superconducting coilgun over his shoulder. Although massive compared to most guns, his weapon was lighter and sleeker than it had any business being. A civilian couldn't build a superconducting weapon that well. I had no doubt our cyber-riders could make one, but no way would it be that well-contained, especially given the power source and cooling system it carried. Jak was holding top-of-the-line restricted military issue.

I scowled at him. "What the hell?"

He met my stare. "Got a problem?"

"We'll get key-clinked in the darkest clink the army has." They didn't take kindly to black marketers stealing their tech.

"Isn't military." He even said it with a straight face. No wonder he was so good at poker.

"Yah, right."

He shrugged. "Got no ID."

All that meant was that whoever sold it to him knew how to remove a gun ID. "Even so."

"Even so." He crisscrossed several clips of extra ammunition across his torso.

I tapped my revolver. "Makes EM pulses. Screw up your electronics."

"Nahya. Protected."

The coilguns I'd used in the army had only managed partial shielding against EMP pulses. The technology had advanced in the years since, though. "You sure?"

"Yah, sure."

I was better off not knowing how he could be so certain that pulse revolvers wouldn't affect his gun. Plausible deniability was off the table for me knowing he had the weapon, but I had no idea if or how he'd used it before, and I wanted it to remain that way.

"Just be careful, yah?" I said.

"Yah."

We set off then, headed into the night.

I stopped in the darkness, silent and shrouded, holding my pack. A few meters away, Ruzik stood on guard duty, alone in the light shed by a torch. It glowed at the entry to the caves where his circle lived. Engravings bordered the entrance, desert vines painted in green and gold. The shape of the archway resembled the keyhole for an antique skeleton key, like many of the arches in these ruins. Whoever had built it probably had no idea their creation resembled the arches in ancient Ruby palaces even more than did arches in the modern palace where the Majdas lived now. These ruins contained memories of our history unmatched anywhere else among the star-flung worlds of humanity.

The rest of the Imperialate considered the Majdas the "true" heirs of Raylicon, the closest genetic match to our ancestors in the Ruby Empire. Except it wasn't true. Here in the Undercity, our genes hewed closer to the ancients than anywhere else. We kept our secrets to ourselves. Beautiful and dark, as magnificent as it was harsh, the Undercity existed like a fantastical world that rarely appeared to outsiders, a separate universe only those born here knew how to reach.

Darkness surrounded the cone of light where Ruzik stood. I knew that beyond him, inside the caves that his circle called home, tapestries softened the walls, rugs warmed the ground, and handmade furniture filled the rooms, all designed by Undercity artisans. None of that showed out here, only Ruzik, armed with a dagger. He looked bored. In my youth, I'd stood guard that same way. Each member of the dust gang I'd run with took a shift of several hours while our circle slept. It was our pact; we protected them and they made a home. Sometimes other gangs harassed or attacked us, but often a shift passed in boredom.

I didn't want to startle him; he'd come out fighting. Instead I whistled like a small lizard.

Ruzik turned in my direction, his hand dropping to the hilt of his dagger.

I walked forward. Jak remained in the shadows, on alert.

Ruzik's posture relaxed as I came into the circle of light. "Eh, Bhaaj. No sleep?"

"Got job." I regarded him. "Need Dust Knights."

He squinted at me. "Now?"

"Yah. Secret rumble."

"Big fight?" He looked more interested at that.

"Maybe." I motioned upward. "Out and up."

His forehead furrowed. "What?"

"Not Undercity. Above."

"Don't ken."

"We go above. Vanished Sea."

He stared at me as if I'd grown a second head. "To the desert?"

"Yah. Desert."

Ruzik stood processing that idea. I waited, not pushing. Very few of my people ever left the Undercity. We'd lived here so long, we'd changed. It wasn't just that we didn't think like people who lived under a sky; our actual neurological process had become adapted to this life. The first time I'd gone aboveground, my brain couldn't process the sight of the sky, desert, and horizon. I literally couldn't see it. It had taken about fifteen minutes for me to comprehend enough so I could walk to the army recruiting center in Cries, but it had taken me years to truly adjust. Even now, when I lived in Cries at the top of a tower, I still felt more at home in the aqueducts.

It wouldn't surprise me, however, if Ruzik and his gang had visited the desert. They were more daring than most and filled with insatiable curiosity.

"Why desert?" he asked.

"Visit starships. Ancient ruins."

He snorted. "Plenty of ruins here."

"Not ships."

"What is ship?"

"Brought our ancestors here."

"To the Undercity?"

"To the world. Raylicon." He'd know what I meant. Although very few of my people understood the concept of a planet, I required the Dust Knights to learn to read, write, and do math. Most found math easy, especially spatial perception, since we constantly used those skills, navigating the aqueducts in the dark. Reading took more time for some, but it came easily to Ruzik. He loved astronomy, even if he wasn't yet convinced its wonders actually existed.

"Why need Dust Knights?" Ruzik asked.

"Need to defend." I grimaced. "Above city wants me dead."

His puzzlement vanished. "We protect." He thought for a moment. "Tower and Byte stay here. Protect circle. Angel, come with."

"They asleep?"

"Yah. I wake." Mischief sparked in his gaze. "Angel will curse."

I smiled. "Jak did too."

Ruzik nodded as if Jak had reacted in the only sensible manner. "You stay here." With that, he strode into his home. I paced while I waited, agitated. Someone wanted to get rid of me, scare me off the investigation, or put me in a hospital where I couldn't keep poking around. Shooting me in a garden at night with no one else around took a certain level of planning. Throwing a knife in broad daylight was sloppier, suggesting they felt more pressure. I had no idea what was going on with the explosion in the tunnel, and that business with gas in the flyer looked like an act of desperation. They were in one hell of a hurry to stop my investigation. Why?

A rustle came from the shadows. I instinctively reached for my gun even as Jak walked into the torchlight.

"They come with?" he asked.

"Ruzik, yah." I dropped my hand. "Maybe Angel."

"We ready?"

"Almost." Tapping my gauntlet, I turned off my shroud. "Max, get me security at army headquarters in Cries." No way could we reach the ruins without alerting anyone this time, now that the army knew people had trespassed there. I didn't want anyone shooting us.

"I can do that," Max said. "But you will get a low-ranking aide at the night office. They won't understand why you want clearance. So you'll tell them to contact the Majdas. First they will want to do a background check, to verify your story, which will take time—"

"All right, I get it. Put me through to Majda security."

"Will do." Then he said, "I have the palace."

A woman's voice snapped out of my comm. "Major Bhaajan? This is Lavinda Majda. What's up?"

Ho! The colonel definitely wasn't a night security officer at the palace. She must have ordered the staff to put me through to her if I contacted them. "I'm going to the Vanished Sea starships. Can you clear me?"

"At least you're asking this time." She didn't sound pleased.

I looked up at the sound of footsteps. Ruzik, Angel, and Tower were walking out of the cave. Tower took her place on guard by the entrance, and Ruzik and Angel came to stand with Jak.

"I'm bringing three people," I told Lavinda.

"Who?"

"Protection."

"I need names. I have to put them into our system."

Ruzik stiffened and Angel scowled. Jak shook his head at me.

"I can't give you names," I said. "They won't come if you put them in your system. If I go alone, then this time when someone tries to kill me, I could end up eating dust."

"We'll send you guards," Lavinda said.

"Not a chance. The last time I trusted Majda, I damn near crashed into the City Arts Tower."

"I'm sorry." She sounded like she meant it. "But I can't clear you without knowing more."

I had no intention of giving her names. So I just said, "Fine. Out," and turned off my comm.

"Still go?" Angel asked.

"Yah." I indicated my pack. "With shroud." It probably wouldn't hide us from the guards now that they were on the alert, but at least they'd know we were coming. They wouldn't shoot me unless Lavinda told them to. I didn't think she would, but regardless, I had to act now, before these slimy bastards could hide, steal, or destroy whatever they were after at the ships.

My comm hummed. Startled, I looked down. Normally people couldn't locate me from outside the Undercity, but I hadn't yet turned my shroud back on.

"Max, who just commed me?" I asked.

"Colonel Majda."

Well, damn. "Put her through."

Lavinda spoke on comm. "Major, wait."

"I don't have time."

"Why?"

"I'll send you a report tomorrow." I couldn't say more on the comm. Gods only knew who else I'd be telling.

"If I give you clearance and whatever you do out there goes haywire," Lavinda said, "it's on my head. It could damage my career and my relationship with my family."

"I understand I'm asking a lot. But it's important." I'd worked for Majda for over two years. All that time proving myself had to mean something. "I'm asking you to trust me."

She swore under her breath, a lively assortment of expletives. I'd have to learn those. Max would quit saying I lacked originality.

Finally Lavinda said, "I'm putting clearance through for you and three other people, from the Undercity I assume."

"Yes, that's right."

She paused. "All right, it's done. The lieutenant at the site knows you're coming."

I closed my eyes with relief. "My thanks."

"Major, I can't guarantee the night guard out there isn't involved with whatever is going on," Lavinda said. "I heard about what happened with the flyer. I'm sorry. Neither Vaj nor I had anything to do with it. Someone sabotaged the craft while you were talking to us."

I hadn't expected an explanation. I hesitated, unsure how to respond without saying too much. I settled on, "Thanks for letting me know."

"Just be careful. Over and out."

"Over and out." I tapped off my comm and toggled on my shroud.

"You sure about this?" Angel asked.

"Could walk away," Jak said.

"Nahya." If the Majdas weren't involved, that meant someone was acting against the military I'd sworn my loyalty to as a soldier and still served as a civilian. I may have never felt comfortable with the Majdas, but they served the Imperialate well. Or so it appeared. If they were involved in this mess, then they'd lied to me big time and damned if I would let them sweep this away. Yes, they were more powerful than sin, but tough. I wasn't quitting.

"We go," I said.

None of them looked surprised. We headed for the desert.

✥ CHAPTER XVI ✥
BENEATH THE ANCIENT SEAS

We followed hidden back passages through the sleeping Concourse. On the main boulevard, a few nightclubs were still going, but our path remained dark and isolated. Ruzik and Angel knew the route well enough that I suspected they'd done this before. I couldn't shroud all four of us with one jammer, so we stayed out of sight until we reached the lobby at the end of the Concourse. A few lights shone there, glowing on the automated vendors selling water, food, and touristy items. A young couple sat slouched against the wall, sleeping. The smell of booze touched the air. The woman opened her eyes, waved at us, and went back to sleep. Apparently if you drank enough, even four Undercity thugs didn't faze you.

We walked up the stairs to the archway. At the top, we stood in front of the molecular airlock with its rainbow sheen.

"Ready?" I asked.

Angel had an odd look. She turned to me. "Time to go above."

"Yah," I said. "Time."

Ruzik spoke. "We do black belt tests at Cries Tykado Academy."

"What the hell?" Jak said.

I understood what Ruzik meant. He wasn't only talking about the tests. He used the word *academy*, a four-syllable word, but he wasn't ridiculing the school. He simply said its name, accepting that people in Cries spoke in a different matter. For the first time in history, one of our athletes offered to go to the city and work with a team there. The academy testers had planned to come to the Rec Center on the

Concourse, a neutral location. Ruzik's offer had great import—in the same way as what he and Angel were about to do, coming aboveground as my bodyguards as if this were perfectly normal rather than unprecedented in the known history of the Undercity.

"You sure?" I asked.

"Yah, we go," Ruzik said. "Meet them as equals."

I nodded my approval. "And so you are."

"Good," Jak growled. "We done with proclamations?" He exaggerated all four syllables of his last word. "Now we go beat up slicks at ships, yah?"

Angel laughed and Ruzik smiled. "Yah," Angel agreed. "Go rumble."

"Hope not," I muttered. I'd had enough rumbling these past few days.

We stepped through the membrane. The film slid along my skin, and then we were out, under the night sky. It arched above us, a deep black dome glistening with stars. In the distance, to our right, the towers of Cries gleamed. The desert spread out everywhere else, silent and vast, bathed in starlight.

Angel stared at Cries. "Sparkles."

"Pretty," Ruzik agreed.

"Yah," I said. They were taking this remarkably well, another reason I suspected this wasn't their first time out here. It helped that night surrounded us, hiding the blue sky with its sun and the true breadth of the desert. With the stars shedding their light across the landscape and our Undercity vision adapted to the dark, we could see well enough.

Ruzik motioned toward Cries. "We go there?"

"Not there." I indicated the land ahead of us. "Desert."

We set off running.

Breezes rustled our hair. We slowed to a walk as we reached the sand dunes. A little flying dragon trilled in the distance, its call drifting on the air, and the sweet scent of desert vines tickled my nose. The great silence of the desert muted our passage. We'd left Cries behind, until it was no more than a faint glow on the horizon to our right. Behind it, the Saint Parval Mountains rose into the sky, their peaks a jagged silhouette against the star-swept sky.

We followed what had once been the shoreline of a great ocean.

As we went further, lights became visible in the distance. We continued on, and the domes of the Vanished Sea starships seemed to rise out of the desert. We didn't shroud our approach, since it wouldn't be possible to hide well enough to evade detection, but we probably didn't show yet on a visual scan. We all wore black, blending with the night. Still, the guard there would have sensors that picked up our heat signatures, heartbeats, even the whisper of our feet in the shifting sands.

We kept walking.

The three ships grew larger. A hatchway glowed on the nearest hulk, and its light showed who else waited for our arrival—a stocky woman with her weapon out and ready. She wore chameleon fatigues, which had chosen a pattern that matched the desert, and she had the bars of a lieutenant on her shoulders. When I realized she held an ADS14 heat gun, relief flickered over me. ADS weapons were meant to control rather than injure. Her gun would heat up our skin enough to make us back off, but it wouldn't do any real harm. She wasn't armed to kill.

I kept my revolver holstered and walked into the light with my hands out from my sides. Jak didn't pull the coilgun off his shoulder as he came forward, and Angel and Ruzik left their daggers sheathed.

"Halt there," the guard said. "Identify yourselves."

I stopped. "I'm Major Bhaajan. You should have received clearance for me to enter the ships with these three guards."

She looked me over, scanning my revolver, then checked out Ruzik and Angel. She didn't seem concerned by the daggers, but when her gaze reached Jak, she scowled. "That coilgun looks like military issue. I thought your guards came from the Undercity."

"The Majdas gave us clearance," I told her, hoping that would be enough.

"I'll need to see your ID," she said.

ID sent, Max thought.

Jak, Ruzik, and Angel remained at my side, intent on the guard. Lights flickered on her gauntlets while she received my ID. Her stance relaxed and she spoke in a friendlier tone as she lowered her gun. "Which ship do you need to visit?" She seemed more curious now than wary.

I'd decided to start my search where I'd seen Ken Roy working yesterday. I motioned to the right. A second ship rose behind this first one, and beyond it, a third ship curved out of the ground. "The last one, the vessel on the end."

"That's the biggest." The lieutenant motioned for us to follow her. "They all look pretty much the same inside."

Her reaction intrigued me. I'd expected her to be more impassive or wary. Then again, maybe she liked having visitors. The night shift here was probably as boring as spit.

We walked alongside the ruins, silent in their ancient presence. Our footsteps rustled and the call of a pico-ruzik whistled in the sky. At a distance, the ships had looked as if they were glowing, but up close, I realized someone had strung lights along their hulls. I doubted the guard normally kept them lit; it made more sense to leave the outside dark and stay inside the craft, monitoring the area with the security equipment. Tonight, however, she'd turned on the lamps for all three ships. They looked festive, as if she were welcoming us to a party.

At the third dome, the lieutenant stopped before a rounded hatch and tapped in a code on a modern panel the army must have installed. As the hatchway shimmered into a molecular airlock, she stepped aside. "You can go on in."

Angel glanced at me. "I stay here."

I nodded, accepting her offer to act as a lookout.

Inside the ship, lamps lit the deck, the round bulbs strung along the bulkheads, each with the insignia of the Pharaoh's army on its stem. They looked like glowing flower buds.

Ruzik and the lieutenant took up positions on either side of the entrance, watching each other with obvious curiosity. Jak walked around, checking everything. The cabin was about thirty meters across. If any barriers had ever partitioned off the interior, they were gone, and nothing remained of whatever devices had equipped this craft. One area looked like it might have been a cockpit. A solid cylinder stood there, maybe a stool to sit on, and the pitted remains of what might have been controls glinted on the bulkhead in front of it. The dimensions were too large; no human sitting on the perch could reach the controls. A few other cylinders of different heights and diameters rose in various places, seemingly at random.

What struck me most were the patterns engraved in the

bulkheads, all silver, blue, and gold lines. They looped in overlapping circles that resembled wheels, crossing in so many places, you couldn't tell where one ended and another started. It reminded me of the "op art" I'd read about, which relied on illusions to fool the observer, creating a sense of movement or vibration. These gleamed in the light. I rubbed my eyes and squinted at them. The designs weren't moving, they just gave that impression.

"Dizzy." Jak stood at a bulkhead and traced his fingertip along the curves.

I joined him. "Seen before."

He glanced at me. "Where?"

"Can't remember." I *almost* recognized the curves. It was like the visual equivalent of catching a whisper at the edge of your hearing, words not quite loud enough to understand.

From the outside, the ship had looked half buried in the desert, but the deck where we stood was level with the ground. That suggested more of the ship lay below us, underground. I turned to the lieutenant. "Does this ship have another deck?"

"One other, yes." She came over to us. "Would you like to go down?" When I nodded, she knelt by a circle in the center of the deck and tapped a code against its edge. The circle slid aside, revealing darkness. When she tapped another code, lights came on below.

I peered at the lower deck. It looked just like this one. "How do we get down?"

She stood up next to me. "Professor Roy uses a ladder. I think he left several down there."

Jak snorted. "That's no help up here."

Ruzik came over, regarding the lieutenant with curiosity. "You made a hole."

"Need to go down." I looked around for materials to make a ladder.

Ruzik didn't bother. He crouched down, grabbed the edges of the circle, and lowered his body into the hole until he was hanging there.

"Wait!" the lieutenant said.

Ruzik let go and landed with a thud on the lower deck. It didn't seem much different than dropping from the midwalk of a large canal to its floor, except that here his landing didn't send dust swirling in the air. Instead, it vibrated and echoed through the ship.

"Strange acoustics." Jak spoke the Cries word in the Undercity dialect.

The lieutenant called down to Ruzik. "You all right?"

"Fine." He stood below us, looking around. "Empty." He didn't have to raise his voice. With the silence of the desert and the shelter of the ships, no sounds invaded this space. We'd have heard him if he whispered.

"Safe." He looked up. "Maybe."

"Maybe?" I asked.

He said, "Aboveground," as if that explained why nothing here would be safe.

"Ladder?" I asked. I wanted to drop down the way Ruzik had done, but the wound in my abdomen still ached.

"I check." He walked out of view.

I knelt next to the hatchway. "Ruzik?"

He came back and held up a knotted contraption constructed from desert vines. "Ladder."

"Toss up," I said.

Ruzik hefted up one end and I caught it. It was indeed a ladder woven from vines, with rungs and everything.

"I'll get some clamps," the lieutenant said. "I can attach it to the rim here."

As the lieutenant went to a pile of modern equipment by one bulkhead, Jak dropped to the lower deck. His athletic grace reminded me of our youth. He didn't have the muscular bulk of fighters like Ruzik or Angel, but he moved faster. Although he'd never enjoyed the rough-and-tumble as much as he liked games of chance, he was one hell of a fighter.

I went to the hatchway that opened into the desert. Angel was still outside, pacing back and forth as she scanned the area. She turned to me. "Eh, Bhaaj."

"We go down in ship," I said. "Lower level."

She didn't look surprised. The Undercity existed as a series of levels, from the Concourse down through the various canals all the way to the Down-deep, where the inhabitants had become so accustomed to the dark, they could no longer endure lights without protective goggles.

"I keep watch," Angel said. "Trouble comes, I let you know."

I nodded, satisfied, and went back inside. The lieutenant had clamped the ladder to the rim of the hatchway in the deck. When she gave it a hearty tug, it stayed in place.

"Thanks." I climbed down, then stepped off at the bottom and looked up. Her head was silhouetted against the light from the upper deck.

"You good?" she asked.

"Yah." I didn't want her down here while we explored. "Can you stay on guard up there?" Angel would keep an eye on her.

"All right." She sounded puzzled. "On guard against what?"

"Probably nothing. But three people came out here yesterday without clearance."

"I heard about that," she said. "I'll keep watch."

I turned to Jak and Ruzik. "We search."

"For what?" Ruzik asked.

Good question. "Don't know. I search. You guard."

Ruzik nodded, accepting the role of guardian with the ease of a leader who had spent his life protecting his circle. Jak, who had spent his life learning to clobber people at games of chance, seemed more intrigued by the ship. I turned in a circle, looking around. Those etched curves covered every surface of this deck, red, blue, diamond, gold, silver, copper, and bronze, especially in an area that looked like another cockpit. Instead of panels, this "cockpit" had a denser set of curves, as if they themselves were the controls. The beauty of it took my breath. That the patterns remained clear even after six thousand years said a great deal about both the construction of the ships and the efforts the army took to preserve them.

Jak came over to me. "You think that trio yesterday came to see this?"

"It's hard to say." I walked with him to the cockpit. "Max, can you bring up your recording of their conversation yesterday? What exactly did they say about finding the lower chambers?"

"Here it is," Max said.

A man's voice rose into the air. "Without Bialo, we can't go any further. Only he can reach the under-chambers from here."

Jak snorted. "They thought they could get to this deck from out there when the ship had both a guard and Ken Roy working here? Are they stupid?"

"No." I thought about the attempts against my life. "Desperate, yes, but I don't think they're fools. I get more the sense of smart people without experience in covert operations."

"Bialo hardly strikes me as a genius," Jak said. "He's tactless, underestimates people, and he can't play cards worth shit. The only time he's taken home winnings was that night you showed up, because you made him leave before he could gamble it all away."

"He's overconfident," I said. "But he follows through. If they came here expecting him to reach these under-chambers, whatever those are, then he can probably do it."

Ruzik stood listening to us. When I paused, he said, "Angel liked."

We both blinked at him. "You mean she liked Daan Bialo?" I asked.

"Yah." Ruzik shrugged. "Said he has good mox."

She thought Daan had charm? Seriously? "City slicks have city mox." I didn't mean it as a compliment.

"His mind," Ruzik told me. "Like Angel."

"He feels moods?" Jak asked.

"Yah." Ruzik spoke as if it were perfectly normal for Daan Bialo to be an empath.

Huh. I hadn't picked that up. Then again, I had no clue how to use whatever minor abilities I possessed. Something tugged at me about all this, but I couldn't figure out what. "Max, who said that about Bialo, that he could get into the under-chamber?"

"The man Bessel."

"Bessel!" I yelled. "That's it!"

Jak looked at Ruzik and Ruzik looked at Jak. "Loud words," Ruzik told him.

"Too much." Jak agreed. "Bring down ship."

I grinned and tapped my temple. "Loud word, good thought. Bessel. Bessel *function*."

They regarded me, waiting to see if I had something to say that made sense.

"Math." I motioned at the curves on the bulkheads. "Bessel functions, spherical harmonics, Laguerre curves, all those gorgeous eigenfunctions."

Ruzik frowned at me. "Jibber."

"It's *not* gibberish." I studied the curves. Yes! They showed stylized math functions using a system of curvilinear coordinates unfamiliar to me, one that distorted their appearance from what I knew. But I'd seen plots like this in my classes on differential equations, quantum theory, and Selei transforms. I'd also seen them in neuromathetics, that bizarre discipline we'd inherited from our Ruby Empire ancestors, an abstract combination of neuroscience, quantum physics, Hilbert space mathematics, and psychology. Our ancestors had learned it from the libraries on these ships, but they hadn't really understood it. Although we'd lost a great deal during the dark ages, some ideas of neuromathetics had survived, what we now called Kyle theory.

"Why is his name Bessel?" I paced across the cabin. "It can't be coincidence."

Ruzik spoke to Jak. "Jibber?"

"Not sure," Jak told him. "Bhaaj thinking."

"Ah." Ruzik nodded, apparently willing to accept the concept that I could think.

I stopped in front of them. "Ruby Empire science."

"Eh?" Ruzik asked.

"Dead science," Jak clarified.

Was it? I went back to pacing. Neuromathetics involved the quantum wavefunctions that described a human brain. That by itself wasn't a big deal; any physics student worth their salt could learn to calculate atomic and molecular wavefunctions. Where neuromathetics lost me was when it applied Hilbert space theory to the wavefunctions that described a thought. What happened when you transformed those functions to a different space, a "thought" space, just like we could transform functions that described the position of an electron to a space that described its momentum? You got Kyle space. I needed to find a theorist I could grill. I had an engineer's mind; I dealt best with concrete puzzles, not abstract mathematics.

"Max," I said. "Did you discover anything else about Bessel? You said he was a computer analyst as well as a personal assistant. What does he analyze?"

"He develops financial models to maximize investment profits."

"Oh." That seemed to be pretty much what everyone in the High Mesh did or wanted to do. "Nothing about him being a mathematician?"

"He must be, and a good one," Max said. "His models are quite successful."

"What about that facial recognition analysis you were doing? Is he a Vibarr?"

"One moment." Then Max said, "Yes, the analysis shows a high probability he is a member of a noble House, with Vibarr as the most likely."

"Hah! I knew it. They're challenging the Majdas."

"Seriously?" Jak said. "You think the Vibarrs want a war with the Majdas?"

"Financial war," I said.

Ruzik was listening closely. "You ken all this?" he asked Jak.

"Yah, some," Jak said.

"The Vibarrs started some project here," I said. "I don't know what. But something went wrong. Now they're afraid of losing control."

"Control of what?" Jak waved his hand at the ship. "A bunch of curves?"

"Maybe we're looking at this wrong," I said. "Or in the wrong place. They said 'under-chambers.' Ken Roy said something about that, too, about mysteries below the ships."

Jak looked around. "I thought this was the lowest level."

I went to stand under the hatchway to the upper deck. "Lieutenant?"

Her face appeared above me. "Yes?"

"Does this ship have a third deck below this one?"

"Well, no. Anything below where you are standing is buried in the desert."

"I think Professor Roy has gone under the ships."

"I don't know," she said. "I'm on at night and he works during the day."

Jak came over and scowled at me. "I hope you don't plan on dragging this Roy fellow out of bed."

I was tempted. But I didn't want to make Ken a target. "Lieutenant, can you help us look for a hatchway here? You know more about how to work them."

"Sure." She climbed the ladder to us. "I rarely come down here. There's no need during my shift."

"Sounds exciting," Jak said.

She spoke wryly. "Like watching sand dunes is exciting."

"Does anyone come out here during your shift?" I asked.

"Never. Except you." She glanced around the ship. "I suppose this place is interesting in a museum sort of way. It doesn't have much to see, though."

Ruzik came over to us. "Found another hatch."

"Show," I said.

He took us across the deck and indicated a circle in the floor. "Goes down, maybe."

The lieutenant knelt and tapped a pattern on the circle. "It does look the same."

Max, I thought. *Are you getting a record of the codes that open these hatches?*

Yes. However, I received a message from Majda security telling me that any records I make here are confidential and may not be distributed to anyone besides you, under penalty of my being erased as an EI.

Gods! I'm sorry. Erasing an EI was like killing it. I had backups of him, but they weren't the real Max. *Don't take any risks.*

No need to be sorry. It's standard army procedure. I'll be careful.

The lieutenant tried several codes. On the third one, the hatch slid open.

I knelt next to her. "Any lights down there?"

"Let's see..." She tried another pattern, with no success. She played her fingers across the rim for several moments, different patterns—

Light flooded the area below us.

"Hah!" She grinned at me. "There you go."

I peered into the chamber. It reminded me of caves in the Undercity, those where my people lived. A rock formation stood to the left of this hatchway, a cone of some sort. An artist had carved it into a totem of lizard heads stacked up on one another, several with their mouths open in roars, fangs bared, and others with their eyes closed as if they slept.

Ruzik looked down the hatchway. "Like aqueducts."

"It's a storage area," Jak said. "I see boxes. Or something."

Ruzik went to a nearby bulkhead, grabbed another ladder from a pile there, and came back to us. "You climb," he told me. "Need more healing."

So it came to this, the student took care of the teacher. He was right, though; I shouldn't jump. After I climbed the ladder to the cave, Jak dropped down next to me, making the coilgun bounce on his shoulder.

"I guard," Ruzik said. "Up here."

"Yah, good," I said. That put Angel on the first level and Ruzik on the lower. The lieutenant was up there too, but at least I had one person I trusted on both levels.

My breath caught as I looked around the cave. Ancient sculptors had carved the stalagmites rising from the ground into beasts with horns curling around their ears, and they'd sculpted the stalactites hanging from the ceiling into great winged lizards. In places where a stalactite met a stalagmite, forming a column, the builders had formed them into arches that supported the ceiling. Mosaics inlaid the arches, gleaming silver, gold, bronze, blue, purple, white, and red. Crystals also glittered in the stone everywhere, blue, white, and the purple of amethyst, not the perfect gems created in labs, but natural stones. The floor, level and smooth beneath our feet, was engraved with more of the math curves.

"Gods," I murmured. "This is gorgeous."

The cave contained nothing else—except three coffins against the far wall.

✢ CHAPTER XVII ✢
HIDDEN KEY

The boxes sat on a ledge that jutted out from the far wall at waist height. Jak and I approached with caution. Up close, they looked less like coffins and more like ornate containers constructed from a glossy black material and engraved with unfamiliar symbols. Rounded moldings ran along their edges, elegant despite the layer of dust that covered them. Each box had a transparent lid that rang when I tapped it. Crystalline bars lined their tops, all with intricate workings inside, gold and copper gears, crystal levers, ebony rods. A bronze crank engraved with spirals jutted out from the side of each, and bronzed hinges held the lids closed.

"Strange," I said. "Who would put these under a starship?"

"Probably whoever left the ships here," Jak said. "Or maybe our ancestors."

"They do look ancient." I tugged on the crank of one, but I couldn't move it. "Stuck, too."

Jak ran his finger along one of the lids, leaving a trail in the dust. "It seems dead."

I grimaced. "Or *for* the dead."

"Maybe we're looking under the wrong ship," Jak said.

I went back to the hatchway, where the lieutenant was watching us. "Anything there?" she asked.

"Just those boxes. Do you know if the other ships have chambers like this?"

"I can go look, if you'd like."

"Yes, thanks."

After she left, Jak said, "She's friendly." He sounded surprised.

I smiled. "Not all city slicks are arrogant. A lot are just normal people."

"Maybe. Still, Angel should follow her."

"Good idea."

He tapped his gauntlet, and Angel's voice came out of his comm. "Yah?"

"City guard comes up," Jak said. "Go with, yah?"

"Will do," Angel said.

"Good." Jak tapped off his comm.

Ruzik's head appeared in the hatchway above us. "The third box. Look. Not same."

Puzzled, I went to the third box. Someone had wiped it clean of dust.

"Good see," I told him. Even without enhancements, he had damn good eyesight. I pulled on its lever, and this one moved. The lid of the box opened on bronzed hinges.

"Hey." Jak set his hands on the rim. "I could lie in there."

"No!" I pushed away his hands. "Whatever happened to Mara Quida and Chiaru Starchild may be connected to these. We don't know what these do. What if it exploded you?"

He regarded me with something strange in his eyes, an intensity that for years I'd thought meant he was angry. I understood it better now. Whatever I'd said stirred up strong emotions, the kind he and I almost never expressed. "Eh, Bhaaj," he said. "Don't worry about me."

"Can't let you blow up. Need you to pull up the ladder when we leave."

He laughed, a good-natured sound. "For you, Bhaajo, I'll pull up the ladder."

I smiled, remembering we were married. Sort of. "Eh, Jako."

He touched my cheek. "Name is Mean Lean Jak."

"Yah, that too." It was, after all, how everyone else knew him. "I think the High Mesh isn't just trying to make new tech-mech."

"Maybe steal tech from these ships."

"Yah. But what is it?" I recognized nothing here. "Whatever blew up the tunnel affects matter on a molecular level, like a quasis field."

"A what?" Jak asked.

"Quasis," I said. "It fixes the wavefunction of matter. The military uses it during space combat to protect fighters from strikes and large g-forces."

Jak squinted at the boxes. "These aren't going to protect star fighters."

"No reason to put the pilot in a box. Their entire ship goes into quasis."

"And anyway, the military already has quasis tech." He touched the lid of the box. "Maybe they got it from these."

I considered the idea. "I don't think so. Our technology for space combat comes from our modern development of science. None of the engineering depends on the libraries of these ships. That only applies to neuromathetics."

"Mind sciences."

"Yah. Kyle." I felt like I was missing something.

My gauntlet comm hummed. Startled, I tapped on the comm. "Bhaaj here."

"We've checked the other ships," the lieutenant said. "Neither has a chamber underneath."

Angel spoke. "One deck on first ship. Two on second. Nothing else."

"Thanks," I said. "Come on back."

"Over and out," the lieutenant said.

A clang came from above us.

I looked up. "What the hell?" The hatch had closed.

Jak went over and pulled on the ladder. It fell down around his feet, minus the clamps that had held it to the rim of the hatchway.

I touched my comm. "Lieutenant, come in."

No answer.

I tried another channel. "Angel?"

No response.

I switched channels again. "Ruzik, answer."

Nothing.

Jak was stabbing at his own gauntlet. "I'm not getting any signals, either."

"Max, why aren't they answering?" I asked.

"I'm not sure," Max said. "I can't link to their comms. My signals are blocked."

The lights went out.

"Gods damn it," I said. "I'm really sick of people screwing with us."

"The lieutenant must have contacted the High Mesh." Jak sounded ready to hit someone.

"I think this is unlikely," Max said.

"Why?" I flicked panels on my gauntlet, trying to turn on its light. Nothing happened.

"I ran the recording of her last communication through my voice analyzer," Max said. "It shows none of the tension I would associate with someone in the process of betraying you."

The lieutenant hadn't struck me as false, either, but I didn't trust her anyway. "How accurate is your ability to analyze a voice?"

"It's reasonable," Max said. "For an EI in a gauntlet. Which isn't that sophisticated."

"Angel sounded normal, too." Jak's voice came from across the cave, along with the drumming noise of his fingers playing across his gauntlet.

"Is your light out, too?" I asked.

A man spoke in a deep, resonant voice. "Neither the light nor the comm are working."

"Eh, Royal," I said, greeting Jak's EI. "Can you reach Ruzik?"

"My sensors are blunted. I can't tell if he's there."

Max, toggle me into combat mode, I thought, testing my neural link. *I need my IR vision.*

Done, Max thought. Your biomech web is operational.

The cave became visible again, as a dim red glow created by the heat. The temperature was dropping, which meant the glow would soon fade and turn bluer. Jak's body blazed white over by the wall he was examining.

"You find anything?" I asked.

"These walls are porous." He scraped his fingers along a rocky projection. "Like stone lace. It reminds me of the Maze. Maybe we can make it to the aqueducts."

"It's kilometers away." I went over to him. "And the Maze is almost impossible to navigate even when you can see."

"Send one of your beetles," Max said. "If it's possible to reach the Undercity, the bot has a better chance of doing it."

"Smart idea." I took the red bot from my jacket. "Go, little droid."

It hummed away and buzzed around the cave until it disappeared into a crevice in the wall.

"Can you see anything?" Jak asked.

"You," I said. "You're like a fire on my IR. Try yours."

Royal answered. "It doesn't work. Whatever fried his comm is also jamming his other tech."

"Why isn't it jamming mine?" I asked.

Max said, "You have a military system that you regularly update through legal channels."

"What, are you saying mine isn't as good?" Jak growled.

"You get it on the black market?" I asked.

"A cyber-rider designed it, years ago." He ran his fingers across the curves engraved in the wall. "She does get a lot of her tech-mech on the market."

"You need an upgrade," Royal told him.

"First we have to get out of here." Jak continued searching for an exit.

I went back and studied the hatch in the ceiling. My IR vision blurred details, but it looked firmly in place. I couldn't jump high enough to reach it, and I didn't see any way to climb up there. The ceiling was smooth around the hatch, and none of the rock formations were close enough to access that part of the ceiling.

"This cave must have another exit," I said. "One that goes up to the desert."

Jak turned toward me in what, for him, must have been complete darkness. "Why?"

"Bessel said Daan Bialo could get here from the desert. If they can go in, we can go out."

Jak walked forward with one arm stretched out. "That also means if someone is out there right now, they could get in here while we're trapped."

I reached toward him. "They didn't know how to find it. Apparently they need Bialo."

"He could be with them." His hand bumped my wrist. "Or someone else who knows how to get into this place."

Taking his wrist, I drew him to my side. "We need to get out of here."

"Royal, did you get my comm working?" Jak asked.

"Not yet," Royal said. "It's getting worse."

"Max, what about my beetle?" I asked. "Has it found a way out?"

"It's traveling underground through a series of conduits. They go farther out into the desert, however, rather than toward the Undercity or up to the surface."

"That's no good," Jak said. "We need to find something we can use."

We started a detailed search, Jak working on one side of the cave while I did the other, looking for crevices, tunnels, conduits, any exit large or small. I found a few holes big enough for a beetle but nothing a human could fit through. I couldn't squeeze behind the coffins, which made it a lot harder to check the walls there.

"Someone had to put these boxes here," I said. My IR vision showed them as slightly bluer than their surroundings, which meant they were cooler. The difference wasn't enough to feel, but it made me wonder. Air in the aqueducts tended to be cooler than on the surface. I pushed my hand behind one of the boxes, running my fingers over the cave wall.

"I found a hole." I kept speaking so Jak could follow my voice. "Behind a box."

He came over, stopping when his hands hit the casket next to me. "Is it big enough for us to fit through?"

I felt around the opening. "Not a chance." My hand hit a much smaller box crammed onto the ledge behind the casket. "That's odd."

"You find a door?"

"Nahya." I picked up the box, which was a couple of handspans wide, and managed to get it out from behind the box. Even in my IR vision, it glittered. I lifted the lid. "It's a jewel box."

"Down here? Whatever for?"

"Hell if I know." I drew a medallion out of the box. It had what looked like an old-fashioned photo in its frame, but I couldn't see the details with my IR vision. "I think this is a picture of two people."

Jak stood next to me, staring off into the dark. "That's an odd thing to put here."

I rummaged through the box. "It's all keepsakes, holocubes, necklaces, that sort of thing."

"We should examine them all."

"Yah. I don't think carrying this is a good idea, though." We needed our hands free and able to maneuver, and my jammer took up too much room in my backpack to leave room for the jewel box. "We'll have to come back to check it out. I'll take the medallion and see if I can identify who it belongs to. Maybe they can tell us why this box is here." I slipped the necklace into my jacket pocket and returned the jewel box to the ledge.

"First we have to get out of here," Jak said.

Max spoke. "The beetle has found a route that goes toward the Undercity."

"Good." Relief trickled over me. "Is it large enough for people?"

"It's too small. Also, the bot had to go several kilometers into the desert before it found the passage to the Undercity. It's worse than the Maze. You'd never make it out there and back."

"Strange," Jak said. "Why all these underground mazes?"

"They crisscross the desert." I spoke absently as I explored the opening behind the casket, pushing the wall to see if anything moved. "They go all the way east to the ruins of Izu Yaxlan in the desert and all the way north to the Temple of Tiqual."

"Seriously? How the blazes did you know that?"

Damn! I'd let myself be distracted by this puzzle and the fact that Jak was one of the few people I trusted. I straightened up, facing him in the darkness. "I didn't just tell you that."

"Fine," he said. "I don't know it. How do you?"

"I figured it out during my investigation last year when we were fighting that ancient EI. General Majda doesn't like that I know. The information is secured." I shrugged. "Not that it really matters. The routes are blocked, apparently including any path from here to the Undercity."

"What routes?" His grin flashed. "Never heard of them."

I smiled. "Let's find one of these routes that doesn't exist and get out of here."

We continued exploring. The wall felt solid behind the middle box, but the third had a larger hole. We might be able to squeeze through if we could move the casket. I tried shoving it, and the lid slammed closed. When I pulled on the lever, the lid opened but nothing else happened.

Max, tell me the codes that the lieutenant used to open the ship hatches. I thought to him instead of speaking to make sure our connection still worked.

It depends on the location of your fingers, he answered. Put them in the position you would use to play a piano.

What's a piano?

An instrument. Never mind. Try the position you'd use for an old-fashioned computer keyboard.

I rested my fingers on the rim of the coffin. *What else?*

It also depends on the frequency and strength of the tap. Try three taps with your thumb, lightly, two harder with your index finger, three twice as fast with your smallest finger, two at the initial speed with your fourth finger, but half as hard, and three fast with your index finger.

I tapped the pattern. Nothing happened. *Did I do it right?*

You did it harder and faster than the lieutenant.

I entered the code more gently. Still nothing. *Was that right?*

I think so. Do you want to try the other patterns?

Yah, let's do that.

With Max's help, I tried all the patterns, tapping the rim of the box, its sides, the bottom, inside, all to no avail.

Jak continued to search the cave. I didn't realize he'd finished until he laid his hand on my arm. "Maybe you're drumming it in the wrong place."

I looked up with a start. "Did you find anything?"

"No luck. You have any with the box?"

"Maybe, if we can move it." I slid my hand over its engravings. They felt rounded by the years, though not much given their age. No wind, rain, or sun could affect them here, and the army probably had protections to keep them from degrading. "It would take forever to try every code on every part of this thing." I rested my hands on the rim and leaned against the box, closing my eyes. I'd barely slept for an entire Raylicon day. Exhaustion was taking its toll.

Jak stepped closer, offering the support. "You all right?"

"Yah. Just give me a second to rest." I remained standing, so I wouldn't doze off, and let my mind wander the way I'd learned during combat, when I desperately needed rest and couldn't sleep. Just a few moments to recharge...

The box hummed.

"Ho!" I jerked away from the rim and stepped back. Fast.

A glow came from the bars that bordered the top edge of the coffin, and sparkles ran along the gears inside like trains of luminance, casting their light across Jak's face.

"It's alive," he said.

"Or something." I touched one of the bars, and it thrummed against my fingertips.

"What did you do?" he asked.

I squinted at him. "I started to fall asleep."

He grinned. "You sleep, the box wakes up?"

"Can't say. I relaxed my mind. The box woke up. I don't know if it's connected."

Jak pushed the box—and it easily slid aside, uncovering the opening in the wall.

"Ho!" I said. "That worked."

"Weird." Jak peered at the lights sparkling inside the bars that lined the top of the casket. "Try thinking to the box again. See what happens."

"Think what?"

"I don't know." He laughed. "Ask it to make a steak. I'm starving."

What the hell, why not? I closed my eyes and imagined food in the box. Opening them, I found the box just as empty as before.

"Oh well." Jak scrutinized the hole he'd uncovered by moving the box. It had a ragged appearance, as if someone had broken pieces of rock out of the wall. The edges were sharp enough to suggest that had happened recently.

"Come on." I grabbed the edge of the hole and lifted myself through, feet first, easing into the area beyond. When I tried to straighten up, my head hit the ceiling, forcing me to stay bent over. A cone of rock stood to my left, and a stalactite hung from the ceiling like a stone icicle. Beyond them, ragged walls formed a tunnel with outcroppings partially blocking the way. It would be a tight fit, but we could probably get through.

"Looks passable," I said.

"You got your other beetle?" Jak asked.

"Good idea." I took the green bot out of my pocket. "Max, see if it can find where this tunnel ends."

The beetle hummed off into the darkness.

Jak squeezed in next to me and stood up, also leaning over. "Tight fit."

"Yah." I looked back at the box. "We should leave that light on."

"You got any idea how to turn it off?"

"I could try thinking at it."

"Like with the steak." He sounded amused, reminding me of Max. I smiled. "Come on. Let's go."

We made our way along the passage, which curved to the left. A noise scraped behind us as if the box were moving back into place against the wall—and the light vanished.

"Well, shit," I said.

"Yah." Jak didn't sound concerned.

Living in the Undercity, we'd made our way in the dark our entire lives. During my army years, I'd seen soldiers panic when forced to deal with places this dark and cramped. Claustrophobia never bothered me; closed spaces felt safer. Open vistas were another story; it had taken me years to adapt to all that distance.

A stalagmite blocked our way. I squeezed past it, easing along in the dim light of my IR vision. "Max, has the green beetle found a way out?"

"Not yet. This passage does continue, however."

"Any barriers?" Jak asked.

"So far, nothing you can't pass," Max said.

We kept on, navigating the obstacles. My neck and back ached from staying bent over.

"I think we're going upward," Jak said. "It feels warmer."

My IR did look brighter. "Max, has the beetle found an exit?"

"Not yet."

We kept going—until the passage ended at a vertical chute. It was so narrow we could climb it by squeezing our way up, pressed against the sides. After about two meters, I hit the top, literally, with my head. A rocky ceiling blocked the way. I braced myself in the chute, my knees and legs pushing against its walls so I could use my arms. When I shoved at the surface above my head, nothing moved. The green beetle buzzed around my hands, also looking for a way out.

"What's wrong?" Jak asked below me.

"We're stuck." I banged on the ceiling with my fist. "This has a lid."

"Hard to breathe." His voice sounded more distant, as if he had climbed back down to the passage. "You're knocking dust on me."

"Sorry." Grit saturated the air, making my breath rasp. It felt sandy. The dust in the Undercity and the sand above in the desert were essentially the same, both silicates with traces of aromatic benzene compounds, but the sand felt rougher.

"We must be close to the surface." I slid my palms along the ceiling, pressing here, pushing there. Nothing. I tried tapping in the codes for the hatches in the ship, with no luck.

"Be careful," Jak said. "It's all dunes out there. If you open the lid too fast, sand could pour down on us."

I stopped banging the ceiling. "Got any ideas how to open this?"

"Did Bessel and crew say anything about it yesterday?"

"They were looking for a way in. They didn't know how to find it." That probably meant this exit didn't show from the surface. "Max, do you know where we are?"

"I'd estimate about four hundred and eighty meters west of the third ship."

Jak said, "It felt like we went farther than half a kilometer."

Royal answered in his deeper voice. "We did. The passage doubled back several times."

"I don't think humans created this passage," Max said. "It seems natural, though in places it does look like machines widened it enough to let a person get by."

"Whoever used those ships is bigger than us," Jak said. "At least, based on the cockpit."

"If that area of the ship is a cockpit, then yes, they are probably much larger," Max said. "They would never fit through these passages."

"You think the army made this tunnel?" I asked.

Royal answered. "Not the modern army. The passage is ancient."

"I didn't detect that," Max said. "How do you know its age?"

"I'm basing my estimate on the texture of the rocks Jak touched on the way," Royal said.

"Bhaaj probably didn't touch the open areas as much," Jak said. "She can see them in IR."

"Maybe this exit uses Ruby Empire science," I said.

"Science is science," Jak said. "Even that Kyle crap."

"Even so," I said. "Our ancestors came up with some pretty bizarre disciplines."

"Daan Bialo seems like an odd person to depend on for knowledge that sophisticated," Jak said. "He's not exactly the brightest laser in the pack."

"Yet they need him." I didn't understand it, either. "He must have a talent we aren't seeing."

"He won the poker hand we saw him play," Max said.

"He's good at figuring out if someone is bluffing," Jak said. "His problem is that he won't stop when he's ahead, and he never stays ahead for long."

An idea was forming in my sleep-deprived brain. "Jak, is he good at bluffing other people?"

"Not really. His tells are too easy to read."

"So his only real talent at poker is that he reads the other players well."

"Ah. I see," Max said. "Angel is right; he's probably an empath."

"I'd guess a strong one," I said.

"Which helps us how?" Jak asked.

"I don't know." I rested my forehead against the wall of the chute and closed my eyes. *Open,* I thought. I formed an image in my mind of the rock barrier above me sliding to the side.

Nothing.

Open. This time I thought in Iotic. It made no difference; the ceiling stayed put.

"You all right up there?" Jak asked.

"Yah. Nahya. I don't know." I felt stupid trying to "think" something open. "I wish I knew what I did to activate that box in the cave."

"I have your physiological records," Max said.

"Was anything different about me during those moments?"

"Your heart beat slowed. Your brain produced alpha waves."

That sounded like a start. "What's different about alpha waves?"

"People tend to be calmer and more creative in that state," Max said. "It's easier to meditate. It can also occur during REM sleep, but you weren't asleep. Being in an alpha state can relieve stress and aid your mind-to-body coordination. However, you're also likely to make more mistakes, since you're paying less attention to detail."

"In other words, I was more relaxed."

"Yes." Max paused. "Actually you were producing a mix of alpha, theta, and delta waves."

I hadn't expected that. "I thought delta and theta only happened during sleep."

"Theta waves are a stage you pass through when going into a deep sleep. Some people produce them in a trance or meditating. They are also associated with the sense of well-being you have when you start to wake up."

I thought of the way I fell asleep every time I tried to do the empath exercises Adept Sanva had given me. "Does any of this connect to empathic ability?"

"Delta waves are the ones most associated with empathy. Humans mostly produce them while asleep or meditating, neither of which applied to you. People also seem better able to feel empathy while producing alpha or theta waves."

"Well that helps," I said. "I can't be an empath unless I'm asleep."

"You're always an empath," Max said. "Your brain doesn't produce only one type of wave at a time. Usually it's a mix. Some people have more delta activity than others when they are awake, and those people tend to have a higher capacity for empathy."

"I had no idea." I'd never been that interested, given that for most of my life I'd assumed I had no Kyle ability. My military records still listed me as having none; no one but the Majdas and Adept Sanva knew those records were wrong. "I'd always thought it was gamma waves that enhanced empathic ability. Whatever those are."

"Gammas relate to simultaneous processing of data from different areas of the brain," Max said. "They are associated with universal love, altruism, and other states people associate with higher virtues. You might say they relate to spiritual emergence."

I snorted. "No gammas for me, then. My spiritual consciousness is zero."

"Actually, you were producing them at one point after you activated the box."

"You're kidding."

"I don't usually," Max said. "Though I have been working on my sense of humor. But no, I'm serious. It seems you interact with these machines when your brain produces alpha, theta, or gamma waves, I'm not sure which. When you are fully awake and problem-solving, you tend to be in a high beta state. That may be why you can't work the mechanism above you right now."

"It's not a mechanism. It's a rock ceiling."

"Actually, it appears to be tech encrusted with sand that has hardened over time."

I rubbed my eyes. "So you're saying we can't get out unless I—" Unless I did what? "I have to meditate or something?"

"I'm not sure. What did you do when you activated the box in the cave?"

I thought back. "I tried this thing I used to do when I was sleep-deprived during extended periods of combat, sort of half sleeping."

"Can you do that here?"

"It's hard to relax when you're trying to make yourself relax."

Jak spoke from the tunnel below. "Think about that game we used to play in the grotto."

I remembered. In our youth, we often went to a grotto sparkling with crystals that reflected in its poisonous water. We'd curl together on the tapestry we brought and imagine secret thoughts for each other, then make love and fall asleep. When we awoke, we'd guess what secrets the other had been thinking. We were rarely wrong; it was as if we shared a mind.

I closed my eyes and tried to calm my body. I was wedged so tightly into the chute, I didn't even slip when my muscles relaxed. I imagined sleeping next to Jak, not in the grotto, but under the open sky on the planet Parthonia, in a field of flowers and waving grass, with the gentle sun overhead, easing out of our worries and into bliss...

"Bhaaj!" The voice stirred my mind.

"What?" I opened my eyes, groggy. "Jak, is that you?"

"Yah, it's me. You all right up there?"

"Sure. Why? What's wrong?"

"You've been asleep for almost three minutes, even after that scraping started."

"Asleep!" Then I realized what he'd said. "What scraping?" I pressed my hands against the ceiling—and it moved. When I pushed it to the side, it slid out of the way. Sand poured all over me.

"It worked!" I averted my head and coughed, trying to clear my nose. "Shit!"

"It's raining sand," Jak said.

"How do you know what rain is?" I rasped. "It doesn't exist on Raylicon."

He laughed, sounding more relieved than anything else. "I do have an education, Bhaajo, even if I didn't go to the university."

I'd always liked that about him, that he read so much. I looked up past the trickling remains of the sandfall—to a starlit night. "We're free!" I clambered out and stood beneath a sky rich with stars. They didn't twinkle as much as on planets with thicker atmospheres, but they glittered in more vivid colors. No glow showed on the horizon from Cries; it was late enough that the light pollution laws had gone into effect, requiring all buildings to go dark on their exteriors for ten hours during the forty-hour night.

In the opposite direction, the starships hulked in the desert, completely dark. We were indeed about half a kilometer away, farther than I'd been yesterday while I eavesdropped on Bessel, Sav Halin, and Detective Talon. Although dunes surrounded us, this small area had less sand.

Jak climbed up next to me. "This exit doesn't seem like it's been used in ages."

"Someone has been in that cave," I said. "They dusted off the third box."

"They probably reached it through the ship."

"Yah." It could have been Ken Roy or whatever other scientists studied the boxes. Bessel and the others knew about the chamber, though, so either they'd been there or they had information from some mole who was helping them.

"We need to get back to the ships," I said. "Find out what's going on before it's too late."

✤ CHAPTER XVIII ✤
SAND MESHES

"I don't see squat," I muttered.

With my mind linked to the green beetle, I flew over the ancient starships. I couldn't locate anyone down there, not Ruzik, Angel, the lieutenant, or anyone else.

Max, disconnect me from the beetle, I thought. The overlay of its view disappeared. I wasn't actually close to the ruins, but instead kneeling behind a dune about fifty meters away from them.

"What about the hatches on the ships?" Jak asked, crouched at my side.

"They're all closed."

"The ships look dark." He sounded pissed. "The lieutenant betrayed us."

"Maybe. But what about Angel? The lieutenant would have had to do something about her." In hand-to-hand combat, Angel could best pretty much anyone. I'd taught the advanced Dust Knights how to disarm opponents with guns, and Angel and Ruzik were wicked good at it. "I think someone else is out here, screwing with us."

Could be, Max thought. The beetle just found two people on the far side of the ships.

Ho! *Link me back up.*

Suddenly I was hovering above the first ship. Two people stood below, one on either side of the closed hatch. I could barely see them. They were probably wearing skin suits that matched the temperature of their surroundings, making them hard to distinguish with IR vision.

Max, bring me closer, I thought.

They could detect the beetle if it gets closer. Also, they are using some sort of smart-dust. I'm not sure what it does, but it's all around them.

On a planet? Ships in battle used "smart-dust," clouds of tiny droids that beleaguered the enemy. The dust corroded ships, hacked into their systems, disrupted their sensors, and in general harassed the offending vessels. Using it on a planet would cause more destruction than made sense, at least in this situation.

Smart-dust "grains" are little droids, I thought. *They're big enough that I'd see them clearly.*

Maybe smart-dust is the wrong word. It's floating around them.

That sounds like the spy dust corporations use for industrial espionage. It's actual dust.

It's hard to tell. The substance barely registers on the beetle's sensors.

We need to get closer.

You're sure you want to risk it?

Yah. But take it slow.

The beetle edged toward the two figures until I could see them better. Damn. That was Bessel and Daan Bialo.

Stop, I told the beetle, which was the same as telling Max, since we were all connected. *Max, try linking me to their dust.*

I don't know if it has that capability.

If it's anything like what the corps use, each grain has a picochip. All the grains can link together to form a rudimentary AI.

If I try to break into their network, I could end up getting hacked instead.

You always run that risk. You never get caught.

Usually I'm dealing with known systems with standardized protocols, like at the Majda palace. This is an unknown and probably experimental system composed of many tiny brains coded in ways that may be alien to me.

I have faith in you, Max.

Is that Bhaaj-speak for "Do it anyway?"

I'm afraid so.

I will see what I can do.

While he worked, the beetle hovered. Bessel and Daan still looked blurred, but I realized now it was because a translucent cloud of dust surrounded them.

They're communing with the dust, I thought.

If you mean, they're using neural links, Max thought, I'd say you are partially correct.

Why partially?

I doubt they can talk to the dust. It's not sophisticated enough.

Can you get me into the network without their knowing?

I can get you in. However, they will know you are there.

That's no good. Then again, maybe it didn't matter. *Max, if they knew I'd hacked their dust, could they do anything to me?*

Yes, I believe so. I don't think the dust incorporates safety codes. If you connect your brain to its network, it could kill you. And since I am essentially part of your brain, if you die, so do I.

Gods. What is it with these people? Imperialate law required anyone creating a mesh system to incorporate safety protocols that prevented the code from injuring humans. It told me a lot about the High Mesh, none of it good, that they chose to leave out such a fundamental protection.

Could the dust actually harm us, though? I asked. *If a grain only carries a picochip, that's far less power than my beetles have. And my bots couldn't kill anyone.*

Your beetles can't kill because you haven't weaponized them. However, that isn't what I meant. The danger isn't from a single grain, but the combined effect of them all. If several sent messages to your brain at the same time, they could cause a neuron to fire. If thousands sent messages, they could cause many to fire at once, sending you into a convulsion. If millions did it, the convulsions could kill you.

I grimaced. *Okay, let's not link to them.*

We have another problem. You've overused our neural link, specifically the accelerated firing of your neurons that speeds communication.

Translate that into plain talk.

You're thinking too fast. It can also damage your brain.

All right. Drop me out of enhanced neural mode.

Done.

I didn't feel different, except for a slight sense of dullness. *Max, that dust probably drifts around more than we can see. Is my beetle picking up grains?*

I'm sure it has. You and Jak probably have, too. It's why your tech-mech isn't working. It seems to affect mechanical more than biological tech, given that your biomech web still seems to be functioning.

So why doesn't it know we're hiding behind the dune? What one grain knows, they all know.

I think its range is limited. You're too far away for the dust on your body to link to the cloud brain. Without that, the grains have to act on their own. By themselves, they're pretty dumb.

Good. Disconnect me from the beetle. Then let it go dead for three seconds.

If I do that, it will drop out of the air like a rock.

That's right. It's like knocking on the door. Set the beetle to escape after the three seconds.

Done.

Abruptly I was with Jak behind the dune again. Across the desert, the clink of my bot hitting the ground cracked in the deep silence of the night.

"You hear something?" Jak asked in a low voice.

"Yah. My beetle. I'm using it as bait." Only a few seconds had passed while I talked strategy with Max. Or with myself, if I accepted his claim that he was a part of my brain, which I wasn't sure I did, but we could leave that for another time. "Bessel and Daan are on the other side of the first ship."

"Angel must still be inside."

"I think so. The lieutenant also." I peered around the side of the dune, to make it harder to see my head silhouetted against the sky. Sure enough, Bessel and Daan appeared, searching the area on this side of the ships, which meant my beetle had mostly likely succeeded in taking off again, frustrating their attempts to locate it. Although the blur of dust surrounded them, I could tell Bessel carried a rifle.

Jak lifted his coilgun, sighting on the two men. "Easy shot."

"No." I laid my hand on his arm. "No killing."

To my relief, he didn't argue, he just lowered the gun.

"I'm surprised they aren't trying to hide," Jak said. "Or at least evade us."

Max spoke in a low voice. "They probably assume you're trapped in the cave."

"They shouldn't assume anything." If I were their CO, I'd have their hide.

"They seem pretty inexperienced," Jak said. "But they still have the advantage. We can't get any closer without showing ourselves."

He had a point. The army kept the region around the ships clear of rocks and dunes. As I studied the area, the hatchway on the third ship opened and a woman stepped outside.

"Shit," Jak muttered. "That's Talon."

The detective motioned Daan and Bessel over, and they stood conferring together. I strained to hear their words. My tinnitus had almost cleared up, but even the faint ringing interfered with my ability to listen. *Max,* I thought. *Can you crank up my hearing?*

No. You need to finish healing or it could do permanent damage.

I grimaced with frustration. Almost nothing worked tonight. After Talon went back inside the ship, Daan and Bessel resumed their search along the ruins.

"It doesn't make sense," Jak said. "They aren't even using their gauntlet sensors."

I told him about the spy dust. "I'll bet it's screwing up their tech-mech, too."

"That's a pretty crappy defense, if it also works on them."

"Indeed," Max said. "They should have coded it for neural recognition."

"You mean tell it how to distinguish friends from foes?" I asked.

"Essentially," Max said. "It should recognize their brain waves."

"We need to get Ruzik and Angel out of there." Jak rested the mount of his coilgun on his shoulder. The readout on his weapon glowed dimly, just enough to show its full charge. Whatever had gummed up our tech-mech hadn't yet penetrated the gun's shielding.

"Jak, no lethal force." I said. "You kill anyone here, it's murder, plain and simple."

"Not them." He motioned toward the desert south of the ships. "I can make a distraction."

"Ah. Smart idea."

Jak sighted on the dunes and fired, his shoulder mount absorbing most of the recoil. Although the gun produced no flash or smoke, the explosive projectiles went at supersonic speed, with a great cracking sound. When they hit the desert, the dune exploded in a geyser of sand.

Bessel and Daan spun around, staring to the south. "What the fuck?" Daan yelled.

"For gods' sake," Jak muttered. "He's as bad at sneaking around as he is at playing poker."

Bessel grabbed Daan and they sprinted toward the third ship. As Talon opened the hatch, Bessel pushed Daan inside and followed him. Talon fired her automatic rifle, hammering the desert where Jak's shot had landed. Jak and I took off in the opposite direction, to the north, running in a crouch behind the dunes. Talon fired again, this time closer to where we'd been a moment ago. With a grunt, Jak skidded to a stop and fired to the south, sending up clouds of sand and filling the night air with grit. Yah, good. I hoped it played havoc with their spy dust.

Talon returned fire, aiming to the south. When she stopped to reload, Bessel stepped out and took over with another gun. Jak and I sprinted in the other direction.

"Where go?" Jak asked.

"First ship." Given how Bessel and Daan had focused on that one, Angel and the lieutenant were probably trapped inside.

"Take too long to go around," he said.

"Not if I cut across the open ground." Talon, Bessel, and Daan were all in the third ship, which I hoped meant they couldn't detect me, given the problems with our tech-mech. I climbed over the dune and slid down the other side. Sprinting across the open area, I kept the bulk of the second ship between me and the third ship. Talon and Bessel had stopped shooting. I suspected they fired more to prevent combatants from approaching than because they expected to hit anyone in the dark.

I reached the hatchway of the first starship and tapped on its panel. Of course the damn thing wouldn't open. I couldn't bang against the hull or yell for Angel, not without alerting Talon.

Jak came up beside me. "Need combo code."

"Yah." I tried the combinations Max had recorded from the lieutenant, but none worked.

"Come on," I muttered. "Open!"

"Maybe it needs brain waves," Jak said.

"I don't have time for weird go-to-sleep shit." Someone fired a burst of shots from the other side of the ships, moving in our direction. "Can you distract them again?"

"Yah." Jak faded into the dark.

If Angel and the lieutenant are in there, Max thought, the lieutenant must have entered the combination that opens the hatch. Maybe the hull remembers it.

Of course this panel knows. I tried another combo, with no success. *Unfortunately, I don't.*

I don't mean the panel. I mean the hull itself, or at least the sand-weaver web on it.

What? More shots came from the south, Jak's coilgun it sounded like.

I've been trying to figure out why the army cleans the webs off these ships.

They corrode the hull.

They covered these ruins for thousands of years and the hulls survived just fine.

Are you saying the webs remember stuff? I don't see how.

They sense movement. That's how the sand-weaver knows it caught dinner. The web also remembers patterns that lured in its prey. If anything walks on the web, it learns the motions that resulted in that success and recreates the patterns to tempt in more prey.

You think it remembers the code taps? No wonder the army was always cleaning the hulls.

I don't see why not. The taps are small, like the motions of their prey.

So how do I get the web to give me the code?

I'm afraid I have no idea.

I ran my palm over the sand-weaver mesh. *All right, sneaky web, I'm an unsuspecting prey. Entice me into your trap.* I tapped a code against the web. Nothing happened, except I heard more gunshots to the south. Moving fast, I tried other codes, with no success.

Tap harder, Max suggested.

I used more force. Still no luck. Frustrated, I did the same code again and again—

The web began to pulse, just slightly. I wouldn't have noticed if I hadn't been so attuned to the feel of it under my fingers. It was giving me back a code, not the one I'd just tapped, but a similar pattern. I memorized the sequence and tapped it into the access panel.

Nothing. Someone fired a burst of shots, this time even closer. Another few moments and they would reach this side of the ship. I tried again—and the hatchway irised open.

Ho! Finally something had worked. I edged my way inside, keeping my revolver drawn. I couldn't see squat. *Max, what happened to my IR filters? Turn them back on.*

They don't work, he thought. *The dust—* His thought cut off.

Max?

I spoke in a low voice. "Angel? Lieutenant? It's Bhaaj."

"About time," Angel growled in the darkness.

"Where are you?" I asked.

Two figures stepped forward, into the starlight pouring through the open hatchway.

"You all right?" I asked.

"Yah, fine," Angel said.

"Someone locked us in here," the lieutenant said. "My gauntlets don't work."

"You hear those people firing?" I said. "They've got some dust that screws up tech." I edged to the hatchway, scanning the area outside while I kept the lieutenant in my side vision. Somewhere to the south, more bullets hammered the night. I didn't know how much ammo Talon and Bessel carried, but Jak was probably almost out of his.

We stepped outside and moved along the northern edge of the ships. "How many hostiles are out there?" the lieutenant asked.

"At least three," I said. "Maybe more. They were trying to open the hatch on your ship when we distracted them."

Angel stepped past me, her knife drawn. "Enough of this." She sounded pissed.

"We need to get back to the city." *Max,* I thought. *Can you contact the red beetle?*

No answer.

"Max?" I asked. "Can you hear me?"

"Yes," he answered. "It's the conduits from your gauntlet to your wrist socket that aren't working. That's why you can't access the neural functions of our link."

It sounded like pretty soon my gauntlets wouldn't work at all. "Can you reach the red beetle we sent out into the desert passages?"

"No luck."

"And Ruzik?" Angel asked.

"Third ship," I said.

"We get him," Angel said. "Finish off these slicks."

"Armed with what?" the lieutenant asked. "Your knife? Against automatic rifles?" Apparently she understood at least some of the Undercity dialect.

Angel didn't answer, but her gaze glinted and so did her dagger. The lieutenant had the sense not to push it. The gunfire was more sporadic now. Talon didn't seem to know our location, which meant the dust hadn't warned her. If this was technology created by the High Mesh, their R&D department needed an overhaul.

When we reached the third ship, I caught Angel's arm. "Slick inside."

She slowed down, and I brought my EM pulse revolver up by my shoulder.

"If you fire that," the lieutenant said behind me, "it will trash my heat gun. Its electronics aren't shielded against the directed EM pulses your gun produces."

"Sorry." I didn't even know if my gun still worked.

"Damn it, Major." Anger crackled in her voice. "I don't want anyone hurt. Your friend with his let's-pretend-it's-not-a-fucking-stolen-super-gun better be exploding sand and not people."

"I don't want to hurt anyone," I said. "Neither does Jak." I hoped.

"I can't believe you got Majda to okay this," the lieutenant muttered.

She and I both. I didn't want Lavinda to pay the price if we screwed up here. "I'll be careful. You have my word."

Angel said nothing, just kept edging toward the third ship, staying within the cover created by the curving bulk of the second ship. The staccato bursts of the gunfight had ceased.

We moved forward, slow and careful. Closer to the hatch—

Detective Talon lunged out of the ship and fired straight at us.

✥ CHAPTER XIX ✥
IN THE DUNES

I threw myself sideways in the instant Talon's boot appeared in the hatchway, a fraction of a second before she fired. She aimed at me, apparently assuming I was the greatest threat. This time she used a pulse revolver, and its serrated bullet slammed the ground, just barely missing my foot when it blasted a small crater in the rocky soil. As I crashed into the second ship, I fired at Talon, but she was already ducking back into the ship.

"Gods damn it," the lieutenant said behind me. "Nonlethal force, people."

Angel stayed in the front, utterly unfazed by the gunfire. When she stepped forward, I grabbed her muscled bicep and pulled her back into the protected dent where the hull of the second starship curved in to meet the bulk of the third.

"Stay here," I said. "Cover."

"Can't stab shit from here," Angel growled.

An explosion came from the south, probably Jak's coilgun. No one returned fire. Talon lunged out for another shot at us—and Angel threw her knife.

The blade whirred through the air like a flash of starlight. It hit Talon's right arm, and the detective grunted as she dropped her gun and jerked back into the ship. Never pausing, Angel sprinted forward, scooped up the detective's revolver and her dagger, and darted back to us, her actions so fast, I barely had time to breathe.

"Well, I'll be fucked," the lieutenant said. "You're wicked good with that knife."

"Eh?" Angel continued to scan the area, her fist gripped around Talon's gun.

"Talon," I yelled. "We have your weapon. Come out. Bring Daan with you."

In response, Talon leaned out just enough to fire a machine gun in our direction. She wasn't moving as steadily as before, and we were still in the cover of the ships, so she missed. It didn't matter; she'd made her point. We didn't have her damn weapon, at least not all of them.

"We get Ruzik," Angel said.

I spoke in a low voice. "Max, can you locate Ruzik or anyone else in that ship?"

"My sensors aren't operating well," Max said. "I'm getting life signs from two people on the top level, but I can't tell if anyone is on the lower deck."

"Two armed fighters with good cover, and one more in the desert," the lieutenant said. "They have at least two automatic weapons. We have two revolvers, and maybe your friend's coilgun, but he must be almost out of ammo. It's crappy odds, Major."

"Yah, but we're better at this," I told her. At least, I hoped we had that advantage. "What is it about those three caskets? Are they why these people want to kill us?"

"I have no clue," the lieutenant said. "I didn't even know they were there."

Angel stepped forward. "Get Ruzik."

I pulled her back. "You go out, you get shot. Need better way in."

"That ship has no other way in," the lieutenant said.

"What about the sand-weaver webs?" I asked. "Can they affect electronics inside the ships, or do they just pick up tapped patterns and give them back?"

Silence.

"Lieutenant?" I asked.

"I have no idea what you're talking about," she said.

"Fine," I said. "Could this thing you have no idea about affect equipment inside the ship?"

Another silence.

"Lieutenant, we're almost out of time." No more shots came from the south, so either they'd quit fighting or they were dead. No, Jak couldn't be dead; I'd feel it. The curve of the third ship wouldn't give us much cover if someone moved to the dunes opposite us.

"Sand-weaver meshes can't activate anything," the lieutenant said. "Their webs pick up vibrations and give them back to you. They might try to echo music, if it shakes the mesh. That's it."

"We'll have to go in ourselves, then," I said. "I'll go first."

"No," Angel said. "You stay. I protect." With that, she took off for the hatchway.

I swore under my breath and sprinted after her, with the lieutenant bringing up the rear. I expected Talon to fire, but she didn't appear in time. We stopped at the hatchway and edged into the ship, our weapons ready. Starlight flooded the interior—the empty interior.

"Where they go?" Angel asked.

I glanced at the lieutenant. "Any way they could hide in here?"

"Just the lower deck," she said.

"Ruzik." Angel's eyes glinted. "He kill."

Damn! If Ruzik was trapped down there, he'd be more pissed than a cop chasing a dust rat back to the aqueducts. So much for the lieutenant's nonlethal force.

"Come on." I went to the hatch for the lower level.

The lieutenant joined me. "They couldn't have opened it. They don't know the codes."

"They know a lot they shouldn't. They must have someone on the inside at Majda."

"That someone is a traitor." The lieutenant knelt and tapped in the code for the hatch. As it slid open, we all moved back. No sound came from below.

"Angel, you stay here," I said.

She turned to me, her gaze dark. "I go. Get Ruzik."

"Need you here." I tilted my head at the lieutenant. "Not trust."

Angel clenched her fists, but she didn't refuse. The lieutenant said nothing. She had to realize I hadn't ruled her out as the person who warned Talon and crew we were here.

"You go first," I told the lieutenant. "Call out if it's safe."

Her face was pale in the starlight. We both knew I'd just made her a target for anyone down there. Even so, she lowered herself through the hatchway and dropped to the deck. The thud of her landing vibrated through the ship. No other sounds came up to us, no words, no fighting, no gunfire.

"Lu Ten, move back," Angel called. She waited, then fired Talon's gun down the hatch. Bullets slammed into the deck below.

"Stop!" I grabbed her arm. "Hit someone."

"Ruzik not under." She tapped her temple. "I'd know."

"Hit Lu Ten."

"Nahya. Aimed at other place, not her."

"Lieutenant?" I asked. "You all right?"

"I'm fine," she said. "Why did you fire?"

"Threaten enemy," Angel said. "Warn them. Behave."

"For fuck's sake," the lieutenant said.

"Is anyone there?" I asked.

"No one," she said. "This deck is empty. They must have gone into the cave."

I spoke softly. "Max, can you analyze the lieutenant's voice for stress?"

"She exhibits tension," Max said. "However, I don't think she is lying or being coerced."

"You want me to open the lower hatch?" the lieutenant called.

"Can you?" I asked.

Taps came from below, then more, then again. "Damn it," she said.

"What's wrong?" I asked.

"This one is jammed shut," she said.

"They might have gone out the way Jak and I did," I said. "Along the tunnel."

"Need to find Jak," Angel said.

"Yah." I hadn't heard any gunfire for some time.

"Let down the ladder so I can climb up," the lieutenant said.

I didn't move. If I closed the hatch, she would be trapped until either her shift or this fight ended and someone let her out. She might escape if she had the Kyle ability to work the ancient tech-mech, but it seemed unlikely. The army wouldn't waste an empath on night duty here. Although I didn't want to trap her if she had nothing to do with Talon, neither did I want to worry about her stabbing me in the back, literally as well as figuratively.

Angel was watching my face. "Bring Lu Ten."

"You trust?" I hadn't expected that.

"Not foe." She shrugged. "Slick, yah. But trust."

Angel had a good sense of people. And she'd been trapped with the lieutenant for some time in the other ship. If Angel trusted her, that told me all I needed to know. I let down the ladder, and the lieutenant clambered up to us. As she stood up, she spoke firmly to Angel. "No more shooting in the dark, all right?"

Angel frowned at her.

"Not shoot at her," I told Angel.

"Nahya hit," Angel told her. "Ken."

The lieutenant looked at me. "I didn't get that."

"She said she knew she wouldn't hit you."

"How could she know?"

"Empath," I said.

The lieutenant's forehead creased. "That's not possible. She's from the Undercity."

I'd become so accustomed to knowing that one third of our population were empaths, I'd forgotten almost no one else knew, only a few people high in the military or government.

I said only, "Let's go."

The three of us stood outside, by the third ship. It not only provided partial cover, it was also closer to our temperature than the desert. Even if Talon or her people still had working IR vision, they'd have trouble seeing us against the hull.

I scanned the empty dunes. No one. "Max, have you managed to contact Royal Flush?"

"He still isn't responding," Max said.

It could mean anything. Probably the dust was interfering with Jak's tech. Very few people knew how to get in touch with Royal, and normally he responded only to Jak. He'd never let me down, though. If Jak was injured or worse, Royal would let me know. I tried not to think what else his silence could mean, that he was also injured. Or worse.

"They were in the south," I said.

"No more shooting," Angel pointed out.

"No more ammo." I hoped that explained the silence.

"It sounded like suppression fire," the lieutenant said. "They were going for neutralization of the enemy rather than a kill."

Angel repeated the word, exaggerating syllables. "Neu-tra-li-za-tion? Nahya. Smash!"

The lieutenant squinted at her. "What?"

I said, "She thinks you're being sarcastic with the word neutralization, that you're trying to avoid saying they might be dead."

The lieutenant exhaled. "Gods, I hope not."

"Need choose," Angel said. "Find Ruzik, find Jak, find slicks. Which?"

Good question. Jak and Bessel were probably in the desert, whereas Talon and Daan, and I hoped Ruzik, were underground. I had no doubt that Angel and Ruzik were more experienced at underground combat in the dark than Talon and her crew.

"We go get Jak," I told Angel. "You find Ruzik and other shooters."

"Yah, good," Angel said.

I described the exit from the tunnel Jak and I had used to escape the cave. She set off then, running to the west in a zigzag path across the open area around the ships. No shots flared from the dark, and within seconds, she'd disappeared into the dunes beyond the cleared region.

The lieutenant motioned toward the south. "We should go that way."

"Yah." I walked with her alongside the ship. When we reached its edge, I scanned the desert to the south, a rolling landscape that made me think of a sleeping giant lying half buried in the sand. The dunes glinted where starlight reflected off flecks of crystal. Although they didn't offer great cover against bullets, they could conceal us, which would help.

Together we sprinted across the bare stretch of land between the ships and the dunes. It took only seconds to cross that open area, but it felt endless. We scrambled up the closest dune, slipping in the sand, and slid down the other side into the valley between it and the next ridge.

"How did the army clear the area around the ships?" I asked. Given the large size of the dunes, they must have moved a lot of sand.

"They didn't," the lieutenant said. "That area has always been clear."

I supposed it could be natural; the character of the Vanished Sea varied. Sometimes the land stretched in swaths of rocky ground with outcroppings sticking up like skeletal fingers, and other times it rolled in these dunes that seemed to go on forever when you were in them.

"Max, can you locate where we heard the last gunfire?" I asked.

"Roughly," he said. "Go east about two hundred meters and also head south."

Moving southeast, we stayed behind a large dune. We kept sliding down its slope, which meant we had to angle our way up again. My calves ached from walking in the sand. I was tempted to tie my boots to my belt and go barefoot. Spiky stone-vines spread their tendrils everywhere, though, with poisonous thorns. If they stabbed my foot, I wouldn't walk anywhere for days. We left a trail, but at least the sand muffled our steps.

The lieutenant spoke in a low voice. "Do you have water?"

I unhooked the bottle from my belt and handed it to her. She obviously hadn't expected a hike in the desert. Maybe that supported Angel's trust in her. At this point I didn't know what to think. I just wanted to find Jak. Alive.

"You need to go more south," Max said.

I angled southward. The land looked as clear to me as a black-and-white image. Those of us bred in the Undercity had more photoreceptor cells in the retinas in our eyes, enhancing our night vision. Silver radiance flooded the landscape, and the sky was glorious, with the Milky Way stretching above us in a sparkling arch.

Max spoke again. "This is where I estimate the last shots came from."

I let out a relieved breath. No one was lying here, wounded or dead.

"Major, look." The lieutenant knelt down several meters away. "I found a trail."

I joined her. Footsteps did indeed show in the sand, headed northwest.

"Do your visual filters work?" I asked. "Anything that lets you see this better?"

"None of my tech-mech works." She stood up next to me. "I'm good at tracking, though. I'd say two people went this way."

Two people. Jak and Bessel? "Lead on. I'll follow." I wanted her walking in front of me, where I could keep watch on her.

We resumed our trek. The desert smelled wild here, away from the sterile atmosphere of the ships. The pleasing scent of the resin that protected the rock-vines wafted on the breeze, more delicate than the plants that produced it, faintly smoky, like a campfire.

"Bhaaj," Max said. "Your path is drifting south too much."

"Lieutenant, are you still following the trail?" I asked.

She turned to me. "I think so. It's hard to see."

I caught up to her and we peered at the ground. Something had disturbed the sand, smearing it out, as if more people had joined the original two walkers. Except not all the prints looked like they came from feet. If I hadn't known better, I'd have said the larger impressions were from gigantic three-toed claws. Hell, maybe I didn't know better.

"These look like ruzik prints," I told the lieutenant.

"I thought you said he was in the ship."

"I don't mean the person." I looked up at her. "Real ruziks. The big lizards."

She stared at me. "You think they dragged off your friend and Bessel?"

"I can't say. I've never seen one." I didn't know much about the creatures, except that ancient warriors supposedly rode them, which I found hard to believe. "If they're like the smaller lizards in the Undercity, they won't attack humans. They don't care about us as long as we don't bother them." I sincerely hoped neither Jak nor Bessel had pissed them off.

"I see two different trails." She motioned to the south. "One goes out that way, deeper into the desert." Turning west, she said, "This one comes from human feet, I'm almost certain."

It didn't look as obvious to me, given how blurred the prints were, but I didn't trust her enough to split up and let her go on without me. "Let's go west, then."

We set off together. The silence of the desert enveloped us, huge and vast. A creature cawed somewhere, its cry riding on the wind. Every now and then, stubby foliage crinkled under our feet.

Wait. I stopped, listening. Was that a voice in the distance?

The lieutenant came back to me. "Did you hear that?"

"I think it was Royal Flush."

"Who?"

"Jak's EI."

She straightened up. "Then we're going the right away."

I hoped so. I hadn't heard Jak, just the EI. We started walking again.

A man's voice drifted on the air. "Are you sure?"

"No," another man said. "I can't tell."

"I don't know either," a third said, his voice deeper than the others. "My ability to determine our direction is corrupted by the spy dust."

I let out a breath I hadn't realized I was holding. The third speaker was Royal, the second was Bessel—and the first was Jak. I stopped and closed my eyes, swept with relief.

The lieutenant shifted her feet, the sound whispering in the sand. I opened my eyes to find her watching me.

"This Jak," she said. "He's more than a friend, isn't he?"

"Husband," I told her. "Sort of."

"I hadn't realized."

Neither had I, at least not until the past few days.

We hiked up the next dune. Near the top, we lay on the ground and inched forward until we could look into the valley between this ridge and the next. Two men stood at the bottom, Bessel holding a machine gun and Jak with the coilgun slung over his shoulder. No ruziks were in sight, which most likely meant I'd misread the tracks in the dark. I felt sorry for Bessel; with Jak, he'd caught a far more dangerous animal. Bessel should never have allowed him to keep the coilgun, not even if he believed Jak had run out of ammo. Jak was probably letting him think he had the upper hand to see what he could find out from the younger man.

Some of their words drifted to us.

" . . . need to go north," Bessel said.

"We're east of the ships," Jak said.

"That's not true," the lieutenant murmured. "We're southwest of them."

Bessel said, "I'm almost certain we're south of them."

"Royal, can't you tell?" Jak asked.

"No," Royal said. "I can't tell shit."

Max spoke in an almost inaudible voice. "Royal is lying. Even with damaged tech, he could track where they've gone. We are south and west of the ships."

"EIs can't lie," the lieutenant said.

Ah, such naivete. I'd never heard an AI lie, but EI systems as sophisticated as Max and Royal were another story, especially when they'd been evolving for so many years, Max with me and Royal with Jak. I had no doubt Royal could tell any falsehood he deemed necessary to protect Jak.

"They're trying to confuse Bessel," I said. "Keep him separated from Talon."

"We need to get closer," she said.

"They will see you as soon as you start down this dune," Max said.

"You should go," I told the lieutenant. "Pretend you've come to help Bessel. Say Talon shot me, Angel is trapped, and Ruzik disappeared. Talon is looking for him while you look for Bessel."

She stiffened. "Are you nuts? This Bessel person won't believe that."

"Sure he will." Bessel's inexperience was painfully obvious. "You distract him. I'll come around from a different direction."

"He has no reason to believe I'd help him."

"Why not? I came here with three Undercity thugs, including Jak down there, the owner of Raylicon's notorious casino. Of course Talon—a respected corporate officer—came to the rescue."

"Your husband is the casino king?" She sounded as if she didn't know whether to be appalled or fascinated. Then she blinked. "What does that make you?"

"Never mind." I motioned toward them. "Just go."

"Well, why not?" she muttered. "You have Majda clearance. This is all surreal anyway." She stood up and strode boldly down the slope, sliding in the sand. "Hey!" she shouted.

Bessel spun around and jerked up his machine gun. "Stop there!" he called.

"It's me," she said. "Lieutenant Ackerson."

"Come down slowly," Bessel said. "You make a fast move and I fire. You understand?"

"Yes, sure." She slowed down, holding her hands away from the innocuous heat gun on her hip. I headed south behind the dune, close to the top of the ridge so I could keep watch on them.

"I see you caught one of them," the lieutenant said. "Good. I was worried about you."

Bessel's aim faltered. "What happened to the others?"

"The younger woman is still trapped in the first starship. Talon killed the PI and went after the other man that came with them."

"Damn it!" Bessel said. "I told Talon I couldn't be involved if they hurt anyone."

I wondered if he realized he'd just told the lieutenant his threat to shoot her was a bluff. I hoped Jak didn't believe Talon had really killed me.

The lieutenant continued her approach until she reached him, all the time fabricating a tale about how she'd searched the dunes by herself. I kept moving, south of them now. Bessel was facing east, and I wanted to get behind him, which meant I'd have to leave the concealment of this ridge. Would he see me? In the dark, humans tended to have better peripheral than straight-ahead vision, but given his above-city eyesight, he probably couldn't see well in any direction.

I edged over the top of the dune and down the other side. Bessel lowered his weapon as he spoke with the lieutenant. He seemed to accept her story, too willing for his own good to believe that everyone from the Undercity was a criminal, ready to attack the good people of Cries.

I paused, too worn out to ignore my exhaustion. Sliding my hand under my pullover, I felt my bandaged torso. Damn. I was bleeding again. The meds in my body masked the pain and the stimulants kept me going, but I couldn't keep this up for much longer.

The lieutenant continued to distract Bessel, "catching him up" on the situation. I crept across the open desert. Although Bessel had his back to me, he kept glancing around. I went flat to the ground during his scans. Although Jak never turned in my direction, I recognized his stillness. He knew I was here. I doubted I could go much closer without revealing myself. I'd only have seconds then to reach Bessel and disarm him. My enhanced speed might still work, given that my internal hydraulics were mostly biological. Unfortunately, I had to ask Max to find out, and right now I could only speak to him, which I couldn't risk. Blasted spy dust. It would be valuable if they could figure out how to make it affect only the enemy, instead of happily gumming up everyone's tech.

Gritting my teeth, I inched forward, slow and silent.

"We'll return to the ships," Bessel was saying. "We should get moving."

"I can't see where I'm going in the dark," Jak told him.

Yah, right. Jak had better night vision than me.

Bessel motioned with his machine gun. "Just walk. I'll tell you where to go."

Keep stalling, I thought.

"Fine." Jak spoke as if he were uneasy, which sounded so fake I would have laughed if I hadn't been trying to be invisible. He limped toward the west.

"The other way." Bessel did another scan of the terrain.

I lay flat on the ground, trying to blend with the desert.

Bessel turned to the lieutenant. "Did you hear someone?"

"No, just us," she said.

I couldn't keep this up much longer. As soon as Bessel was facing away from me, I jumped to my feet and sprinted toward them, raising my gun—with enhanced speed. Yah!

I knew the moment the lieutenant saw me. Her posture tensed, just barely.

"What the hell?" Bessel swung around—

I fired once, twice. I hated shooting when I was running; it was never accurate, contrary to all those corny adventure shows the city kids loved. Fortunately, I wasn't trying to hit anyone. The bullets slammed the ground and sand jumped into the air. Bessel fired his machine gun, but with me dodging back and forth through a haze of grit, his shots went wild. More sand leapt into the air.

It took only seconds to reach Bessel. I tackled him, crashing into his body. As we fell, I rolled him over my hip, throwing him on his back. He lost his gun, but he managed to jump to his feet. Grabbing my arm, he spun me around while he tried to trip me. As I twisted free, he scooped up his gun, losing precious time. He had no time to aim; he just swung the thing at my head. I was already twisting away, so the blow slammed my torso—and one of my ribs broke with a great crack.

Ach! Pain exploded in my upper body. Gritting my teeth, too pumped with adrenalin to stop now, I yanked the gun out of his hand and threw it toward Jak. My nanomeds went to work, flooding my body with more painkillers. I'd pay the price later, but right now it kept me going. Catching Bessel in a tykado hold, I threw him hard and slammed him onto the ground.

Bessel groaned and stayed on his back. I stood there, a straggle of hair in my face, staring at him, my fists clenched. With a groan, he climbed to his feet, watching me, his body tensed.

"I'd stay put," Jak said in a conversational voice. "It's never wise to piss her off. And this gun of yours still has a few rounds left."

I glanced over to see him aiming his captured machine gun at Bessel.

"Eh," I told him.

"You all right?" Jak asked.

"Yah," I lied. I'd need more than a few hours in the hospital this time.

"So." The lieutenant considered Jak and Bessel. "Either of you see any ruzik lizards?"

Jak blinked at her. "Well, uh, no."

Bessel stared at her in disbelief. "You're working *with* these two assholes?"

"I serve in the army," she said coldly. "They cleared these people to come out here. Not you, just them. You're trespassing on a secured site and committing gods only know what other crimes."

"Well, shit." Bessel made it a statement on life and the universe in general.

"Come on," I grated out. "We need to find the others."

✥ CHAPTER XX ✥
QUARRIES

We searched the entire area where Jak and I had come up to the desert from the tunnel. The ancient hatch had closed; we couldn't find it even when we stood on the open space where we'd climbed out of the passage. Jak and the lieutenant continued to look, but I had to stop. My meds couldn't completely numb my injuries, and I slowed us down. I sat on a rock and Bessel sat on another across from me with his wrists locked behind his back. He looked as tired as I felt. I didn't think my rib punctured my lung, but it hurt like hell. It would have been a lot worse if my meds hadn't upped my dose of meds. I kept my revolver out, hoping Bessel didn't notice that the "ready" light on its grip had gone dead. Spy dust: the gift that kept on giving. At least my meds still worked, which made sense since they were biological molecules.

So we sat, at an impasse. To distract myself from the pain, I said, "I wouldn't have expected a member of the Vibarr noble House to take work as the personal assistant for a corporate exec."

Bessel raised his head. "What?"

"You aren't in the line of succession," I continued. "Otherwise, you'd never have agreed to go undercover, working for Lukas Quida. You're only part Vibarr, an illegitimate child."

"Go to hell." He sounded like he was gritting his teeth.

I felt like I was there already. "Bessel isn't your real name. You picked it for your cover." I studied his face, trying to read his tells. "Your files list you as a mesh analyst, but that's not quite right. You like math. I mean, you *really* like it. That's why the Vibarrs picked you for this job. And you hoped it would help you move up in the hierarchy of the House."

His mouth opened. Then he closed it. "How did you figure all that out?"

I hadn't, not for certain, until he just verified it. "I'm good at my job. So are you. Math, I mean." I motioned toward the starships in the east. "Talon and her bosses wanted you to decipher all those curves inside the ships. You're the brains, the scholar." I thought of the way he'd fought me in the dunes. "You've learned martial arts, but you've never used it to defend yourself before."

"You can't know that." He sounded more like he was trying to convince himself.

"Sure I can." The way he fought reminded me of the students from the Cries Tykado Academy. Undercity gangs rumbled to survive; city kids considered it a sport. Bessel was well trained, yes, and I was exhausted, but the reason I'd bested him was the slight hesitation in his responses. "It's the same with the way you shoot. Your family encouraged you to learn. Maybe you joined them in hunting for sport. But you never expected to shoot a person."

He spoke coldly. "I'm perfectly capable of defending myself."

"Yes, you are." I was thinking as I talked, judging from his reactions how close my words hit to home. "You joined this project because you wanted to solve the puzzle of the ships. You never thought you'd be involved in criminal actions, especially not murder."

"Murder?" He stared at me. "What are you talking about? I haven't killed anyone."

"What do you call what happened to Mara Quida and Chiaru Starchild?" I was really guessing now. I was also getting pissed. "If their deaths aren't murder, I don't know what is."

"They shouldn't have died!" His voice broke. "I swear it. We don't know why it happened."

His response felt like a punch to the gut. Until this moment, I hadn't realized just how much I'd hoped to find Quida and Starchild alive. "Your work killed them."

"No! I just solve the equations. I swear it. I had no idea the quarries could operate on their own. None of us knew."

Quarries? I didn't think he meant prey. Rock quarry didn't make sense, either; there weren't any within hundreds of kilometers. I took a guess. "You came up with that name yourself, didn't you? Because quarries sure as hell aren't what the military calls those boxes in the cave."

"I don't know what the military calls them," he said. "Mara came up with the name quarry."

So he did mean the coffins. "Quasis box." I pretended I knew what I was talking about. "They produce a quasis field when someone gets into them."

His forehead creased. "What are you talking about?"

Damn. I'd guessed wrong. "I meant the quasis produced by the boxes."

"It isn't the same."

Well, then, what was? "I know it's simplifying things. But the quarries do fix the quantum wavefunction of whoever uses them."

He frowned. "You understand wavefunctions? That can't be right."

"Why can't that be right?"

"You're from the Undercity."

Not this again. "And of course we're all too stupid to learn quantum theory."

"I didn't mean that. But you have no schools there, right?"

He had a point, at least in terms of formal schools. He was also being an idiot. "How do you think I became an officer in the Pharaoh's Army? You can't without a university degree. I'm a mechanical engineer. Of course I learned physics."

He squinted at me. "But not really, right?"

"What do you mean, 'not really'?"

"I mean, you didn't really complete all the requirements for your rank, right?"

"You know, I really get sick of this fucking attitude." I was too tired to be diplomatic. "How else would I have received my commission or promotions?"

He spoke awkwardly. "I figured it was a program meant to give your people representation in the army, even if it meant letting you slide on requirements."

"Then you figured wrong." *Temper*, I told myself. *Don't lose your cool. Keep him talking.* "I had to meet every requirement and then some. No one ever let me slide on anything."

"I'm sorry. I don't intend to insult."

Could have fooled me.

"I don't understand you," Bessel said. "How did you get out of the cave? We locked the hatch in the ship. You had no way to open it. The only other exit is impossible for you to use. You can't activate the quarries, and if you can't move them, you can't get past them. Even if you did manage to reach the tunnel, you couldn't get out at the end."

"Why not?" If he knew I came from the Undercity, he also knew I'd grown up underground. "It was easy."

"That can't be true." He yanked on his bonds as if he needed to gesture with his hands to give his protest more power. "You can't operate the ancient machines."

I saw what he was getting at now. "Because only Kyle operators can do that."

"You're not a Kyle." He shook his head. "You don't have the neural structures or training. Hell, none of us have the training. Daan Bialo has no idea what he's doing. I was surprised to find out he was a Kyle. He isn't from any noble House. My genetics aren't pure Vibarr, so I don't have enough Kyle DNA to activate the machines." Anger crackled in his voice. "No way in hell could anyone from the Undercity do it. We're talking genetics here, Major. None of those dust gangers you brought tonight have the right DNA, and we know you aren't a Kyle. We've seen your army records. You have no trace of Kyle ability."

I remained still, showing no reaction, but my pulse surged. He'd just answered my question about the Majdas. Vaj and Lavinda both knew my army records were wrong, that I did have Kyle ability, but they were the only ones. Had they been involved with the High Mesh, they wouldn't have held back that information, not when it could be vital to dealing with me. I couldn't even fault Bessel's assumption that the Undercity population didn't include Kyle operators. I hadn't expected many of my people to be psions, either.

I said only, "You shouldn't have access to my records. Stealing classified files is a crime."

He just looked at me, but he had a terrible poker face. He was finally realizing his words implicated him in both treason and murder.

A lizard whistled in the dark. I whistled back. A moment later, Jak appeared with the lieutenant and Angel, materializing out of the night like ghosts haunting the desert.

"Eh," Angel said. She had Bessel's machine gun slung over her shoulder.

"Ruzik?" I asked.

"Nowhere." Her answer held a world of tension. I knew her tells; she might appear impassive to the others, but she was afraid, not for herself but for Ruzik.

"We didn't find anyone," Jak said.

"They're probably trapped underground." Bessel had it right; Daan Bialo wasn't trained to use his abilities. I'd literally had to put myself to sleep to free us. Ruzik was probably a stronger psion than Daan, but the others had no clue and he certainly wouldn't tell them.

"We should check the cave first," I said.

Jak motioned at Bessel with his coilgun. "Get up."

Bessel stood, moving slowly to keep his balance with his hands locked behind his back. "I know you're out of bullets," he told Jak.

Jak tapped the control panel on the gun—and the menu lit up, showing the status of his magazine. He had two shots left. "I programmed it to show a false empty."

Bessel stared at him. "What for? You could have captured me. I'm out of ammo."

Jak just shrugged. He didn't need to say he let himself get captured.

"You weren't trained for this," I said to Bessel. "You never expected any of it to go so far."

"Never. Mara Quida was my sponsor at the Desert Winds." Grief crackled in his voice. "She's an amazing person. I admired her. I would never have hurt her."

"Then what happened?" Jak said. "Where is she?"

Bessel looked as if he felt ill. He said nothing.

Ah, hell. My voice tightened. "You've seen her body, haven't you?"

He turned a stark gaze on me.

My anger was growing. "You all played with technology you didn't understand. Those coffins under the ships—and I do mean coffins, even if that wasn't their original purpose—the High Mesh turned them on and people died."

Bessel gaped at me. "You know about the Mesh, too?"

Yah, surprise. I'm good at what I do. "The Mesh tried to get control here, but you all botched it. Even that spy dust isn't ready. Sure, it's better than the military version, except for one 'little' problem. It screws up your tech, too." I let out a breath. "I believe you never meant to hurt anyone. But the monsters you got into bed with will do anything to get what they want."

Bessel spoke in a strained voice. "We never expected you to figure any of this out."

I met his gaze. "What happened to Mara Quida and Chiaru Starchild?"

"I don't know!" Anguish showed on his face. "I swear, we didn't intend to use the quarries."

"They disappeared from their homes. They weren't anywhere near the cave." Insight hit me. "They're both strong Kyle operators, right? That's what activated the quarries."

"They couldn't have activated the quarries," Bessel said. "They were too far away. Your brain waves have to interact with the machinery. You have to be right next to it."

"What are you talking about?" Jak asked.

"The explosions in the Quida and Starchild mansions," I said. "They're connected to those coffins we found in the cave. Those boxes somehow blew up Mara Quida's bedroom and Chiaru Starchild's kitchen. And I'll bet they exploded the tunnel with Daan Bialo in it."

"Daan?" Bessel asked. "Nothing happened to him. He's with us tonight."

"That's because I figured out it was about to happen." I hadn't figured out shit, I'd acted on instinct and been lucky. "I threw him out of the way."

"You witnessed the explosion?" Bessel's voice snapped with a sudden intensity. "Where? When? How did you survive? How did you know it was happening?"

Good questions. I spoke slowly, thinking. "Quarry. Quantum stasis and something else. That's what the name means, isn't it?"

Bessel just looked at me.

"Listen, asshole," Jak told him. "Answer her questions. Cooperate, or the cops will hit you with every fucking charge they can bring against you."

Bessel swung around. "How would you know? They're more likely to lock you up."

The lieutenant spoke. "He's right, Del Bessel. I can speak for you to the authorities, let them know you helped with the investigation. Otherwise, you're looking at a long prison sentence."

He stared at her. After a moment, he turned to me. "Quarry means quasis carrier."

"Carrier?" I hadn't expected that. "How can quasis carry anything?"

"Like the carrier of a signal. Fix the wavefunction and recreate it in a new place."

The implications finally penetrated my sleep-deprived brain. "Holy shit." No wonder they were willing to kill to keep this knowledge to themselves.

"What the hell?" Jak said at the same time the lieutenant asked, "What does that mean?"

"Think about what quasis does," I said. "It fixes the wavefunction of whatever it affects. Everything in the universe is described by a quantum wavefunction. We look solid because the wavelength is so tiny, even our best instruments can't observe it. But in theory you could calculate it for any object. That's what the quarries do, right? They map out the wavefunction of their target."

"That's right," Bessel said in a subdued voice.

"So what?" Jak said. "It sounds like an incredible waste of bandwidth."

I spoke quietly. "Because if you digitally transmit that map to some other place and recreate the wavefunction there, you're producing an exact copy of whatever that wavefunction defines."

"I still don't get it," the lieutenant said.

"Jump from place to place," Angel said.

Apparently she'd been learning Cries-speak. It didn't surprise me, especially after what happened in the tunnel with Daan. She'd want to do whatever she could to avoid it happening again, including understanding the people involved.

"It's a bit like old-fashioned three-D printing," I said. "Except you're producing an exact copy down to a molecular level. You make a copy of the person in another place."

"Printing people is impossible," the lieutenant said. "The copy dies."

"That's because three-D printing can't perfectly replicate a living organism," I said. "It isn't sophisticated enough to make a copy identical to the original down to an atomic level. But suppose you had an *exact* map of the organism? That's the quantum wavefunction. If you could transmit that map, you could make an identical copy at the receiving end." The more I thought about, the more convoluted it seemed. "That's assuming the receiver had the necessary materials and energy. If they did, they could reproduce the organism by placing every molecule in exactly the right place and state. They'd produce a clone of the original in a new location."

"That's ridiculous," Jak said. "Even if you could reproduce an organism from its wavefunction—which I don't believe you can, not with our current technology—that doesn't mean it would be alive when you finished."

"No," Bessel said, his voice strained. "It doesn't."

I stared at him, feeling ill.

"It sounds bonkers," the lieutenant said. "How would you deal with the moral implications? Is the copy the same person? Is it self-aware? Do you keep both copies? Gods, if you sent the quantum map through Kyle space—" She stopped, drawing in a sharp breath.

"Hell and damnation," Jak said.

The lieutenant didn't need to finish; we all knew what she meant. If you sent the quantum map through Kyle space, you could reproduce the person anywhere a Kyle gateway existed. It meant you could instantaneously transport human beings across interstellar distances.

"If it worked," Bessel said. "It would be a technological breakthrough that dwarfed any humankind has created since we found our way to the stars."

I made myself stop gritting my teeth. "But it doesn't work, does it? It kills instead."

He answered in a flattened voice. "That's putting it kindly."

I forced myself to speak calmly. "You figured out the theory. But understanding equations and using technology are worlds apart. This tech is ancient. No one understands it. What possessed you to use it at all, let alone on people?"

He met my hostile stare. "You're assuming we tried to transfer people. We didn't."

"Yah, right," Jak said. "What, someone tricked you into using the boxes?"

"No!" Bessel said. "None of us knew this could happen. It's just— we woke up the quarries. We poked them in Kyle space." With a shudder, he added, "They poked back."

The lieutenant said, "You mean those boxes in the cave are alive?"

"No. Maybe." Bessel exhaled. "Hell, I have no idea."

I went over to him. "You need to tell me exactly what you've done. In detail."

He hesitated. "I figured out what the quarries do by translating the symbols in the ships."

"Why hasn't anyone else?" I thought of Ken Roy. "Like the scientists who come here."

"They work a lot more slowly."

Jak spoke coldly. "Apparently for good reason."

Bessel winced. "We didn't plan on trying the process on living organisms."

"What process?" I asked. "What did you do?"

"I discovered that only Kyle operators can operate the quarries. The only Kyles in the High Mesh were Daan Bialo, Chiaru Starchild, and Mira Quida. So they helped us figure out the boxes. Our contact on the Majda staff arranged for us to enter the cave when no one else was out here at the ships." Bessel held up his hand as if he were holding a small object. "You link what you want to copy to the quarry and activate the quarry. It makes a new version of the object inside itself."

"That sounds way too easy," Jak said.

Bessel hesitated. "We just tried transferring a rock from Mara's house, to see what would happen. She used her mind to activate the quarry."

I stiffened. "And that caused the explosion? Why would she do it during the gala?"

"No, not at the gala," Bessel said. "We did it days before the gala."

It still made no sense. "A rock can't appear out of thin air. You need materials to build it."

"That's Talon's field," Bessel said. "Her degree is in chemistry. She analyzed the rock and provided the necessary minerals in the quarry box so it could replicate the rock."

I couldn't help but be intrigued, despite the fact that we were stuck in the desert with people trying to kill us. "Did it work?"

Bessel shifted his weight. "Yes and no."

"Not an answer," Angel said.

"The quarries only work," Bessel said, "if you send the quasis map of what you want to transfer through Kyle space."

"Why only Kyle space?" Jak asked.

"Because location there is determined by your thoughts," Bessel said. "So the object isn't moving through space. If you're thinking about transferring the object between two different places, those places are on top of each other in Kyle space. Also, it lets you transmit the map with better accuracy and precision than with three-D printing."

"So how did Mara send it from her house?" I still wasn't coming clear to me.

Bessel had guilt written all over his face. Definitely not a poker player. "With a console in her bedroom. We placed the rock on the console and she used the Kyle mesh to contact the quarry."

"Is that why Mara's room blew up?" I still wasn't coming clear to me. "I thought you said this happened before the gala."

"It did. A copy of the rock appeared in the quarry here, like we'd hoped." Bessel stopped, then said, "The copy immediately disintegrated into dust."

I tensed so much, the tendons in my neck felt like steel. "What about the original?"

He spoke with difficulty. "Apparently the process eliminates the original, maybe so no duplicates exist. The original blew up, just a small explosion."

Jak looked ready to shoot someone. "In other words, both the copy and the original were destroyed."

"Yes." Bessel ground out that one word.

"So you tried it on a human being?" I asked. "Are you fucking insane?"

"We didn't!" Bessel said. "The box activated itself."

"Itself?" I asked. "What does that mean?"

"No one set it up to do a transfer." He took a ragged breath. "It happened several days later, with no warning. It tried to transfer Mara from her bedroom into a quarry box here."

"Not good," Angel said.

No shit. She was a genius at understatement.

"Did it?" the lieutenant asked. "Transfer her, I mean."

"We found dust in the quarry, like with the rock," Bessel said. "More this time, enough to account for a human being."

I stared at him. "Are you saying it tried to make a copy of Mara Quida, and that copy turned to dust? And then it blew up the original Mara in her mansion?"

Bessel answered in a hollow voice. "Yes."

"Gods almighty," the lieutenant said.

"That couldn't happen." I didn't want to believe any of this. "Why would the quarry try to transfer her? And what materials did it use to build the copy of her body? If none of you planned it, doesn't that mean no one put any chemical or biological material into the quarry to use in making a copy of a human being?"

"That's right." His hand shook as he pushed back his hair. "So the quarry pulled material from the cave wall behind the boxes. It constructed her body out of rock. It did the same to Chiaru Starchild. Both times, the copies disintegrated."

"And the originals?" I didn't want to hear the answer, but I had to know.

"Detective Talon found no trace of Mara or Chiaru in their houses," Bessel said. "Just dust flung around the room. She wouldn't have realized what it meant if she hadn't seen what happened when we tried to send the rock. She analyzed the dust herself." Grimly he said, "It was all that remained of them."

"She *knew*." I was so angry I could barely speak. "Talon gods damned knew. And she's setting up Lukas Quida for his wife's death." I felt as if I were going to explode. "These ships have been here for thousands of years. Didn't it occur to you that they're off limits for a reason?"

"Of course it occurred to me!" Bessel said. "We were sure we were being careful." His voice shook. "You act as if it's fine for the military to hide this knowledge, to control all access to discoveries that could literally transform human existence. You call that moral?"

I wanted to punch something, *anything*. "You all fucking sacrificed your morals and the lives of two people to further your power."

"Bhaaj." Jak spoke quietly. "This isn't the time."

I drew in a deep breath, trying to steady my pulse. "Why did it only transfer members of the High Mesh? The quarries have been here for thousands of years. Why not transfer other people?"

"They weren't active before," Bessel said. "We activated one to study it. Daan did, actually, but he didn't know why or how he managed it."

"Daan's in danger, too." I described the explosion in the tunnel. "Was a quarry active then?"

"We were working on it," Bessel said. "Without a Kyle operator, we couldn't do anything. We were talking about how much we needed Daan's help."

"You must have done something," Jak said. "It wasn't like the quarry randomly picked any Kyle operator. Why only your three?"

"Feels moods," Angel said.

"All three were empaths, yes," Bessel said. To me, he added, "So are you, apparently." He sounded as if he still didn't believe it.

"Not the people," Angel said. "Box feels moods."

Bessel squinted at her. "Did you say the box?"

"She's right," I said. "The quarries know when an empath links to them."

"If that's true," Bessel told me, "and you're a psion, it should have tried to transfer you."

I stared at him. My need to solve this had just abruptly turned very, very personal.

"We have to destroy the damn boxes," Jak said. "Now!"

"No, wait!" Bessel said. "Even if we could get down there, destroying the boxes could boomerang on every Kyle who has ever used one."

"The box didn't do anything to Major Bhaajan," the lieutenant said. "Not even when she was using it."

"I don't think it's enough to be an empath," I said. "Mara, Chiaru, Daan—something they did activated the quarry. Something I *didn't* do."

"It doesn't make sense," Bessel said. "You were right here. Mara, Chiaru, and Daan were all too far away. They could only have interacted with the quarry by using the Kyle mesh."

"How?" the lieutenant asked. "That cave under the ship doesn't have a mesh console."

"Maybe the quarry itself acts as a console," I said.

"It might," Bessel said. "We don't really understand how it works."

"Mara Quida had a console in her bedroom," I said. "Starchild had one in her kitchen."

Max spoke for the first time since we'd started grilling Bessel. "Neither record of the Quida and Starchild disappearances show either of them using their console."

Bessel jerked as if someone had struck him. "Who the hell is that?"

"He's my EI," I said. "Max, in both cases, no record exists for the few moments when they disappeared. That could happen if they and their surroundings went into quasis. It's the same as you not having a record of what happened with Daan down in the tunnels."

"Daan Bialo didn't have a console," Jak said.

"Tried to send wealth," Angel said.

We all turned to her. "What do you mean?" I asked.

Angel tapped her gauntlet. "Used this. On his arm. Send away his winnings."

It sounded like she meant he tried to transfer his winnings from his chip to some account. Probably he wanted to make sure that if anyone caught us, he had nothing incriminating on his person. The transfer itself could draw attention, but given how rarely he won, he might not have realized that. However, gauntlets didn't normally include a Kyle console. It took more tech-mech than most people could carry on their wrist.

"Normal gauntlet?" I asked Angel.

She shook her head. "Big tech-mech. Like Hack uses."

I swore under my breath. Hack *did* have a minimal Kyle gate. And yah, I remembered when I tried to sense Daan Bialo while Angel and I were taking him home. He'd been thinking some shit about copying his winnings. Ah, hell. The lunatic had wanted the quarry to copy the disk with his credits, to increase his wealth. He'd tried to employ some of the most sophisticated tech-mech in the known universe to counterfeit money. A gauntlet couldn't carry much of a Kyle system, though. That could be why the quarry's attempt to copy Daan instead of the disk hadn't worked as well, letting us escape.

"So you're saying when Mara Quida, Chiaru Starchild, or Daan

Bialo accessed Kyle space, it alerted the quarry?" the lieutenant asked. "Why only them?"

Why indeed? I needed an answer before the quarry blew me up, too.

"What means Kyle?" Angel asked.

"Thought place." My exhausted brain finally made the connection. "The quarry took Quida and Starchild, and tried to take Daan, because they were thinking about the quarries when they accessed Kyle space. Your thoughts determine your location there. That meant they were right next to the quarry. Apparently that activated some ancient, corrupted coding in the machine."

Jak swung around to me. "If that's true, then any empath who's been in contact with a quarry is at risk."

"He's right," Bessel told me. "You're the only other psion thinking about it."

The lieutenant squinted at me. "Why didn't it explode you, then?"

"I wasn't using a Kyle gateway," I said. "You have to contact the box through Kyle space."

Jak came over to me. "Do you *ever* use a Kyle gateway?"

"Never." I spoke dryly. "I'd have no clue what to do." Fortunately, the same was true for Angel and Ruzik.

"The families of Mara Quida or Chiaru Starchild could be in danger too," the lieutenant said. "Even if they aren't thinking about the quarries, they were close to the people killed by them. That would put them close to the quarries in Kyle space."

"Only if they use a Kyle gateway," Bessel said. "But no one else in Mara's family is a psion. Same for Starchild."

Something tugged at my mind, something important—

"You stay away from that Kyle crap," Jak told me. "Don't even think about it."

That was like saying don't think about a pink ruzik. Of course then I couldn't think about anything else—

And then it hit home. "Not me. Lavinda Majda!"

They all blinked at me.

"You mean Colonel Majda?" the lieutenant asked. "You think she's involved?"

"We have to warn her!" I said. "Now!"

"Why?" Bessel asked. "What does she have to do with this?"

I gulped in a breath. "The palace is going to update their security mesh today. I'm supposed to help. They haven't been using the Kyle gateways because someone broke into their mesh a few days ago." Of all the results I might have expected from my cracking Majda security, I'd never have guessed it could end up protecting Lavinda by forcing them to turn off the system. "They're bringing it back up this morning. Colonel Majda is in charge."

"I don't see the problem," Jak said.

"She's an empath!" I said. "A strong one. And an accomplished Kyle operator."

"The quarry shouldn't affect her," Bessel said. "It only happened when Mara and Chiaru were thinking about the project. Colonel Majda knows nothing about it or the people involved."

I couldn't tell them Lavinda was grieving for her lover, Chiaru Starchild. "I talked to the Majdas yesterday, both Lavinda and the general. I told them everything I'd learned."

"General Majda?" The lieutenant squinted at me. "I thought she wasn't on Raylicon."

"She arrived a few days ago. She'll probably be present when Colonel Majda plugs into the Kyle. They're having security problems at the palace. If Colonel Majda accesses Kyle space, she'll be thinking about everything I told them." And Chiaru. *Especially* Chiaru. "That damn quarry is active down in the cave. We have to turn it off!"

"How?" Bessel said. "*I* sure as hell don't know."

"Don't you see? It will try to transfer Lavinda Majda—which means we'll get another detonation, except this time it will be in the Majda palace." Which meant the explosion would hit *both* Majda sisters, as well as their security staff. "Max, you have to contact the palace! Tell them not to use the Kyle gateway, none of them, especially not Colonel Majda."

"I can't," Max said. "My comm doesn't work."

I looked around at everyone, desperate. "Do any of you have access to the mesh?"

"I've lost all contact," the lieutenant said.

Bessel grimaced. "None of our comms work."

"How did you get here?" I asked.

"We came in a flyer."

"Who is 'we'?" Jak asked.

Bessel turned to him. "Detective Talon, Daan Bialo, and Ti Callen."

"Ti-fucking-Callen?" I asked. "You mean the circus whatever? Why?"

"I don't know." Bessel raked his hand through his hair. "Talon piloted the flyer. She let us out in the dunes and went on to land somewhere else, I'm not sure why."

"So you didn't know where she landed," Jak said. "She wanted an escape that didn't implicate her if this all went bad. She'd strand the rest of you here to be caught or killed."

"No. She wouldn't do that." Bessel sounded as if he were reaching the limit of what he could handle. I even felt sorry for him. The House of Vibarr had taken miserable advantage of his brilliant mind and desire to better himself. He was the only Vibarr who would be implicated, though gods only knew how many innocent people would pay the price of their greed.

"You think Talon already left?" I asked.

"I doubt it," the lieutenant said. "I'd have heard her take off. A flyer landed while we were in the ship earlier, and I heard that even with bulkheads muting the sound."

"Do you know where she landed?" I asked.

The lieutenant considered. "To the south, I'd wager."

"You can't use the flyer," Bessel said. "It will only recognize Talon's activator."

"Then we find Talon and get her activator," the lieutenant said.

I rubbed my eyes, struggling to think. We had so little time. Majda would start the update in little more than an hour. Even if we could get back into the cave, we didn't know how to deactivate the quarry. We had to warn the Majdas, which meant we had to find Talon. If she was trapped underground, she could either be in the cave or stuck in the exit passage, unable to open the hatch at its end. Over a kilometer separated those two locations. We didn't have time to check both.

"Angel." I spoke in a rasp. "Ruzik. You feel his mood?"

"Some." Angel said. "He's calm."

Calm. Good. "Where?"

"Close, I think."

I turned to the lieutenant. "What are we closer to, the starships or that hatch in the desert?"

"That's easy." She motioned to the east. "The ships."
"Then that's where we go."
I hoped to the gods I'd just made the right choice.

✥ CHAPTER XXI ✥
LEGACY OF THE RUBY EMPIRE

The third ship was still dark and the hatch to the lower deck wouldn't open.

Jak raised his coilgun, aiming at the hatch. "Everyone go outside."

"Gun not work," Angel told him.

Bessel spoke uneasily. "Look at the charge button. It's lit."

I saw it too, the small blue light that indicated Jak's coilgun was primed.

"It has good shielding." Jak aimed at the hatch.

"No!" The lieutenant stepped forward. "If you shoot that thing in here, it could destroy a substantial portion of the ship. This deck would fall into the lower deck, which could collapse into the cave and probably kill anyone trapped there."

Jak didn't move, and I could tell how much he wanted to fire, not to open the hatch, but to blast this symbol of Cries authority. The anger didn't go away now that we in the Undercity were improving relations with Cries; it only made it worse because it took the Imperialate discovering we had something they wanted for them to care at all.

"Jak," I said.

"Go out of the ship," he said.

"Not going anywhere," I told him.

Angel met his hard gaze with her own. "You'll kill Ruzik."

Bessel motioned at me. "She's linked to the quarry. If you destroy it, that could send her into convulsions, give her a stroke, or just plain pulverize her brain."

"Gods-fucking-damn it." Jak lowered the gun. "You all got a better idea?"

The lieutenant turned to me. "Your gun worked in the desert. It would do far less damage."

I drew my revolver and fired. The bullet slammed into the center of the hatch with a boom that vibrated through the ship, shaking the deck.

"Hey!" Bessel jumped back.

The lieutenant checked the hatch. "It's cracked. You got any shots left?"

"Step away." As soon as she moved away from the hatch, I pressed the stud—

And nothing happened.

"Great," I muttered.

"No more ammo?" Jak asked.

"No, it still has shots." I tried again, with no more success. "Dust."

The lieutenant went over and rammed her heavy boot heel into the hatch again and again, like a jackhammer. Her bio-hydraulics must still have been working, because her motions blurred with enhanced speed.

The hatch broke in a great crack, the pieces falling to the deck below. The lieutenant jumped back, but when nothing else happened, she leaned over the opening. "Doesn't look like anyone is down there." She dropped to the lower deck. "It's empty," she called. "The ladders are gone, too."

No ladders. She needed me down there if we had to use the quarry for any reason, like getting into the tunnel. Morning was coming too fast; I couldn't waste time waiting around until they decided if I should struggle my way down to the lower deck. I eased through the hatchway, dropped—and almost screamed when I landed. *No pain,* I told myself, gritting my teeth. *You feel no pain.* It was bullshit, but if I thought it enough, maybe I could make it true.

"I'm upping your pain meds," Max said. "Also, I'm having your nanomeds use more resources in their repair of your rib."

I didn't answer, just steeled myself. Yah, my meds could fix the broken bone. With Max forcing them to accelerate their healing, they'd probably already partially repaired it. But I was going pay a dear price, draining what little energy reserves remained to my body.

The microfusion reactor that powered my biomech hydraulics and reinforced my bones had so many safeties, it might still be operating, but even if that were true, it couldn't create physiological energy reserves. I'd have a healthy rib and be dead from sheer depletion of my body.

An hour more, I told myself. *Just keep going an hour more.*

Angel jumped down next. Jak stayed up top to guard Bessel and watch for anyone coming at us from that direction. Starlight filtered through the hatchway, enough to show the lieutenant working on the hatch to the cave. I shivered in the cold air. My climate-controlled clothes weren't working. It had to be that. I wasn't in trouble. If falling down a cliff and getting hit by a knife didn't stop me, I could handle a broken rib.

"It doesn't look like this hatch got much of the dust, with the upper one closed." The lieutenant stood up, watching me. "How do you want to do this? Get Talon's flyer and fly to the palace, or get you to the quarry so you can deactivate it?"

Decide, I thought. If I went down there, I had nearly an hour to turn off the quarry, but I had no idea how to do it. Even if I thought I'd deactivated it, I could be wrong. The High Mesh hadn't realized it was active when it tried to transfer Mara, Chiaru, and Daan. Reaching the palace would take longer, but all we had to do was warn the Majdas. If we were right, then as long as Lavinda didn't access Kyle space, she'd be safe.

I answered in a low voice. "If they're down there, get them up here. We'll knock out Talon, get her flyer controls, and go to the palace."

Relief flickered across her face. Apparently I wasn't the only one with doubts about my ability to work with the boxes. She nodded to me, then knelt again and tapped the rim on the hatch in a code. It slid open with a hiss.

"Detective Talon?" the lieutenant called out. "You down there?"

Talon's voice came from below. "Yes. Can you catch the ladder if I toss it up?"

"Sure." When the ladder came sailing up, the lieutenant easily grabbed it out of the air. She clamped it to the rim of the hatch and let down one end. "You're all set."

"Who is with you?" Talon asked.

"Bessel," the lieutenant said. "We had to shoot Major Bhaajan and the man with her. The other woman is locked in another ship."

Rustles came from below, what sounded like someone climbing the ladder. Angel and I moved back in the darkness. No sound came from the upper deck; whatever Jak was doing to keep Bessel silent was working.

Light suddenly flared around us. Ah, no! With my vision so attuned to the night, I went blind. Someone must have set off a handheld flare, which only used chemicals, not circuits the dust could fry. I whipped up my gun, but I managed to stop my reflexes before I fired. Even if the revolver worked, I could just as easily hit Angel or the lieutenant.

"Don't shoot!" someone shouted.

Someone else ignored them. A bullet grazed my waist, or at least that's what it felt like. With a groan, I stumbled backward, dropping my gun. I couldn't think, couldn't breathe, couldn't see. I would have passed out if I hadn't been in combat mode, pumped full of stimulants. What hit me had to have come from an old-fashioned gun without any tech-mech the dust could foul up. Although it didn't tear apart my body like a modern pulse bullet, it hurt like the blazes.

I backed into a bulkhead and braced myself against the barrier. Another gunshot rang out and hit a bulkhead somewhere. Squinting, I struggled to see. Angel was fighting someone. A large man— Ruzik!—grappled with someone else. Who? I clamped my hand on my waist where the bullet had torn my side. The smell of blood saturated my senses, and my palm felt slippery.

Talon. Ruzik had taken on Talon. She tried to roll him to the floor, and he twisted out of her hold. Angel went to the circus, also known as Tandem Walkerdale, punching her hard and ducking away. Even as Walkerdale struck at the air where Angel had been a moment before, Angel kicked like a dancer and slammed her foot into Walkerdale's head. Ruzik sparred with Talon, street boxing, pummeling her with power punches, going full out in a way I'd never seen from city-trained fighters. Talon and Walkerdale fought well, but Ruzik and Angel fought dirtier, as deadly as they were graceful.

As my eyes adapted, I saw Daan making a fast exit, climbing the ladder to the deck above. Well, good. Jak could hold him with Bessel. If I could just . . . think. I slid down the bulkhead until I was sitting on the deck. Ruzik had knocked out Talon and it looked like Angel was finishing off Walkerdale. The lieutenant lay on the deck, still and silent.

"Get the flyer activator." I rasped out the words. "From Talon."

Angel came over and knelt next to me. "You got to hold on."

"Yah." Bracing myself, I tried to push back up the bulkhead. "Got—activator?"

"Acta-what?" Angel helped me stand up.

"For fly thing."

"Not ken."

"Lieutenant?" I rasped out the word.

Ruzik moved away from Talon's still form, keeping watch on her and Walkerdale as he stepped over to the lieutenant. Angel kept her body turned toward them even as she held me up.

"Lu Ten alive?" I asked.

Ruzik turned to me. "Yah. Breathes. Not awake."

"The other two?" I asked.

"Sleep, also."

We couldn't leave the lieutenant with Talon and Walkerdale. Gods only knew what they would do to her if they recovered first. I had no intention of killing anyone, which meant we had to bring the lieutenant with us.

"Wake up Lu Ten," I said.

"Bhaaj." Jak spoke from the deck above. "Can you get up here?"

"Yah. I'm fine," I lied.

Ruzik shook the lieutenant. "Wake up, city slick."

I limped over to them. My head felt light, dizzy. Gods I needed to lie down. I knelt next to the lieutenant. She opened her eyes and stared at Ruzik.

"Lieutenant?" I asked. "Can you understand me?"

"Yes." She sat up, pressing her hand against her shoulder. "I'm all right."

I doubted it, given the blood leaking from her shoulder all over her hand. "Can you walk?"

"I think so."

I spoke to Ruzik. "Get her up, yah?"

Max spoke. "Bhaaj, your meds are releasing more painkillers and stimulants."

"Good," I muttered.

"It's not good," he said. "It will keep you going now, but when you crash, your internal organs could start to fail."

"You got a better idea?"

After a pause, he said, "No. You all need to leave this place as fast as possible."

"Right."

As Ruzik helped the lieutenant up, I checked on Talon and Walkerdale. Although both were unconscious, neither seemed in trouble. They'd recover soon. I went through Talon's jacket and found the activator, a handheld wedge. I held it up. "Activator. We go."

No one argued. With Angel helping me, and Ruzik helping the lieutenant, we climbed to the upper deck. It felt excruciating, taking forever, though logically I knew no more than a few minutes had passed since the flare blinded us.

"Bhaaj, you can do it," Jak said.

"Of course I can," I mumbled as I crawled onto the deck. With his help, I stood up, swaying.

The flare was dying below, dimming enough that I could see better. Jak had both Bessel and Daan Bialo, with Bessel's hands still locked behind him. We should have locked Daan too, but we only had one set of restraints. He stood watching us, his face as pale as starlight.

I limped over to him. "Don't use the Kyle functions of your gauntlet."

Daan tried to look innocent. "What Kyle functions?"

"Bialo, you're a crappy liar," I said. "It's for your own safety. One of the quarries is awake. If you access the Kyle web, it will try to transfer you, like it did with Quida and Starchild. You want to get exploded?"

"No." His face turned even more ashen. "I don't think my gauntlets work now, anyway."

I looked from him to Bessel. "Do either of you know how to reach Talon's flyer?"

"I can," Daan said.

"Good." I pushed him toward the exit. "Go."

We all walked out into the chilly desert night beneath the glorious starscape that ruled the sky. Jak stopped, facing northward—

And raised his gun.

"Hey!" the lieutenant said. "What are you doing?"

"Nothing is out there to shoot," Bessel said.

Jak ignored them, sighting on the desert beyond the ships, his gun aimed in the direction of the long trek to the Undercity.

I recognized his hardened expression. "Jak, no."

He pressed the firing stud.

The bullet ripped through the air with a huge crack. It hit ground and exploded, shattering the silence, followed by the thunder of the desert collapsing into the tunnels below. Jak fired again, and another explosion ripped through the dunes. More ground fell, obliterating the cavity-ridden conduits beneath the desert.

"Are you insane?" Daan yelled.

The ground shook under our feet and the thunder continued as more tunnels collapsed.

"Stop!" the lieutenant shouted. "You're obliterating it!"

"No," Bessel said. "How could you destroy those ruins?"

Angel and I just stood there. Jak had shot far enough away from the ships that he didn't harm them, but whatever paths might have led from here to the Undercity, no matter how convoluted, were gone now, crushed into debris.

Jak's stare burned with a furious intensity as he turned to the others. "The aqueducts are ours." His voice rumbled like an echo of the falling ground. "For thousands of years. We take care of the Undercity. *Us.* Not Cries. Not the military. Not Skolia. Not nobles, royalty, or the Assembly." His gaze was so intense I could almost feel it searing my skin. "Never will any of you come from this place to invade the Undercity. *Never.*"

I said only, "Yah." I'd buried my resentment for years. It was the only way I could work with the powers of Skolia, the only way to convince them to deal with me rather than trying to wrest what they wanted from my people with no care for our culture or identity. I hid my anger, but it had never cooled. It burned within me like a furnace.

Jak met my gaze and nodded. We understood each other.

I laid my hand on his arm. "No more shoot."

He lowered his gun. "No more ammo."

"Good boom," Angel told him.

He slung the empty gun over his shoulder.

I turned to the others. "We should go."

Daan stared at me. "Just like that? 'We should go' after he fucking blew up the desert?"

"You want to stay?" I asked.

He stared at me, at Jak, back at me. "No."

"Surreal," the lieutenant muttered. She headed south, and we all followed.

During our hike to find the flyer, my night vision mostly returned. Talon had set the craft down far from the ships to avoid the effects of the spy dust, or so we hoped. I could only think of the time rushing past. It was almost morning, at least in terms of when people got out of bed, despite the darkness. Majda would launch their security update regardless of whether or not I showed up. They needed a Kyle operator to work on the Kyle mesh, and that meant Lavinda.

The pain of my wounds receded some as the meds did their work, but my mind kept going around in circles. As much as the Vibarrs were the greatest financial rivals to the Majdas, both Houses kept politics out of their challenges. They had too much at stake. But if the House of Vibarr caused the death of Colonel Lavinda Majda, heir to the Majda throne, it would be a political assassination as well as a personal disaster. If the blast caught the General of the Pharaoh's Army, it became treason at the highest level, involving noble Houses with power that rivaled the elected Assembly. It could tear apart the Imperialate.

The lieutenant managed to walk on her own after Jak used his undershirt to bandage her shoulder. He was good at that, given all the times in our youth we'd been injured in fights. The temperature continued to drop, and we all shivered even with climate-controlled clothes. We kept going because, well, it was either that or die. Talon had to get rid of us or risk life in prison, even execution. The worst of it was that she could get away with murdering Angel, Ruzik, and Jak because no formal record existed of them in Cries. Powerful people knew Jak, sure, but they weren't about to admit an association with the Undercity's crime lord. Although records existed for the lieutenant and myself, Talon could easily blame our deaths on unknown Undercity gang members or drug punkers or whatever.

The flyer finally loomed ahead, large and dark. Very large, in fact, more than I'd expected.

"What's wrong with it?" Daan asked.

"Good question," Bessel muttered.

"What do you mean?" the lieutenant asked.

"It doesn't look right," Daan said. "It's too big."

"Moving," Angel said.

Ho! I saw it now, too, the back of the craft shifting—

I stopped. The others stopped with me, except Ruzik, who continued on for a few more steps, then realized we weren't with him and came back to us.

Jak was watching my face. "What is it?"

"Ruzik," I said.

He came over to me. "Yah?"

"Not you." I motioned toward the flyer. "Your namesake." We weren't close enough to see the shadowed forms clearly, but I had no doubt.

"Saints almighty," the lieutenant said. "She's right."

"I don't understand," Bessel said. "What are you talking about?"

"Ruziks," I said. "Two of them, I think."

"*What?*" Daan stiffened. "They'll kill us! We have to get out of here."

"Calm down," Jak told him. "They won't attack unless you attack them. They probably think the flyer is some weird-smelling creature that invaded their territory."

"A colony of them does roam the desert south of the starships," the lieutenant said. "But we almost never see them, not even from a distance. They avoid us."

"How are we going to get to the flyer?" Bessel asked.

Good question. "Anyone ever approach them?" I asked.

"Not that I know of," the lieutenant said. "I've never seen one up close. Supposedly warriors rode them during the Ruby Empire."

"I've heard tales about them," Bessel said. "Each ruzik formed a bond with its rider."

"The hell with that," Daan said. "This isn't some child's tale."

"I need my arms free." Bessel's voice shook. "In case we have to run."

I doubted we could outrun a ruzik, but he had a point. Jak

apparently agreed, because he released him, and Bessel let out a strained breath.

"Feel them," Angel said.

"Are you crazy?" Daan said. "Why would you touch one?"

"I don't think that's what she meant," I said. "She feels their minds."

Ruzik didn't bother to comment—he simply headed toward the flyer. Angel joined him and they strode across the sand, which was flat here rather than the rolling dunes.

"Hey." I limped forward, trying to catch up with them.

The others came too, though Jak had to prod Daan with his gun. Maybe Daan didn't realize the gun was out of bullets, but I suspected he'd have moved even if Jak just scowled at him.

As we approached, the ruziks took form out of the silvery night, watching us now instead of the flyer. They resembled the Tyrannosaurus rex, and some scientists believed they were engineered from the DNA of Earth dinosaurs. Others thought they were native to Raylicon. As we drew nearer, their differences became more obvious. Their scaled forearms were much larger and longer than for a T-rex, enough that a ruzik could easily use them to run on the ground. The claws on those massive limbs were as big as my lower arm, daggers that could tear a human to shreds. Scales covered their bodies. They looked monochrome in the starlight, but holos I'd seen showed them glittering in gold, green, and blue. They had a terrifying beauty, the most magnificent animals on Raylicon. I didn't believe our ancestors had ever ridden these creatures.

We stopped a few meters away, none of us daring to go closer. They smelled of musk, spice, and citrus. One of the animals snorted, and the other shifted its weight, scraping the sand with its clawed feet. Plumes of condensation curled up from their snouts into the cold air. They watched us out of large eyes, one on either side of their great heads.

"Gods," Bessel whispered. "They're glorious."

"Yah," I murmured. I just hoped they didn't eat humans.

I didn't realize Ruzik was walking again until it was too late to stop him. He halted below one of the animals. His namesake lowered its head, and mist from its nostrils swirled around his body. He stayed perfectly still, letting it explore him. Angel came up to his side, and the other animal butted her shoulder with its snout. I felt an odd sense then, a curiosity that wasn't my own. At my side, Daan Bialo exhaled, and I actually felt him relax.

"What the bloody hell are they doing?" the lieutenant said. She sounded about as relaxed as a desert lion with indigestion.

"I think those animals are Kyles," I said. "Sort of." I didn't sense anything human, not emotions as I knew them, but they recognized a kinship in Ruzik and Angel. "Come on." I limped forward. "They'll let us by."

Everyone else stayed put. Then Daan caught up with me. His terror had gone, shaded into a respectful fear. The others finally moved as well, their steps whispering in the sand.

The lieutenant came up alongside me. "You've got guts." She motioned at Jak. "Then again, you're married to him."

I smiled. "After that, big lizards are child's play."

Their smell saturated the air, sharp and pungent. I stopped below one of them and held still, my heart beating so hard, surely it could hear that thump. The ruzik watched me with one eye, then turned its head to look with the other eye. Softly, so carefully, I laid my hand against its gigantic head. Its scales felt glassy, yet also pliable. It whistled, a sound I'd heard in the desert tonight.

"We go in," Ruzik told the animal in front of him. With care, he stepped around the beast and walked along its side toward the flyer.

I lowered my hand. Taking a deep breath, I went past the ruzik, doing my best to show no fear. I put my hand in my pocket and folded it around the activator.

When I reached the flyer, I tapped the activator. The hatch opened with a snick that vibrated in the night. One of the ruziks snorted and the other whistled. After Ruzik and I moved aside, the others in our party came forward, walking as if they were on a plane of glass that could shatter if they even breathed too deeply. Daan climbed into the flyer, followed by the lieutenant, then Bessel. Jak paused, looking at me, then boarded. I stepped up after him and turned to see Ruzik and Angel, still outside. I waited, but neither of them moved.

"You come?" I asked.

Ruzik looked up at me. "We stay."

"You sure?" I didn't want to leave them here, and not only because

I had my doubts about hanging out with the local dinosaur population. Talon and Walkerdale would come looking for us soon.

"Stay in desert," Angel said. "Not go back to ships."

"Come home later," Ruzik said.

"All right." I couldn't force them to board. I also trusted their instincts for self-preservation. "Be well." I tapped the hull panel and the hatch snapped closed.

Everyone else had crammed into the cabin. It had two passenger seats, a pilot's seat and a copilot's seat. The lieutenant was pulling up a smaller emergency chair from the deck between the two passenger chairs that looked barely big enough for a fifth person.

"Anyone know how to fly this thing?" I asked.

"I've tried a few times in a simulator," the lieutenant said. When no one else offered, she shrugged and squeezed into the pilot's chair. I handed her the activator.

"You take the copilot's seat," Jak told me. "See if you can contact anyone." He motioned at Bessel and Daan. "I'll keep watch on them."

Given the way they darted glances at him and then quickly looked away, I suspected he didn't need his monster gun to intimidate them into staying put. His presence was enough.

I slid into the copilot's chair. As I fastened on the safety webbing, pain stabbed through my rib cage and abdomen. I moaned, unable to stifle that sign of weakness. With my jaw clenched, I scanned the controls. The comm looked standard. Nothing happened when I tapped its panels.

"Comm is down." I glanced at the lieutenant, who was working at her controls. "Will it fly?"

"I'm not sure." She paused as one panel lit up. "It might."

"It *might*?" Daan said behind us. "Meaning what? We 'might' stay in the air?"

"I can't say." The lieutenant continued to work, activating some controls while others stayed dark. I kept working on the comm, with no luck. Nor could I open the panel that would let me check the interior components.

"All right," the lieutenant said. "I think I can get us at least partway to Cries."

"Partway?" Jak asked. "Then what?"

"We'll crash into the desert, the mountains, or the city." She spoke matter-of-factly. "If we fly low enough, I might be able to land instead of crashing."

"Great," Daan muttered. "Just great."

I pushed a tendril of hair out of my face. "We have to go to the palace."

"I don't know if I can get high enough," the lieutenant said.

"We have to." I forced myself to keep talking. "If I can't get the comm working, we'll have to warn them in person."

"Majda security won't let us into their airspace," Bessel said. "If we can't tell them why we're coming, they'll shoot us down."

"No. They won't. I'll find a way to signal them." Sure. I could create a few galaxies, too. *Stop it,* I told myself. *You can manage. Just a little longer.*

"This is crazy," Daan said. "If we die, we can't warn anyone."

"You can let us out at the city limits," Bessel said. "We'll warn them."

"Yah, right," Jak said. "So you can warn your people they still need to kill us? Not a chance."

"Everyone hold on," the lieutenant said. "Prepare for takeoff."

The engines rumbled, and the front screens cleared to show the desert silvered by moonlight. When she turned on the exterior lamps, they only flickered. The ruziks backed away from the rumbling ship, and one reared high on its massive back legs, its front arms clawing at the air. The roar of its challenge vibrated through the flyer.

"Saints almighty," Bessel said.

I thought of Ruzik and Angel. Gods, I hoped I hadn't made a mistake in leaving them.

Jak spoke in the Undercity dialect, his accent heavier than usual. "Trust them, Bhaaj. Trust their instincts."

I nodded, grateful for his presence.

The lieutenant taxied across the desert. The craft shook, I hoped from the uneven terrain rather than because it was in trouble. She managed to gain enough speed to lift off and soar into the air. My thrill of relief didn't last long; the craft's exterior lights went off, leaving us to fly in the starlight. The desert passed below in a plain of darkness.

"Can you see well enough to fly?" I asked.

"On instruments, I can manage." She didn't look as confident as she sounded.

"Can you turn on the heat?" Daan asked. "It's freezing."

"I'll try." I worked at the environmental controls, with no success. Finally, in frustration, I smacked my palm on the panel. It lit up, both the air conditioning and heat buttons glowing blue.

Hah! Welcome to the Bhaaj school of mechanical repairs. I turned off the air conditioning and tried to raise the cabin to room temperature. It wouldn't go high enough, but it hummed as if it were working. "That might do it."

"Can you get anyone on the comm?" the lieutenant asked.

"Not yet." I kept working on the panel, to no avail. I ran my fingers along its edges, trying to pry it open. After several attempts, I loosened the panel enough to pull it free. The circuits inside looked fine. No obvious signs of spy dust showed, which I hoped meant less of it had reached the flyer. I blew on the circuits, wiped them with my fingers, even licked my fingertips and ran them over the components to pick up dust. Still no response.

"Bessel," I said. "Do you know how long the spy dust remains active?"

"About six hours," he said.

In other words, too long. I looked back at him. "Any idea how I can clean it off?"

He shook his head. "Sorry. It's not my specialty."

"I think blowing on it helps," Daan said.

"I tried that." I sat back, thinking. We had to let Majda know we posed no threat. Normally they'd escort an uninvited craft to an alternate landing site and arrest everyone onboard. Given the complications with this investigation, however, they'd be even less inclined than usual to take risks. They might shoot us down.

"Lieutenant, do the exterior lights on this craft work?" I asked.

"Not much." She tapped several panels and the lamps outside flickered, strobed, cut out, then strobed again. She grimaced and turned them off. "It's better without."

"Can you pulse a code with them?" I asked.

"I don't think they're consistent enough to relay a message."

"Try Morse code." Some Skolian ships had adopted the Earth code because of its simplicity.

She checked her controls. "This flyer does have Morse code. I don't think the lamps are steady enough to do it, though."

Jak spoke from the passenger seat. "Even if it doesn't succeed, just flashing the lights will warn them we're having trouble."

"It might stop them from shooting us down." I hoped.

The lieutenant nodded, her face grim. "Will do. Let me know when you want to start."

"Copy that." I leaned back and closed my eyes, taking a moment. It seemed only seconds before the lieutenant said, "We're nearing the city."

"They must be trying to contact us," Bessel said. "Every craft has to link to the grid."

I leaned forward, working on the comm. It showed no indication it was receiving or sending signals. No lights glowed, nor did it make the low hum of an operating system.

"Go around the city," I suggested. "We'll be in less violation of traffic ordinances."

"I've got a traffic drone on approach from the south," the lieutenant said. "It must be telling us to connect to the mesh or land."

Jak snorted. "It's probably trying to give us a ticket."

"Keep going," I said.

The flyer continued on, with the lights of the city shimmering on our left. It wasn't a good sign; glowing buildings meant the mandatory nightly blackout had ended. People would be getting ready for their morning work shifts. The Majdas were probably gearing up for the security update.

"How far are we from the mountains?" I asked the lieutenant.

"We're over the northern foothills." She was gripping the wheel so hard her knuckles had turned white. She smacked several panels and the outside lamps strobed, flaring in the night. It made it hard to see where we were going. Within seconds, she tapped them off again.

"Can you navigate?" I asked.

She grimaced. "Nav is getting weaker. I'll need to see better when I land."

At least we had the forward screens. The mountains were rising ahead of us. "To reach the palace, you need to get higher and more to the south."

She glanced at me. "I don't suppose you have its coordinates."

"I do," Max said. "I'm sending them to your nav system."

"Got it," the lieutenant said. The mountains loomed like monoliths silhouetted against the starry sky. She tapped on the lamps, and they flashed in the night. "What message do you want to encode? Keep it simple."

"Try this," I said. "'Help us. Urgent. Bhaaj.'"

When she entered the code, the lights did flick on and off, long flashes alternating with short, but then they strobed randomly, destroying the pattern.

"How am I going to land?" she muttered. "I can't see shit."

"The palace has a pad on its roof," I said.

"What palace?" Daan asked. "We aren't even close."

Max spoke. "Actually, we should be quite close. I'm sure they are trying to contact us."

"At least they haven't fired," Bessel said.

The lights kept flickering, sometimes getting the pattern, other times flashing at random.

"Got an escort," Jak said.

I heard them, too, the rumble of other engines. The front screen didn't show any aircraft ahead of us, but I glimpsed a flyer on the left, maybe one on the right, too. I couldn't see well at all. I was so damn dizzy . . .

Nausea swept over me, and I groaned as I slumped in my chair. The lamps outside were dimming again. Darkness swirled in my vision.

"Don't pass out," Jak said. "Bhaaj! Wake up." He pressed my shoulder. Groggy, I opened my eyes. The lamps outside hadn't dimmed; they were still blinking their ragged Morse code. Jak had leaned between the two forward seats, bending over me.

I tried to sit forward, then fell back with a moan.

"We have to get her to a hospital," the lieutenant said.

"I'm fine." I was lying so badly, I didn't know why I bothered, but it came out anyway.

"Right." Jak stayed put, his hand on my shoulder, as steady as a rock.

"Holy shit!" Daan said. "That's amazing."

"What?" Then I saw it. In the ragged, pulsing light of the flyer lamps, the palace had come into view. Amazing indeed—and way too close. We were headed straight for its beauteous self.

"Can you get more altitude?" I rasped.

"I'm trying!" The lieutenant pulled on her wheel with one hand and tapped furiously with the other, working both the manual and automatic controls. As the palace loomed closer, we climbed a bit.

"Time to land," I mumbled.

"I've never landed, not even in a simulator," she said. "This would be a good time to pray."

I held my breath as she just barely skimmed above the palace. The craft bucked unsteadily—and slammed onto the roof, completely missing the landing pad. A great tearing sound ripped through the flyer, and the impact threw us forward and to one side. I jerked against my safety webbing, crying out as agony flared through my body. I fought to get free. "Jak!" He'd been standing when we crashed. I twisted around—and saw him climbing to his feet from where he'd hit the deck.

Voices came from outside. The hatch snapped open, not by any effort from us, since we were all trying to crawl free of the crumpled seats, which were tilted sideways. Several guards stood outside, their guns aimed at us.

"All of you out!" an authoritative voice bellowed. "No weapons, or we shoot."

"Don't." I thought I spoke loudly, but the words scraped out as a whisper.

"They're Undercity!" a woman said. The unmistakable click of someone readying a power rifle to fire snicked through the air.

"Don't shoot!" I yelled. I moved out into view, standing on the sloping deck. Blackness threatened to sweep over me. "You have to warn Colonel Lavinda Majda!" I forced out the words. "She *must not* access the Kyle web. If she does—could kill her. It will explode!"

"You won't be getting near any Majda," a hard voice told me.

I felt their distrust, anger, and suspicion. My vision was so blurred, I couldn't even tell who had spoken. They weren't going to listen—

"Bhaaj?" a man said. "Is that you?"

"Ah, saints." I barely got the words out.

The group of officers in the hatchway parted, letting a man step forward. He stood there, dark-haired and dark-eyed, a lean figure in simple black trousers and shirt. He needed no uniform; his authority permeated the air. The guards moved aside for him.

"Randall!" I gulped in a breath. Randall Miyashiro, Majda's tykado wizard, the seventh-degree black belt. Seeing him gave me a final surge of energy. "You have to warn Lavinda Majda! If she accesses Kyle space, it could cause an explosion like what killed Mara Quida and Chiaru Starchild. It will pulverize her and anyone nearby."

He was already activating his comm. "I'm sending the message."

"Good," I whispered.

I collapsed then, and darkness closed in.

✣ CHAPTER XXII ✣
THE LOST SEA

Lavinda Majda attended the tykado demonstration when my students tested for their belts. Professor Ken Roy came as well, and sat with me in the risers set around the open area where the fighters were warming up.

I'd decided to have both Angel and Ruzik test for their black belts. Given how well they'd dealt with the situation at the starships, two nights ago, they'd proved they were more than ready. Both were doing stretches in an area set aside for students to warm up.

Today I felt almost human. I'd spent the last two days, nearly one hundred and sixty hours, recovering. I went to the Undercity a few times when the boredom got so bad I thought I'd go crazy if I stayed in bed any longer. Mostly, though, I rested. Sometime during all that, Angel and Ruzik returned from the desert. They went about their business as if nothing had happened, preparing for their tykado exams. They said nothing about what they did after the flyer took off. I didn't push. They would tell me in their own time.

Neither of them seemed fazed by their surroundings today at the Cries Tykado Academy. If I hadn't known this was their first time visiting Cries, I'd never have guessed. In the tournaments we'd done at the Rec Center in the Concourse last year, they'd dressed in what they always wore, dark trousers and sleeveless muscle shirts. Today they established another first, though only they and I knew the significance. They wore the white uniforms common to all tykado students, a V-neck top with long sleeves and trousers. They tied red belts around their waists.

I'd purchased the uniforms for them. Prior to today, no Dust Knight had ever agreed to accept or wear the uniform. However, I trained them, so by the unwritten laws of the Undercity, they owed me their oath. We made a bargain. Ruzik and Angel accepted the uniforms in exchange for their service as my bodyguards at the starships. It seemed an absurd bargain, clothes in exchange for saving my life, but it made sense in the Undercity.

I would have given them the world if it had been within my power.

They were testing with two students from the city, a young woman and man, both also in their twenties. The board of judges consisted of three tykado masters, the top two instructors from the Cries Tykado Academy—and Randall Miyashiro. He did us a great honor. As much as I knew this didn't mean he would work with my students in the future, I couldn't help but hope. It would be incredible if he could spare even a fraction of his invaluable time for the Dust Knights.

Each of the four candidates gave a prepared statement about why they wished to earn a black belt. The city students talked about how tykado helped them overcome obstacles in their life, everything from developing a sense of self-worth to becoming humble. It seemed to me they spoke forever, so wordy, but their statements were well given and heartfelt.

When it came time for Ruzik, I went so tense, I felt as if I'd stretched tighter than the string on a curved lute. Neither he nor Angel had ever spoken more than a few words at one time. I'd practiced with them, my excuse for going to the Undercity when I was supposed to be in bed. Working with me, however, and speaking to a crowded studio were two very different matters. Although they'd practiced phrasing their words so people from Cries could understand, I was relieved to see the academy had brought a translator.

Ruzik spoke about poverty and survival, of the violence and beauty in the Undercity, and of the spiritual sense tykado allowed him to find even in his darkest times. His speech was short, his sentences terse, but the words had a power of life and death. The entire room went silent. When he finished, the masters nodded to him with respect.

Angel went next. She spoke in short sentences, as terse as Ruzik, but with a lyricism she had no idea she possessed. She talked about the first time she had come aboveground and seen the sky. She described its endless wonder, the incredible colors, and how at first she couldn't even absorb the sight. Then she spoke of how tykado evoked that wonder for her, the sense of becoming one with a new world she had never imagined. Her audience sat mesmerized.

Their choice of subject matter touched me at a deep level. Ruzik and Angel used tykado in a way the city students would never know, if they were fortunate. For Dust Knights, tykado wasn't just a sport, it offered a means of survival. Yet today they spoke of their spiritual connection rather than of the attack and defense as everyone expected. The spare beauty of their words stunned me.

The students had taken a written test earlier, one Ruzik and Angel studied for at great length, not only the questions about form, function and philosophy, but also how to *take* a written test, something we never did in the Undercity. As with the speech, they found it difficult. Although they'd spent two years learning to read and write the Cries dialect, I hadn't realized until that night at the starships that they also spoke it, or at least understood when others did. We didn't know yet if they'd passed their exams; that would come later. Only the physical tests remained.

The students gathered on the mats and bowed to the instructors, who had them stretch and do exercises. Ruzik and Angel barely broke a sweat. For people who ran and trained every day, often for hours at a time, it was child's play to do one hundred push-ups and sit-ups. They next went through their stances, the basic positions for defensive and attack footwork. Then they showed their mastery of defense-and-attack patterns, finishing with a pattern they'd designed themselves. Sparring with their instructors came next. Both Ruzik and Angel made it look easy. I didn't get the sense they considered this part a test. For them, fighting just to show you could fight was something done for fun, in contrast to real fighting to protect your territory or challenge another gang. At the end, they showed their ability to break various blocks and bars. The process went on for hours, with few rests, a form of endurance testing.

It felt odd to sit rather than work with them. I needn't have worried about their preparation; they were well beyond the city students, not only in their ability to do tykado, but also in strength and fluidity. The sheer grace of their moves was joy in motion.

During a break, Ken said, "It's beautiful to watch them. It's like they're dancing."

"They enjoy it." I regarded him. "I heard you've been working on the quarries."

Ken nodded. "The army rushed through my clearance. They wanted to make sure those boxes were dismantled and couldn't activate." He gave me an appraising stare. "No one is telling me what happened, why they suddenly needed these 'quarries' moved and neutralized."

"You took them apart?" I tried to sound casual, rather than saying, *Yah, I want those mothers broken into tiny little pieces so they can't blow up people.*

"Completely." He considered me. "Do you know why it was such a priority?"

I didn't have the authority to talk about the High Mesh, so I just said, "People were going to the ships who shouldn't be there. The army wanted the ancient tech in a safer place, and in a form that couldn't harm people."

"Harm how?"

I just sat there. After a moment he smiled and said. "All right, Major. No more questions. We moved them to the temple Tiqual out in the desert. It's better protected."

"Good." It was an immense relief. If our ancestors had ever mastered the quarry technology, that knowledge had been lost long ago. Their machines no longer worked properly. Hell, maybe they'd never worked. That might be why they stored the quarries under the ships, out of the way.

"We do hope to figure them out someday, if we can manage it safely," Ken said. "A fellow named Bessel is going to work with us."

"Good. He's smart." To put it mildly.

"He's also under some sort of house arrest." He studied my face. "I wonder why."

"I'm sure a good reason exists."

He waited.

Oh, what the hell. I could tell him one truth. "He went to the ships without permission, to study them. He feels it's a crime for the army to hide the knowledge they contain. He believes it's the heritage of the entire human race."

"He has a point." Ken nodded, more to himself than to me. "Whatever happened convinced the army to expand the circle of people working on the ruins. They asked me for recommendations. I suggested some Imperialate scientists, and also a few from the Allied Worlds of Earth."

It made sense to invite people from Earth. They could see connections we might never realize. I doubted our government liked the idea, though. "It's hard to imagine them letting anyone from Earth see the ruins."

"Well, I only convinced them for two scientists, John Rather and Dean Hartley from the Tennessee Valley Interstellar Workshop. Maybe you've heard of it?"

Well, yah. Who hadn't? TVIW was a part of history. The "workshop" started in the early twenty-first century as a small group of visionaries who dreamed humanity would someday reach the stars. It had grown over the decades until they became experts in Earth's burgeoning program of interstellar travel. They were the ones who discovered the star drives that took our siblings from Earth to the interstellar community. "It's a good choice."

"I agree." He glanced across the room. "Someone has noticed you."

Startled, I followed his gaze. Lavinda Majda was seated on the tiers against the opposite wall with her aide and also a new bodyguard. The colonel inclined her head to me, a rare public acknowledgment. I nodded back, on my best behavior today.

After the physical tests, while the students were cooling down, I stood with Ken. When Lavinda headed in my direction, Ken tactfully left to talk with some other people. Lavinda and I met under the graceful archway that exited the room.

"My greetings, Major," she said. "You look much better today than the last time I saw you."

I winced. "I'm afraid I don't remember anything after I collapsed in the flyer."

She strolled with me into the hallway beyond the testing room. "The palace doctor treated you. I don't know how you kept going. Your injuries were extensive."

"Ah, well." I shrugged. "I have good biomech."

"Yes, you do." She regarded me steadily. "But a lot of it wasn't working. And biomech only affects the physical. It can't give strength of character."

I hadn't expected her to imply anything positive about my character, given how often I annoyed her family, breaking all sorts of unwritten rules about how to behave with royalty. "I had to stop you from using the Kyle gateway."

She spoke quietly. "You saved my life and that of my sister Vaj. You did a great service, not only for my family but also for the Imperialate. You have our deepest thanks."

I'd never known how to accept thanks, especially from someone so highly placed, so I just returned her nod, Undercity-style. Then I thought, *She deserves better from you than silence.*

"I'm glad I could help," I said.

She smiled, which I'd noticed royalty did as rarely my people in the aqueducts. "So am I."

We entered a small room, a serene place with blue walls and window mosaics designed from colored glass. The floor had no chairs, only white rugs bordered by woven gold vines. Parchment screens stood around the room with delicately painted mountains and deserts.

As much as I wanted to find out what had happened with the palace security updates, I couldn't risk pushing the subject. So instead I asked, "Have you figured out how Tandem Walkerdale comes into all this?"

"Ah, yes, our illustrious circus spy." Lavinda walked with me toward an alcove. "She was the High Mesh contact on Metropoli. They wanted to steal more than the quarry tech; they wanted the quarries themselves. She planned to move them through Metropoli. It's why Mara Quida got the Metropoli contract. When Quida disappeared, Walkerdale showed up to find out what happened."

It made sense. From what I'd gathered, the Scorpio CEO was also part of the High Mesh. "Walkerdale wasn't the one who attacked me after the gala, right? That was Sav Halin, the reporter." Supposed reporter, but I couldn't reveal that I knew that Halin worked for the Majdas, or at least, used to work for them. Yesterday the news conglomerate had fired Halin, and I didn't doubt the Majdas had also shown her the door.

"It looks that way," Lavinda said. We reached the alcove and sat on a blue banquette set under tall windows. "Halin and Detective Talon were the only ones in the Mesh with true covert training. Talon spent five years in the Fleet after she earned her chemistry degree at the university."

"What about Walkerdale? She claimed she did covert ops for the military."

"She lied." Lavinda shook her head. "What operative, even former, gives away her cover so easily?"

I'd wondered that, too. "My EI claims she's a magician in the circus."

Lavinda smiled at my incredulous expression. "That was actually her real cover. She's the financial equivalent of a mercenary. Corporations hire her to do their dirty work."

"In a circus?"

"I think its incongruity is the point. She could move the quarries through the circus because no one would think to look there. She planned to disguise them as part of her show." Her smile faded. "Gods only know what would have happened if she'd actually tried to use them. That's one performance I sure as hell never want to see."

I grimaced. "You almost did."

Her tone became guarded. "You have always had an ability to make leaps of logic most people never see. Whatever it was that led you to think that I in particular might be in danger, I thank you for your discretion."

I spoke with care, not wanting to overstep. "I'm sorry about your friend Chiaru."

"Yes," Lavinda said softly. "As am I." She seemed to give herself a mental shake. "Hell of an arrogant move for the Mesh, trying to murder the Majda investigator."

That was unexpected. Sure, I worked for the Majdas, but I hadn't thought they saw me as the Majda anything given how often I got on their bad side. That seemed especially true now; I was almost certain Lavinda knew I was the one who cracked their security network.

"What will happen to the High Mesh?" I asked.

"Talon and Halin will go on trial for attempted murder, breaking into a secured military site, and probably other charges as well. Security charges will also go against Bessel, Daan Bialo, and

Walkerdale." Lavinda spoke dryly. "The prosecutors are still figuring out who to charge with what in regards to the deaths. Talon and Halin will almost certainly get prison time. Walkerdale too, but not as much since she didn't try to kill anyone." She paused. "We don't have much on Daan Bialo. His employers at Scorpio Corp also got him one hell of a lawyer."

"You think he'll get off?" It annoyed me, but not as much as I expected. The High Mesh had used him big time, for his Kyle ability, and they damn near got him blown up.

"He'll get fines, probation, a demotion." Her voice hardened. "Jo Muller will go to prison."

It took me a moment to place that name. Jo Muller was Lavinda's bodyguard, the one I'd seen at the gala and again in the park in Cries. "She was the mole at the palace?"

"If by mole, you mean she betrayed our trust, then yes. She picked up Halin in the flyer that morning after the attempt on your life. She's also the one who gassed you in the other flyer."

"I'm glad you caught her." I didn't want to imagine Muller's fate. The same could happen to me if the Majdas ever charged me with cracking their mesh.

Lavinda was watching my face. "We found clear evidence that Muller compromised our security. So our security people believe she is also the one who broke into the palace mesh."

I kept my voice neutral. "Then your people have completed the security updates?"

"Yes, after the techs dismantled the quarries and did more safety checks than I can count." She continued to study me. "I find it odd. I've worked with the palace system for decades. That break-in during the night seemed too sophisticated for Muller. And no damage was done, unlike her other attempts to compromise our systems."

Stay calm, I told myself. "That's good it caused no damage." I'd never intended any.

Her gaze never wavered. "I'm assuming we won't have any more problems in that area."

I met her stare. "I'm sure you won't."

We sat for a few excruciating moments. Then she said, "That must have been quite a fight at the starships."

"I hope it didn't cause too many problems."

She shrugged. "The ships are fine. We can fix the broken hatch and repair the bullet holes."

"And the desert?" Jak's final shots had collapsed the tunnels beyond repair. My red beetle may have explored that maze of ancient passages, but I'd never know; the army had caught the little drone and wiped its memory clean before they gave it back to me. Same with my green beetle. It didn't matter. I knew enough to guess at the rest, that before Jak destroyed the passages, an ancient route from the ships to the Undercity had existed, even if it was clogged and forgotten in modern times. Now no one would ever use it. The military could dig new tunnels if they wanted, but I doubted it was worth the expenditure, besides which, they probably knew my people would harass any such efforts now that they knew the ancient passages had existed.

"Perhaps," Lavinda said, "some damage is better left alone."

I breathed more easily. "Thank you."

"Lieutenant Ackerson spoke highly of how you conducted yourself."

"Ackerson?"

"The lieutenant who helped you at the Vanished Sea starships."

Ho! I hadn't expected her to say anything positive. "She seemed a bit, uh—taken aback by my methods."

Lavinda smiled. "Most people are."

I wasn't sure what to make of that, so I said nothing.

"This Vibarr fellow who calls himself Bessel," Lavinda added. "He is a brilliant young man."

"Then he is a Vibarr?"

"Half Vibarr. His father is a commoner. His mother is a younger Vibarr cousin who had Bessel out of wedlock. Caused a scandal for the father, but the mother did acknowledge her son and give him the Vibarr name."

"I had the sense Bessel was trying to prove himself to his family."

Lavinda frowned. "He shouldn't have to. His intellect is incredible, but they don't care unless he uses his intelligence to make money for their house."

"The Mesh used him, playing on his insecurities." My anger surged, adding an edge to my voice. "None of the Vibarrs or corporate top execs—none of the true powers behind the Mesh—got

Catherine Asaro

involved. They let their flunkies commit the crimes while they stayed hidden. So they're all free, while Bessel takes the fall."

"Not quite." The way she said those two simple words, so cool and precise, spoke volumes about what her House intended for the true powers of the High Mesh. "Now we know who to watch." Her voice turned to steel. "We'll catch them."

I was glad I wasn't a Vibarr, dealing with the Majdas in that terrifying arena where the noble Houses fought with each other with weapons designed of power and influence rather than projectiles or explosives. "I heard the army offered Bessel a plea deal."

"Yes, house arrest in return for working with the corps assigned to the ships."

It could never make up for the two deaths, but at least now his mind would neither be wasted nor misused by people with no scruples. "He feels a lot of remorse for what happened."

Lavinda exhaled—and her mask of reserve slipped. Pain showed on her face, a deep pain, the kind that never truly left you. With difficulty, she said, "Telling Inna Starchild what happened to Chiaru—it wasn't easy."

Watching her, I suspected that was the understatement of the year. Lavinda could never acknowledge her grief, not in public, not to her family, and especially not to her husband Paolo. I'd met him a few times, always in the controlled environment of the palace. Although it wasn't a love match, I had the impression he and Lavinda treated each other well. He'd given up a great deal to marry a Majda heir; before that, he'd lived as a modern man and a successful architect. He still worked as an architect, but he could never leave the palace. He lost his freedom on the day of his wedding. I had no doubt that in return for his agreeing to live in the ancient manner, Lavinda respected their vows, though she loved someone else and could never love Paolo in the way he might want.

The greed of the High Mesh had claimed a high price. At least this all offered new insights into our origins, especially since our scientists were going to work with Earth researchers who knew more about our ancestors. Although it could never take away the grief, it did provide another step toward understanding the ancient mysteries of our world.

✤ ✤ ✤

I found Lukas Quida in a garden behind the mansion he had shared with his wife and now lived in by himself. He sat in an open gazebo. The walls and roof were white trellises intertwined by vines. As I approached, walking along a bluestone path, he must have heard my footsteps. He turned and stood up, watching me.

I stopped at the three stairs up to the gazebo and bowed to him. "My greetings, Del Lukas."

He indicated the bench where he had been sitting. "Please. Join me."

I went up and sat with him on the bench. A breeze ruffled our hair and stirred the vines on the lattices. "This is beautiful," I said.

He stared out at the gently rolling lawns. "Mara and I used to sit here together."

"I'm sorry for your loss." I thought I would have liked his wife. Although I didn't agree with her choices regarding the High Mesh, she wasn't the one who'd broken the law. As with Bessel and his love of knowledge, her interest in the Mesh was also for the scientific treasures they might uncover. And she had mentored Bessel, the only person who supported and encouraged him rather than using his genius.

Lukas spoke with pain. "The cosmos, fate, a deity in heaven, the pantheon of our ancestors, whatever you believe in—they have no sense of justice, that they should take someone so worthy of life."

"I don't know if this helps or not—but I found something you might like to have." I reached into my pocket and took out the medallion I'd picked up in the cave under the starships. It showed an image of Mara and Lukas with their arms around each other, smiling in the sun. "The people working on the project left a box of keepsakes of their loved ones, each person picking something they valued over all others, to honor their hopes for the project. This is what your wife chose."

Tears formed in his eyes. "I wondered where this had gone. I was so upset when I couldn't find it." He took it from my hand. "I've always loved this picture. That was such a wonderful day we spent together." He looked up at me. "It means a lot to know she chose this medallion."

I spoke gently. "She didn't die in vain. What happened will help future scientists solve the secrets of our ancestors. The work she began may someday change human life."

His voice caught. "Thank you, Major."

I couldn't tell him the rest, about the avarice and thirst for power that had led the House of Vibarr to fund the High Mesh. Their secret cabal had cost more, in human terms, than I knew how to quantify. However, I also knew one more fact: The Majdas would make sure the High Mesh paid dearly for his wife's death.

The sunrise soothed the ragged edges of my thoughts. I walked across the rocky desert far from any settlement, alone under the brilliant sky, with its red and gold bands on the horizon and the arch of purple overhead. The last stars of the fading night were giving one final glimmer before dawn washed away their gleam. Stone-vines curled in silver lace across the land. I had no idea why Ruzik and Angel had sent word through the whisper mill for me to meet them here. They should be at home relaxing, recovering from their tykado exams yesterday while they waited to hear whether or not they had passed.

I saw no one. Wind stirred my hair, which I'd left loose around my shoulders. I stopped and listened to the vast silence of the land. Except the Vanished Sea never truly fell silent. Somewhere a flying lizard called out, its voice carrying across the desert like the spirit song of ancients who had lived and died here so long ago.

I realized I was no longer alone. In the distance, three animals were approaching, silhouetted against the sunrise. Large animals. They glinted in the predawn light, with iridescent sparks of green, gold, and blue glinting on their bodies.

Ruziks.

I went still, like a statue hiding in plain sight. The beasts galloped across the land, powerful and deliberate. I knew so little about these rulers of the desert. They stayed away from humans, and in return we left them alone. As they came nearer, they slowed to a walk. I saw them more clearly now, the giant heads, their large eyes, the huge tails. One walked on its massive back legs, with its front legs in the air, and the other two walked on all fours. Something didn't look right—those two each had an extra ridge on their backs—no, not a ridge. Ho! Those were *riders*.

The animals continued their approach, looming larger and larger. I held still, waiting until they stopped in front of me. Ruzik was sitting on the one in the middle and Angel rode the animal to his right. The third came down on all fours, standing like a beast from a mythological tale.

"Eh, Bhaaj," Ruzik said.

"Got a big lizard," I said.

The animal without a rider came forward, watching me out of one giant eye, its head turned sideways. It lowered its snout and shoved my shoulder. I swayed back, then regained my balance. Its breath curled around me, smelling of musk and lemon.

"Eh," I told it. I laid my hand against its head. The ruzik whistled, a sound much lower than the cries of the smaller lizards, almost a rumble. I stood quietly, letting it smell me. I should have been afraid, yet I felt only curiosity. No, curiosity wasn't the right word. I had trouble defining the emotion, as if it belonged to someone else. The ruzik was deciding if it wanted to accept me.

The animal pushed my shoulder again, harder this time. I stepped back and waited. It turned its head to look at me with its other eye. With another whistle, it straightened up to its normal height, then higher still, onto its back legs, towering, its giant claws glittering in the dawn. If it decided to attack, I wouldn't have a chance. It could kill me with one swipe of those claws. No matter. Nothing could have frightened me away from this glorious moment. I'd never known an animal with such majesty.

The ruzik came down again, less than a meter away. It slowly lowered its bulk to the ground, folding its front and back legs under its body. Then it waited.

"You honor me." I stepped forward and set my palm on its back. A bony ridge ran down its neck and another crossed its lower back like a natural saddle. I understood the invitation, the rarity of what it offered. For a moment, I stood with my hand resting on its scales. Then I climbed onto the animal and settled into the indentation in its lower back. The ruzik stood, and the ground seemed to drop away beneath us. My breath caught. I looked at Ruzik, the human one, and he grinned. Beyond him, Angel lifted her chin, her gaze radiant.

"Good way to celebrate new belts," I said, giving them the good news. They'd passed their exams and were now first-degree black belts. And celebrate was just the right word. Their achievement deserved three syllables.

They nodded, accepting the congratulations Undercity-style, with no words or excessive emotion, but I saw the gleam of satisfaction and yah, relief, in their gazes. Ruzik laid his hand against the shoulder ridge of his mount, and the animal stepped around until it faced the sunrise. I put my hand on the ridge of the ruzik I rode, but nothing happened. So I tried pressing. It responded then, turning to join Ruzik's mount. Angel bought hers around and together we walked toward the sunrise. The wind blew across my face and swirled my hair around my shoulders. It took me a moment to realize I'd been holding my breath. I inhaled again.

"Press inward," Ruzik said. "With knees."

I tried his suggestion and the ruzik walked faster. Another press, and it speeded up again. I took a deep breath, filling my lungs with the clear desert air—and pressed *hard*.

We took off then, thundering across the desert. I tilted my face up to the red sky, glorying in the ride, one that no one had taken in thousands of years. Freedom coursed through us, the freedom to run beneath the sky of a world that had become more ours than Earth would ever be.

We rode across the desert in joy.

❖ APPENDIX ❖
Mathematical Methods and the "What if?" of Science Fiction

by Catherine Asaro

In *The Vanished Seas*, the idea of Kyle space depends on a mathematical concept called Hilbert space. I'll describe here what that means and how I played with those ideas for the story.

To start, we'll define a "vector space." Consider the three-dimensional world we live in. If you want to tell someone your exact location, you can do it by using three numbers. Imagine you are sitting in a room. You can describe your position by saying how far you are from some point in the room. We will choose the corner where two walls and the ceiling meet (assuming they are all perpendicular). We call that corner the *origin*. You say the top of your head is two feet from the wall in front of you, three feet from the wall at your right, and seven feet from the ceiling. Those three distances define your coordinates relative to the corner. Specifically, your coordinates are (2, 3, 7). You've described your location in "coordinate vector space," which is just the three-dimensional universe where we live.

It's possible to specify the coordinates with arrows. One arrow starts at the origin (the corner described above) and points along the seam where the wall in front of you meets the ceiling. It extends for two feet and ends at the point we'll call *X*. The next arrow starts at *X* and comes straight out from the wall along the ceiling, parallel to the wall on your right, for three feet. The point where it ends is *Y*. The third arrow goes straight down from the point *Y*, perpendicular to

323

the ceiling, for seven feet. It should touch your head. That is point Z. So in this case, $X=2$, $Y=3$, and $Z=7$. The arrows are called vectors.

We can define the location of any object by figuring out the numbers (X, Y, Z) that indicate the location of the object relative to some origin. Once we know X, Y, and Z, we know the exact location. To make the process more general, define three arrows (x, y, z), each with a length of one. Then *any* point P can be described by $P=Xx + Yy + Zz$. The position of your head would be $P = 2x + 3y + 7z$.

The arrows (x, y, z) are mutually perpendicular vectors with unit length. They are called orthogonal coordinate vectors, and we say x, y, and z *span* coordinate space. The word "span" means that any location can be described using just these three unit vectors, multiplying each by appropriate numbers and adding them together.

Mathematically, other "vector spaces" exist. Some have an infinite number of dimensions! I'll describe here the type I play with in this story. As it turns out, the solutions to certain differential equations act in a manner analogous to the unit vectors described above. If we draw the solutions to such an equation, we get a family of curves, all of which have similar properties. To see what this means, consider the vibration of a string on a musical instrument. It is fixed at its endpoints and goes up and down in a wave with periodic peaks and valleys. These are called *sinusoidal waves* and give the solutions of the equation that describes the motion of such a string. The more peaks and valleys in the wave, the higher the pitch; that is, it has a higher frequency. Only certain frequencies work, however—those where an exact number of peaks and valleys fit along the length of the string. We say the frequencies are *quantized*. An infinite number of possible waves still exist, going to higher frequencies as we cram in more peaks and valleys. The functions that describe these waves are called *eigenfunctions*.

Many differential equations follow this behavior. Each has a family of eigenfunctions as solutions. We call the eigenfunctions "vectors" because they behave in a manner analogous to the x, y, and z unit vectors above. Just as the location of any point P in three-dimensional space can be described by the sum $P=Xx + Yy + Zz$, so any function $P(x)$ can be described as a sum constructed from a family of eigenfunctions. We add them up with each vector weighted according to its contribution to the total result. However, we have an infinite set of eigenfunctions! So they span a space with an infinite number of dimensions. Universes defined by such vectors are called Hilbert spaces.

Think of it as preparing a dish for a meal. We add ingredients together, varying the amount depending on the recipe. If you have an infinite number of ingredients, you can make any dish in the universe. For a particular recipe, you use only a few ingredients; the contribution of the rest is small (say a pinch of salt) or zero. So it is with eigenfunctions. The number needed to create the wavefunction is infinite, but the main contributions usually come from a small number of eigenfunctions, with the others adding corrections or having no effect.

A well-known family of eigenfunctions are the curves $\sin(n\pi x/L)$ and $\cos(n\pi x/L)$, which can describe functions that repeat like a wave. The value of 2L is the length of one cycle or *period* of the wave, and $\pi = 3.14159\ldots$ is the number pi. The number n takes the values $n = 1, 2, 3\ldots$ on to infinity. These are seen in an area of physics called *Fourier analysis*. We write a function P(x) as a sum of those "vectors." For example, a triangular wave looks like a triangle repeated over and over. It is used in many disciplines, such as electronics, and can be written as

$$P(x) = \frac{8}{\pi^2}\sin\left(\frac{x\pi}{L}\right) - \frac{8}{9\pi^2}\sin\left(\frac{3x\pi}{L}\right) + \frac{8}{25\pi^2}\sin\left(\frac{5x\pi}{L}\right) - \ldots$$

The sum goes on forever, but the contributions of the waves for large frequencies (large n) are tiny. The constants $(8/\pi^2)$, $-(8/9\pi^2)$, $(8/25\pi^2)$ and so on specify the contribution of each sine wave to P(x).

For the spatial vectors, the values of X, Y, and Z depend on the origin. In the example we started out with, if we define the origin as a different corner in the room, then X, Y, and Z would be different from (2, 3, 7). The choice of origin should be sensible. If I wanted to specify my position in a room in New York, it wouldn't make sense for me to choose the origin at a bar in Toledo. Likewise, the description of P(x) using eigenfunctions depends on which family of functions we use. For example, the radial position of an electron in the hydrogen atom uses Laguerre polynomials, whereas Bessel functions are better suited to describe the radial position of a free particle in spherical or cylindrical coordinates.

The three unit vectors *x*, *y*, and *z* are mutually perpendicular; that is, they intersect at right angles. We say they are *orthogonal*. Eigenfunctions are also orthogonal, but here the meaning becomes more complicated. Roughly speaking, two functions are orthogonal if they have no overlap. This is a simplification because it doesn't actually mean that no part of the functions overlap; rather, it means that when certain operations are performed on the functions (integration over their inner product), the result is zero. If we have two copies of the same eigenfunction, they have one hundred percent overlap. If we scale that overlap so it equals one, the functions are normalized. It's the same as taking the length of the *x*, *y*, and *z* vectors to equal one. We call such a family of functions an orthonormal set of eigenfunctions.

Quantum Dreams

Quantum physics predicts that any object can be described as a wavefunction. For example, electrons sometimes act like particles and sometimes like a wave. Both descriptions are valid! If we shoot tiny particles through a double slit, they diffract as if they were a wave. Any "solid" object can also be defined in that manner, including humans. You might say, "If we're all waves, why can't we see the wave properties of our bodies? People don't diffract when they go through a double doorway." The answer is that the wavelength for a macroscopic object like a human is so tiny that we can't (yet) see it even with our most advanced technology. Quantum theory may seem nonintuitive, but the model gives results that match what scientists observe in the real word. In fact, it's one of the most successful scientific models ever developed. It allows us to describe what's happening at the atomic level, yet on larger scales it agrees with classical mechanics, that is, with what we see in our world.

For particles such as electrons, we can use wavefunctions to investigate their energy, position, momentum, and other properties. Wavefunctions that describe the spatial behavior of a system depend on position variables. Some variables are part of what we call a conjugate pair. A result of quantum theory called the Heisenberg uncertainty principle specifies that we can never know the value of both conjugate variables exactly; the more certain we are of the value of one variable, the more uncertain the value of the other. For example, the better we know the position of an electron, the more uncertain its momentum. Time and energy are also conjugates. We can give a highly accurate number for the lowest energy of the electron in a hydrogen atom, but we can't say *when* that measurement was made; the number is always the same regardless of when we determine its value.

We find the eigenfunctions that describe quantum behavior by solving the Schrödinger equation. Its solution produces families of orthonormal eigenfunctions. To model the system, we take sums of those eigenfunctions just like we needed sums of sine waves to describe a triangular wave. In theory, the spatial part of the wavefunction that describes the electron in a hydrogen atom exists everywhere in space. It is centered around the nucleus, but its tails extend to infinity, becoming negligible at large distances. We can use the wavefunction to find average values for properties of the electron, such as its position and momentum.

Quantum theory can describe any collection of particles. The more particles are involved, the more complicated the problem. For example, a student can learn to calculate the wavefunction for the hydrogen electron with only pencil and paper, needing no computer. For a system even as simple as three particles, it is no longer possible to solve it by hand. A collection of just twenty particles requires intensive computer work. In theory, the behavior of any system can be determined by solving the Schrödinger equation as long as we include a term in the equation for *every* particle in the system. We don't have the computer resources yet to do any system of substantial size, but our ability to solve such equations has grown over the years. Someday we should be able to solve even human-sized systems.

In theory we could calculate the wavefunction that describes a human brain during a thought. It would most likely be localized around the brain, with tails that trail off to infinity, rapidly becoming tiny. What does that mean? We can't really isolate thoughts; they blend into one another and we can also think about more than one thing at once. One way to specify a thought might be according to how long it takes to complete an idea. It could be a single idea, going to the store perhaps, or a mingled thought about fixing the car and feeding the cat. More complicated thoughts could be broken into individual components. We could describe what goes in the brain at a specific moment as a "slice" of a thought. Although the structure of a brain is pretty much fixed, it isn't identical from moment to moment. As we think, neurons fire and other chemical reactions take place. At each instant, the collection of all those particles can be described by a quantum wavefunction. A thought could be described as the sum over the wavefunctions for all the slices involved with a particular idea. Voila! We have a mathematical description of a thought.

The "What if?" for this story is this: Suppose we apply the vast machinery of Hilbert spaces to wavefunctions that describe a thought. To do that, we need to know how to transform from one type of space to another.

Transformations

In their simplest form, transforms take a function depending on one variable and turn it into a function depending on a different variable. One of the best known is the Fourier transform that turns a signal described by its behavior at various *times* into a function described by its behavior at various *frequencies*. Conceptually, a transform is analogous to a caterpillar turning into a butterfly. The cocoon acts as the transform, causing the change. Just as the characteristics of the caterpillar determine those of the butterfly, so the characteristics of the original function determine those of its transform. Many types of transform exist, and they operate between many types of spaces, often involving conjugate variables. For example, we can transform a function that depends on position to one that depends on momentum.

A difference exists between caterpillars and functions, however; you can do an inverse transform on a function to turn it back into one that depends on the original variable. It would be like the butterfly spinning a "reverse" cocoon that would transform it back to a caterpillar! The ability to go back and forth is an entertaining aspect of what I call Kyle space in the book.

The wavefunction for a particular thought varies with position.

The fictional "Selei transform" converts it into a function that varies with thoughts in a particular location. That wavefunction would be localized on that thought and its tails would be other thoughts less and less related to the main as you move away from the main peak. So here is the game: If we can describe the wavefunction for a certain thought at all positions, then we can transform it into a space that describes the wavefunction for all thoughts at a certain location. The closer the thoughts are that gave rise to the function in our universe, the "closer" the peaks of their transforms are in thought space, aka psiberspace or Kyle space. The Kyle operators in the books have brains that are neurologically better developed to interact with psiberspace. They use gateways that transform their thought processes from our universe into the thought universe and then reverse transform their thoughts back into our universe.

Kyle space has other fun extrapolations that can be found in others of my books, such as *Spherical Harmonic* (and its essay at the end of the book). Also, it is possible to play other "What if" games with wavefunctions that describe human beings. I will leave it to the reader to find out what those are in this novel. Enjoy!

TIME LINE

Circa BC 4000	Group of humans moved from Earth to Raylicon
BC 3600	Rise of the Ruby Dynasty
BC 3100	Raylicans launch their first interstellar flights Rise of the ancient Ruby Empire
BC 2900	Ruby Empire declines
BC 2800	Last interstellar flights Ruby Empire collapses
Circa AD 1300	Raylicans begin to regain lost knowledge
AD 1843	Raylicans regain interstellar flight
AD 1871	Aristos found Eubian Concord (aka Trader Empire)
AD 1881	Lahaylia Selei born
AD 1904	Lahaylia Selei founds Skolian Imperialate
AD 2005	Jarac born
AD 2111	Lahaylia Selei marries Jarac
AD 2119	Dyhianna Selei born
AD 2122	Earth achieves interstellar flight with the inversion drive
AD 2132	Allied Worlds of Earth formally established
AD 2144	Roca born

AD 2169 Kurj born

AD 2203 Roca marries Eldrinson Althor Valdoria (*Skyfall*)

AD 2204 Eldrin Jarac Valdoria born (*Skyfall*)
Jarac Skolia, Patriarch of the Ruby Dynasty,
dies (*Skyfall*)
Kurj becomes Imperator (*Skyfall*)
Death of Lahaylia Selei, the first modern Ruby
Pharaoh, followed by the ascension of Dyhianna
Selei to the Ruby Throne

AD 2205 Major Bhaajan hired by the House of Majda
("The City of Cries" and *Undercity*)
Bhaajan establishes the Dust Knights of Cries
(*Undercity*)

AD 2206 Althor Izam-Na Valdoria born
Major Bhaajan solves the case in *The Bronzed Skies*.

AD 2207 Del-Kurj (Del) and Chaniece Roca born
Major Bhaajan solves the case in *The Vanished Seas*

AD 2209 Havyrl (Vyrl) Torcellei Valdoria born

AD 2210 Sauscony (Soz) Lahaylia Valdoria born

AD 2211 Denric Windward Valdoria born

AD 2213 Shannon Eirlei Valdoria born

AD 2215 Aniece Dyhianna Valdoria born

AD 2219 Kelricson (Kelric) Garlin Valdoria born

AD 2220 Eldrin and Dehya marry

AD 2221 Taquinil Selei born

AD 2223 Vyrl and Lily elope at age fourteen and create
a political crisis ("Stained Glass Heart")

AD 2227   Soz enters Dieshan Military Academy
(*Schism* and "Echoes of Pride")

AD 2228   First declared war between Skolia and Traders
(*The Final Key*)

AD 2237   Jaibriol II born

AD 2240   Soz meets Jato Stormson ("Aurora in Four Voices")

AD 2241   Kelric marries Admiral Corey Majda

AD 2243   Corey Majda assassinated ("Light and Shadow")

AD 2255   Soz leads rescue mission to colony on New Day
("The Pyre of New Day")

AD 2258   Kelric crashes on Coba (*The Last Hawk*)

AD 2259   Soz and Jaibriol II go into exile (*Primary Inversion*
and *The Radiant Seas*)

AD 2260   Jaibriol III born, aka Jaibriol Qox Skolia
(*The Radiant Seas*)

AD 2263   Rocalisa Qox Skolia born (*The Radiant Seas*)
Althor Izam-Na Valdoria meets Coop
("Soul of Light")

AD 2269   Vitar Qox Skolia born (*The Radiant Seas*)

AD 2273   del-Kelric Qox Skolia born (*The Radiant Seas*)

AD 2274   Aliana Miller Azina born (*Carnelians*)

AD 2275   Jaibriol II captured by Eubian Space Command
(ESComm) and forced to become puppet emperor
of the Trader empire (*The Radiant Seas*)
Soz becomes Imperator of the Skolian Imperialate
(*The Radiant Seas*)

AD 2276   Radiance War begins, also called the Domino War
(*The Radiant Seas*)

AD 2277   Traders capture Eldrin (*The Radiant Seas*)
Radiance War ends (*The Radiant Seas*)

AD 2277–8 Kelric returns home and becomes Imperator
(*Ascendant Sun*)
Jaibriol III becomes the Trader emperor
(*The Moon's Shadow* and *The Radiant Seas*)
Dehya stages coup in the aftermath of the
Radiance War (*Spherical Harmonic*)
Imperialate and Eubian leaders meet for
preliminary peace talks (*Spherical Harmonic*)
Jason Harrick crashes on the planet Thrice
Named ("The Shadowed Heart")
Vyrl goes to Balumil and meets Kamoj
(*The Quantum Rose*)
Vyrl returns to Skyfall and leads planetary act
of protest (*The Quantum Rose*)

AD 2279   Althor Vyan Selei born (the second son of
Dyhianna and Eldrin)
Del sings "The Carnelians Finale" and nearly starts
a war (*Diamond Star*)

AD 2287   Jeremiah Coltman trapped on Coba
("A Roll of the Dice" and *The Ruby Dice*)
Jeejon dies (*The Ruby Dice*)

AD 2288   Kelric and Jaibriol Qox III sign peace treaty
(*The Ruby Dice*)

AD 2289   Imperialate and Eubian governments meet for
peace negotiations (*Carnelians*)

AD 2298   Jess Fernandez goes to Icelos ("Walk in Silence")

AD 2326   Tina and Manuel return to New Mexico
("Ave de Paso")

AD 2328   Althor Vyan Selei meets Tina Santis Pulivok
(*Catch the Lightning*; also the duology *Lightning
Strike, Book I* and *Lightning Strike, Book II*)

✢ ✢ ✢

Taken together, *Lightning Strike, Book I* and *Lightning Strike, Book II* *are* the story told in *Catch the Lightning*, but substantially rewritten and expanded for the e-book release. The e-book version of *Primary Inversion* is rewritten from the original and considered by the author as the best version.